Victoria Bernadine (a pseudonym) is, as the saying goes, a "woman of a certain age". After twenty-something years of writer's block, she began writing again in 2008. She began with fanfiction about a (now-cancelled) TV show called Jericho and particularly about the characters of Heather Lisinski and Edward Beck. From there, she expanded into writing original fic and she hasn't stopped since.

Victoria enjoys reading all genres and particularly loves writing romantic comedy and post-apocalyptic science fiction. What those two have in common is anybody's guess.

She lives in Edmonton with her two cats (The Grunt and The Runt). *A Life Less Ordinary* is the first novel she felt was good enough to be released into the wild.

Victoria can be contacted through Love of Words Publishing Inc. (loveofwords@shaw.ca) or through her brand new blog at:

http://victoriabernadine.wordpress.com/.

A Life Less Ordinary

Victoria Bernadine

Love of Words Publishing Inc.

Cover Design by Patrycja Pawlik.

For information, contact Love of Words Publishing Inc., loveofwords@shaw.ca .

ISBN 978-0-9918102-1-5

m/d/y/#
12-10-12-0001P

A Life Less Ordinary

EPISODE ONE
Minus Thirty-one Days

"All I ever wanted was a life less ordinary."

Manny lay flat on her back, eyes wide, staring at the ceiling while she waited for her clock to hit 6:00. Another day of work, she thought. Another day older and deeper in debt.

She had the alarm timed to the millisecond. The jarring noise had barely begun when she clicked it off. She sighed then threw back the covers and got out of bed.

She padded into the bathroom, glanced without interest in the full-length mirror that doubled as her shower doors and took her morning inventory.

Plain face? Check.

Looking tired? Check.

Thirty pounds overweight? Check.

Dark circles under deer-caught-in-headlights eyes? Check and check.

She shook her head at her limp, mousy hair and wondered when she'd gotten so old.

She sighed in resignation then conjured up her Perfect Fantasy Man—or Harvey, as she liked to call him—to give her a morning lift. She cocked her head to one side as she stared into the mirror and imagined him standing behind her. She smiled at the handsome man, and he smiled back, putting his hands on her shoulders. Everything about him was warm, in stark contrast to the cold shades of grey in which she lived her life. He had warm brown eyes, warm brown skin, and a warm smooth voice that always reminded her of golden honey. Today his hair was black with greying temples, and yes, even that seemed warm to her.

He was perfect, everything she considered ideal in a man—and extra-perfect, of course, because he was a fantasy. Just the thought of trying to establish a relationship with an actual man felt too much like work.

She sighed and Harvey disappeared.

"Instead I ended up in a rut—everything planned and executed to the minute."

She finished her shower and padded out to the kitchen wrapped in a worn terrycloth robe just as the coffee pot finished perking her morning coffee. She pulled a white cup out of the cupboard, filled it and took it with her to the bedroom, where she drank her coffee while she dressed and pulled her hair into its habitual bun high on the back of her head. At 6:45 sharp, she was back in the kitchen where she rinsed out the cup and put it on the rack next to the other three cups from earlier in the week; they marked the passage of time like scratches on a prison wall.

She walked out the door at 6:55 as usual, called good morning to Mr. Abinash from next door, as usual, got into her car and drove to work. As usual. She walked in at 7:37, called good morning to those of her staff already at their desks, and settled herself in her office.

As usual.

She sighed silently as she logged on to her computer and realized she couldn't remember the last time she'd had a sick day or had come in late. Even her car and traffic and the sometimes-harsh Edmonton winters had given up trying to throw off her schedule.

She sighed again as she rifled through her stacks of

paper, searching for the information she needed to review before the staff meeting at nine. The last staff meeting before their new boss arrived at ten, and Manny went back to her old position. She'd enjoyed being the boss and thought she'd had a good chance to win the promotion. If she was honest with herself, though, she hadn't really been surprised with the decision to offer the job to Steph. If she had the energy, she'd almost wonder why she didn't even care that much.

"I told myself it was security. But all I was doing was sleeping with my eyes open."

Manny glanced up as her assistant energetically bounced in.

"Morning, Manny."

"Morning, Roxie. How was your evening?"

"Great—went to that new Robert Downey Jr. movie—*rrrooowwwrrrr!* Phil wasn't too impressed with my drooling though."

Manny laughed. "I'd expect not. I guess I need to go see it then."

"Yeah, sure. When was the last time you actually went to a movie in the theatre?"

Manny paused, considering the question then shrugged carelessly. "Can't remember, actually."

Roxie shook her head in exasperated fondness and sat down in front of Manny's desk. She leaned forward and lowered her voice. "So, the new boss starts today?"

"Yep," Manny replied absently, reviewing the e-mails in her inbox.

"Are you going to be okay with this? I mean, you—"

"Of course I'm okay with it. Steph's a nice person, bright, energetic, competent, levelheaded, full of new ideas. She may have a bit of a learning curve ahead of her, but she'll do just fine. She may be just what we need around here. Perk us up a bit."

"Yeah, but you—"

Manny took her hands off the keyboard and turned to

face Roxie directly. She gave her a reassuring smile and calmly held her gaze.

"I'm okay with it," she said. "Really. I didn't want to be the boss anyway." She paused then continued. "Everything's going to be fine. You'll see. A new boss will be fun!"

Roxie grimaced cynically and Manny shook her head in mock disapproval.

"We should get to work," she urged gently.

Roxie nodded and stood. "Yeah, that at least never changes. But Manny..."

Manny raised a quizzical eyebrow.

"It should've been you."

~~~~~

Manny couldn't stop her mind from wandering during the staff meeting, finding Craig's voice even more monotone than usual. Or maybe the information was more monotonous than usual.

Or maybe you just don't feel the need to pay close attention since you didn't get the promotion.

Manny raised an eyebrow as she glanced towards Harvey sitting across the table from her. He looked very handsome in a well-cut expensive suit and gold silk tie.

I should still pay more attention, she replied primly and turned her attention back to Craig's dry voice.

"The quarterly forecast clearly shows–" he droned, and she mentally rolled her eyes and glanced back across the table where Harvey grinned wickedly at her. For a moment, she allowed herself to get lost in his dark, mysterious eyes.

"Manny?"

She blinked and looked up at Craig. "Yes?"

"What's your opinion?" he repeated.

"I'm sorry–I was thinking of something else. My opinion on what?"

Craig frowned at her, obviously displeased. "The budget allocations," he snapped, and Manny flushed and shifted uncomfortably.

Wonder what he'd say if you told him your <u>real</u> opinion?

Shut up.

~~~~~

Craig preceded Manny into his office then stood behind his desk and watched as she closed the door and sat down at the table. He frowned at her.

"It's not like you to not pay attention in a meeting," he said.

Manny sighed and shrugged. "Sorry, Craig."

"This isn't about losing out on that promotion, is it?"

"Not intentionally, but now that you mention it—"

"I've already explained it to you. We had no concerns that you could have done the job."

"That's a relief, especially since I've *been* doing it."

Craig gave her a warning look at her slightly sarcastic tone and continued, "We want to go in a new direction. We decided we needed somebody fresh, not burdened by the years of history and 'how things used to be'. We needed somebody—"

"Young?"

Craig's lips tightened. "New ideas, Manny. Somebody with new ideas, to take your area from the status quo to high achievement."

"Our status quo *is* high achievement."

"Higher, then." Craig paused and stared hard at her. "Are you going to be able to work with Steph?"

"Of course. I'm nothing if not professional and dedicated to my job."

Craig nodded, his eyes boring into hers. "And I appreciate that. I'd hate to think you're not a team player."

Manny flushed but held his gaze for several beats. Craig seemed satisfied by what he saw and nodded to indicate the conversation was over. Manny walked to the door, then paused and turned back to him.

"Craig? Do I have any chance at all of moving up in

this company? I mean, I've been here for fifteen years—"

"There's always a chance, Manny. You'll just have to wait and see what comes up." He gave her a thin smile, then sat and turned his attention to his computer.

Manny left thoughtfully; she knew a brush-off when she heard it.

~~~~~

Manny walked in her door, looking tired and feeling worn out. She wondered ruefully why the only thing not on a schedule was the time she could leave the office. She dropped her purse on the table and hung up her coat and keys. With a tired sigh, she walked into the living room and plopped into the armchair. She closed her eyes as Harvey walked out of the kitchen with a glass of white wine and began to rub her shoulders. He again looked impossibly handsome, this time wearing a sweater and jeans. She sighed in imagined bliss, and looked at him with sad eyes.

You have no idea how much I wish you were real.

In a blink, he was gone—and the phone was ringing. For a split second, Manny considered not answering it.

There's your chance to talk to a real person, Harvey murmured.

Probably a telemarketer.

Probably Rebecca. Or Daisy. They'll worry if you don't answer.

All right, all right.

Manny heaved herself to her feet and walked to the phone.

Maybe I'm glad you're imaginary after all.

She caught a glimpse of his grin as she answered the phone.

It was Rebecca, asking her to go out the next night.

"I don't know..." Manny sighed.

"Oh, come on—you'll have fun! And seriously—you haven't gone out with us in months!"

"I've been tired..."

"You've been tired your whole life I think. You need to

break out of this rut you're in! Come out for a few drinks and dancing with me and Daisy. Who knows, maybe you'll meet a good-looking guy and be swept off your feet into a red-hot love affair."

Sounds like a plan to me.

Yeah, 'cause that'll happen.

"I'd love to go dancing," Manny said to Rebecca, "but the guy is just a figment of your imagination."

"Only because you don't put any effort into it. Seriously, it's not healthy to do nothing but work and go home. That's how people go crazy you know."

"Huh. You mean next thing you know I'll be talking to my imaginary friend?"

Harvey grinned wickedly and Manny abruptly turned her back to him.

"Exactly!" Rebecca said. "Come on—what do you say?"

"Okay, okay," Manny sighed. "Tomorrow night—the usual place?"

"Yep—and sound like you're actually looking forward to it, okay?"

"I'm sorry. I *am* looking forward to it—it'll be fun."

~~~~~

Manny laid in bed, staring up at the ceiling and waiting for sleep. She plucked restlessly at the blanket and wished she could relax. Tomorrow was Steph's first staff meeting. Today she'd reacquainted herself with everyone in the office then spent the rest of the day with Manny being briefed on the details of the work of the branch and any current issues she'd need to resolve within the next few days. That meant Manny's own work had been delayed, and tomorrow it would be delayed again—and Manny would have to leave early in order to meet Rebecca and Daisy at the lounge for drinks before heading to the club.

Manny took a deep breath and slowly let it out. It wouldn't be too bad, she staunchly told herself. Steph was young, energetic, and had a shrewd intelligence almost obscured by the cleavage-revealing shirts, short skirts and a figure that could stop traffic—and probably did. Manny wondered if Craig truly understood what he'd gotten himself in for by promoting Steph rather than Manny.

Cleavage and legs.

She mentally rolled her eyes at Harvey's dry, cynical tones.

Maybe—but that's not really fair to him, is it? He's not a bad guy.

But he is just a guy.

She does bring a new perspective—a new way of thinking about things. She's not a bad choice—and I can't argue with Craig's idea that shaking things up could make things better.

And where does that leave you?

No worse off than I was before.

And no better.

If you're not going to be helpful...

Harvey glanced down at his suddenly ruffled shirt opened to the middle of his muscled chest and skin-tight breeches. He glanced back at her with a ruefully amused smile.

Watched the <u>Ice Pirates</u> again, did you?

Oh, shut up—it's a classic no matter what anybody else thinks!

I'm just sayin'—if I was real and regularly wore pants this tight, I'm not sure I'd be of any use to you. If you know what I mean.

Manny groaned and shook her head, and Harvey blinked out of existence. She wondered when she'd managed to lose control of a figment of her imagination—one she'd eventually felt compelled to name after an invisible rabbit.

She groaned again, rolled over and pulled the covers over her head. It was going to be another long day tomorrow.

Complete with dancing.

Minus Thirty Days

Manny calmly considered Steph as she spoke to the staff in the boardroom. Steph had a short haircut that emphasized her high cheekbones and flawless skin. She was dressed to the hilt in a well-tailored suit that flattered her stunning figure. She was young, late twenties at most, Manny figured, and she was going to go far. Manny estimated she'd last two years in the new job and no more than three. There was no doubt in Manny's mind that Steph would be running the company by the time she was forty-five.

Manny's age.

Not for the first time, Manny vaguely wondered where her own life was going. With a silent sigh, she refocused on Steph's introductory pep talk.

"...and I'm looking forward to working with all of you."

Steph beamed at everyone, and her smile didn't waver even in the face of the awkward silence that filled the room. With a determined glint in her eyes, Steph turned to Manny.

"And I'm particularly looking forward to working with you, Manny," she continued. "I know I'm going to learn so much from you. Why, you're practically an institution around here! You've been here forever; you know everything there is to know about how this branch and the entire organization operates. I mean, you've been working here, in the same role, for fifteen years! That's amazing—and shows us how dedicated you are, and how much you're needed in your position. From what Craig told me, I don't think we could function without you! And I know I speak for everyone in this organization, from the President on down, when I say we look forward to having you with us, doing what you do, for the next fifteen years!"

Oh. My. __Fucking.__ God.

~~~~~

"And that's when I did it."

Rebecca and Daisy sat at the bar on either side of Manny as she sipped a beer. They were listening intently to her story of the staff meeting.

"Did...what?" Rebecca asked cautiously.

"I quit."

"WHAT!"

Manny winced at both the volume of the screech and the fact that it was in stereo, directly in her ears.

She shook her head. "My God—another fifteen years? I can't even—not another day!"

"You didn't just walk off the job, did you?" Daisy asked incredulously.

"I offered two weeks' notice. Steph told me I could leave today." Manny shrugged. "So I did."

"I take it she wasn't impressed," Rebecca said drily.

"Hah! That's putting it mildly! On the other hand, I'm not sure she actually *cares* all that much. It just looks really, really bad for somebody to quit on her first full day on the job. I think she just wanted to have the problem...well, not solved, but out of sight as quickly as possible." Manny shrugged again. "In two weeks, it'll be like I was never even there."

Daisy frowned at the trace of bitterness in Manny's voice even as she asked, "So what are you going to do now?"

"I've already done it," Manny replied calmly.

"What have you done?" Daisy asked.

"I'm cashing out my pension. Rebecca, you can sell my house. I've decided I'm going to have a mid-life crisis, and by God, I'm going to have it like a man!"

"What the hell—?" Rebecca asked, at a loss.

"I'm going on a road trip. Hopefully with a young man in a hot red convertible—but I'll take whoever shows up."

Daisy stared at her, stunned. All she could think to say was, *"Huh?"*

"I put the personal ad online today," Manny continued. Manny handed Daisy a slip of paper covered with her familiar scrawl.

Daisy read it out loud for Rebecca's benefit. "*SWF, 45, having mid-life crisis, seeks travelling companion with own money for six-month road trip to destinations unknown. Don't worry—no sex wanted or offered. Young men preferred but really don't give a damn. You have a month to respond then I'm leaving with or without you. Hot red convertible will be considered an asset.* ROSE!"

"Now I know you're pissed if you're calling me Rose," Manny said ruefully.

"I'm your sister—I'll call you whatever the hell I want!" Daisy snarled.

Rebecca finally found her voice again. "Have you lost your ever-loving mind?"

"No," Manny said seriously. "I think I've finally found it."

Minus Twenty-one Days

Zeke shuffled into his living room wearing a t-shirt and boxers, a cup of coffee lovingly cradled in his hands as if it was more precious than diamonds. He settled himself at his desk, took a sip and closed his eyes in bliss. With a yawn, he scratched at the stubble on his cheek then turned on his computer and logged into his writer's account at *What Women Want.*

Time to check in on the reaction to his latest blog, he thought. He was actually rather proud of it; "In Praise of Older Women" had been a *tour de force*, even if he did say so himself. He settled in and had just begun to read the comments when his cell phone rang.

"Yeah?" Zeke answered, his New Zealand accent, as usual, more pronounced in the morning.

"Have you seen the comments on your latest blog?"

Zeke leaned back in his chair with a fond smile. "Good morning to you too, Leah. Yes, I slept well, and not alone—my date with Dixie went really great last night, thanks for asking."

On the other end of the phone, Leah rolled her eyes in

exasperation at her husband TJ as she replied, "Whatever. Take a look at the comments."

"Yeah, I'm starting to go through them now."

TJ leaned closer to the speakerphone and said, "Remember you live with Dixie–your dates always end well."

"That's what you think," Zeke muttered to their amusement as he focused on the comments. He read avidly, occasionally snorting in exasperation or laughing or scribbling a note about something he wanted to respond to later.

"Hey–how'd it go yesterday?" Zeke asked as he worked.

"Embarrassing," TJ groaned.

"The nurses were all impressed with you, though," Leah said, a thread of humour in her voice. "They said that was the fastest they'd ever seen anyone fill up that little cup."

"Doesn't sound impressive to me!" Zeke laughed.

"Me either," TJ agreed wryly. "They probably felt sorry for you, Leah–perhaps I'm always that quick on the draw."

Zeke sputtered a laugh. "So what were the results?"

"Nothing so far," Leah replied. "We meet with the doctor in a couple of weeks, once my tests come back."

"Well, I'm sure everything will be fine. Sometimes it just takes a while to get pregnant."

TJ and Leah exchanged a glance. "Yeah, sometimes," TJ agreed slowly.

"Some pretty good battles going on this time on my blog, huh?" Zeke said, changing the subject as he continued reading and making notes. His voice was deadpan, belying the huge grin on his face.

"Come on, Zeke!" Leah said. "We both know this is the most reaction you've ever received! I knew that blog was gonna be controversial, but *this*–"

"Surpasses even your wildest hopes?"

"Yes!"

Zeke continued scanning the comments as he said, "Which part do you think did it? My witty jabs at cougars? My even wittier comments about the drones and drudges?"

"Probably both—and probably the fact that your 'praise' is anything but. Especially when you get into women's mid-life crises."

Zeke shrugged even though Leah couldn't see him. "I call 'em like I see 'em."

"I know—it's why I hired you and why I publish you even though you really haven't got a clue what women want."

"That's not what Dixie told me last night. Or this morning." Zeke's voice was unbearably smug and Leah rolled her eyes again.

"Yeah?" she said. "Give some pointers to TJ then."

"Hey now!" TJ protested.

Leah grinned at him, then leaned over and gave him a quick kiss.

"Sorry, honey—couldn't resist," she said. "Especially after your performance at the clinic yesterday!"

TJ pouted until she kissed him again, this time a bit more thoroughly.

"Okay, lovebirds—I'm still on the line," Zeke groaned. "So, Leah, does this mean you want me to do a follow-up to this piece?"

"Better than that. Wait 'til you see—"

"*Whoa!*"

"Got to that part, huh?" Leah chortled.

Zeke stared in disbelief at his computer screen. "Is this ad for real?"

"Oh, yeah," Leah said gleefully. "I've checked it out."

"Huh?"

"I called the number and spoke to..." Leah shuffled through the paper on the table in front of her then picked up a small piece with some notes scribbled on it. "I spoke to 'Manny'. She's really having a mid-life crisis, she's really heading out on a road trip and she's really looking for a travelling companion."

Zeke flopped back in his chair with a huff. "Is she suicidal or nuts?"

"She just sounded kind of frazzled."

"Let me guess. You want me to interview this woman and–what? Make her the face of the pathetic older woman I just wrote about?"

"I want you to go with her."

Minus Fifteen Days

"Even though I still think you've lost your mind, I can't say I'm sorry you're throwing everything out," Rebecca said, making a small moue of distaste as she lifted yet another grey skirt out of the closet.

"Me neither," Manny sighed. "When did I stop buying colours?" She frowned as she checked over a grey blazer before tossing it on the donation pile.

"You never bought bright colours," Daisy objected mildly as she rifled through the shirts Manny stored in her chest of drawers, "but you used to buy strong ones."

She glanced at the other two who were giving her puzzled looks. "You know–black, red, white."

"Oh–and you had that jewel tone period, remember?" Rebecca said brightly. "Those strong blues and greens."

Manny smiled fondly. "I remember."

"But no patterns."

"Not by my face anyway," Manny agreed, tossing another grey blazer on the donation pile.

"Do we get to go shopping with you?" Rebecca asked.

"If you can meet me–sure," Manny grinned. "But I'm not waiting for you."

They worked in silence for a few moments before Rebecca said, "I have to leave around five. Jaime's bringing Tris over tonight and said she wanted to talk to me–alone."

"That doesn't sound good," Manny said.

Rebecca shrugged as she tossed another non-descript skirt onto the rag pile. "It's probably another rant about The-Currently-Evil-One."

Both Daisy and Manny snorted.

"The divorce is still on then?" Manny asked.

"So far today," Rebecca agreed and made a show of checking her watch, "but it is only noon."

"This has to be tough on Tris," Daisy said sympathetically and Manny nodded in agreement.

Rebecca sighed. "She hasn't said anything, but then she doesn't usually say anything to me." She lowered her voice conspiratorially. "She doesn't like me much." She laughed lightly, but her eyes showed the bewildered pain that lay beneath her words.

"She likes you just fine," Manny protested, then bit her lip. "I'm sorry—that was stupid."

Rebecca shrugged, determinedly focused on the skirts. "She's her mother's daughter," she said, and pressed her lips into a thin, tight line.

Daisy and Manny exchanged significant glances then turned back to their friend, who after a moment sighed and met their eyes.

"I know—I know—it's not all on them. It's never only one person's fault. I'm a responsible adult and I have to take my share of the blame for failing to bridge the gap between me and my daughter, and me and my granddaughter. Blah, blah, blah. I *get* it."

"Nobody's judging you," Manny said gently.

"Why not? *She* does." Rebecca angrily threw another skirt on the donation pile and glared at the clothes, her hands on her hips.

They stood in tense silence until Manny said tentatively, "Are—are you *pouting?*"

Rebecca's startled gaze met hers. She blinked, nonplussed, before she frowned and put a hand to her mouth.

"Oh, my God—I am!" she exclaimed and started to

laugh. The other two joined in. After a moment, they sobered and grinned at each other.

Rebecca sighed. "Seriously, it's really not their fault. Especially Tris. I mean, she's only ten for God's sake! And I'm her grandmother—it's just...unfortunate that her personality is so much like her mother's."

"At least *they* get along," Manny said with forced optimism.

Rebecca rolled her eyes at her. "Always a silver lining, huh? You get that from *your* mother."

They lapsed into silence and worked steadily until Rebecca said quietly, "I sometimes wonder if I would have been more successful with Jaime if your parents hadn't died when she was so young."

"Okay, come on," Manny said, "you weren't *un*-successful! I mean, she's not in jail—she's smart—okay, she hasn't really held a job, but you've supported her—I mean, you're rich, and The-Currently-Evil-One is also rich. But she's not...you know, living on the street!"

Rebecca and Daisy blinked at her.

"No..." Rebecca said slowly.

"Anyway, you did just fine," Manny continued. "You were just a child yourself—and after our parents died, you were really all alone, well, except for us, of course. But I mean, his parents—and *your* parents—"

"Don't," Rebecca said sharply.

Manny frowned at her. "All I'm trying to say is—you've gone from a disowned, homeless pregnant teenager—with the deadbeat dad heading for the hills—and look at you now! Successful, wealthy, with a daughter who may not like you much, but she's at least a functioning human being. And Tris—regardless of your personality clashes—she's your granddaughter! And that can only be a good thing!"

Rebecca nodded glumly. "You're right," she sighed. "And I love them, of course—just like they love me. Really—like we have a choice!"

"Rebecca," Manny chided.

"You know what I mean. I just...I just wish we *liked* each other more, you know?"

The three friends worked in silence for a few moments.

"You never liked your mother either," Manny said thoughtfully.

Rebecca glared. "I liked her just fine until she threw me out of the house!"

"You *know*—"

"Don't! My God—don't you talk to me about my parents!"

"You know what your dad was like!" Manny protested. "I just don't think you should always blame your mother for your father's actions."

Rebecca glared at her. Manny stared calmly back, the air crackling with tension.

"What are you trying to say?" Rebecca snarled.

"That it's genetic. Or something. This—this—tendency to blame the mother for the sins of the father."

Rebecca looked stunned. "Do you think that's what this is all about?"

"She was asking you about her dad the other day, wasn't she?"

"Yeah."

"And you told her...?"

"The truth. His name and what happened. You know, everything she already knew."

"Well, maybe she's just...resentful about what her dad did, and—well—she only has you to take it out on."

Rebecca stared at Manny in wide-eyed silence.

"Or maybe I'm full of shit," Manny continued, "I don't have any kids; what the hell do I know?"

Rebecca stared for another moment before she reluctantly grinned and laughed. "Hey, it's as good a theory as any I've managed to come up with." She shook her head. "Enough about me. Have you had any responses to your ad?"

"Tons. Tons! I've set up meetings with the four that seem the most promising and we'll see how it goes."

"Well, if you choose one, give me their name and I'll have Max do a background check on them," Daisy said.

"That seems like a little bit of overkill," Manny murmured.

"You're my only sister. I'm not about to let you leave town with a total stranger and not have some idea about who, and what kind of person, they are. Besides, Max owes me. I've gone above and beyond for him more times than I can count." Daisy shrugged. "Plus he likes you."

"He's not going to be tracking my credit card records is he?" Manny asked, her eyes wide.

"If I ask him," Daisy replied primly, then grinned. "Only if you don't call me every couple of days and let me know where you are and if you're okay. And e-mails won't be enough! Anyone can send an e-mail."

"I'll call. Don't worry."

"So when do you meet these people?"

"Tomorrow at the coffee shop on the corner."

"Good luck."

~~~~~

Jaime was sitting at the kitchen table reading the morning's newspaper when Rebecca breezed in later that evening.

"Sorry, Jaime," she said, "I wasn't expecting you until closer to five-thirty."

"That's okay," Jaime drawled, bored. "I'm used to waiting for you."

Rebecca's step faltered slightly, but she recovered quickly and continued to the stove. She filled the kettle as she considered ways to respond to Jaime's comment before she decided there'd be no point. She replaced the kettle on the stove and turned on the heat before she turned to Jaime with a determined smile.

"Tris in the family room?"

Jaime shrugged. "I assume. Either that or her

bedroom."

Rebecca nodded and thoughtfully contemplated her daughter. She'd tried to give Jaime a good life: safe, secure and protected. She'd worked hard—maybe too hard, she acknowledged. She'd made sure Jaime never came into contact with the fleeting lovers Rebecca had had over the years; she'd never found a man she trusted enough to introduce to the most precious person in her life.

Perhaps she should have told Jaime she loved her more often, Rebecca mused. Jaime, however, was apparently more interested in the paper than in speaking to her mother, and Rebecca heaved a silent sigh.

"So," she said with forced cheer, "you said you wanted to talk to me about something?"

Jaime glanced up, then nodded as she folded the paper and laid it aside. The kettle began to whistle as Rebecca took two cups out of the cupboard and took the lid off the teapot. She warmed the pot then turned to Jaime with an expectant, quizzical look.

Jaime calmly met Rebecca's eyes and said, "I'm going to hire Max to look for my dad."

Rebecca stilled. She blinked when she realized Jaime was waiting for her to say something.

"Oh," was all she could manage as she turned back to the teapot.

Jaime snorted in frustration. "Oh? Is that all you can say? *Oh?*"

Rebecca shrugged, her eyes resolutely on her hands as she made the tea.

"You're thirty years old. You're more than old enough to make your own decisions. What else is there for me to say?"

"I don't *get* you, you know. You make no goddamn sense."

"The feeling is mutual," Rebecca muttered under her breath. She carried the teapot and two cups to the table and frowned at Jaime.

"Why do you say that?" she asked aloud.

Jaime threw herself back in her chair with a huff, her arms crossed tightly across her chest.

"You've never once blamed him, or said anything truly bad about him to me. You've never even called him a name! You can't be this perfect! You *must* have hated his guts! You must *still* hate him! I know I hate Blake right now, and he's at least in Tris' life. Are you really this...this *noble* and *perfect*?"

The words would have been flattering if Jaime's lip hadn't been lifted in a sneer. Rebecca stared at her daughter, her stomach roiling with anger and nausea at having to think about everything that had happened to her over thirty years ago. She carefully poured herself some tea with shaking hands; she added honey then sat back, cradling the cup, taking comfort from its weight and heat.

"Of course I'm not perfect," Rebecca said, doing her best to keep her tone neutral. "Of course I was angry—who wouldn't be?"

She swallowed, her throat clicking. Then she thought, *no.* Jaime was an adult; had been for a very long time now, and a mother herself since the age of twenty. Jaime wanted to know how Rebecca had felt; perhaps it was time to tell her. To *truly* tell her.

"Your father got me pregnant then buggered off for parts unknown the day after I told him," she said slowly. "His parents refused to believe he was responsible. My parents disowned me. If it hadn't been for the Mankowskis, I would have had to have you on some street corner in that shitty little town! As it was, I was a wreck for the first year—more!—of your life. I—I did lots of things I'm not proud of—lots of things that still make me ashamed when I think about them. I did my best to hurt the only people in my life who had proven they loved and accepted and believed in me no matter how much I fucked up.

"I'm talking about the Mankowskis, of course. Mrs. Mankowski tried to talk sense into me—and I said things to her and Mr. Mankowski that I'll regret until the day I die. Everyone but them thought I was white trash–and trust me, I did my damnedest to live down to expectations! Everyone but the Mankowskis thought I would end up with a houseful of brats, all with different fathers, living on welfare, and drinking and whoring myself into an early grave. And looking back, that's exactly what would have happened if I'd continued the way I was going.

"But the Mankowskis not only gave me a home–they also gave me tough love. You were about a year, year-and-a-half when they sat me down and laid out my options."

"Options?" Jaime asked faintly, her eyes wide.

"They offered to support me if I wanted to go to school. They'd help me out if I wanted to get a job. They even–" she clamped her mouth shut, blinking back tears. She took a small sip of hot tea as she struggled to compose herself.

"They even...?" Jaime prompted.

"They offered to adopt you if I thought that was what was best. The only thing they *wouldn't* do was let me continue to throw away my life and yours–for nothing. They warned me they'd try to take custody of you if I continued the way I was going.

"At first I was furiously angry and I felt horribly, horribly betrayed–again. But once I calmed down–and, yes, sobered up–I took a cold, hard look at myself; realized they were right. I cleaned up my act, enrolled in the same university as Daisy, and life was beginning to–to turn right side up again."

"And then they died," Jaime said flatly.

"Yes. And then they died, and it was my turn to be the strong one, to help Daisy and Manny work through their grief and come out the other side."

Rebecca barked out a harsh, bitter laugh, a tinge of hysteria in the sound. "*Perfect*? *Hell*, no, I'm not perfect! And if I've never said a word against your father in your hearing that doesn't mean I haven't said plenty out of it.

But no. I don't hate him. Hate implies I give a damn about him. I don't. I'm indifferent. I've made a good life for us in spite of him and what he did.

"If you want to find him—then find him. I hope he's grown into a decent man—for *your* sake."

"I want to hear *his* side of the story," Jaime said stubbornly and Rebecca wondered what, exactly, Jaime hoped to hear him say.

She took a sip of tea, her eyes steady on her daughter's face. She carefully set her cup on the table.

"Then I hope you find him."

Minus Fourteen Days

The coffee shop wasn't very busy. Only a couple of tables were occupied, with several more people standing in line. Manny sat rather nervously at her table sipping her third vanilla latte and wondering if she was as crazy as Rebecca and Daisy claimed. This would be her fourth interview today of a potential travelling companion and she hoped this guy would be more of a possibility than the other three she'd already met. Oh, they all seemed nice enough, but Olive had been jittery and they'd quickly realized their personalities would never mesh well enough to travel together for six months. Isaac had had a predatory, speculative gleam in his eyes as he looked her over—and she hadn't needed Harvey to tell her to stay as far away from *him* as possible.

Darius was very sweet and charming, just eighteen, but he couldn't pay his own way, and Manny wasn't about to support him for six months. He'd shrugged and accepted her decision with an adorable smile and she offered to call Daisy's boss, Max, to see if he had any work that Darius could do. Darius had thanked her and even paid for their lattes, and they'd chatted for a good forty-five minutes before he'd finally gone on his way. Yes, he would have been a good choice—and she might change her mind if she didn't find anyone before she left in two weeks.

You can always go by yourself.

I know. But it would be more fun with someone else.

You'll have me.

Manny glanced at Harvey sitting in the chair across from her. He was dressed casually in jeans and a button down shirt open at the throat to show the strong lines of his neck and chest.

You're not real.

Harvey winked at her. **Just checking.**

She shook her head and Harvey blinked out of existence as the door opened and a darkly handsome man walked in. He paused in the doorway and removed his sunglasses as he glanced around the small room. Securely hidden in her corner, Manny considered him.

Tall; over six feet. Dark. Handsome, with large, dark eyes and full pouty lips. His black, tousled hair and dark stubble on his face gave him a sexy, scruffy appearance. He was slim, with broad shoulders, narrow hips and long legs encased in jeans.

I'll bet he has a great ass.

I'll bet you're right.

He's like a younger version of me.

Manny blinked at the man standing in the doorway and realized Harvey was right. Oh, they didn't exactly look alike, but they had similar colouring, and a similar underlying confidence and arrogance in their stance. Probably something natural when you're that naturally gorgeous, Manny thought ruefully, or, in Harvey's case, that *unnaturally* perfect.

I'd almost be jealous...if I was real.

But you're not–and he's quite something. I wonder who he's here to me...eeet.

Her internal dialogue trailed off as the stranger's gaze met hers. He gave a half smile and headed towards her.

Shit. Manny could feel her eyes getting bigger as he came closer. She fought the urge to look behind her–but only succeeded because she knew she was sitting in the corner with her back against the wall.

This could be interesting.

Shit!

She looked up and up as the stranger stopped at her table.

"Manny?" he asked.

<u>And</u> an accent! Now I really am jealous.

Why the hell did I wear these sweats and this sweatshirt? Why didn't I check my hair before he arrived? Why didn't I at least try to look presentable for these things?

Because you're getting rid of all your boring work clothes, you haven't bought casual clothes in ten years, and your hair hasn't been out of that bun since the year 2000?

Oh. Right.

Manny pulled herself together. She gave him a half-smile of her own and stood. "Yes. Manny Mankowski." She held out her hand. "You must be Zeke."

Zeke nodded and shook her hand. His grip was warm and firm and lasted exactly long enough to be polite without being too friendly before he released her hand.

Obviously not love at first sight.

Shut up.

"Did you want to get a coffee or anything?" she asked, getting herself under control. She was forty-five years old, for God's sake, and he wasn't the first handsome man she'd met up close and personal.

He <u>is</u> the first one you've met outside of a work context in over fifteen years.

Please shut up.

"No, no thanks," he said.

They sat down, and Manny nervously played with her latte while they assessed each other.

"Manny Mankowski?" he finally said, breaking the awkward silence. "Your parents ran out of ideas, did they?"

Manny huffed a short laugh. "It's a nickname. My real name is Rose." She made a rueful, self-deprecating face. "It doesn't suit me."

They lapsed into another awkward silence.

This bodes well, Harvey said, watching with avid interest.

"So..." Zeke said, gesturing helplessly, "how does this work?"

"Well, we just...talk. See if we have anything in common; see if we can decide if we could spend six months travelling together. So far, nobody else has worked out."

"Yeah? Have you had many people answer your ad?"

"A lot, actually, but counting you, I've only met with four of them. Most of the people who responded were obviously nut jobs, another pool of them just wanted to wish me luck and tell me how much they wished they had the courage to do what I'm doing. Almost everyone else backed out when I insisted they would be paying their own way. So, the only ones I've actually met at least told me they were willing to pay their own way and confirmed it when we met. Well, except Darius, but he was so sweet I didn't have the heart to be annoyed with him. Anyway, obviously most people get turned off when I remind them I won't be supporting them for six months."

"No free ride then, I take it."

"Is there ever a free ride?"

"I guess not."

"So what is it?"

"What?"

"Money problems or women problems? Or–I'm sorry, I shouldn't assume–maybe it's men problems?"

I'll break down in tears if he's gay.

I'll join you.

Zeke blinked at her in surprise. "None of the above. And if you're asking if I'm gay, the answer's no."

There really is a God–and He apparently loves you.

"I wasn't asking—I just didn't want to presume."

"Hmmm. So, tell me about yourself."

"I thought the ad was pretty self-explanatory."

"If you're this talkative all the time, it could be a very long six months."

"I'm sorry. I'm...to be honest, I'm a little nervous. I never thought anybody would answer the ad. I mean, not to actually meet with me, and here you're number four."

Zeke gave her a polite smile. "So, tell me about yourself."

Manny sighed. "I'm forty-five and trying to put some spark back into my life. I've spent the last fifteen years being defined by my job—so much so I've lost sight of who I am without it. I don't know if this road trip will help me rediscover myself, but I think I'll enjoy giving it a try. Now, tell me about *your*self."

"I'm thirty-five. I'm a freelance multimedia developer and can basically work from anywhere. I'm originally from New Zealand—"

"I was trying to place the accent."

"Yes. Anyway, I'm originally from New Zealand and even though I've seen a lot of this continent, I wouldn't mind seeing more of it. This seemed like it could be fun."

"I think so, too." She paused and considered him thoughtfully. "I'm guessing it's women problems."

Zeke heaved an exasperated sigh. "I'm guessing *your* reasons are women problems, too," he said.

Ooooh. Ouch, Harvey winced.

Manny blinked at Zeke, brows raised.

"Wow," she said. "Okay. Well, if you're this forthcoming all the time, this could be a long six months."

"I'm sorry," Zeke said, "but I don't think my reasons for answering your ad are all that important."

Manny frowned. "Except we're both thinking about leaving town with a total stranger. Even though we can both leave at any point—one reason for having your own money—you don't want to have a miserable time, even if it's only for a few days."

Zeke cocked his head to one side and considered her thoughtfully before he answered. "Oddly, I don't think we'd have a miserable time, although I have a sneaking suspicion we'd fight a lot."

Manny chuckled slightly. "That assumes I'd care enough to argue with you. Look, if we agree that you're the one, then I suggest you think of me as an older sister–or...or your aunt. If we go on this trip together, I don't care what you do. If you decide at some point to not continue, then I'd like to know as soon as possible so I can make other arrangements if necessary."

Zeke leaned back in his chair, his arms crossed as he considered her carefully. There was a speculative gleam in his eyes that puzzled her although it didn't alarm her the way Isaac's had. Whatever was going on in his head, Manny instinctively believed he would never hurt her.

"What do you expect from me," Zeke asked slowly, "if I go with you?"

Manny shrugged. "Companionship, mostly. I don't mean we're joined at the hip. I mean, what I'm hoping is if I want to take a tour of an historic site, for example, that you'd go with me–at least occasionally. Basically do things with me while we're travelling. I'm trying to get out of my comfort zone, try new things, meet new people. I'd like somebody to be with me while I do that. I can do it alone but it's sometimes more fun with someone else there."

Zeke frowned. "Don't you have any friends?"

Manny shrugged but she couldn't quite meet his eyes. "Sure–but they all have to work, or they have families, or they just have no desire to bum around for six months. Or they don't have the money to bum around for six months."

"No boyfriend of your own? Or–I'm sorry, I shouldn't assume–no girlfriend?"

Manny chuckled again. "Neither one. And it's boyfriend, by the way. I haven't had one of those in...decades, I think. It certainly feels that way. And I was never any good at all that..." she waved vaguely, "*stuff* anyway."

"Stuff?" he asked, amused.

"You know. Relationship stuff. I guess it didn't help that I never wanted to be married or have kids—but I did expect to at least have sex on occasion." She shrugged. "I was wrong."

"Is that on the agenda for this trip?"

"Sex?"

"Yes."

"Well, I'm not intending to have sex with anyone. And like the ad said, no sex is offered or expected from whoever I take with me."

"That's good to know. I have to tell you—I...I like younger women."

"You and every other straight man on the planet. So, you're trying to say my virtue is safe with you?"

"Like you were my sister," he said with a charming smile, "or my aunt."

Shit—and he's got a great smile, too. I've got a bad feeling about this.

Those are just hormones. Remember them?

...I can't believe I created you.

"Well, that's a relief," Manny said drily. "Now, are you going to tell me the truth?"

Zeke sighed and shrugged, but avoided her eyes, "Women problems."

Manny hummed. "Well," she said, finishing her latte, "I think you'll do." She met his gaze steadily, seriously. "I'm leaving in two weeks—you can let me know any time up to the night before I leave if you'd like to go with me. Think it over, try to work things out with your girlfriend, and let me know. You have my phone number and my e-mail address." She stared hard at him. "I won't be chasing you down for an answer," she warned. "I'm not going to phone you in a couple of days asking if you're going to come with me or not. Let me know—or don't."

Zeke blinked at her, then raised his eyebrows in amusement. "Pretty cut and dried."

"I'm too old and tired for games," Manny said, "even if it's only to go on a trip."

They stood and headed outside. She smiled and held out her hand. "Either way, it was nice to meet you, and if I don't see you again, good luck with your girlfriend."

"Thanks," he said. She watched him walk away.

Told you he'd have a great ass.

Never doubted it for a minute.

~~~~~

Leah watched with amusement as Zeke paced around her boardroom.

"I'm telling you, she won't last a week! A more...prudish, repressed woman I have yet to meet! I doubt she's done anything just for fun in her life!"

"Doesn't mean she won't go the full six months," Leah replied mildly.

"Oh, please! She wears her hair in a bun! A *bun*! And if her face has seen makeup in the last ten years, I'll eat my socks! She'll get scared at the first loud noise and skitter home to safety." He shook his head. "This is a non-story. Trust me."

"Well, I think you should still take the trip. You can write this blog you're currently working on if you want to—but you'll probably be wrong." She frowned thoughtfully. "You know...I wonder if she'd be interested in writing a guest blog."

Zeke stopped in his tracks. "*What?*"

"Sure," Leah said, gaining enthusiasm. "That's not a bad plan B. She could write updates of her journey—I mean, my subscribers are absolutely rabid about this—and absolutely passionate about you going with her if the poll results and the comments are anything to go by. Half want you to expose her as pathetic; the other half want you to be surprised and humbled and knocked off your high horse."

"Hey!"

"Some love you; some love to hate you–but they all want you to document this woman's adventure–no matter how long it lasts, or what you learn."

"Well, it's a non-story–I'm telling you. She probably won't even make it out of town. I doubt she's ever been anywhere!"

"That's...actually kinda sad."

Zeke shrugged. "Yeah, well–those were the choices she made."

Leah frowned at him. "You don't know what she's faced in her life. You shouldn't be so judgmental."

Zeke grinned at her. "Hey, that's why you pay me the big bucks, you know–because I'm so judgmental."

"You know, if I didn't know that sometimes you can actually be a really nice, understanding guy, I'd think you were the biggest jerk that ever walked the planet."

He shrugged again. "People don't want to read the blog of a nice guy."

"But they would love to see you taken down a peg or two."

"Oh, like any tightly wound old lady could do that!" he scoffed.

Leah gave him a reproving look as she stood and walked over to him, a hand cupped around her ear. "Do you hear that? That's the sound of fate taking aim right–" she poked him hard in the middle of the forehead–"*there.*"

Zeke rolled his eyes as he rubbed the spot she'd poked. "Yeah, yeah, yeah. Look, I gotta go. I have an interview in an hour on the other side of town." He gave her a wicked wink followed by an equally wicked grin. "Believe me, my next blog is gonna be a scorcher!"

"Yeah? Dixie gonna be okay with that?"

"Hey–what she don't know–"

"Won't hurt you?" Leah asked drily.

"Exactly."

~~~~~

Zeke smiled at the woman behind him as he waited for Dixie to answer the phone. "I don't know how I let my phone run down," he said, then turned away when he heard Dixie's questioning 'hello'.

"Hey, babe, it's me. I'm running a bit later than planned tonight, doing research for tomorrow's blog. I should be home in about an hour, maybe two."

"Research, huh?" Dixie said skeptically.

"Yeah. Don't be mad, sweetheart. I'll make it up to you when I get home."

"I'll bet. Fine."

"See you later, babe." He hung up the phone and handed it back to the attractive blonde holding a glass of wine and smiling charmingly at him. He grinned back. "Thanks for that. Now, where were we?"

Two hours later, Zeke pulled in the driveway at the back of the house and headed towards the front door, whistling cheerfully. He grinned to himself as he tried to decide what would be the best way to make it up to Dixie for him getting home late. He frowned as he came around the corner and saw the boxes piled on the front porch. He took a close look at them and his eyes widened when he saw his name written in black felt pen on them, with a white envelope taped to the top one. He hesitated, swallowed hard, then picked up the envelope and slowly opened it.

The message was printed in block letters and simply said, 'NEXT TIME USE YOUR OWN DAMN PHONE.'

~~~~~

Zeke sat slumped at TJ and Leah's kitchen table, playing with the glass in front of him. TJ and Leah watched him, concerned, taking sips from their own drinks as they listened to his story.

"How she managed to get the locks changed at this time of night—" he shook his head, staring down at his glass.

"I'm sorry, man," TJ said.

"Me, too," Leah said. "I really liked Dixie."

Zeke nodded and sighed. "Yeah. Me, too. You know the sad part? I was really trying this time. I mean, I wasn't cheating. For the first time since...in a long time, I felt...She's...she's sweet, you know what I mean? I thought we really had something."

"If you feel like that," TJ said, "then go back tomorrow and try to work it out. Explain to her what you were doing."

Zeke shook his head. "I told her I was working. She obviously didn't believe me." He paused, running a finger around the rim of his glass. He glanced up at Leah.

"Is that offer to leave town still open?"

Minus Six Days

I'm getting worried.

Manny glanced over at Harvey, who was currently painting her living room dressed only in a pair of low-riding jeans. She took a moment to admire the impossibly well-defined muscles of his torso as they moved beneath the skin of his back and sighed. Who else, she thought, would happily help her paint her living room and not mind that she herself was sweating up a storm, tendrils of hair escaping from its tight bun to plaster themselves to her cheeks and forehead, all while she was wearing the only pair of sloppy sweats and t-shirt Rebecca and Daisy had left behind after they cleaned out her closets? Anyone other than a fantasy man would run screaming for the hills, she thought ruefully, and who could blame them?

What are you worried about?

We only ever seem to talk anymore—or else I'm helping you work. You haven't had me rescuing you from pirates in months.

Hey–you're the one who complained about the breeches!

I'm just wondering if the romance has gone out of our relationship.

Sadly, the only fantasy I want right now is somebody helping me paint who looks as good as you do with his shirt off.

I aim to please.

I should hope so–you're <u>my</u> fantasy after all.

The doorbell startled her, and she glanced at her watch as she headed to the door. She opened it to find Rebecca on the other side, dressed in old jeans and a t-shirt and yet somehow still looking gorgeous, a sparkle in her bright blue eyes, her auburn hair adding a glow to her smooth cheeks.

"If I didn't love you like a second sister, I'd hate your breathing guts," Manny said and stepped aside to let Rebecca into the house.

Rebecca laughed. "Well, that's good to know...I think. What brought that on?"

"The fact you look gorgeous in anything you wear and I always manage to look like a schlub."

Rebecca laughed again. "Well, thanks," she smirked, "but even I couldn't pull *that* look off." She gestured at Manny's sad outfit then critically assessed the progress Manny had made in painting the room. "I'll start on the opposite wall?"

"Good a place as any," Manny agreed. She watched as Rebecca poured paint into the pan and took up a roller. "I really appreciate this, you know."

Rebecca shrugged. "That's what friends are for–to help you out even when you're losing your ever-loving mind."

"Thanks for the vote of confidence there, Rebecca."

"Hey–I have a very real worry that this guy–what's his name again?"

"Zeke."

"Right–Zeke. Look, besides the fact he might turn out to be a serial killer, have you thought about what you're going to do when this road trip is over? You still need to work, and you're selling this place, so you'll need somewhere to live, and just where do you think you're going to find another job that paid as much as that one?"

Manny determinedly shook her head. "I'm not thinking that far ahead."

"See? This is what I'm talking about! That's not like you! You've got things planned years in advance! Sometimes to the very hour!"

"That's because nothing—and I mean nothing—ever changes for me! That's the point! That's why I need to do this! I'm almost positive I didn't used to be like this. I don't remember worrying or planning years in advance when I was in my early twenties. I used to...I don't know...just *live*."

Rebecca painted in silence for a moment then slowly said, "You were still reeling from the deaths of your parents. You and Daisy both. I think your early twenties were—well, you'd had it proven to you when you were seventeen that there's no such thing as a guaranteed future. You both lived life in the moment for a while there."

Manny bit her lip. "It was...hard," she acknowledged softly. "For all of us," she added, glancing at Rebecca.

"It's still hard," Rebecca sighed, "and it's been almost thirty years."

They worked in somber silence for a few minutes, then Manny shook off her melancholy mood.

"Regardless of the reasons why I was different in my early twenties, I don't want to be this...*this*...person anymore. I want to know who I could be—or who I want to be—or..."

"Or?"

"Or who I *am*. I've been my job for so long, I can't remember who I am without it." She stared at Rebecca, stricken. "I don't want to die as this person."

Rebecca put down her roller, walked to Manny and pulled her into a tight, comforting hug. "I'd prefer it if you'd say you want to *live* as a different person," she said gently.

Manny gave a choked laugh and nodded.

Rebecca stood back, her hands on Manny's shoulders. She searched Manny's eyes then nodded briskly. "Okay. I won't argue or try to talk you out of this. Just...be careful, okay? And if you run into trouble, you call, okay? I'll be there."

"I know," Manny nodded. "And I'll be careful."

They went back to painting and worked in silence for several minutes then Rebecca asked, "So, when's this guy getting here?"

Manny glanced at her watch. "In about fifteen minutes or so–if he's on time." She glanced slyly at Rebecca. "Don't worry–you'll like him."

"Oh?"

Manny nodded. "Tall, dark and handsome–just the way you like 'em."

Rebecca laughed. "Well, in that case I'd better not tell Jackson about him."

Manny laughed as well. "I'm not sure he's in Jackson's league–but he's pretty darn close."

"Now I'm intrigued...and possibly a little jealous."

Manny grimaced. "Don't be–Zeke likes younger women."

"Him and every other straight man on the planet."

Zeke was exactly on time. Manny led him in to the living room and was rewarded and amused by Rebecca's reaction to him and his reaction to her. She struggled not to laugh out loud at the appreciative gleam in his eyes and charming smile that curved his mouth. He might like younger women, Manny thought as she watched them greet each other, but he also appreciated beauty when he saw it. In an odd way, it was a mark in his favour.

The doorbell rang again, and Zeke looked at her with raised eyebrows.

"That'll be Daisy," she said and hurried to answer the door.

While Rebecca's reaction to Zeke amused her, Daisy's reaction sent her off into a fit of giggles she couldn't seem to stop. Daisy's wide-eyed, mesmerized stare and breathless "hel-*lo*" made Manny laugh even harder. Zeke was somewhat nonplussed by her amusement, while Daisy just gave her a disgusted look. However, Manny's laughter seemed to snap Daisy out of her dazed fascination, and she became once again a mature woman instead of a teenager.

"Okay, okay," she sighed as Manny got herself under control. She turned to Zeke. "Thanks for sending me all the information I asked for, Zeke." She waved the envelope she carried in her hand at Manny and Rebecca.

"He's definitely who he says he is. Ezekiel 'Zeke' Powell, freelance multimedia developer. Born in New Zealand, and been in this country for the last fourteen years. No criminal record, no bad debts, no court orders or restraining orders against him in either country. He also has a healthy bank account and an excellent professional reputation."

"Good lord—are you a cop?" Zeke asked incredulously.

"I work for a very good private investigator, actually." She turned to Manny. "As far as Max can tell, he's as safe as anybody else."

"Well, that's a bit lukewarm, don't you think?" Zeke protested.

The women ignored him.

"Great!" Manny said. "Thanks, Daisy. Tell Max I owe him one."

"He's already eager to collect," Daisy replied drily. "He mentioned something about a roast duck dinner when you get back."

"He's got it," Manny said. She turned to Zeke who still looked slightly insulted. "Okay, here's the deal. I'm leaving a week from today. I bought a small travel van—bed, stove, a mini-fridge, and a little bit of storage."

Zeke looked alarmed and opened his mouth, but she

forestalled him.

"Don't worry—your virtue is safe with me. We'll be staying in hotels and motels most of the time. The van is just in case we get stranded or if the passenger wants to have a nap, or we don't want to stop to eat—or we need a little space away from each other."

"Just one question," Zeke said. He gestured at Rebecca and Daisy. "Why aren't the two of you going instead?"

"I can't be away for six months," Rebecca replied, "that's an eternity in the real estate business. Besides, my daughter's going through a divorce right now and I need to be here for her and my granddaughter."

"And my husband and kids might have something to say about it if I were to leave for six months," Daisy said drily.

"Ah. Okay. Then a week it is."

Manny nodded, satisfied.

Daisy stepped up close to Zeke, getting into his personal space. Her face was set, blue eyes steely.

"Just for the record, Zeke—Max and I didn't find anything on you, but I'm telling you something right now: this is my baby sister you're traipsing off with. Anything happens to her that she doesn't want or like—and I'll hunt you down like the dog you are. Got it?"

Zeke stared at her for a moment, then, "*Traipsing*?"

Daisy took a step back but didn't break eye contact. "Just remember that."

He nodded quickly, his eyes wide.

Manny cleared her throat uncomfortably. "Well," she said, her voice a bit higher than usual, "now that that's settled—let's get back to work."

"Work?" Zeke asked incredulously.

"You don't have to, of course, but we," Manny indicated Rebecca and Daisy, "have a house to paint."

Zeke hesitated, then shrugged and smiled. "Why not? I have nothing better to do today."

He took off his jacket and ignored Rebecca and Daisy's

appreciative sighs, although he shared a surprisingly comfortable and amused glance with Manny before getting a pan and a roller.

I'll bet he'd look almost as good as me if he took his shirt off, Harvey murmured.

Go away.

~~~~~

Later that night, Daisy sat at a slot machine in her local casino, playing without paying too much attention to what she was doing. She was thinking of Manny's road trip and trying to keep calm about it. Zeke seemed like a nice guy although...*unhappy*. She'd asked Manny about it while they were making coffee in the kitchen, and Manny told her Zeke had recently had some issues with his girlfriend. Daisy wondered if that meant Zeke would cut his trip short—or back out entirely—if things changed with his girlfriend. She didn't know which would be worse: Manny leaving for six months with a stranger, or Manny leaving for six months alone.

Both options made her shiver with apprehension. Daisy had her family, her husband and kids, and, of course, Rebecca, but Manny—Manny was her *sister*, a different kind of bond than any of the others, and her only true link to the parents they'd lost so long ago. They had history that even Rebecca didn't share.

"Why the hell am I not surprised?"

Daisy started with a little screech, and stared, wide-eyed at her husband.

"Jesus, Hub—you scared me!"

"Yeah, because you can't see anything but that damn machine! As usual!"

Daisy gave an exasperated sigh. "Don't start. Have you tracked me down just to give me hell, or do you need me for something? For a change," she added sarcastically.

"Don't *you* start. Did you forget? Jakob played soccer tonight and Janika had a volleyball game."

Daisy sighed tiredly. "No, I didn't forget."

"Then—look at me!" Hub hissed furiously. She turned a bland face towards him but kept playing her machine. "Then why are you sitting here, instead of going to their games?"

Daisy stopped playing and turned to face him fully.

"Because they're your children, too," she snarled, "and you haven't been to a single game for either of them this year!"

"You could have just asked instead of—of—of taking a runner to the fucking casino! Again!"

"I *have* asked you! I've also told you and begged you and even tried forcing you! Shockingly, you're always busy!"

She smacked the cash out button with more force than necessary and walked rapidly to the ticket-cashing machine, Hub hard on her heels.

"So you come here—abandon your children—"

"Oh my God—I've been gone for two hours! You've been emotionally gone for the last five years!"

Hub growled, "I don't appreciate being pulled away from work—"

"Yeah? Well, I don't appreciate being a single parent while I'm still married! It's time you picked your head up from your work and started paying attention to your children! And while you're at it, you'd better start paying attention to me, too! Before it's too late."

Minus One Day

TJ and Leah anxiously waited for the doctor to arrive. TJ glanced at Leah as he took her hand and gave it a reassuring squeeze.

"No matter what he tells us, we'll find a way to have a baby," he told her softly.

She smiled although she remained tense and alert.

"I know we will," she said and squeezed back.

TJ shifted his chair closer to hers and kept a firm, warm grip on her hand, their fingers laced together, as the door opened and the doctor walked in carrying a file.

He greeted them with a gentle smile as he sat at his desk. He opened the file, then met their anxious stares.

"As you know, the test results have come back." His gaze shifted to TJ. "I'm sorry. Your sperm count is very low. Which means Leah's chances of getting naturally pregnant by you aren't good."

TJ and Leah's faces fell, devastation in their eyes. The doctor gave them a reassuring smile.

"There are, of course, many other options you can explore. A donor, perhaps IVF, fertility treatments, adoption. There's no need to decide immediately, of course. I'll pull together some information on the options for you to review, if you'd like. Please. Take your time, think things over. There's still a very slim possibility you could conceive naturally, but–I'm sorry–the odds are extremely low."

TJ glanced at Leah. She looked as sick as he felt. He gave her a twisted smile.

"I...I guess you can't call me Stud anymore," he joked weakly.

Leah stared blankly at him before she half-chuckled then burst into tears. TJ pulled her to him and held her as she sobbed into his shoulder.

~~~~~

Zeke sat in the spare room at TJ and Leah's house, his laptop open in front of him. He stared at the blank screen, the blinking cursor, for a few moments and thought about everything that had happened in the last two weeks leading up to tomorrow's departure. He thought about Manny, Daisy and Rebecca; about TJ and Leah's disappointment; about Dixie's decision. He took a sip of his beer, drew in a deep breath, and began to type.

Is it ever too late to change? To make an effort to grasp life in both hands and wring every ounce you can out of it?

Rebecca put the finishing touches on her outfit just as the doorbell rang. She greeted Jackson with a smile and a kiss, then led him by the hand into the living room where she fixed him his favourite drink.

Sometimes change happens without our consent or even our knowledge.

Daisy checked on each of her sleeping children in turn, and smiled at the sight of their tousled heads on their pillows. They each looked much younger than seventeen and fifteen. She quietly shut the door on Janika's room, and walked out to the living room. With a significant look at Hub, she grabbed her purse and left the house.

She strolled from her car to the casino, and smiled when she saw her favourite slot game was free. She sat down, fed a twenty into the machine and ordered a drink from the waitress. She sighed, leaned back and began to play.

Sometimes it happens because of past mistakes.

Zeke glanced at the small framed picture beside the computer. It showed him with a huge grin on his face, his arms around a smiling Dixie. TJ had taken it just a few months ago, when they'd been here for a barbecue. He turned the picture face down and returned his focus to the computer screen.

Sometimes it's completely out of our control.

Leah shifted and made herself more comfortable snuggled up with TJ in their king-sized bed. He absently stroked her arm as he stared sightlessly at the ceiling. She opened her mouth, hesitated, then resolutely closed her eyes.

And sometimes it's a conscious decision, to throw away everything known and safe and secure, and face the new day knowing only one thing: today will be different from yesterday.

Manny stood in her empty, freshly painted living room and turned in a slow circle as she admired their hard work. She made a conscious effort to breathe calmly before, with a final deep breath, she turned off the lights and left the room.

EPISODE TWO
Day 1

Manny finished pinning her mousy hair into her habitual bun and scowled at her shapeless sweats and t-shirt. She wasn't a clotheshorse by any stretch of the imagination, but she had to admit she couldn't wait to start replenishing her wardrobe. For now, all she could do was shake her head. She grabbed her duffel bag and backpack and headed to the living room. She'd just placed her bag on the living room floor when the doorbell rang.

"I'll get it!" Daisy called and hurried to the door.

Manny's stomach curled with nerves as she finished stuffing her laptop into her backpack then glanced at Daisy and Zeke as they walked into the room.

"Ready?" Zeke asked, rubbing his hands together. He looked attractively scruffy with his tousled black hair and five o'clock shadow and for a split second Manny wondered if Rebecca was right, and she'd lost her mind.

Chickening out?

She glanced at Harvey then met Zeke's eyes. She frowned slightly at his half-amused, half-expectant expression. She suddenly realized he was convinced she was about to tell him she'd decided to stay.

...never.

Good girl.

She put her hands on her hips and glanced around. "I think I've covered everything. Daisy, you have enough money to pay the bills until Rebecca sells the house..." She glanced back at Zeke and nodded. "Yeah. Yeah, I'm ready."

Zeke smiled and nodded back. "So where are we going first?"

Manny reached into her backpack and pulled out a small zip-lock bag filled with folded slips of paper.

"You can have the honour of deciding," she said as she opened the bag and held it out to him.

Zeke stared, eyebrows raised. "What the hell is this?"

"Our itinerary. Well, mine anyway. If there are any places you'd like to see we can just add them in." She shook the baggie invitingly. "Pick one."

Zeke stared at her in stunned disbelief. "Are you *nuts*?" he exclaimed. "We could be criss-crossing the continent a hundred times!"

Manny nodded with a bright smile. "Exactly. Pick one."

Zeke looked at Daisy who only shrugged helplessly.

"Don't look at me," she said. "I don't know where the hell this idea came from."

Zeke shook his head, but his lips quirked into a reluctant smile. He reached into the baggie and pulled out one of the pieces of paper. He unfolded it and said, "'San Francisco/San Jose—we have to see the Winchester House.'"

"Oh, awesome!" Daisy said. "I wish I could go with you to that one!"

"Too bad you can't get away," Manny said wistfully.

"Yeah, well, Hub would throw a fit," she said drily. "He had a fit when I told him I was coming over this morning to see you on your way."

Daisy and Manny exchanged a silent look that spoke volumes. Zeke raised an intrigued eyebrow but said nothing.

"But you'll join us sometimes?" Manny asked a little wistfully.

Daisy nodded. "Whenever I can. Wherever I can. And if you need me–I'll be there."

Manny's eyes filled with tears. "I know," she said, and hugged her tightly. "I'll keep in touch," she promised.

"You damn well better, if you know what's good for you," Daisy choked out. "Don't make me have Max track you down! You wouldn't like it if Max has to hunt you down."

Manny laughed a watery laugh as they parted. "I'm sure I wouldn't."

She was still wiping tears away as she waved good-bye while they pulled out of the driveway. She stared resolutely out the passenger window and sat in silence while Zeke drove them out of town.

~~~~~

"Hey, Stacey," Daisy said to the woman who answered the phone, "I'm looking for Hub. Is he around?"

"Sorry, Daisy," Stacey replied in her bright, cheerful voice, "he's out of the office for the afternoon."

Daisy frowned slightly. "Oh? I could have sworn he said he was going to be in the office all day."

"The meeting must have slipped his mind," Stacey said breezily. "Is there a message? Do you need him to call you right away?"

"No. No, I'll talk to him when he gets home."

Daisy thoughtfully hung up the phone and stared off into space with a frown.

She glanced towards the door as it opened and Max walked in. He was tall, still trim even in his fifties, craggy-featured and soft-spoken. He always looked like he'd slept in his clothes while at the same time he was intimidating with his shaved head, aquiline nose and bright, shrewdly intelligent green eyes. Daisy had been terrified of him when she'd first started working for him immediately after Janika had started kindergarten. Ten years on, any fear had long ago subsided and now he was just as much friend as he was boss.

"Manny get off all right?" he asked, his sharply observant eyes taking in her expression.

"Hmmm? Oh. Yes. Right on time, in fact."

Max gave her a reassuring smile. "Don't worry too much. This Powell guy checked out."

"Or he just hasn't been caught yet," Daisy replied drily. She shook off her mood and smiled at him. "New case?"

Max nodded and slumped into a chair beside her desk.

"Jaime's hired me to find her father," he said bluntly.

Daisy blinked at him in silence.

"*Rebecca's* Jaime?"

Max nodded.

"Oh."

"You knew him, didn't you?" Max asked.

Daisy shrugged. "Everyone knew him. Small town, you know. He's probably not going to be hard to find—the last I heard, his family's still living there. I'm sure they'll know where he is. It'll probably only take one phone call."

She cocked her head and considered him thoughtfully.

"Why did Jaime *really* hire you?"

Max sighed. "To check on her mother's version of events."

"You're kidding," she said flatly.

Max shook his head. "Oh, finding her dad is part of it, but for some reason she thinks Rebecca's lying about what happened thirty years ago. She thinks Rebecca has deliberately kept her away from her father all these years."

"It's only taken her thirty years to come up with this theory?" Daisy snorted inelegantly. "That's her father's side coming out. He never was the brightest bulb in the light socket."

Max frowned. "So why did Rebecca—?"

"Because he was freakin' *gorgeous*."

Max huffed and rolled his eyes. "Seriously?"

"Seriously. He was the best-looking boy in town, Max!

Every girl in high school had a huge crush on him, even those who already had boyfriends. Well, except those who had crushes on each other." She stared off into space, her expression softening with the memories. "Devon was tall, black hair, dark brown eyes, great cheekbones and a sexy smile, even at eighteen. Plus he was in his last year of high school—an 'older' man." She chuckled ruefully.

Max raised an amused eyebrow and shook his head in mock disapproval.

"Athletic?" he asked.

"Oh, yeah. Track and field, football, baseball, hockey; you name it, he was good at it. His parents put him on pretty much every team they could find. Drove him everywhere so he could participate. I heard he even got a partial scholarship. Considering our backwater school, that was pretty impressive."

"So, how did he hook up with Rebecca?"

Daisy sighed and leaned back, tapping a pen on the arm of her chair.

"Rebecca was always beautiful, but in those days she was....*shy*. Too scared to speak before being spoken to. But she was—and is—smart. I mean, *scary* smart. She skipped a grade and would have graduated with Devon if...

"Well. Anyway. Long story short, schoolwork was a breeze for her; Devon wasn't the brightest and he—basically—" She hesitated, frowning. "Looking back, it's just so *obvious*, but then again, she was only sixteen and no other boy had ever paid that level of attention to her. Anyway, she did his homework for him. Helped him cheat on his exams. How the hell he thought he'd survive university..."

She shook her head.

"I can see now that Devon was very deliberate in his approach and he'd chosen carefully. Rebecca was...vulnerable, easily convinced he was madly in love with her when in reality, he was using her in order to finish high school with the least amount of effort. I think the sex, for him, was just a bonus...and probably just another strategy he used to bind Rebecca more closely to him. She was completely in love with him, and Manny and I knew pretty much everything about their relationship. But Devon kept Rebecca a deep, dark secret—how he managed *that* was a miracle all by itself when you live in a town as small as ours!"

Daisy sighed heavily. "Anyway. The end result was that when Rebecca got pregnant and named him as the father—nobody believed her. Especially not her parents, who disowned her and haven't spoken to her since. His parents laughed her out of their house."

She frowned at Max. "Which part of Rebecca's story does Jaime doubt?"

Max shifted uncomfortably. "She doesn't think her father ever knew Rebecca was pregnant. She thinks he never would have abandoned his child."

Daisy blinked at him in silence. Then, "Wow. Delusional at thirty. *Wow.*"

Max shrugged. "That's not for me to judge. She doesn't seem dangerous, so I'll find him for her." He smirked at her. "Even if all it takes is a phone call."

Daisy chuckled slightly, then frowned thoughtfully.

Max cocked his head as he watched her. "You look like you have something on your mind."

Her frown deepened. "I'm not sure—it's more like a faint...discomfort."

"About?"

She silently stared off into space.

"Daisy?" he prompted when it appeared she had no intention of breaking her silence.

She jumped slightly at the sound of his voice. She seemed to make a decision when she met his eyes. Her lips tightened, her eyes hardened, and she gave a brisk nod.

"I want to hire you."

Max's smirk widened. "You can't hire me, Daisy; you get my services for free. What's going on? Do you want me to dig deeper on that Powell guy?"

She shook her head. "I want you to follow Hub."

Max's jaw dropped. "*Hub?*"

Daisy nodded and leaned forward, resting her tightly clasped hands on the desk. "He's always been a workaholic, but something's been different lately. Small things–his secretary tells me he's one place; he tells me another. He's been particularly moody lately, getting angry at almost everything I do. He's never been super involved with the kids, but now he only remembers them when I ask–or force–him to do something with them. Which means the kids barely see him and...and I'm not sure how that's affecting them. I just–I just need to know if there's something going on I need to know about. That's all. And then I can deal with whatever the problem is–if there is one that's...well, outside of our relationship."

"You don't think you should just sit Hub down and ask him what's going on? Maybe he's having trouble at work."

Daisy shook her head. "We haven't been talking much lately, and when we do, it just turns into an argument."

Max thoughtfully considered her then said, "I just don't want you to blame me if I find something you don't like."

Daisy raised an eyebrow. "Why would I blame you? Are you sleeping with him?"

Max laughed. "If I were, I'd make sure he wasn't being followed. In fact, I'd be able to catch me in the act..." He frowned, replaying what he'd just said. "Okay, that sounded way better in my head."

Daisy laughed. "I'm sure it even made sense."

Max airily waved away her comment. "Yeah, it did."

He sobered and sighed, looking at her with sympathy.

"I'm sorry, Daisy. I'm sorry you feel you need me to do this."

Daisy smiled sweetly at him. "Me, too. But it's better than doing nothing. And if he won't tell me what's bothering him, well, then I guess I just need to find out what's going on in another way."

Max nodded and stood. "I'll see what I can do," he said.

"That's all I ask."

~~~~~

"Are you always this talkative?"

Manny glanced over at Zeke. It was the first thing he'd said in the last hour. Not that she'd been exactly chatting up a storm as she drove. She raised an eyebrow.

"Are you?" she asked.

Zeke sighed, shook his head and looked out the window. "This is gonna be a *long* six months..." he muttered.

Manny winced. "I'm sorry. It's just...it's been a very long time since I've tried to create a purely social relationship. And just as long since I've had anything even remotely interesting to talk about. Honestly? I just have nothing to say right now."

Zeke eyed her thoughtfully. "Okay. How about we play a game then?"

Manny shrugged. "Okay."

What the hell, she thought. It had to be better than driving in this strained silence for the next six months.

"Okay," Zeke said, shifting so he faced her more fully. "This game is called 'Ask Me Anything'. We take turns asking each other questions. The first one who refuses to answer buys the next tank of gas."

This could be either dangerous or extremely entertaining, Harvey said, one eyebrow raised.

Possibly both.

Manny hesitated for a moment, then gave a determined nod.

"Okay," she agreed. "You start."

Day 2

"Who the hell would have figured she'd answer every question!"

Zeke paced rapidly around the gas station parking lot,

his free hand waved in the air to emphasize his point even though his listeners couldn't see him. Leah and TJ shared amused glances as they leaned closer to the speakerphone and laughed as he continued.

"This is the third damn tank of gas I've paid for–and this crappy van drinks it like it's running on beer!"

"If that van runs on beer, you're driving a fortune!" TJ quipped.

"Oh, ha–ha. See how much you laugh when you get the bill, funny man!"

"It'll be worth it if your readership keeps up," Leah said. "They're going nuts on last night's blog."

"I did reach new heights of cruelty," Zeke acknowledged smugly.

"Or do you mean new lows?" TJ asked.

"Whatever," Zeke shrugged, "so long as people are reading."

"Keep it up," Leah said. "Well, not necessarily the nastiness–but people want to know about everything."

"Especially about vans that run on beer!" TJ added, and Leah rolled her eyes and lightly smacked him on the shoulder.

Leah said, "When you have a chance to check the comments, you'll see that people are hoping for funny stories, not just cruelty."

"I'll do that," Zeke promised, "and I'll make sure I'm not always so nasty. I need to keep the readers on their toes, and besides, she's so...she's like...she's just like a maiden aunt. I mean, you can't be too nasty to her or she'll–I don't know–make you write 'I will respect my elders' a thousand times. But if you're good, she might give you cookies and milk."

"Oh, man," TJ groaned, "I feel for you, I really do."

"Hey, I still don't think she's gonna last more than a week, and she may definitely bore me to death long before then. Not a word–not *one* word, I tell you–for over an hour! Who knew a woman could go that long without talking?"

"Watch it, bud," Leah warned. "Anyway, just do your best to tolerate her—and do your best to make sure you have material for your blog!"

"Will do."

~~~~~

Who do you think he's talking to? Harvey asked curiously.

None of my business.

Well, look at him. He's pretty animated.

Maybe it's his girlfriend. Maybe it's one of his clients—he does still have to work, you know.

Hmmmm. Maybe...You gotta admit, he knows how to rock a pair of jeans. Jesus, his legs go on forever!

...Are you going to be like this the whole time?

Look, you're forty-five, not dead! What's it gonna hurt to let your hormones have a party? He'll never know.

I'll know—and I'm the one it's gonna hurt when I forget that it's only my hormones having a party. We've been here before, remember?

That was a long time ago. And one bad experience—

I'm not thinking about this anymore. Got it?

...Yeah, 'cause I've always listened to you before.

~~~~~

Zeke wondered at the rueful grimace on Manny's face as he walked towards her, and felt a stab of fear as he wondered if she'd overheard his conversation with Leah and TJ. It wasn't just that he didn't want his assignment to be finished before it had truly begun; it was also what he'd said to Leah and TJ: he might reach new highs—or lows—of snark and sarcasm in his blogs, but he truly didn't want to hurt Manny. She really was like an old maiden aunt, creeping tentatively out of her safe cocoon that was probably festooned with flowers—with a name like Rose, how could it not?—ready to bolt back to safety at the first hint of danger or anything else that could potentially knock her out of her calm and steady path.

Which made the fact she'd thrown away everything safe and secure that much more puzzling for him. He wondered what would happen when she realized just what she'd done; he wasn't sure he wanted to be there to witness the meltdown when she did.

The object of his thoughts gave him a half-smile and tossed him the keys.

"Your turn to drive," she said.

"Okay, Auntie Em," he replied, thankfully changing the course of his thoughts.

She froze in mid-step. "*What* did you just call me?"

He gave her a cheeky grin, his eyes dark and dancing with amusement.

"Hey—you *said* to think of you as my maiden aunt—"

"Or your sister!" she protested.

He cocked his head as he considered her carefully, taking in her mousy, not-quite-blonde-not-quite-brown hair pulled into a tight bun, the shapeless sweat pants, and the equally shapeless t-shirt. He decisively shook his head.

"Nah—you don't look anything like me. So, Auntie Em it is."

"That's what you think," she growled as she yanked open the van door and clambered inside, "or do you want me to start calling you Dorothy?"

"Maybe when we get to Kansas," he shrugged, and Manny laughed in spite of herself.

Maybe this trip wouldn't be so bad after all, Zeke thought as he pulled out of the parking lot.

Day 7

It took them four days to get out of Alberta by way of the Rockies, with a side trip to the badlands. They toured Jasper and Banff and hiked a couple of short trails at each location. Manny was panting like a steam engine by the time they were done.

Zeke's blog that night was about the value of keeping

in shape.

They toured Kananaskis then headed east to Drumheller. Zeke's jaw dropped when he saw the badlands and they spent a full day touring the museum, and going on a walking tour even though the weather had turned blustery again. Springtime in Alberta, Manny sighed, and Zeke ruefully agreed.

But the area was ruggedly beautiful and breathtakingly desolate, and he admitted he wished they were staying longer as they reluctantly put the badlands in their rear view mirror.

Everywhere they went, Manny snapped pictures of the scenery and buildings and interesting people, but she seldom spoke unless spoken to, and while she was friendly to strangers, she never, as far as Zeke could tell, initiated a conversation.

His next blog talked about loneliness and social isolation.

From Drumheller they headed to the Crowsnest Pass and Frank Slide, another site that caused Zeke's jaw to drop. The rocks looked fake, like Styrofoam, and if it weren't for the sheer scale of the site, Zeke would have believed they were driving through the world's largest movie set.

They toured the interpretative centre, and Manny blinked away tears at the story of a town devastated by a mountain collapsing on top of it. As they left, Manny told him about a field trip she'd taken many years earlier where they'd found a rock almost two miles from the site, evidence of the force and power of the slide.

Zeke's blog that night talked about empathy and soft hearts too easily bruised.

By the time they were two hours out of San Francisco, they'd been travelling for a week, and they were both tired of moving.

Manny glanced over at Zeke, where he sat relaxed behind the wheel.

"Do you want to find someplace to sleep?" she asked. "Make it to San Francisco tomorrow?"

Zeke considered the suggestion. A part of him was anxious to get to their destination, if only because they intended to stay in one place for a few days. But it was already dark, and San Francisco wasn't going anywhere.

"Sounds like a good idea," he agreed.

Manny opened the glove compartment and pulled out her guidebook of the area. "There's supposed to be a bed and breakfast near here. I'll call; see if they have any room."

"Rooms," Zeke quickly corrected.

Manny rolled her eyes so hard Zeke imagined he could actually hear them.

"Seriously, you need to relax. In case you haven't figured it out by now, your virtue is beyond safe with me, puppy."

Zeke laughed incredulously. "What did you call me?"

"Puppy," Manny said distractedly, trying to dial her cell phone while holding her penlight on the page with the number of the bed and breakfast. She glanced at him as she hit send and lifted the phone to her ear.

"You know," she told him as the phone rang on the other end, "wide-eyed and stupid and too young to take seriously."

"I am thirty-five years old!" Zeke protested.

"Biologically, maybe," Manny grinned then turned her attention to the person who answered the phone.

Day 8

Manny walked into the dining room and smiled rather tentatively at the elderly woman sitting at the table. The woman was exotically beautiful, her skin a rich brown, her eyes dark, and her face bright with intelligence, wit, humour and curiosity.

"Good morning, Ms Mankowski," she greeted with a warm smile and Manny couldn't help staring at the sound of her smoky voice.

"Good morning," she replied.

"I'm Leila. Welcome to my home. Help yourself to whatever you'd like and have a seat at my table."

Leila waved a wrinkled but still graceful hand towards the sideboard where there was a coffee pot, cups, sugar and cream, as well as tea and juice.

Manny smiled again and thanked her. She sat rather hesitantly at the table with her filled cup of coffee. Leila smiled at her, a friendly twinkle in her eyes. Manny did her best not to stare as she smiled back rather shyly and took a sip of her coffee.

My God, she's beautiful! Harvey breathed.

I know! Look at that __skin__! It's so clear. And she sounds like Lauren Bacall, too.

"You're staring," Leila said, gently amused.

Manny's eyes widened and she flushed guiltily. "I'm sorry. I didn't mean to be rude." She sighed ruefully. "I hadn't realized just how much my social skills have withered away." She squared her shoulders and smiled at Leila. "I was admiring your complexion and your voice. They're both beautiful."

"Thank you," Leila replied, her eyes dancing with amusement. "I appreciate that, especially about my complexion, since I've spent most of my life in the sun. I'm from Hawaii," she added at Manny's curious frown.

"Oh! I've never been there," Manny said wistfully.

"It's beautiful and everyone should experience it at least once."

"How did you end up here in northern California?"

"A combination of things, but mainly because my grandchildren are here. Once I started having trouble walking, it made sense to move where I had family who could help take care of me." Leila gestured ruefully at the cane beside her and Manny glanced over at the wheelchair sitting discreetly in the corner of the dining room.

Manny grimaced in sympathy. "I'm sorry." Something

struck her and she frowned slightly. "You moved here to be near your grandchildren? Does that mean your children...?"

Leila laughed huskily. "Oh, no—my son isn't dead if that's what you're worried about. He's also here in northern California, but he doesn't approve of my husband and while he was at my wedding, he's currently not speaking to me." She shrugged gracefully. "He'll forgive me sooner or later."

"Oh," Manny said, feeling almost ridiculously relieved.

Leila considered her thoughtfully. "You seem like a nice girl, Ms Mankowski."

Manny blushed and squirmed slightly at the compliment.

"Please—call me Manny," she mumbled, looking down at her coffee cup.

"But isn't your name Rose?" She shrugged at Manny's startled look. "I checked the register. I'm always curious about who's eating breakfast with me."

Manny nodded and grinned sheepishly. "I can understand that. And yes, my name is Rose, but I've never been very Rose-like. Everyone calls me Manny."

"Even your mother?"

Manny laughed. "No, but my mom and dad were the only exceptions. Everyone else—even my sister—calls me Manny."

Zeke walked into the dining room as she finished speaking. He smiled at them, giving Leila a smile with extra charm as he wished them good morning.

"Good morning, Mr. Powell," Leila greeted.

"Zeke, please."

"Leila."

"Nice to meet you. I want to compliment you on your establishment here. It's a beautiful house."

"Thank you," Leila nodded graciously. "The house is a hundred and fifty years old and far too big for me. I'm very glad my grandchildren came up with the bed and breakfast idea."

"Don't you find it odd, though, to have strangers in your house?" Manny asked.

Leila shrugged. "Some are stranger than others, I'll admit, and some have caused a few moments of concern. However, I truly believe that a stranger is simply a friend you haven't met yet. My grandchildren knew I couldn't get out into the world as easily as I used to, so they decided to bring the world to me. I have to admit, for the most part, we've loved every minute of it!"

They smiled at each other in perfect harmony.

"Breakfast will be served shortly," Leila continued.

Zeke nodded and turned to Manny. "What's on the agenda for today, Auntie Em?" he asked with a raised eyebrow.

Manny mock-glared at him. "I told you not to call me that!"

Zeke's grin was challenging. "If I'm a puppy, then you're definitely my old maiden aunt. So—Auntie Em it is."

Leila laughed. "That's rather sweet, actually."

"If you say so," Manny sighed. "Makes me feel ancient, though."

"Better than *being* ancient. Trust me, I know!"

Manny looked embarrassed and stricken, and Zeke watched with interest as she blushed and stammered a garbled apology.

"No need to apologize," Leila assured her with an airy wave of her hand. She directed a suddenly serious look at Manny as she said, "Enjoy your youth—and from where I'm sitting, you *are* still in your youth." She reached over and gently tapped the back of Manny's hand. "Don't make yourself older than you are."

Manny stared at her with wide eyes, unable to think of what to say in response.

Leila smiled, sat back and nodded decisively. "Now, what's on your agenda for today, Manny?"

Manny bit her lip then said, "We're going to San

Francisco today. I have a whole list of sights to see and things to do, including a Victorian house tour, Fisherman's Wharf and Alcatraz."

Zeke rolled his eyes. "Ugh," he said, but he winked when he met Leila's questioning gaze. She sternly suppressed a smile but her eyes danced at him.

Manny rolled her own eyes back at him. "You can do what you like once we get to San Francisco," she sniffed, "I have *plans*."

Leila chuckled. "Do you have a place to stay in San Francisco?"

"Not yet," Manny replied. "I'm sure we'll find a place when we get there."

"Well, I have another bed and breakfast there, in one of the Victorian houses. We can't take many guests but I happen to know we have two vacant rooms right now. How long are you planning on staying?"

"I don't really have a time when we have to leave." She glanced at Zeke. "I'm planning on staying until I've seen and done everything I want to see and do. There's also a ghost tour, and Coit Tower—and shopping! Ghirandelli chocolates...shoes..." she trailed off, staring off into the distance with a dreamy smile.

Zeke stared at her in growing consternation. "Oh, *man*..."

Manny deliberately ignored him. "I'm not sure what *he's* going to do—and I don't care—oh, except Winchester House!" She turned to Zeke with an excited grin. "You have *got* to go with me to that one!"

She was practically vibrating with enthusiasm.

Zeke stared at her, taken aback. "Old maiden aunt is right!"

Manny wrinkled her nose and stuck her tongue out at him.

Leila laughed, and gently tapped the back of his hand. "You should keep an open mind, young man. You might be surprised by what happens when you do."

Zeke grinned wickedly. "You're very sweet, Leila, but a little naïve. My idea of a good time involves loud music and women who–" He stopped, suddenly disconcerted as he realized what he was about to say to a woman who was old enough to be his grandmother. *Great*-grandmother, if he wanted to be cruel.

Leila laughed delightedly. "I've been around, young man, and I'm virtually unshockable. I'm not surprised you like women who..." She trailed off and raised her eyebrows suggestively, "and with those criteria, there's more than enough to keep you entertained in San Francisco. But I also recommend you do at least some of the activities Manny has planned. You'll enjoy yourself–I promise."

Zeke glanced over at Manny and shrugged. "I make no promises that I'll enjoy myself but I'll escort her on all of the activities she has planned."

Manny beamed at him.

"Except the shopping," he added quickly.

"Fair enough," she agreed. She turned her grin to Leila. "This is going to be *awesome!*"

Day 9

Leah and TJ sat in their living room surrounded by pamphlets and reference books their doctor had provided or recommended. They were each studiously reading a pamphlet on different fertility treatments and options, and TJ, for one, felt like he'd fallen down the rabbit hole. The options were so varied, he had no idea how they'd ever decide which one–or ones–to pursue.

He finished his pamphlet and tossed it on the coffee table with a groan. He rubbed his eyes as Leah glanced up and smiled at him.

"What was yours?" she asked.

"In vitro fertilization–yours?"

"Intrauterine insemination."

"What's the difference?"

Leah raised her pamphlet. "Turkey baster." She

gestured at the pamphlet he'd tossed down. "Petri dish."

"Ew."

Leah shrugged. "Well, the old-fashioned way isn't going to work," she said breezily.

"I know," TJ said and subsided into brooding silence, lost in his own thoughts. Leah watched him, her mouth turned down in a concerned frown.

TJ looked at her with solemn, sad eyes. "I'm sorry, Leah."

Leah smiled at him and shook her head. "Not your fault."

"Well, technically–"

"I mean," Leah chuckled, waving his words off, "it's not something you did deliberately. I'm pretty sure the doctor would have mentioned a vasectomy."

TJ shrugged and nodded. "Or you would have noticed a scar," he conceded.

"Depends on the skill of the doctor." TJ stared. "Or so I've heard," she quickly added.

TJ slowly smiled then laughed.

"Still," he said, his smile slowly fading, "it *is* my fault–whether deliberate or not."

"No," Leah said firmly. "It's not your fault. It isn't *anyone's* fault. It just...*is.*"

Leah moved to sit beside him. She put her arms around him and rested her head on his shoulder.

"I love you, you know," she said softly. "For *you*–and not because you're supposed to give me children."

TJ swallowed heavily. "What about my money?" he joked weakly, his voice choked.

Leah smiled against his shoulder. "We-ell, that doesn't hurt. Naturally."

"Naturally," TJ agreed solemnly and kissed her.

Leah smiled softly. "I love you."

"I love you, too. And...whatever you want to do about..." he gestured vaguely at the pamphlets strewn over the coffee table, "...all of this...Money's no object, you know."

"I know."

"I just want you to be happy."

"I know," Leah assured him, "and I just want *you* to be happy. We'll decide together; we'll do what we're *both* comfortable with, not just me. Okay? But I am not going to lose you over this."

TJ hugged her closer and kissed her again. "And I'm not going to lose you," he promised. "We'll figure something out," he vowed softly.

She smiled sweetly at him. "No doubt about it," she agreed firmly.

Day 10

Rebecca opened the front door and greeted Jaime and Tris with a smile.

"Tris, why don't you go to your room while I talk to Gramma," Jaime said after the obligatory chat about what was new since the last time they'd seen each other.

Rebecca raised an eyebrow but kept silent until Tris closed her bedroom door.

Jaime jiggled her leg in a fit of nervous energy then blurted, "Look—Mom—Max found my dad."

Rebecca froze, her eyes widening as she stared silently at her daughter. She felt suspended, caught in time and her memories.

For a moment, she was once again sixteen-going-on-seventeen, being disowned by her father, the door being closed in her face by her mother. She was once again hysterically sobbing, pounding on the Mankowskis' door, expecting it, too, to be slammed in her face, her only two friends turned away from her just like her family had turned away.

Instead, Mrs. Mankowski had taken one appalled look at the broken child on her doorstep, and bundled her inside. They'd dried her tears, coaxed the story out of her, and tucked her into bed with Daisy and Manny. Manny had been only fourteen, almost fifteen; Daisy the same age as Rebecca, and neither had known what to say or do. So they'd just hugged her close, and told her everything would be all right.

She hadn't believed them.

The next morning she could hear the Mankowskis' whispered conversation in the kitchen, but she couldn't make out the words. She'd been in that suspended state between waking and sleeping, and the low murmur of voices had been unusual, yet soothing. Then she heard Mr. Mankowski leave the house.

Jaime was almost a year old before Rebecca learned that Mr. Mankowski had gone on the warpath that day. He'd talked to her parents; told them to accept the baby and her.

They refused.

He told Jaime's father, Devon, to man up, and at least acknowledge the baby and support his child.

Devon left town that afternoon.

Rebecca had always thought the Mankowskis could forgive anyone anything. It turned out they couldn't forgive a boy who deserted his child, or parents who disowned their pregnant daughter.

Rebecca had thought she'd gotten over the pain of it all.

Until now.

She blinked, and wondered if she looked as green as she suddenly felt.

"All right," she said slowly, wondering what Jaime was hoping she'd do or say; wondering what Jaime *wanted* her to say or do.

"I...I'm going to go and meet him." Jaime said, her chin raised, her eyes glittering defiantly.

Rebecca stared at her and realized she was looking at a stranger. Her own daughter—it had been just the two of them for so long and they'd gone through so much—and she couldn't recognize this young woman sitting in front of her, looking at her like she, Rebecca, was the one who had abandoned Jaime before she was born.

Or was she simply projecting, she wondered dazedly.

"All right," she said again and wondered why this had knocked her so far off balance. It wasn't like she wasn't expecting it; Max was very good at what he did, after all, and Devon probably hadn't been that difficult to find.

Jaime waited, carefully watching her mother. She continued speaking after she realized Rebecca didn't have anything else to say.

"Can you look after Tris for me? I—I just want to meet my dad and get to know him before introducing him to his granddaughter."

"All right," Rebecca said for the third time.

"Great! I've got Tris' stuff in the car. I'll go bring it in. I want to hit the road early tomorrow."

"When will you be back?"

Jaime shrugged as she stood and picked up her purse. "However long it takes me to get to know my dad." She grinned, and Rebecca could see the little girl she used to be. "I'm going to get to know my dad!"

"Does he know you're coming?"

Jaime rolled her eyes. "*No*, Mom. But I'm sure once he sees me, he'll want to get to know me—and we have thirty years to catch up on, after all. I'll call and let you know how it's going."

Rebecca nodded and walked Jaime to the door on numb legs.

"Yes. I...look forward to hearing all about it."

Jaime brought in Tris' suitcase and then left with an airy wave to her mother. Rebecca closed the door and leaned against it. She wondered how Jaime's father would react to the child he'd denied so many years before. Would he be sorry about what he'd done? Would he open his arms and heart to her now? Rebecca hoped he would, for Jaime's sake. She and Jaime had their conflicts, but she was still Jaime's mother, she loved her, and she wanted her to be happy. If finding her father would do that, then Rebecca wouldn't stand in her way.

Not that Jaime would let her anyway.

Rebecca took a deep, shuddering breath, squared her shoulders and walked down the hall to check on Tris.

Day 11

Daisy carried the teapot into the living room while Rebecca carried the tray filled with cups, honey, and spoons. Daisy watched her thoughtfully as they set everything on the coffee table and settled themselves comfortably on the couches.

"What does Jackson have to say about all this?" Daisy asked with a thoughtful frown after they'd fixed their tea and Rebecca had filled her in on Jaime's visit the night before.

"He doesn't know."

Daisy stared at her, dismayed.

"Yet," Rebecca clarified. "He's out of town on business right now, then he's taking the kids on a holiday to Mexico. I won't even see him before he's gone again."

Daisy relaxed. "Ah. Well, lucky kids—not even teenagers yet and travelling the world."

"Helps to have a rich dad."

"Yeah, well, I wouldn't know."

"Me, neither. Anyway—would Janika or Jakob—or both—like to stay with Tris after school? I mean, I still have to make a living, too—"

"I'm sure they would."

"And I'll pay them, of course."

"They'll be home in a minute or two—you can talk to them yourself. They're more than old enough to make their own decisions—at least in this particular case."

Rebecca chuckled. "I can't believe Jakob's seventeen!"

Daisy nodded glumly. "I can't believe my baby's fifteen. Where does the time go?"

Rebecca shook her head. "I don't know, but I'm pretty

sure we're experiencing lost time on a regular basis. Tris is ten. *Ten!* Closer to eleven, actually. Damn!"

They subsided into depressed silence while they poured more tea and added honey.

Rebecca sighed as she took a sip of her tea, then asked with a sudden grin. "What do you think Manny's doing right now?"

"I know what she's *not* doing," Daisy replied drily.

"Zeke?"

"Exactly."

They snickered.

Rebecca shook her head and said, "That girl–she has the self-control of a nun."

"If she can spend six months with a guy like that and she *doesn't* make a pass at him? She'll be more than a nun–she'll be a saint!"

"I know I'd be tempted–and I'm happy with Jackson."

"Oh?" Daisy asked archly. "*How* happy?"

Rebecca smirked into her cup. "Very. Extremely. Wonderfully. Pick one. Pick them all."

They were laughing conspiratorially when Jakob and Janika walked into the house, calling greetings to their mother as they opened the door.

"Hey," Daisy said when they came into the living room, "how was your day?"

"Okay," Jakob shrugged and Janika nodded. They greeted Rebecca with smiles.

Janika had her mother's colouring and her father's bland good looks, while Jakob was his grandfather all over again, tall, dark, roguishly handsome with the same wicked gleam in his eyes. Who knew that was genetic, Rebecca thought with fond amusement.

"Hey," she said now, "we were just talking about you. Do you guys have a couple of minutes?"

They both nodded.

"Great! Well, I'm going to be looking after Tris for the next little while, and I was wondering if one or both of you would be interested in helping me out?"

Jakob and Janika exchanged glances and shrugs.

"Sure," said Jakob. "What do you have in mind?"

"Well, definitely after school on those days she isn't going over to a friend's house," Rebecca said thoughtfully. "The occasional evening and weekend as well."

Jakob thought about it. "Between the two of us, we should be able to manage that, right, Janika?"

"Should," she agreed. "We do have games, though, and practices—but Tris can always come with us if they overlap and if she'd like."

"That's great!" Rebecca said, rubbing her hands together. "What's the going rate for babysitting these days?"

Jakob winced. "Tris is our friend—and you're...you know, *you*, Auntie. I...I don't feel right getting paid to help you out."

"Same here." Janika nodded.

"That's really sweet, and ordinarily, I'd take your offer and leave it at that. But this isn't a one-hour deal or even a couple of days. This is on-going for, well, I don't even know how long. Jaime might be back tomorrow, she might be gone for a couple of weeks. But during the next few days, I have business commitments I can't break or reschedule. So, how about this: I'll give you each a pre-paid credit card—say, a thousand dollars? You can use it for yourself or to do things with Tris and whatever. Just let me know when the cards get low, and I'll put more money on them."

"That's way too much!" Daisy protested.

Rebecca laughed and waved away Daisy's objection. "Nothing's too much for my granddaughter! Besides, I trust you kids. Plus Tris knows and likes you, and I'm not going to lie to her about paying you to look after her. The cards are also for entertainment costs if you want to go to a movie, or go shopping, or whatever it is kids do these days for fun."

"Well," Janika said slowly, "I'd prefer to think of it as an expense account then, rather than you paying us to look after her."

"That's fine," Rebecca shrugged. "Whatever you'd prefer. I'm just glad you can help me out."

Jakob grinned. "No worries. Always happy to help you, Auntie."

Jakob and Janika went to their respective bedrooms to start their homework. Rebecca and Daisy watched them go with fond smiles.

"You raised good kids," Rebecca said to Daisy.

"I'm not sure if I should take any credit," Daisy said thoughtfully. "Maybe they were just born that way."

"Come on—take the credit. Milk it, baby, milk it, and hopefully you'll be able to continue to milk it into old age."

They laughed then Daisy sobered as she leaned back and stared thoughtfully at the teacup cradled in her hands.

"I may need to milk it sooner than that," she said softly.

Rebecca's eyes widened at Daisy's tone. "Why?"

Daisy glanced down the hall to her children's closed doors. "I don't want to talk about it now. Maybe in a few days. I'll call you, okay?"

Rebecca slowly nodded, her eyes wide. "All right," she said slowly, curious and suddenly worried, but she allowed Daisy to change the subject. Besides, she knew Daisy would unburden herself soon enough.

Day 13

The days were, Manny was told, unusually warm for the time of year.

She wasn't complaining.

She soaked up the sun as she and Zeke wandered the streets of San Francisco, and after the first few days, her legs began to get used to the constant workout of constantly walking both up and downhill.

For the most part, Zeke accompanied her on her daily

excursions, and watched her with a distantly observant albeit slightly mocking expression. He held himself aloof from her excited and wide-eyed enjoyment of the tourist sites and of the city itself and appeared to be deliberately holding himself back from truly enjoying himself. It almost felt like he was taking notes, she thought ruefully, he watched everything so carefully. It puzzled her but then again, she sometimes watched him just as carefully. They were still strangers to each other after all and still trying to figure each other out.

On the few occasions Zeke had begged off from accompanying her, Manny had taken the opportunity to do more shopping. During their journey through Alberta, she'd replaced the baggy sweats and t-shirt with some jeans and new t-shirts, and now she added shorts and tank tops to her wardrobe. When she pulled on a pair of the new jeans and a tank top in her room, she almost didn't recognize herself.

Harvey gave a slow whistle. **Looks good,** he said.

These jeans are so...low! And this top clings to my tummy bulge too much.

Stop worrying. Nobody's looking at you anyway.

...aren't you supposed to help build my self-esteem?

That was <u>meant</u> to be comforting. You're the only one who's looking for flaws and therefore you'll be the only one to see them.

...I'm not sure that's actually logical.

You do realize you're arguing with yourself, right?

Fine. Okay. Whatever.

Now, be honest. Look at this outfit. You actually have a waist. And those jeans make your legs look longer than they are. You also look ten pounds lighter. Come on. Admit it. You look really good in this outfit. And years younger!

Manny considered Harvey's words with a frown, and tried to see herself objectively.

Okay. I don't look <u>horrible</u>.

It was as far as she was willing to go.

Her skin was beginning to turn a golden brown, her mousy, not-quite-blonde-not-quite-brown hair getting bleached by the sun. As always, she ate with a hearty appetite, and her initial physical discomfort had faded to a pleasant ache brought on by exercise and sun.

Leila's second bed and breakfast was lovely, a large Victorian house nestled in the heart of San Francisco. Leila's grandson managed the place and served not only breakfast but also supper for those people who wished to eat at the house with the family.

Everyone ate at one long table, in a warm, friendly atmosphere, and Manny had become cautiously friendly with her fellow guests.

There was the young gay couple on their honeymoon from British Columbia; the two middle-aged sisters who had more enthusiasm for sightseeing than even Manny could muster; and the elderly man and his wife who were in San Francisco for a granddaughter's wedding and had initially been rather shocked by the newlyweds, and had subsequently been anxiously worried about giving offense. The young couple were in love with each other and everyone around them, and they'd quickly eased the elderly couple's minds and easily befriended everyone staying in the bed and breakfast.

Manny subsided into a position of sitting quietly at the table, listening to the conversation flowing around the room. She envied Zeke his casual ease with the others, and wondered when she'd turned into somebody with nothing worth saying.

It sometimes made her feel very cold, lonely, small...and old. Much older than the elderly couple, and centuries older than Zeke and the newlyweds.

What am I doing here?

You're re-learning how to connect with people.

I have nothing to say to any of these people! How can I reconnect if I can't participate in the conversation?

But you're listening with interest.
...that doesn't help much.

**Small steps, Manny. You didn't get here overnight—
you're not going to get out of here overnight either. Give
yourself some slack. And relax. This isn't like being on
the job. Nothing is dependent on you succeeding or
failing.**

Except my happiness. And my mental health.
...point taken.

Harvey was almost constantly with her, usually casually
dressed in jeans and a button-down shirt, or, on occasion,
well-fitted t-shirts. He was always impossibly perfect, but it
was oddly comforting to see him from the corners of her
eyes during everything she did or experienced. Perhaps it
was a sign she'd been alone too long although she
preferred to think he was simply a way to ease the
loneliness caused by leaving Daisy and Rebecca—and
everything else in her life—behind.

That night at supper, she listened to the conversations
flowing around her, and by the end of the evening, she'd
agreed to go the next day with the sisters on a guided tour
of the city.

She might feel awkward and lonely, but she was
determined to enjoy seeing the sights on this trip, no
matter what.

Day 14

TJ spooned around Leah and breathed in her scent.
They'd spent yet another evening reading pamphlets and
books and web sites they'd dug up during the day related
to fertility issues, treatments and options. TJ's head
pounded from once more weighing and debating the pros
and cons of each option and trying to decide what would
work best for them. Money was no object—they had that
advantage at least—but there was still something inside him
that hoped against hope that there must be a simpler
solution than the ones they'd been discussing. Even, he

thought wistfully, that the doctor had made a mistake.

"Look," TJ said softly, "I'm going to go to another doctor–get a second opinion."

Leah frowned, and twisted to look at him in the darkness of their bedroom. "Do you really think the clinic–the most highly respected fertility clinic in town, in case you'd forgotten–would make such a simple mistake?"

"It happens all the time. Besides, what does it hurt?"

Leah frowned as she slowly said, "Okay...or is this just because you want to get your hands on those girly magazines again?"

TJ pulled back and dramatically placed a hand on his chest. "You wound me! I only have to think of you and let nature take its course."

Leah laughed, rolled over to face him fully, and kissed him. "You flatterer–you're too good to me," she teased.

"And don't you forget it," TJ replied, giving her a smacking kiss.

"Anyway," he continued, his arms loose around her, his hands resting comfortably at the base of her spine, "I'm going to get a second opinion, and then, if the results are the same, see if there's anything that can be done–you know, surgically maybe–to improve things. I mean maybe I have a–a–a blockage or something–something that's simple to fix."

He shrugged sheepishly at Leah's skeptical look. "I know, I know–but at least we'd know for *sure*."

Leah placed her hand flat on his chest and smiled a little sadly at him. "If it'll make you feel better," she agreed. Then her smile changed, became suggestive.

"In the meantime," she purred seductively, sliding her leg over his, "maybe you should get some practice in for when you're all alone again with that little cup."

He slid his hands sensuously down her back to cup her bottom and pull her closer against him.

"Well, practice does make perfect," he agreed, and Leah chuckled as she kissed him.

Day 16

Manny and Zeke left the bed and breakfast at mid-morning to join the Victorian house walking tour that was scheduled to leave from a nearby hotel.

The late start had given them time to see the rest of their fellow boarders off that morning, and Manny, to her surprise, had been hugged by all six of them, especially the two sight-seeing-obsessed sisters. Those two pressed their e-mail addresses on her, promised to friend her on Facebook and asked her to send them updates on her travels.

She watched everyone leave with a mixture of relief, sadness and bemusement, and wondered if she'd have anything worth telling them if she did e-mail them updates. So far, she thought ruefully, she'd been mostly just sitting like a lump while other people did the talking and the doing.

Like now.

Zeke had been sidetracked by a darkly lovely young woman who'd struck up a conversation with him after he held the door for her as they all entered the hotel.

From their body language and facial expressions, she knew they weren't simply discussing the sights of San Francisco or the upcoming walking tour.

You know, if you sidle over a little closer you'll be able to hear what they're actually saying.

Manny slid an exasperated glance at Harvey.

I already know what they're talking about, she replied primly.

Well, maybe you could learn something.

Like what? And for what reason? So I can give men advice on how to hit on other women? Again?

You could use those moves to hit on a man, you know.

Oh. Yeah. Because _that_ *always ends well.*

You always did give up too easily.

...I'm not talking about this anymore.

...**Fine. But sooner or later–**

Enough!

Zeke glanced over at her and frowned. He turned back to the young woman he was talking to.

"Give me a second?" he asked with a charming smile.

She agreed with a smile that was equally charming.

Now that's a come-hither smile!

Manny couldn't remember the last time she'd looked at a man like that. She wasn't even sure if she'd *ever* looked at a man like that.

Not even at Zeke...are you sure you're not dead from the waist down?

Shut. The hell. Up.

Manny forced a smile as Zeke came to a stop beside her.

"Listen," he said, putting a hand on her shoulder and urging her to move a few steps away from the others waiting for the tour to begin who were now milling around the lobby. She flinched slightly from his touch and was grateful when he didn't appear to notice her reaction.

She glanced up at him, suddenly struck by how tall and broad he really was, how darkly handsome and how expressive his–she blinked–hazel eyes, she realized, rather than brown, were. To his credit he appeared honestly torn, his eyes pleading, and she felt her smile become genuine rather than hurt or sulky.

He's actually rather sweet.

Sometimes.

"Go ahead," she said with an airy wave of her hand before he had a chance to say anything.

He blinked, taken aback.

"Are you sure?" he pressed, his dark eyebrows lowered over his eyes as he frowned. For the first time she noticed how expressive his face truly was.

"You were really excited about this tour," he added.

"And you almost passed out from boredom at the

thought. I was worried you were going to roll your eyes right out of your head."

She glanced with amusement at the lovely young woman who was watching them with patient curiosity.

"I suspect you'll have much more fun with her."

Zeke's grateful smile turned into a wicked grin.

She forestalled whatever he was going to say with a raised hand.

"Spare me–please!" she groaned. "Go. Have fun. I'll see you later."

"Thanks, Auntie Em," Zeke said, gently patting her shoulder.

She shooed him off and watched him go with something that felt rather ridiculously like affection.

Jesus, you really are, aren't you?

Are what?

His Auntie Em!

She sighed and glanced ruefully at Harvey, who was gaping at her while looking impeccably handsome in jeans, golf shirt and sneakers. He at least was willing to go on this walking tour with her.

I know how to do that, she told him now. *I've been Auntie Em to a lot of people; what's one more?*

You could have at least been his sister instead.

Don't be ridiculous–we don't look anything alike.

Harvey put his hands on his hips and actually huffed in exasperation, before he shook his head in disgust and disappeared from sight.

Manny sighed, feeling a sudden chill of loneliness wash through her. She wondered what it said about her when even her imaginary friend didn't want to stay with her.

~~~~~

Late that afternoon, Manny walked slowly back to the bed and breakfast, feeling simultaneously satisfied with the tour while still feeling that cold chill of loneliness and sadness. A part of her wondered what, exactly, she was doing–here, in San Francisco–travelling with Zeke–with her life, in general.

This was what she'd wanted and yet—and yet—and yet she still wasn't happy or any more social than she'd been for the last fifteen years. She still felt awkward and like a stranger in her own skin. She was still frustrated with where her life had gone and terrified about where it would go in the future. She sometimes felt as if she wasn't living anymore, that there was nothing exciting left for her to do, or see—or feel.

She wanted to stand on a rooftop—or, hell, here in the middle of the street—and scream at the sky at the top of her lungs about how this wasn't how her life was supposed to be. She wanted to sob and rage and stamp her feet and demand that somebody somewhere give her...*something* more! Whatever that *something* might be.

At the same time, she wanted to fall to her knees and sob with fear. Fear of what, exactly, she didn't really know, or couldn't accurately describe. Fear of everything, really, she thought ruefully, but mostly she was afraid of the very thing she so desperately wanted: *life*.

She laughed bitterly to herself. She saw Harvey flicker into sight from the corner of her eye, but she ignored him. She didn't need his voice in her head at the moment; her own was more than enough to bear.

As she let herself into the bed and breakfast, she wondered why her plans never seemed to go the way she thought they would. She'd hoped once she left her dead-end job that she would stop feeling this way; this cold, fearful, lonely sadness she so desperately wanted to banish.

"Ah, Rose!"

Manny paused, then backtracked to look into the sitting room she'd just passed.

"Leila!" she grinned and walked to where Leila sat in her wheelchair. Manny carefully took her hand and gently squeezed it in greeting. "What are you doing here?"

"I have a doctor's appointment in a couple of days," Leila said in her smoky Lauren Bacall voice, "and I thought I'd arrive a little earlier and see how you and that charming Zeke are getting along."

Manny chuckled slightly. "We're getting along just fine," she said, perching on the loveseat and leaning forward, her elbows on her knees, her eyes intent on Leila's face.

"I'm glad to hear that." Leila reached over and tapped Manny gently on the back of her hand. "Now tell me everything you've been doing."

Manny tried to give her the short version, but Leila would have none of it. She asked questions about each tour, probing into everyone Manny had met and their conversations, and what she had felt or thought about the people and sights and sounds and scents. Manny found herself remembering things about the last few days she hadn't even realized had impressed her at the time.

Finally Leila sat back with a sigh and a smile.

"Thank you, Rose. I can't get out as much anymore, so thank you for humoring an old woman with her endless questions."

"I enjoyed it," Manny said rather shyly, "I hope I didn't bore you."

"Not at all," Leila said as she cocked her head to one side and observed her closely. "And yet...you don't seem happy."

Manny blinked at her in surprise.

"I–I'm fine," she protested half-heartedly, flushing with embarrassment.

"Are you upset Zeke went off with this–what was the girl's name?"

"I'm not sure, actually. It starts with an L, I think. And no, I'm not upset about it."

"But you look like a woman with something on her mind. Is it another man?"

Manny laughed, "No."

"Ah. A woman, then?"

Manny laughed again, even harder. "No woman

either," she said.

"But there's something weighing on you," Leila said shrewdly.

Manny huffed and sat back on the loveseat.

"Too much," she sighed, "and none of it's of any importance. It's not like I have any problems—not real ones, anyway." She shook her head with a grimace. "It's stupid."

"What's stupid?" Leila persisted gently.

"A mid-life crisis. Just...feeling like life has passed me by." She looked half-pleadingly at Leila although she didn't know what she really wanted from the older woman.

Leila smiled. "What do you think I can tell you?"

Manny hesitated, biting her lip as she stared off into space.

"Tell me it's not over," she finally blurted, meeting Leila's patient gaze.

"What's not over?"

"Anything. *Everything*. Passion—passion to learn and do and know. Life. That there are still things to do and think—that I can still make changes—still make a difference in this world—still *matter*. Tell me—tell me—" to her shame, hot, stinging tears suddenly filled her eyes. "Tell me I'll—I'll—I'll *feel* something again."

Leila tutted soothingly and opened her arms. Manny slid from the loveseat to kneel beside the wheelchair and lean into the offered hug. To her horror, she burst into tears against Leila's shoulder.

"I'd say you've already answered your own question," Leila said and she gently rubbed Manny's back until the tears stopped as suddenly as they'd begun.

Manny leaned back and frowned, sniffling, her nose running, her eyes sore and gritty.

Leila smiled gently at her. "You're feeling something now, aren't you? Your tears are a form of passion, too, you know. You were angry, weren't you, when you didn't get that promotion. And you were afraid—horrified—and that's why you quit your job. All of those are emotions. I'd say you still feel things."

"But those are all negative!"

"But you still *feel* them—and feel them deeply. If you can feel the negative emotions, then you can also feel the positive."

She smiled a suddenly wicked smile, and gently tapped the back of Manny's hand where it rested on the arm of Leila's wheelchair.

"No, it's not over—not if you don't want it to be." She leaned closer. "You know, I married my fourth husband just last month."

Manny stared. "Really?" she breathed.

Leila nodded. She gestured towards her purse on the coffee table and Manny retrieved it for her. Leila opened her wallet and took out a picture of her standing with a distinguished older man in a traditional post-wedding pose.

"James. He's currently away on a business trip," Leila explained and she sounded much younger than her eighty-plus years. She lowered her voice conspiratorially. "A much younger man—only sixty. I feel like I've robbed the cradle. That's why my son isn't talking to me at the moment—although he did attend the wedding."

Manny blinked in stunned silence as she looked from the picture to Leila's sparkling grin, and began to laugh.

~~~~~

Zeke opened the front gate as quietly as he could, wincing slightly as it creaked. It was late, after midnight, and he wondered if Manny was going to take him to task for deserting her not only for the day, but for the night as well. As he carefully closed the gate and soft-footed it up the walk, he decided the day and night had been worth it, even if Manny pulled out her most severe disapproving maiden aunt look—a look she'd already levelled on him several times, and which had been the topic of his last blog.

Yes, he mused, Luciana was a beautiful and charming

young woman, and even though she'd been somewhat disconcerted by his refusal to go back to her place, she'd seemed to enjoy their time together as much as he had. *Definitely* worth suffering through that look.

TJ and Leah would never believe him if he told them there'd been no sex, though. Hell, he could barely believe it himself. He shook his head. Maybe Manny's prudish ways were starting to rub off on him. He shuddered at the thought even as he filed it away to pull out for a future blog.

Zeke winced again as the doorknob rattled under his hand and he ruefully realized he hadn't been this worried about sneaking into the house since he was sixteen and trying to slip past his dad's far-too-sharp ears.

His efforts were wasted; he was hit with what felt like a wall of noise the moment he cracked the door open.

He quickly entered the house and shut the door behind him, his eyebrows lowered dangerously over his eyes. There was a mix of loud music and voices, and even louder laughter exploding from the living room located at the back of the house, and he knew there was no way in hell Manny was sleeping through this racket. He shuddered at the realization that this would only make her prudish maiden aunt face all that more severe in the morning.

He walked into the room with a questioning frown that quickly turned into stunned surprise as he took in the scene in front of him.

Leila was holding court at the head of the table with her three grandchildren, three unknown people who Zeke assumed were her grandchildren's significant others–and Manny, sitting between Leila's two grandsons. Everyone was talking and laughing as they played cards, with the stereo blasting an old rock song. As Zeke watched, a concerted howl of protest went up as Leila laid down her cards with a falsely innocent smile, obviously winning the hand.

In the hubbub of people calculating their scores and

calling out the results to the scorekeeper, Leila glanced at the doorway and grinned.

"Zeke!" she called in welcome, clearly delighted. "Come in! Help yourself to a drink and if you're hungry, there's some food over on the sideboard. I'm afraid we're in the middle of a game, but you can join the next one."

Zeke wasn't sure how to react to the general chaos and he gave Leila a slightly stunned nod at her words.

"Sounds like fun," he said uncertainly and walked over to the sideboard to check out the food. He poured himself a drink, filled a plate with snacks and turned his attention back to the raucous group sitting at the table who were joking and laughing as the next hand was dealt.

"I gotta warn you, Zeke—she's a real shark," Manny laughed, picking up her cards, "she hasn't lost a game yet!"

"I'll keep that in mind," he replied, bemused, and settled in to watch the rest of the game.

~~~~~

As midnight changed into the early hours of the morning, Zeke covertly observed Manny from his position beside Leila and thought this was the most relaxed he'd ever seen her, even though her hair was still in that damn bun. He watched her from beneath his lowered dark brows and wondered what it was about this particular group of people that was bringing out this side of her and whether he could pinpoint it enough to write about it in his blog.

As the final game of the night wrapped up and people began to rise from the table and prepare to leave, Zeke leaned back in his chair and watched as Manny stood to say good-bye to Leila's family.

Leila gently tapped the back of his hand and he started, glancing at her quizzically.

"She'll be all right," she said softly.

Zeke frowned. "I'm sure she will be," he replied slowly.

Leila simply tapped the back of his hand again and sat back with knowing eyes and an enigmatic smile.

EPISODE THREE
Day 24

Manny shifted in the passenger seat, trying to find a comfortable spot. It felt like they'd been driving forever, which felt even longer since Zeke was once more behind the wheel, driving silently and looking thunderous.

With those eyebrows, not hard to do.

Manny bit back a grin at Harvey's words. He was sitting beside her dressed in jeans and wearing a t-shirt that clung to his well-muscled chest and emphasized his arms.

Jealous? she teased.

Well, you have to admit they have a personality all their own.

True. Would you like me to give you similar ones?

She imagined him with Zeke's thick, arched eyebrows and they both winced.

Doesn't work.

Not even close.

She glanced at Zeke who was glowering at the road in front of him. He'd refused to so much as glance at her ever since they'd pulled out the next destination from the bag, and discovered they needed to retrace almost the entire route they'd taken a week earlier. To say he was displeased was like saying Death Valley got a little warm during the summer.

"All right," Manny sighed breaking the heavy silence, "you win."

He glanced at her from the corner of his eyes although his expression didn't lighten.

"Pulling locations randomly out of a hat–or baggie– while pretty fun in theory–isn't very practical," she conceded grudgingly.

"*Thank* you!" Zeke said, smacking the steering wheel in triumph.

"If you start singing *We are the Champions*, I'll hurt you," she warned drily.

"I'm sure I can find something more recent to use in tormenting you."

She rolled her eyes.

"So," she continued after another moment of silence, "are you going to start talking to me again or should I go to the back and have a nap?"

Zeke shrugged carelessly. "I suppose I could grace you with my wit and charm for at least–" he glanced at the fuel gauge–"the next twenty miles."

"Or whenever we get to the next town," Manny agreed.

"Whichever comes first," he nodded, and flashed her a grin.

<u>Now</u> I'm jealous.

Manny glanced affectionately at Harvey.

You're still number one in my heart.

...that may not necessarily be a good thing.

"So, what did you want to talk about?" Zeke said.

"Anything."

"Want to play 'Ask Me Anything'?"

Manny laughed. "At the rate you're going, you'll be paying for the whole damn trip if you're not careful."

"Hah! I'll find something you'll refuse to answer one of these times!"

"And I might find something you *will* answer one of these times!"

Zeke shrugged. "Fair point."

~~~~~

Half an hour later, Manny was considering Zeke with a thoughtful frown. He'd once again had to buy the gas, and Manny was sipping on a coffee while he stood waiting for his turn to pay.

"What?" he asked as they walked back to the van.

"I was just thinking," she said.

"I could tell," he said drily, shaking his head at Manny's outstretched hand and walking to the driver's side.

She settled into the passenger seat again and watched him in silence as they pulled out of the gas station and back on the road.

"What were you thinking about?" Zeke asked when she showed no sign of speaking.

"That you seem to have an awful lot of secrets," she replied.

Zeke shot her a startled glance and opened his mouth to protest.

"Come on," she said, "you always lose the 'Ask Me Anything' game."

He frowned, staring resolutely at the road in front of them.

"You just ask the questions first," he grumbled. "I don't really have that many secrets."

"No?" she asked skeptically.

He shook his head. "No. It's just–"

"It's just you don't want to answer *my* questions– especially when I ask about your personal life."

Zeke glanced at her. She'd sounded almost...hurt.

"I don't answer anyone's questions about my personal life," he admitted grudgingly. "I'm not interested in well-meaning but useless advice."

She cocked her head and steadily met his gaze. "I don't give advice," she assured him quietly.

Zeke stared at her for a moment then turned his attention back to his driving. He swallowed as he shifted in his seat, flexing his hands on the wheel. She'd looked sincere, he thought grudgingly, her eyes clear and blue and honest. He glanced at her again from the corner of his eye, wondering what was different before he realized some strands of her mousy hair had escaped and were hanging beside her face, softening her appearance.

He frowned, wondering if that was all that was different.

"Are you wearing your hair differently or something?" he blurted.

She turned to him, her jaw dropping in surprise. She closed her mouth with a snap. "Uh, no. No, I'm not," she replied.

"Well, something's different," he insisted.

"I'm wearing new clothes," she offered with a puzzled frown, trying to think what she might have changed.

He glanced over at her, and realized that yes, she was in something other than her shapeless sweats and t-shirt. In fact, he couldn't remember the last time he'd seen her wearing them.

He shrugged off his confusion.

"What were we talking about?" he asked.

"Your secrets."

"I don't have any," he said again.

"Which is why I always win the 'Ask Me Anything' game."

"You just have no shame," he sniffed.

"Well, it's not like I've ever done anything to be ashamed about," Manny replied drily, a slightly wistful hint in her voice.

He glanced sharply at her, sensing he was on the trail of something he might be able to use for his blog.

"Come on," he coaxed, "you must have done something!"

"I've lived a very sheltered life," she replied, shaking her head.

"Good God—you're not a virgin! Are you?"

She burst into laughter. "I'm not sure if you're more appalled at the thought of me being a forty-five-year-old virgin, or at the thought that I've actually had sex!"

He grimaced ruefully. "I have to admit, both scenarios are rather disturbing. No offense," he added quickly when she glared at him.

"Anyway," Manny said pointedly, "the bottom line is: I have nothing to hide. I have to admit, the more you refuse to answer any questions about your personal life, the more curious I get."

Zeke hesitated, his hands tightening even more on the wheel.

"I don't really have anything to hide," he said slowly, "but I've left people behind me for a reason."

She considered him thoughtfully. "And once you've left them behind, you never—what? Think or see or speak of them again? You never wonder about the girl you left behind?"

"I—no. No. I walk away and I never look back. Oh, I'll talk about them. Just—not with people I don't know well."

Manny gave him a glimmer of a smile. "Fair enough," she conceded. "Besides, I guess we need to leave ourselves something to talk about later. We still have over five months to spend together."

Zeke gave her a rueful grin. He continued driving in thoughtful silence for a few minutes before he said, "What about you?"

Manny gave him a puzzled frown. "Me? What about me?"

"Don't you—don't you have somebody—anybody—you've left behind? Somebody you've walked away from without a backwards glance?"

Manny carefully considered the question.

"I have people I've left behind, yes," she replied slowly, "but I've never managed to walk away without a backwards glance. Or two." She gave him a glimmer of a smile. "I do have some who got away...although, to be honest, I never actually had them in the first place. I've also had a couple who I should have run away from, but didn't. But nobody recently."

"So," Zeke drawled, trying to lighten her somber mood, "you're looking for some old-fashioned romance on this trip?"

Manny shrugged, leaning her elbow on the passenger door, her head propped on her hand as she looked at him.

"Not really. I've been around that block a few too many times. For whatever reason, I don't attract single men. Or men older than twelve or younger than sixty-five. Or sober men, come to think of it."

Zeke sighed dramatically. "Poor thing," he said sarcastically.

"Your sympathy is overwhelming," she said drily, "and unnecessary. I'm used to it. Anyway, no, I'm not looking for romance on this trip. I just want to have some fun. That's it. See things, do things—just...have a good time."

"Like sex?"

Manny laughed and shook her head. "Honestly? Sex just screws everything up. No, thank you. Mind you, if I should get an offer—" she shrugged.

Zeke grimaced.

"Yeah, thanks, asshole," Manny snapped, suddenly angry.

"No, no, no," he protested, flushing guiltily. "I didn't mean—"

"Whatever. You know what? I think I'll go take a nap." She unbuckled her seatbelt and made her way to the back of the van where she toed off her shoes and slid under the covers on the bed.

Zeke shook his head as he swore under his breath.

~~~~~

Well, what did you expect?
Not __disgust!__

Harvey settled on his side on the bed with a sympathetic sigh. He leaned over her, his head propped on his hand.

You're his Auntie Em, he reminded her gently. **Nobody wants to think of their aunt getting laid. Not even by their uncle!**

...doesn't really make me feel any better.

I know. I'm sorry.

Me too.

With a soft sigh, Manny turned on her side. She resolutely closed her eyes, and concentrated on the sound of the tires on the pavement.

~~~~~

That evening, Manny settled on the bar stool beside Zeke and took a swig of her beer. She closed her eyes in appreciation as the cold liquid slid down her throat and hit her stomach.

"God, that tastes good," she sighed.

Zeke slanted a glance at her and smiled slightly at her look of total satisfaction. She opened her eyes and smiled at him.

"So, you're talking to me again?" he asked.

"Obviously," she said drily. "Of course, I'll talk to almost anyone who buys me a beer."

He raised one expressive eyebrow and she chuckled slightly as she shook her head to forestall whatever comment he was about to make.

He leaned closer and said in a low voice, "Look, I'm sorry about earlier. I didn't mean to hurt your feelings."

Manny considered him thoughtfully. "I know you didn't," she assured him.

"I just—you're my Auntie Em, you know? I don't really want to think about you and...you know..." he leaned even closer and lowered his voice, "*sex*."

Manny blinked at him.

"You do realize you just whispered the word sex, right?"

Zeke flushed and ducked his head as he abruptly straightened in his chair. "Yeah, I know," he groaned.

Manny laughed. "As much as I enjoy watching your discomfort, I'll tell you what. I promise not to ask you about your personal life anymore–just to give you a fair shot at winning the 'Ask Me Anything' game–and I'll also try not to embarrass you by talking about me having sex. Okay?"

Zeke gave her a half-smile. "Of course, that first one kind of defeats the whole purpose of the game, doesn't it?"

Manny shrugged as she took another sip of beer. "I've already discovered your Achilles' heel; I know all I need to do to win is pull out a question about past loves or the girl you left behind. While I like never paying for gas, it's not really a fair game, is it? I'm just trying to level the playing field."

Zeke considered her somberly then turned his attention back to his own beer, taking a sip with a thoughtful frown.

"Look," he shifted uncomfortably, "okay. All right. Her name is Dixie."

He met Manny's puzzled gaze. "The girl I left behind," he clarified.

He hesitated, turning his beer bottle between his hands. Manny watched him and waited in silence.

"We lived together for just over six months, although we'd dated for almost two years before we moved in together. Things were...*good*. I thought we were happy enough. She's a sweet kid–but there was always some underlying tension, some level of distrust...for many reasons."

"On both sides?" Manny asked.

"Mostly hers. She never seemed to believe I...*cared*...for her. Things improved once we started living together, but she never seemed able to truly trust me. The end came because I'd called her from–from a friend's house and Dixie saw a woman's name pop up on the phone. She automatically assumed the worst and when I got home that night, all my stuff was outside, waiting for me." He shrugged, deliberately casual as he said, "I decided it would be best to get away for a while."

Zeke kept his eyes on his hands as he idly played with his beer bottle.

"Did you talk to her at all before you left?" Manny asked, her mouth twisted in sympathy.

He shook his head with a self-deprecating grimace. "There wasn't anything to say," he said.

"Not even you're sorry? Or to explain? Or to try and work things out?"

"No. She'd made up her mind, and I wasn't about to go crawling to her for forgiveness—especially when I hadn't done anything wrong."

Manny subsided into thoughtful silence, her own eyes dropping to her hands on her beer bottle. She quietly picked at the label as she considered Zeke's words.

"What?" he finally demanded, his formidable brows lowered over wary eyes.

She glanced at him and shrugged. "I'm sorry about what happened, and I'm wondering if you're regretting the fact you just walked away? I mean, without another word and without—without trying to—I don't know—understand?"

He gave her a twisted smile. "Get closure, you mean? Isn't that the word of the day?"

Manny shrugged. "Call it what you want. I just wonder if you have unanswered questions—or lingering guilt. Maybe giving her a call wouldn't be such a bad idea."

She took a sip of her beer and steadily met his glower.

He finally snorted and shook his head. "I thought you said you don't give advice," he growled.

She smiled sweetly. "I lied."

Day 25

TJ and Leah walked wearily into their house.

"That was incredibly helpful," TJ sighed as he threw his keys on the side table in the hall.

"She was good, wasn't she?" Leah agreed, toeing off her shoes and hanging up her coat.

"You know, we could have saved ourselves a lot of time and effort if we'd just signed up for the counselling right away."

Leah laughed. "Yes, but you know we would have just done the work afterwards." She walked to him, slid her arms around his neck, and leaned in to him as she kissed him. "We both like to do our own research and make our own decisions."

TJ chuckled. "And we both understand knowledge is power." He kissed her again before leading her into the living room, their hands loosely linked.

"True," she agreed, once they were snuggled comfortably on the couch. Leah thoughtfully stared into space and bit her lip.

"I'm definitely going to recommend the counselling, though," she said slowly. "I've been getting some great responses to my blog entries about our experiences—and I think this can really help other women and couples who are struggling with infertility."

"Well, she certainly helped us determine the best course of action," TJ sighed and wearily rubbed his free hand over his face.

Leah nodded against his shoulder.

"So, a donor?" TJ asked, shifting into a more comfortable position on the couch.

"Yes, if the IUI fails. I guess the next question is whether we want to ask somebody we know, or use an anonymous donor?"

"Let's consider somebody we know, first. Anonymous—I don't know. I think I'd be looking for the differences, you know? Trying to put a face to the father. And what if there are serious health issues?"

"First of all—*you're* the father, TJ. Biology alone doesn't make a father. But if we ask somebody we know, would he want to be part of the child's life? And would that make it awkward for you?"

TJ thought carefully for a moment before he sighed.

"If he's somebody we know well, then he'd already be a part of the child's life. If he wanted to be an uncle figure, then why not? Of course, nothing is ever that simple or that...bloodless, I guess, for lack of a better term. Would you–do you think sharing a child with someone you know–and possibly someone you know well–create a–a bond?"

Leah lifted her head and smiled into his concerned eyes.

"There would probably be a bond of some kind–even if it's only gratitude. You can't pretend otherwise. But it's not like we'd be making the baby the old-fashioned way. I'm not sure how close you can really feel to a turkey baster."

TJ grinned and said, "Well, if you give the turkey baster a name, you might be surprised."

Leah grimaced, and hit him with one of the couch's throw pillows.

TJ laughed and gave her a smacking kiss. He pulled back and said, "What about Zeke?"

"I haven't heard from him lately. Why?"

"No–I mean, as the donor."

Leah's jaw dropped. "He's your best friend!" she exclaimed.

"I know–that's why I thought of him."

"He also works for me. I'm not sure that's a good idea."

TJ grimaced ruefully. "He's got good genes, though." He was suddenly wistful as he added, "It would be a beautiful baby."

"See?" Leah exclaimed. "This is what I'm talking about! Would you be jealous? Would it strain your friendship?"

TJ sighed and yawned. "I don't know. We don't have to decide right now, anyway. I have my doctor's appointment tomorrow; maybe he'll be able to give me better news."

"Maybe," Leah agreed, carefully neutral.

TJ gave her a rueful smile.

"I just want to give you everything you could ever want," he said quietly.

Leah smiled sweetly.

"*You're* everything I could ever want. And don't you forget it."

TJ nodded and grinned as he pulled her in for another kiss.

Day 27

Rebecca answered the phone with a light-hearted hello. She quickly sobered when she recognized her daughter's voice.

"Hi, honey. How are things going?" She felt a knot of dread forming in her stomach. Jaime's phone calls had been sporadic during the weeks she'd been gone, and Rebecca sometimes suspected Jaime only called when she was reasonably certain Rebecca wouldn't be home. That way she could speak with Tris without also having to talk to her mother.

"Nothing's changed, Mom," Jaime replied impatiently. "I haven't met my dad yet."

Rebecca frowned. "It's been a couple of weeks, Jaime," she said as gently as possible.

"I'm getting a feel for this town," Jaime protested. "You never brought me here–I'm curious about it. I'm trying to understand the world you kept me away from."

"Kept you–Jaime! I never took you there because there was no one who wanted to see us!"

"Oh, Mom," Jaime sighed, and Rebecca could imagine the exasperated roll of eyes. "How do you *know* that?"

"Uh–the fact that he denied he was your father?" Rebecca snapped, then sighed. "I'm sorry, honey. I'm just tired. I'm not used to having a pre-teen around the house anymore."

"It's good for you," Jaime said, letting Rebecca's earlier words flow over her.

"When are you coming home?"

"Oh, Mom—I don't know! I haven't had a chance to talk to my dad yet! He's been out of town."

Sure, Rebecca thought sourly. He probably left the minute he was told there was a strange woman in town who looked like him. Jaime had lived in a big city all her life, and while there were many similarities to living in a small town, she'd never truly experienced a grapevine until she experienced the grapevine in a small town. Rebecca had no doubt Devon had known Jaime was there less than half-an-hour after she checked into her motel.

Rebecca returned her attention to the conversation.

"Besides," Jaime was saying, "this is my first holiday alone since I married Blake. I'm really enjoying the freedom from responsibility."

"I'm sure you are," Rebecca said neutrally, "but Tris misses you and—"

"Oh, honestly, Mom! You almost sound like you can't wait for me to take Tris off your hands!"

"Well, she is your daughter," Rebecca reminded her mildly.

"I'm having a good holiday, Mom! Please stop trying to ruin it for me!"

"I'm not trying to ruin anything for you! But you have responsibilities here—a daughter who misses you and wants her mother around."

"It'll be good for Tris to be away from me for a while."

"And good for you, too?" Rebecca asked cynically.

"Look," Jaime snapped, "I don't need you putting pressure on me right now! I'll be home when I've gotten to know my dad. I don't think it's asking too much for you to look after your granddaughter."

"While you're off doing what, exactly?" Rebecca snapped.

"Coming to terms with my past—a past you denied me," Jaime shot back.

"You could have done this any time since you were

eighteen. Why now?"

"When exactly would I have had the chance? Huh? I was married at nineteen and a mother at twenty! I had a baby too young!"

"You had a baby too young?" Rebecca muttered under her breath.

"What was that?" Jaime snapped.

"I said I'm sorry about that, hon," Rebecca sighed, "but you can't just–just walk away from your life and leave everything hanging."

"Why not? Manny's doing it."

"Manny didn't park her child with her mother!"

"I should have known you wouldn't understand, and that you'd be more concerned about how much it inconveniences *you*! You've always put yourself first."

"Jaime!"

"Whatever. Tell Tris I'll call her later."

And Rebecca was left with nothing but dead air.

~~~~~

"She said *what*?" Manny demanded, disbelieving, wiping sleep from her eyes. She adjusted the pillows behind her and made herself more comfortable. She'd been snuggled under the covers on the verge of sleep when Rebecca called.

"That I always put myself first." Rebecca's voice was choked, and she sniffled into a Kleenex.

"Maybe after she got married–but *before* that?"

"You know, I tried to do my best. I never brought men home; I was always here when she got home from school. I tried to make sure she had everything she wanted."

"Well, this is just something else she wants. You to look after Tris while she...I don't know–finds herself by bonding with her father, I guess."

"If he'll let her bond with him," Rebecca said cynically.

"It's been thirty years. Maybe he wants to bond with her."

"You never know, I guess."

Rebecca sighed.

"Thanks for listening, Manny."

"No problem. What did Daisy have to say about it all?"

"Nothing yet–she wasn't home."

Manny frowned. "No? Were they out for supper or something?"

"Hub? Go out for supper with his wife? That'd be the day! No, Daisy was out on her own. At the casino."

"On a Thursday?"

"Manny–she goes to the casino every night."

"What?"

"That's what Hub told me when I called looking for her. He was pretty, um, vocally unhappy about it."

Manny let out her breath in a long sigh. "Damn–is she in trouble?"

"Well, with Hub, anyway. He was really pissed off– although whether it's because she was at the casino or because he was home with the kids–it was hard to tell."

"Yeah, well, I don't have much sympathy for him," Manny said drily.

"Me neither. Hub's been pretty much an absentee father and husband for way too long."

"To be fair, he never used to be. He just seemed to drop out of their lives a couple of years ago. Daisy's especially. When's the last time they did something together?"

"I know," Rebecca sighed. "Listen, I didn't mean to worry you–not about Daisy, or me or Tris. Tell me–what have you guys been doing?"

"Driving, mostly," Manny groaned. "We're headed to a small town in Arizona for a classic film festival that starts in a week or so. Zeke doesn't know why we're going there."

"You haven't told him? Why not?"

"Because it's hilarious watching him get all wound up about what we're doing next. I don't think he handles ambiguity well."

"Or else he just doesn't like having someone else in control," Rebecca suggested drily.

"That's much more likely. You figured him out pretty quickly after only meeting him once."

"Nothing personal–it just seems to be a typical male trait."

Manny laughed. "Speaking about Jackson, are you?"

Rebecca laughed. "Jackson does like being in control– when he thinks it's worth the effort."

"Is he back in town?"

"They got back Monday, but I haven't seen him yet. We're going out for supper on Saturday."

"Are you going to send Tris to Daisy's for the night?" Manny asked slyly.

"That's a better idea than my plan to rent a hotel room for a couple hours," Rebecca mused.

"Although the hotel room has some merit, too."

Rebecca laughed throatily. "Good point." She sighed. "Thanks for listening, Manny. I miss you, you know."

"I miss you, too, Rebecca. You and Daisy."

They ended the call, and to Manny's horror, hot tears suddenly filled her eyes. She really did miss both of them. Which was ironic, she thought, sniffling slightly, since she talked to them more now than she had when she'd been home.

She shook her head, turned off the light, and snuggled under the covers once more. She made a mental note to ask Daisy about her trips to the casino, and to make her tell the truth about her relationship with Hub.

Day 28

Zeke watched Manny with a puzzled air.

He'd expected her to press him on Dixie, to ask him if he'd called to apologize. He'd expected her to express her disappointment at his lack of feelings for his ex-girlfriend.

She did none of it.

As far as Zeke could tell, she treated him exactly the

same: a bit reserved, friendly, accepting his decisions regarding whether he would join her for yet another day of sightseeing. She always asked him what he did on those days he wasn't with her, but she never pressed him for details if it seemed he didn't want to share.

It...

He leaned back in his chair, tapping his fingers on the table beside his laptop.

Not disconcerting.

No.

No maiden aunt with her hair in a bun could ever disconcert him.

No, it was...*distracting*.

Yeah. That was it.

And it was making it difficult for him to write his next blog.

That evening at supper, after they shared the small happenings of their day and Zeke learned more than he'd ever thought there was to know about this nameless small town Manny had insisted on exploring, he decided to confront the elephant in the room.

"So," he said, setting down his beer mug, "let me have it."

Manny blinked. "Let you have...what, exactly?" she asked carefully, a tiny frown line wrinkling the middle of her forehead.

"Dixie."

The frown deepened.

"What about her?"

"You don't want to know if I called her? Or how it went if I did? Or why I haven't manned up and made the call? You don't want the chance to say 'I told you so', or try to play matchmaker—or—or—" he trailed off as Manny clapped a hand over her mouth to muffle her laughter.

"I'm sorry," she managed between giggles.

"I sound ridiculous, don't I?" he sighed.

"Just a little." She grinned at him. "I'm sorry I'm not

living up to your expectations of a nosy, interfering old maid but I have no interest in living vicariously through you. I get enough of that by talking to Rebecca and Daisy. Besides, you're a big boy, Zeke. Last I checked, you could walk and even go to the bathroom on your own. Most of the time."

Zeke gave her his best scowl, which only sent her off into another fit of giggles. He rolled his eyes as he waited for her to calm down, but a reluctant smile tugged at the corner of his mouth.

Manny shook her head. "Have you ever thought that maybe you're expecting me to give you a hard time about Dixie because you think you've done something to deserve it?" she asked, reaching for her wine glass.

This time Zeke's scowl was real.

"I'm just putting it out there," she said, waving his scowl away.

"No," he snapped and reached again for his beer.

Manny considered him thoughtfully, then shrugged. "Whatever you say," she said lightly. "Now, what do you want to do tomorrow?"

Zeke scowled even harder as Manny easily moved on to other subjects.

~~~~~

"So, what's the problem?" TJ asked once he stopped laughing. "And—for the record—my mother was a very nice woman."

"Her son—not so much," Zeke snarled. He shifted to put one arm beneath his head and stared up at the ceiling of his motel room.

"Hey!"

Zeke huffed what might have been a chuckle, then said, "I don't know—doesn't it seem weird to you? I mean, she just dropped her little pithy observation, then moved on. You've been married forever—"

"Don't let Leah hear you say that!"

Zeke ignored the interruption as he continued, "Do

you think she's just gonna pull the topic out when I least expect it and try to convince me to do what she thinks is right?"

TJ sighed. "I couldn't tell you," he said. "I haven't been with the woman virtually non-stop for almost a month. If you can't figure her out, I'm not sure how I'm supposed to. What I can tell you is, she isn't necessarily wrong. You do have a tendency to be...well..."

"Firm in my decisions?"

"Pigheaded is the word I was looking for."

"Hey!"

"I'm just saying, Zeke—I've known you for a long time and I've never known you to be the first one to forgive and forget. How long has it been since you've seen your father?"

Zeke hesitated, then slowly said, "Fifteen years."

"Exactly. And he only wanted what was best for you."

"That's different," Zeke protested weakly.

"Yeah? How many women have you walked away from because they wanted something you weren't prepared to give them?"

"I'm not the marrying kind, TJ."

"I'm not talking marriage, Zeke! I'm talking—I don't know—fidelity! Hell, I'm talking respect!"

"I respected all of them!"

"Just not the relationships?" TJ asked cynically.

"Look, TJ—I know I have a reputation—but I've never cheated on a woman once it got serious and long term—you know that! But I like to flirt and they just couldn't trust me enough to let me be myself, and still be faithful to them. Or believe that I could do both. And no, once a relationship is done, it's done. There's no point hanging around where I'm not wanted, is there?"

"Or where you don't want to be?"

"Either way, the result's the same. The past is past, and there's nothing to be gained in trying to change somebody's mind when it's a lost cause."

TJ sighed. "I suppose so," he conceded.

"But?" Zeke prompted.

"But I'm worried that someday you're going to wake up and regret the people you left behind without a fight."

Day 29

Rebecca took a sip of her wine, her mouth dry from all the talking she'd been doing. She smiled ruefully at Jackson as she daintily replaced her glass on the table.

She hadn't realized how much she'd missed him until she saw him in her doorway. She felt almost light-headed with pleasure and happiness as she looked at him sitting across the table from her in their favourite restaurant, his dark, expressive eyes intent upon her face as he listened to her.

Jackson was still boyishly handsome at forty-six, his thick, unruly black hair in perpetual disarray. He didn't look like a successful businessman, with his messy hair and five o'clock shadow, wearing jeans, t-shirt and sneakers, but Rebecca thought he looked delicious, and more precious than gold.

Even after all this time, she couldn't quite believe they were still together. Jackson was an old friend of Max's and had met Rebecca after he'd separated from his wife and found himself in the market for a new house for himself and his two young children, of whom he had sole custody. The rest, as Rebecca was fond of saying, was history.

She sometimes thought that many of her former lovers would be shocked to find her dating such an unpolished man. She'd been shocked the first time he asked her out, and she'd found herself agreeing, when she'd fully intended to gently refuse. She later told Daisy and Manny that she couldn't say no to his eyes, large, dark and vulnerable, fringed by thick black lashes she would have killed for, and looking as hopeful as a puppy in a window. Over the last two years, those eyes often intently watched her, like she was one of those computer programs he was paid big money to create or fix.

She smiled at him now.

"Jackson, I'm sorry. This is our first chance to see each other since you got back, and here I've done nothing but complain."

Jackson smiled in return. "It's okay. You need to vent."

"But–well, this must be boring for you–hearing about my daughter's journey to meet her father, and the day-to-day trials of living with my granddaughter."

Jackson shook his head. "No, no. I'm just happy you're sharing these stories with me. Finally."

Rebecca frowned. "Finally? I–I'm not sure–"

"We've known each other for almost three years now, and we've been seeing each other for over two–and you've always kept your family strictly off-limits. I mean, I've never even met them! Just as you've always refused to come home with me and meet my kids."

Rebecca flushed guiltily as she began to stammer out a response.

Jackson waved her efforts away. "Oh, I get it–don't think I don't. Dayle and Ryder are around the same age as Tris–believe me–I *get* it. But Rebecca," he leaned forward, his dark eyes intent upon her face, "sooner or later–you have to let someone in."

Rebecca stared, her eyes wide in consternation. "You are in," she protested weakly.

"No," Jackson said firmly, "I'm not."

Rebecca hesitated, her mind whirling as she desperately tried to think of something to say.

Jackson said, "I know this'll take a bit of time for you to get used to, but..."

He reached across the table and placed his hand over hers.

"Listen. Rebecca. I'm not planning on going anywhere. I hope you know that–but I don't want to live in limbo, either. I don't want to always be on the outskirts of your life."

Rebecca swallowed painfully. "Wh–what are you trying to say?" she whispered.

Jackson gave her a sweet, heartbreakingly vulnerable half-smile. "I'm trying to say I love you, and I want a real life with you."

Day 31

"Oh, my God–what did you say?" Daisy squealed.

Rebecca laughed at her reaction, then sobered.

"I didn't say anything. I couldn't think of what to say! This is so...so..."

"If you say this is so unexpected, I swear to God I'll reach across the table and give you such a smack!"

Rebecca grinned. "No, it's not unexpected. I guess. It's just so...I never thought he'd want to move things to a whole different level. He seemed happy with the way things were, just like me. I had no idea he wanted something more than what we had."

She shook her head.

"So when are you going to meet his kids?" Daisy asked. "When's he going to meet Tris? Maybe you should have the kids meet each other at the same time!"

Daisy trailed off as she realized Rebecca was once again shaking her head.

"What?" Daisy asked suspiciously.

"We're not meeting the kids anytime soon," Rebecca said firmly. "God, his kids are around Tris' age! And if there's one thing these last few weeks with Tris have proven to me, it's that I'm too old to start raising kids again! I don't have the energy, and I sure as hell don't have the patience!"

"It's not like they're babies," Daisy protested.

Rebecca gave her an exasperated look. "Would you want to go through the teenage years again?" she demanded.

Daisy grinned. "Personally? Or with my kids?"

Rebecca groaned and waved the question away.

"Forget it! You managed to raise two little saints. You need to bottle your secret and sell it—you'd make a fortune."

Daisy laughed.

"Enough about me," Rebecca said firmly, "let's talk about you."

Daisy raised an eyebrow as she picked up her cup of tea. "Me? What about me?"

"I've called you three times this week."

"You did?"

"Yes. And every time you've been out at the casino." Rebecca looked steadily at her. "Are you in trouble, Daisy?"

"Trouble?" Daisy repeated blankly. "What kind of trouble?"

"You can't be winning all the time! And how can you afford to be at the casino every night?"

Daisy dropped her eyes to her teacup. "I'm fine. I'm not bankrupt or anything."

"How are you paying for it?"

Daisy snorted. "With my paycheque, of course. Don't worry about me, Rebecca. Everything's fine. It just gives me something to do, and I'd rather not sit here either waiting for Hub to come home, or simply staring at him when he is home." Daisy squarely met Rebecca's concerned gaze. "Everything's fine," she repeated firmly.

Rebecca frowned, only half-convinced, but she sat back and allowed Daisy to change the subject.

Day 32

Daisy sat at her desk, typing Max's latest case report, and thought once again that she really needed to encourage him to learn how to use a computer. After all, if she ever won the jackpot at the casino, he'd be out one office manager and then what would he do?

She shook her head as she continued typing then glanced up as the door opened and the man himself walked into the office. He looked unusually grim, even for him, a frown on his craggily attractive face. He carried one of the plain brown envelopes he used to deliver reports to his clients.

He stopped in front of her desk and she felt her heart plummet into her stomach as he fidgeted uncomfortably with the envelope in his hands.

Finally, he took a deep breath, said, "Daisy–" and held the envelope out to her. She stared at it like she'd never seen one before.

She swallowed.

"Oh," she said. "Oh."

She didn't have to ask Max what, exactly, he'd found; his face told her everything she needed to know.

"I'm sorry," he said in his deceptively gentle voice.

Daisy stared sightlessly over his shoulder and made no move to take the envelope from his hand.

"You know," she said numbly, "I didn't actually believe you'd find anything. At least not *that*. I mean, how...cliché..." To her horror, she suddenly began to cry, great, wracking sobs, interrupted only by gasping breaths. Max carelessly dropped the envelope on the desk, and pulled her out of her chair and into his arms. She buried her face in his shoulder, and felt something inside her break as she cried.

The sobs finally slowed, then stopped. For a few moments, she allowed herself to lean into Max's shoulder and let him comfort her. Then with a determined sniff, she pulled away.

"Thank you," she said, not quite meeting his eyes as she turned and pulled some tissue from the box she always kept on her desk. She turned her back, blowing her nose and wiping the last of the tears from her eyes. Max watched silently, his face creased with worry as she turned back towards him with one last swipe with the tissue.

She nodded at the envelope sitting on her desk.

"Is the usual evidence in there?"

"Yeah."

Daisy nodded, her gaze distant as she stared at the envelope.

"Okay. Okay. Okay." She gave herself a shake and added, "Thanks, Max."

She jumped as the phone rang. She took a deep breath and answered, "Springfield Investigations, Daisy speaking...Speaking." She listened intently, paling even further as she did so. She reached out and clutched Max's sleeve. Finally, she said, "Thank you; I'll be there as soon as I can."

She hung up the phone and turned to Max.

"There was an accident during Jakob's phys ed class today. He's been taken to the hospital; they think he broke his leg."

"I'll drive," Max said.

~~~~~

Hub walked into his darkened house and hung up his coat and keys without turning on any lights. He wandered into the living room and stopped short when he saw Daisy sitting in the dark.

"What the—"

"I called your office this afternoon," Daisy said, her voice eerily quiet in the dimness. "Late this afternoon. Jakob was injured during phys ed; broke his leg."

"My God—" Hub began and took a step towards her.

"He's okay. He's in the hospital right now, and I sent Janika over to Rebecca's to spend the night with Tris."

"Was that wise? Her brother just broke his leg! I would think she'd want to be with her mother!"

"You weren't here. In fact, you also weren't at work. You'd left around one-thirty. No one knew where you were, and you weren't answering your cell phone."

"I was at a meeting," Hub snapped.

Daisy gave a watery chuckle. "Really? Is that what the kids are calling it these days?"

She turned on the lamp beside her chair. Hub blinked

in the sudden flood of light, then blinked again as Daisy pushed an envelope across the coffee table and nodded at it.

"I think you can guess what's in there," she said.

Hub stared at the envelope, then his shoulders slumped. He slowly, almost painfully sat on the edge of the couch. He leaned forward, his elbows resting on his knees, his hands loosely clasped together.

He nodded. "Yes. I know what's in there."

Daisy swallowed hard, her throat clicking.

"I think it's time for this farce of a marriage to be over. A neglectful husband and father I could...tolerate. A cheating one? Never."

"Daisy...it just—"

"If you tell me it just 'happened', I swear to God, I will punch your lights out!" Daisy snarled, suddenly enraged. "Stubbing your toe 'just happens'. Breaking your leg 'just happens'! That—" she stabbed a finger towards the damning envelope, "*that* takes planning and a conscious decision!"

She jerked to her feet. "Whenever you can find a place, you can go."

Hub stared up at her. "What about the kids?"

Daisy snorted. "Maybe they'll see you more often when you only have visitation rights."

"Daisy—"

"I've set up the guest room. I'll tell the kids tomorrow. Somehow, I don't think they'll be surprised."

She gestured carelessly at the envelope.

"You can keep those," she sniffed, "I have the originals."

Day 33

"I'm so, so sorry, Daisy," Manny said, appalled.

"You want to know the sad part? I'm not even surprised. I think I suspected for a long time—otherwise I wouldn't have asked Max to follow him in the first place."

"Do you want me to come home? Just say the word, and I'll be there."

"I know. But while I could use you here—no. No. There's really nothing for you to do, except listen to me bitch, and you can do that from anywhere. Besides—and this is going to sound awful, but...I'm almost...relieved."

"Well, as Mom used to say: you can't solve a problem—"

"You can't define," Daisy finished with her.

They laughed.

Daisy sighed sadly. "I could use her and Dad right now."

"Yeah. Daisy, really, I can come home."

"No, I'm okay—and if I'm not—"

"*Then* I'll come home."

~~~~~

Zeke sat in his motel room and stared off into space.

He thought about the things TJ and Manny had said to him. He thought about the people he'd left behind long before, most without a single backwards glance.

He thought about Dixie.

And for the first time, he allowed himself to wonder if he'd be on this trip if he'd just tried to call her. Tried to explain. Tried to make things right again.

He bit his lip before he took out his phone and dialed Dixie's number. He felt a cold sweat break out on his skin as he listened to the ringing of the phone on the other end of the line.

"Why are you calling?"

Zeke jerked, taken aback. "Well, hello to you, too, Dixie."

"It's been over a month and no word from you until now," she snapped. "What do you want?"

Zeke hesitated for a long, silent moment, wondering what the hell he was going to say.

"Zeke?"

He started, and refocused on the conversation. "I—I

don't want anything. I just called to say...I'm sorry. And to tell you—I wasn't cheating. I was doing an interview. If you'd read my blog, you'd know it was strictly business."

Now it was Dixie's turn to be silent. Zeke sat quietly and waited for her to speak.

Finally she said, "Well. I guess...thank you for the apology. And, I guess...I appreciate the attempt at a cover story."

Zeke said softly, sincerely, "It's the truth."

"Maybe. But I don't dare take the chance and believe you."

Zeke closed his eyes and wearily rubbed the bridge of his nose. "I didn't expect you to do anything. I just wanted you to know. I thought you deserved to know. And maybe, if I had talked to you then, instead of...well...maybe things would be different right now."

Dixie hesitated then said, "I guess we'll never know."

Zeke slumped down in his chair. "I guess not," he said quietly. "Good-bye, Dixie."

"Good-bye, Zeke."

He continued to hold the phone to his ear long after she ended the call.

~~~~~

Manny lay on her back and stared at the ceiling. Harvey was beside her, his hands resting on his flat stomach.

So, Daisy and Hub have split.

Yes.

And Jackson told Rebecca he wants more from her.

He has.

Zeke's looking for some way to mend his broken heart, even if he won't admit it.

That's true.

And I'm here. With you. Like always.

Yes.

I'm the one who wanted change...this isn't exactly what I had in mind.

EPISODE FOUR
Day 39

Zeke stared at Manny in consternation. She'd bounced into his room with a broad grin, a glossy brochure clutched in her hands, and excitedly announced her plans for the next week.

"You want to go *where?*" he asked, hoping his ears had deceived him.

"To the Classic Movies Film Festival, being held in this town in Arizona. Oh, God—it's going to be awesome! Four full days—five venues—and every year they showcase a different actor or actress. Last year it was John Wayne. This year—this year it's *Cary Grant*!"

Zeke's lips twitched at the way she almost squealed the name.

"Girly kinda fella?" he asked drily, raising an eyebrow.

"Oh, ha ha!" Manny rolled her eyes then turned her attention back to the brochure she held in her hand, her face lit up with enthusiasm.

"They're showing the only three Cary Grant movies I've never seen! Oh, my God—Cary Grant! On the big screen!"

Zeke couldn't help himself. He burst out laughing at her awed and excited demeanour. He plucked the brochure out of her hand, ignoring her startled and indignant yelp.

"Is there anything else playing or is it All-Cary-Grant-All-the-Time?"

"There's lots playing—I'm going to have a tough time deciding which movies to see and which ones I'll have to miss."

Zeke's eyebrows rose as he read the brochure. He hated to admit it, but he was actually impressed. With five venues playing movies simultaneously, there was literally something for everyone.

"When does this thing start?" he asked, turning the brochure over.

"Friday," Manny said, then quickly lunged and snatched back the brochure. He gave her an exasperated glare that turned into a grin as she turned her back, engrossed in reading the lineup.

"Oooh," she crooned, "All my favourites! Humphrey Bogart! Clark Gable! Oh my God—William Powell and Myrna Loy! Oh, hell," she moaned as she turned towards him again, "I think I've died and gone to movie heaven!"

Zeke shook his head as he doubled over with laughter even as he resigned himself to suffering through four days of endless romantic comedies.

If nothing else, he thought ruefully, he should end up with lots of material for his blog.

~~~~~

Manny had a fairly accurate suspicion about Zeke's feelings, but she was too excited to care.

Cary Grant, she thought giddily, *twelve feet high.*

She almost wished she could swoon. Or squeal like a little girl.

Oh, God, Harvey groaned.

What?

I see lots of tuxedos in my future.

Manny glanced up and blinked at him. He was, as predicted, in an impeccably tailored tuxedo complete with bow tie, his crisp white shirt in sharp contrast to his salt-and-pepper hair, golden skin and deep brown eyes.

You look so good in them, though.

True. But I'm no Cary Grant.

Who is? Even Cary Grant wished he were Cary Grant.

Are we going to have romantic candlelit dinners now?

Maybe. But that's better than the pirates, right?

Harvey smiled at her. **Sometimes the pirates can be fun, too.**

Glad to hear it–there are some Errol Flynn movies, too.

Harvey groaned, and Manny laughed.

She refocused on Zeke.

"You don't have to see the movies with me," she told him. "You can do whatever you like."

"It's no fun watching movies by yourself," he shrugged. "Besides," he plucked the brochure out of her hands once more, "I'll bet there's nothing else to do in this town."

"You'll never know until we get there," she tutted.

Zeke heaved an exaggerated, long-suffering sigh as he threw himself down in his chair in front of his desk. He glanced at his laptop sitting on the desk and his eyes widened as he realized he'd left the blog he was writing up on the screen. He quickly glanced at Manny and was relieved to see she was still focused on the brochure in her hands, her excited smile firmly in place.

"And to think, we still have almost five months to go..." he teased as he reached over and quietly closed the computer.

She wrinkled her nose and stuck her tongue out at him.

"Cary Grant, twelve feet high," she sighed, and wandered out of his room.

~~~~~

Zeke sighed as he picked up the thick program booklet. "Four days of classic movies, twelve hours a day, isn't exactly my idea of a good time."

"Oh, come on," TJ urged, "there has to be something you'll enjoy watching."

"Oh, sure," Zeke replied sarcastically, switching his glower from the program to his cell phone, even though TJ couldn't see it, "but it's not like I'm going to get Auntie Em to watch any of them!"

"It does sound like she's planning on dying from multiple Cary Or-grant-asms."

Zeke stalled, blinking, then said with great feeling, "Ew!"

"Ew? What 'ew'? I'm sure she thinks that wouldn't be a bad way to go."

"That's disgusting for many reasons—not least of which is thinking of Manny with any kind of sex drive!"

"Well, I'll bet you anything she's not going to those movies for the plots!"

"She has been going on about seeing Cary Grant twelve feet high," Zeke admitted thoughtfully.

"Anyway, is she insisting you go to every movie with her?"

"Well...no."

"Okay then. What else is playing?"

Zeke heaved a long-suffering sigh and flipped through the program.

"Well, besides romantic comedies, there are thrillers, mysteries, sci-fi and horror."

"That's quite the combo. Mostly geared towards the male audience, huh?"

"Probably to make up for all the Cary Grant," Zeke replied drily.

TJ laughed. "So? Go to a couple of movies with her, then go to a few you want to see—or don't go to any of them. She seems pretty laid back."

"Oh, she'll agree, but then she'll give me her disappointed maiden aunt look, and I'll cave."

TJ laughed. "How's it going otherwise? You don't seem

quite so–uh–"

"Vitriolic?"

"That's a good way of putting it," TJ agreed.

"She's a nice person," Zeke conceded, "and while I want to make fun of her actions and words, I don't want to make fun of *her*. She's pretty funny sometimes."

"And fun?"

"Yeah," Zeke agreed grudgingly, "and fun. When she relaxes and forgets herself."

He grinned at the sudden memory of the card games at Leila's bed and breakfast in San Francisco. He shook off the memory.

"What about you, TJ? How are you and Leah doing?"

"We're good–although it's beginning to feel like we've spent every minute of every day for the last month talking about fertility treatments and options and what steps we need to take in order to have a baby."

"Have you guys made some decisions about that?"

"Yeah, we've decided on a course of action. I'm just waiting to hear back from my doctor–I went for a second opinion and a full physical a couple weeks ago; they should be getting the results of all my tests any day now."

"You think the best clinic in town made a mistake?" Zeke asked skeptically.

TJ laughed. "Now you sound like Leah! No, I don't think they made a mistake–but my old man always said to never trust just one doctor when they told you bad news."

"Your old man never said that! He said never trust *any* doctor!"

"That, too."

"Well, good luck with all of that, man. Let me know what happens, okay?"

"You'll be the first to know," TJ promised. "Enjoy the movie festival. Who knows? Cary Grant might grow on you."

Zeke simply groaned.

Day 40

Leah heaved a sigh of relief as she walked in the door and tossed her purse on the hallway table beside her keys.

"TJ?" she called as she toed off her shoes.

"In here," he replied.

She padded into the living room and raised an eyebrow when she saw he hadn't yet turned on any lights in the room.

She gave him a kiss hello then teased with a grin, "Too lazy to turn on the lights?"

She reached over to switch on the lamp beside him, but he quickly captured her hand.

"I need you to sit down, sweetheart."

Leah felt the blood drain from her face, both from TJ's gentle tone and the endearment. She turned her hand so she could grip his, a thousand thoughts racing through her mind, wondering who had died or been injured, wondering if something had happened to Zeke. She slowly lowered herself to sit beside him, her eyes desperately searching his in the dimness of the room.

"What?" she asked reluctantly, terrified at what he needed to say.

TJ hesitated, his gaze dropping to the floor as he said slowly, "My doctor called. There's something strange in my blood tests. Some anomalies. He wants me to go for further tests."

"Something strange? What strange? What did he find?"

TJ shrugged helplessly. "He said something about my blood count being low, that it's going somewhere."

"Like where?" Leah winced at her strident tone and struggled to calm herself. "Like...there's internal bleeding or something?"

TJ took a deep breath and resolutely met her eyes. "He suspects a tumor–most likely in the colon, but it could be anywhere. With any luck, it's nothing, but...he wants me to get it checked out. I'm going in tomorrow to get the necessary paperwork, see what I have to do to get these tests done."

Leah stared, her dark eyes huge in her face. She gripped his hand so tightly she felt his bones grind together, but he never winced and his eyes never wavered away from her face.

"Oh God," was all she could think to say.

Day 41

Daisy laughed as Manny went into raptures on the other end of the phone about the first day of Cary Grant movies.

"So, well worth the price of admission?" she teased when Manny took a breath.

"And then some," Manny sighed with pleasure. "And of course there are all the other movies, too. Too bad you—" she stopped abruptly. "Oh, shit—I'm sorry, Daisy! I forgot—"

"That's okay—I tend to forget, too. Hey—it's only been two weeks, and Hub's still here in the house until the end of the month when he moves into his new apartment."

"How are Jakob and Janika doing? I know you keep telling me they're okay, but...tell me honestly."

Daisy sighed, and bit her lip. "They're...not happy. Naturally. Jakob's even angrier since he's finished with sports for the rest of the year, although apparently all the girls flocking around to give him tea and sympathy do help a little."

"Are they blaming you?"

"They're blaming their father. They're pretty grounded kids; uncannily grounded. Half the time I wonder if they were switched at birth because they're so mature. Remember us at those ages?"

"Well, we were definitely flightier, but we were also helping Rebecca with Jaime around those ages, so we had to be a little bit more mature."

"Until university, anyway."

"Oh, yeah," Manny grinned. "Those were some fun days, weren't they?"

"Sure were. And to think, out of all those men who flocked around in those days, I chose Hub." She ruefully shook her head. "If I only knew then what I know now..."

"But you got two great kids out of it," Manny reminded her, "and you had some good times, right?"

Daisy pulled the phone away from her ear and blinked at it before she replaced it and said, "Manny? Are you trying to find the good things that came out of my relationship with Hub? You never liked him!"

Manny bit her lip, then said, "You loved him. What I thought about him was moot. I just thought–you know, your personalities were so different. Hub never was all that...um..."

"Fun?" Daisy asked drily.

"Yes! And I have to say, finding out he's having an affair surprised me. He's never been very spontaneous, either."

"Oh, I doubt very much this was spontaneous. I suspect he weighed the pros and cons and made a very informed choice."

"Except he decided it was worth risking everything he had with you and the kids to be with this woman. That almost sounds like...I don't know..."

"Love?" Daisy's voice broke on the word.

"Oh, God–I'm sorry! I didn't mean–"

Daisy sniffed and wiped her eyes. "No, it's okay. Really. I just–it's still hard to believe, you know? That he's been having this affair for a while; that he was willing to lose his children and his home. And...it just *hurts*."

"Oh, Daisy," Manny groaned in sympathy. "Are you sure you don't want me to come home?"

Daisy chuckled wetly. "Definitely not! I'm living vicariously through you–and I'm still planning on meeting you somewhere one of these days. Maybe once Jakob's out of his cast."

"But the kids are doing okay with everything that's happening?"

"Yeah. Really, honestly, truly–they're doing okay."

"And what about you, Daisy? How are you set financially?"

Daisy hesitated.

"I know you've been going to the casino more often than is good for you," Manny blurted into the silence. "I also know you couldn't be winning all the time. Are you in trouble?"

Daisy bit her lip and said, "Nothing I can't handle."

Manny hesitated, not sure if she should believe her sister or not.

"You'll let me know if you need help, right?" she finally said.

"You'll be the first to know. I promise."

"All right," Manny sighed. "If you need me, call and I'll get home as soon as I can."

Daisy chuckled. "I know. But I'd hate to have you cut your trip short just to come back and hold my hand. Besides, then you wouldn't see Zeke anymore."

Manny laughed. "That doesn't even come into the equation!"

"Too bad," Daisy sighed.

"Oh, God–that's my cue to say good-night, Daisy."

Daisy laughed. "Good-night. And thanks."

"Anytime," Manny said, and smiled as she ended the call.

Day 43

Zeke hated to admit it, but he'd actually enjoyed the movie festival. Manny hadn't forced him to go to every single Cary Grant movie–although it had been close. Zeke hadn't realized just how long and diverse the man's career had been, and as far as he could tell, there hadn't been a truly awful movie in the entire bunch. At least, according to Manny anyway.

After the first day, he and Manny had worked out a fairly equitable approach and between the two of them managed to take in something from every genre presented. His next blog would show him eating some crow, but he figured it was probably about time. He'd been pretty sarcastic in most of the blogs he'd posted over the last month and a half, and he ran the risk of coming across as too pigheaded to be kind.

He could tell from the number of hits, the types of comments, and from what Leah told him, that his reading public was still fascinated by his opinions about and experiences with Manny and her journey. If anything, the traffic to his blog posts was steadily increasing. The possibility that it would stay this popular until their journey was over was highly unlikely, so Zeke was determined to milk this small piece of notoriety for all it was worth.

Of course, online notoriety was a bit of a misnomer, since no one other than TJ and Leah—and Dixie—knew that Zeke Powell and the snarkily sarcastic blogger named Zeep were one and the same.

He grinned as he pulled a chair up to his desk and opened his laptop.

This one should get the comments flying, he thought gleefully, even it was going to be at his expense rather than Manny's. For a change.

He began to type.

~~~~~

Manny padded out of her bathroom, wrapped in a thick bathrobe, rosy from her bath. Her hair was piled on top of her head, long tendrils hanging damply on either side of her face.

She undid her hair, letting it tumble down her back, then laid down on the bed, her arms stretched above her head. She grinned as she thought of the last four days.

I think he enjoyed it in spite of himself, Harvey said.

Yeah, I saw him laughing at __Bringing Up Baby__. Of course, who could resist Cary Grant as an absent-minded

124

professor being slowly driven insane by Katharine Hepburn? I mean, <u>really</u>.

She turned her head to grin at Harvey, who was beside her on the bed still dressed in a tuxedo with a top hat balanced on his perfectly flat stomach.

He sadly shook his head and asked, **Am I going to be stuck in this thing for the rest of your life?**

Manny laughed. *It's only been four days! Maybe you'd prefer this instead?*

Harvey was now wearing white pants with the cuffs rolled up. His chest and feet were bare, and Manny could almost smell the salt air and feel the sunset on her skin.

Harvey raised one eyebrow and said, **Have you been watching those Old Spice commercials again?**

You'd prefer the pirate outfits?

At least then it's implied I've done more than just walk along a beach!

While looking very handsome.

Like that helps.

Wow. Picky yet. You can be replaced you know.

Oh? With Zeke maybe?

What? No! No, no, no.

Why not? He's real and you're in close proximity every day. Who knows what might happen if you're willing to take a chance?

I know exactly what will happen. I'll get all twitter-pated–

<u>Twitter-pated</u>? What–are you twelve?

I'll get all twitter-pated, Manny repeated, deliberately ignoring Harvey's interruption, *he'll remain oblivious until I make a pass at him–probably while I'm drunk–he'll be horrified and run screaming for the hills. Been there–done that–*

That was a long time ago.

Read the book–saw the movie–

Manny–

Bought the t-shirt. Thank you–<u>no</u>. Never fucking

again.

So—what? You're just going to 'make do' with me? I'm not real!

I know! Which makes you perfect in every way! You know that! It's why you exist, after all...I mean, to a certain definition of 'exist'.

That's...

Pathetic. I know. But it's safe.

And almost unbearably lonely.

Manny's eyes suddenly filled with tears and she blinked rapidly until both the tears and Harvey were gone.

EPISODE FIVE
Day 49

Manny yawned as the elevator dinged and she sleepily shuffled out into the lobby. She was meeting Zeke for breakfast, but the reason why she'd agreed to meet at such an ungodly hour had completely slipped her mind at the moment.

Of course, the fact that you were up 'til two a.m. playing the slot machines has nothing to do with it. Or the drinks, Harvey pointed out.

Manny shot Harvey a withering glare but refrained from comment.

She glanced around the lobby and saw Zeke standing at the front desk, talking with great interest and charm to the blonde woman who had checked them in the previous afternoon. The woman was definitely intrigued as she smiled up at him. Manny had to admit Zeke seemed even more rakishly handsome than usual this morning, with his five o'clock shadow and dishevelled dark hair standing up in spikes. His black jeans made his long legs look even longer and his black button-down shirt accentuated his broad shoulders and lean frame.

Oh, oh. This looks like San Francisco all over again.

I think you're right...well, he's a good-looking guy,

and this is Vegas.

Gotta admit, he doesn't seem to discriminate. Blondes, brunettes—redheads, if you count Rebecca.

He likes women. So sue him.

...my, you **are** cranky today...

Manny shook Harvey out of her head as she walked up to Zeke and the blonde woman with a tired smile.

Zeke gave her a slightly guilty look as he introduced her to Alicia, and Manny watched him from the corner of her eye, amused at his lingering look back as they left the attractive young woman and headed towards the breakfast buffet.

Zeke shot her thoughtfully considering glances as they moved through the line waiting to get into the restaurant, but they spoke little until they were inside, had filled up their plates and were sitting at the table.

Manny closed her eyes and hummed with pleasure as she sipped her coffee. She was beginning to wake up but she still regretted her two a.m. bedtime. She opened her eyes and blinked at Zeke's steady albeit slightly pleading gaze he had focused on her.

She cradled her coffee cup in both hands and raised a questioning eyebrow.

"Would you mind if—" Zeke began.

"Go," she interrupted with a half-smile. "Have fun. Play safe."

He smirked slightly. "Always."

"Good to hear," Manny said absently, yawning into her hand. She took a bite of her scrambled eggs and considered him thoughtfully.

"So, does this mean you're over Dixie, then?" she asked slowly.

"Pffft," Zeke shrugged, his eyes sliding away from hers. "What's to get over, really?"

"Ummmm—the fact that she threw you out? And you've never spoken to her about it? You said you cared about her."

"I did," Zeke agreed, his eyes focused on the food on his plate.

"But you're ready to move on? After what? A month? Maybe two? Don't you want to give your broken heart more time to heal?"

Zeke glanced at her, a half-bitter smile on his face. "What broken heart? And you didn't seem worried about this in San Francisco."

"I didn't know you as well then," Manny replied mildly. "Plus I didn't know what had happened with Dixie." She shrugged and picked up her coffee cup once more. "Anyway, I was just checking," she assured him.

Zeke considered her thoughtfully, his head cocked to one side.

"Thank you," he said quietly, "but I can take care of myself. Alicia's beautiful and she's definitely interested in getting to know me a little better. You said we weren't joined at the hip—"

Manny shook her head, waving away his words. "Go," she said again. "Have a good time. I have your cell number if I need to get in touch." She raised an eyebrow. "I assume I'll see you sometime before we're supposed to leave next week?" she asked sardonically.

"Maybe," Zeke teased, then smiled. It wasn't the deliberately charming smile he'd focused on Alicia but one that actually seemed genuine and surprisingly sweet.

"You're a very understanding soul, Auntie Em," Zeke said, his hazel eyes soft.

"Yeah, that's me," she sighed, and took another bite of her eggs.

Wonder what he'd do if you threw a temper tantrum? *Run away.*

...would that be a bad thing?

Hey, he's been really good so far. Really, I can count on one hand the number of days he's left me on my own. I can't really be pissed because he wants to spend time with a beautiful woman. After all, I understand sex is something you can do to pass the time.

Yes. You should try it sometime.

Well, I __am__ in Vegas. Who knows what might happen.

Day 53

Zeke wandered through the casino and tried to ignore his slight feeling of guilt. He kept an eye out for Manny but he knew that after four, almost five, full days, she could be anywhere in Vegas.

He ruefully shook his head.

While Manny loved to sightsee–as he'd first learned to his dismay and sometime amusement as they meandered their way out of Alberta–she wasn't exactly the most social person he'd ever met. It took her time to warm up to people, and even at the film festival, she only spoke to those people he spoke to, or who spoke to her first. He could just imagine how she'd spent the last four or five days–probably wandering diffidently along the Strip, avoiding eye contact, and not speaking a word.

He sternly squashed the feelings of guilt, telling himself he hadn't intended to leave her on her own. But when things had spectacularly crashed and burned with Alicia that first night, he'd wanted a day or two to lick his wounds in private. Who knew she even had a boyfriend, let alone one quite that big and quite that good with a right hook? He rubbed his jaw and winced at the remembered pain.

Then Leah had called with an urgent need for a half-dozen articles for her site after one of her other regular writers had taken another job and left her high and dry. She'd sounded stressed, as had TJ when Zeke spoke to him the next day, but they both assured him they were simply worried about getting ready to start on the potentially long and complicated path towards having a baby.

He paused at a bank of slot machines and frowned.

He'd never find Manny just by wandering around. She hadn't answered her cell phone when he called, and he couldn't remember her room number. He sighed. He'd just have to go to the front desk and leave a message for her.

His steps slowed when he saw Alicia was working, but then he mentally shrugged and walked up to the desk.

Alicia flushed when she saw him.

He greeted her with a rueful smile.

"Listen, Zeke," Alicia said hurriedly, "I really am sorry. I didn't even know Abe was in town–I swear!"

Zeke waved away her apology. "Nothing got broken," he replied, "and you can barely see the bruises anymore. No real harm done."

Alicia smiled gratefully at him. "Thanks, Zeke."

She leaned closer.

"Listen, Abe really is out of town tonight, so if you wanted to get together–just for a drink," she hastened to assure him. "I think I probably owe you a beer at the very least."

Zeke chuckled. "I'll have to let you know. I haven't seen Manny–you know, the woman I'm travelling with–for the last few days, and I want to check in with her before I start making any other plans."

Alicia shrugged. "Let me know, okay? And I think I just saw your Manny heading towards the casino." She nodded her head towards Zeke's right, which was the opposite wing of the casino than the one he'd just explored.

He thanked her and strode in the direction she'd indicated, his long legs making short work of the distance to the casino floor. He walked down the main path, looking down each bank of slot machines without success. He was about to give up when he heard his name being called.

He turned and smiled as Manny walked up to him. Her mousy not-quite-blonde-not-quite-brown hair was, as always, tightly bound in its habitual bun, but he saw her face was again slightly sunburned, her nose rosy. She was wearing blue jeans and a grey tank top that hugged her figure. For the first time Zeke noticed Manny carried her weight in her breasts and hips, and even though she was a bit overweight, her waist appeared quite tiny, especially in that tank top. He frowned slightly, not sure he liked just how much her current outfit revealed of her figure while she was wandering around Vegas on her own. She was, after all, his Auntie Em.

On the other hand, he was surprised at just how happy and, yes, relieved he was to see her. He must have been feeling guiltier than he thought about leaving her to fend for herself. To be honest, he'd barely thought of her at all during the last five days, first because he'd been in pain from Abe's punch, then hungover from all the whiskey he'd drunk that night after Abe had taken Alicia home, and then he'd been too busy working to worry too much about how Manny was spending her time, or what she was wearing while she wandered the Strip.

He greeted her now, though, with real pleasure, then asked, "So, what have you been doing the last few days?"

Manny gave him a distracted smile as she glanced around the casino, and said, "You first."

Zeke considered telling her the truth for all of half a second, then decided to keep the illusion of his last week going for a while longer. Besides, he couldn't really explain about Leah without skirting dangerously close to inadvertently leading her to his blog that was focused on her and this trip.

His grin turned wolfish as he instead said, "If I have to explain it to you, then you really shouldn't be let out of the house."

Manny raised a questioning eyebrow. "Really? For four whole days?"

Zeke preened slightly, making a show of straightening the sleeves of his green button-down shirt. "Impressed?"

"Skeptical, actually. But unless...whatshername decides

to share, I guess I'll have to take your word for it."

Zeke mock-glared at her, his hands on his jean-clad hips.

"Thanks," he said drily. "Anyway, I'll bet what you've been doing can't come anywhere near that!"

Manny tsk'd and lightly patted his arm. He stared down at her hand, startled and suddenly noticing just how much shorter she was than him. This was, he realized, the first time she'd touched him since their trip started.

She said lightly, seemingly oblivious to his startled reaction to her touch, "Well, if I'd known we were in a competition, I might have—oh, hi, Angeline, Reuben!"

Zeke looked to his right and saw two people in their mid-to-late sixties striding briskly towards them. He hesitated between polite curiosity and frowning confusion as the older woman and Manny shared a hug.

"There you are!" Angeline said, leaning back and smiling cozily at Manny. "I was getting worried about you! Are you ready to go to the chapel?"

Zeke whipped his head towards Manny.

"Chapel?" and to his horror, his voice actually squeaked.

"Absolutely," Manny said to Angeline, then met Zeke's wide eyes with an amused grin. "Zeke, meet Angeline Steinberg and her fiancé, Reuben Kingsley. They're getting married today, and I'm going to be a bridesmaid."

She bit back a laugh at the look on Zeke's face as she turned back to the happy couple.

"Have you seen Lionel?" she asked.

Lionel? Zeke thought blankly.

"He's going to meet us at the chapel," Angeline replied. She turned to Zeke with a broad grin. "It's a pleasure to finally meet you, Zeke. I've heard a lot about you. If you have the time, you're more than welcome to join us."

Zeke blinked at her, feeling a confusion that was disorienting while at the same time, surprisingly familiar. It reminded him of walking into Leila's bed and breakfast to find Manny in the midst of a no-holds-barred card game. The world currently seemed to be tilting on its axis in much the same way.

He shook himself out of his fog and said, "Thank you– I'd like that. Are you an old friend of Manny's?"

Angeline laughed, a surprisingly young and musical sound. "Oh, no! We met here at the slot machines the other night. She brought us luck, and we've sort of adopted each other."

"Oh?" Zeke replied faintly, as they began to walk to where Zeke assumed the chapel was located.

Angeline chattered on, "And she's been so kind, humoring us by making all the arrangements and accompanying us wherever we wanted to go. She did the Fremont Street zipline with us."

"Screaming the entire way," Manny confided drily.

Angeline shook her head and continued, "We rode donkeys down into the Grand Canyon, and yesterday we toured Death Valley. Then, of course, there was Area 51 and the UFO watching tour–which was very exciting for everyone!"

"In more ways than one," Manny nodded.

Zeke didn't have a chance to ask her what she meant before Reuben said, "Tomorrow is the ghost tour, and the day after that we're going to hit all the museums we can find."

"Tonight's the wedding, of course," Manny said, "but then we're all going to the high stakes poker room afterwards–mostly for drinks and the ambience because I don't think many of us can afford to actually play at a table. Maybe you can bring, um, whatshername to that. It's formal, though, so you'll need a tux and she'll need a formal outfit."

Angeline slipped a hand in the crook of Manny's arm and said, "It's very hard to organize so many people for all those activities, but Manny just seems to pull it all together so easily."

"Well," Zeke said weakly. "there are only the four of you–"

Manny laughed. "Four? Oh, Lord no! You'll see everyone at the wedding. Lionel, Jack, Simon-Simone and I have to be there because we're in the wedding party, but nobody from the group would miss this!"

Zeke stared at her in utter confusion before his dark brows lowered thunderously over his eyes.

"What the hell are you talking about?" he demanded.

Before Manny could respond, Reuben said, "We're here," and pulled open the door.

Zeke's jaw dropped as he gaped at what at first appeared to be a kaleidoscope of people of all ages, shapes and colours. The tiny chapel was packed, but as he began to make sense of the scene, he realized there were actually only about thirty people in the room.

There was a rather dapper man in his sixties talking to a trio of twenty-somethings of various nationalities but with their hair in matching shades of purple, and each sporting several tattoos and piercings. As Zeke watched, they all began laughing uproariously at what Zeke could only assume was the punch line to a joke. His gaze moved to a group of women standing around a very tall, striking blonde woman. The shorter women were obviously giving commentary on the tall woman's dress, shoes, hair and makeup. Zeke blinked and frowned as he peered closer and realized the tall woman was male. He stared for a moment before admitting that he–or rather, she–was really quite attractive.

Everywhere he looked, he saw a mixed bag of people, mingling together in high spirits and good humour. Well, he thought dazedly, they were at a wedding after all.

He turned as a big, bluff, classically handsome man in his fifties strode up to them, his arms spread wide in welcome.

"Here you are!" he boomed. "I was beginning to wonder if you'd gotten cold feet! I've put your wedding dress in the bride's alcove, Angeline, and Manny, your maid of honor dress is there as well. There's also a woman waiting to do your hair and make-up."

"Shoes?" Manny asked, stopping his words with one raised finger.

Lionel—because Zeke could only assume this larger than life man was Lionel—put a hand to his broad, elegantly clad chest and his eyes widened in mock pain.

"I'm hurt—of course I remembered the shoes! The three of you are going to look absolutely stunning." He turned to Reuben. "We'll do them justice as well. Our tuxes are in the groom's alcove."

He finally seemed to notice Zeke and quickly gave him the once-over.

"Another addition to the menagerie, I see," he said to Zeke with a smile. "Introduce yourself, find a seat—and enjoy the show. You'll need to get a tux before we go to the high-stakes poker room, but don't worry—everyone has to go change. Will you be bringing a date?"

Zeke simply stood, feeling shell-shocked. "Uh, maybe," he finally managed, and Lionel beamed at him.

"Good man. Make yourself comfortable. The wedding will begin soon."

Manny and Angeline hurried off to the bride's alcove, taking the tall woman with them as they left. Zeke took the opportunity to slip back to the front desk and ask Alicia if she'd be interested in buying him that drink at a wedding reception. She stared blankly at him before she slowly agreed.

Zeke slipped back into the chapel just as the wedding began. He hastily sat and watched as Reuben, Lionel and another impeccably dressed fifty-something man took their places at the altar and turned expectantly towards the back of the chapel.

The first bridesmaid was the tall woman Zeke had noticed earlier. She was now dressed in a dark blue sheath dress that ended just below her knees and she was no longer blonde. Instead she wore a chestnut wig with the hair pulled away from her face and then allowed to tumble loosely down her back in thick waves. She was wearing delicately pretty shoes with one-inch heels that exactly matched the colour of the dress. She walked slowly and a little unsteadily on the shoes, biting her lip and frowning in concentration as she walked down the aisle.

Manny was next to step out of the bride's alcove. Zeke thought she was pleasantly plump and decently pretty in the same sheath dress but in a brilliant jewel blue, and with a similar hairstyle as the first bridesmaid. He hadn't realized just how long Manny's hair truly was, well past her mid-back, and he guessed he could now almost understand why she always wore it in a bun.

He looked curiously at her feet and raised an eyebrow. The shoes were the same delicately pretty shoes as the first bridesmaid's, perfectly matched in colour to her dress, but the thin stiletto heels were at least three inches high. He had to admit, they were gorgeous shoes, but they looked far too dangerous for someone like Manny to wear. He idly wondered if any of the people in the chapel were also doctors or at least knew how to deal with a broken ankle. She walked steadily down the aisle and never missed a step.

Once Manny took her place at the altar, the music paused before the wedding march began. Angeline appeared wearing a simple pale yellow lace dress, her own shoes just as delicately gorgeous as her bridesmaids' but with a much lower heel. She smiled rather shyly at everyone in the room and began to sedately walk down the aisle.

She'd only taken three steps when the music abruptly changed to a fast-paced country-rock song, and everyone in the chapel, including the groom and the minister, began to clap and sing along.

Angeline stopped short, her jaw dropping before she burst out laughing. She laughed even harder when Reuben did a shuffling dance down the aisle to meet her then scooped her into his arms and whirled her down the aisle before finally depositing her, flushed, breathless and starry-eyed, at the altar.

Even as he clapped along with the others, Zeke's eyebrows rose even higher as he wondered just what, exactly, he'd missed over the last five days.

~~~~~

Two hours later, the odd group of people Manny had found were milling noisily around the high stakes poker room. They were the only people there and Zeke wondered how Angeline and Reuben had managed to convince the casino to rent them this room for the evening especially since very few in the crowd looked like they could afford to breathe the air in here, let alone lose any money at the tables.

He glanced at Alicia, standing in an out-of-the-way corner of the room, waiting for him to return with their drinks. She was staring around with the same expression he knew he wore on his own face, a mixture of confusion, dismay and amusement. He shook his head in bemusement.

Manny stood beside him, watching everyone with a fond smile.

Zeke leaned closer and murmured, "Why do I have that Dr. Hook song in my head?"

Manny tsk'd mildly then gave him her most fearsome prudish-maiden-aunt look as she firmly said, "They're not freaks."

Zeke found that the prudish-maiden-aunt look didn't have quite the same effect while she was wearing those sexy high-heeled shoes and her hair wasn't in its usual bun.

"Island of misfit toys, then?" Zeke teased.

She tsk'd again, more forcefully this time. "How about just people?"

Zeke shook his head. "How the hell did you fall into this group?"

Manny shrugged. "We all just...met."

"Well, are they friends of Angeline and Reuben? Did they come to Vegas for the wedding?"

Manny shook her head. "No. I told you—we all just...sorta...*met*. Here in Vegas."

"Don't you listen to her," Lionel boomed, and Zeke jumped a little before he turned around. He hadn't realized the older man had walked up behind them.

Lionel continued, "Although it's true we met here in Vegas, I think it was her ability to strike up a conversation with anybody that really drew us all together."

Zeke blinked at him in silence for a moment.

"*Manny's* ability to strike up a conversation?" he asked carefully.

Lionel slung a friendly arm across Manny's shoulders. "And her willingness to get a conversation started between people, and then step out of the way."

Zeke frowned and opened his mouth to ask more questions, but Manny forestalled him.

"Let's get our drinks and rejoin Alicia—she's looking lonely and uncomfortable. I promise I'll tell you all about the last few days once we have drinks in our hands." She glanced with some amusement at Zeke's befuddled expression. "I think you're going to be grateful for a drink or two by the time I'm done."

Zeke was almost bursting with impatience and curiosity by the time they rejoined Alicia with a small entourage in tow. They stood in a circle, Zeke standing between Alicia and Manny, with Lionel and Jack, who'd been the other groomsman; Simon-Simone, who was the other bridesmaid, and Angeline and Reuben.

Zeke and Alicia introduced themselves and learned that Jack was Lionel's life partner, and this was Simon-Simone's first trip to Las Vegas. Lionel casually slipped an arm around Jack's waist as they chatted.

Zeke pounced at the first lull in the conversation.

"Okay," he said to Manny, "enough with the small talk.

Spill! What—who—how did you meet all these people?"

Manny took a sip of her drink and smiled with a half-puzzled, half-embarrassed air.

"Well," she hesitated, "that's a bit of a long story..."

"I think we have time," Zeke said drily, "and you promised to tell me everything. With the way you're squirming, I'm beginning to think you have something to hide."

Manny shot him a mock glare, then shrugged and said, "Well, I guess I should start at the beginning, then." She nodded at the newlyweds. "I met Angeline and Reuben when we were playing on neighbouring slot machines and we struck up a conversation."

Angeline said, "I was having so much fun talking to Manny that I got distracted and accidentally hit the maximum bet button." She leaned closer to Zeke and conspiratorially lowered her voice as she added, "I don't *ever* play at the maximum bet—I can't afford to lose that much. Plus I was down to my last twenty dollars for the day. I screamed when I realized what I'd done, let me tell you!"

"Really loudly," Reuben agreed with a wince. Angeline smacked him lightly on the shoulder.

"Thankfully, she got the bonus," Manny told Zeke with an affectionate smile at the happy couple.

"And she ended up winning the jackpot," Reuben finished with a grin.

Zeke raised an eyebrow. "The jackpot?" he asked, lifting his drink to his lips.

"It was one of those progressive machines," Angeline explained modestly. "Eleven million dollars."

Zeke spewed out his drink, although he thankfully didn't get any on anyone except himself. Manny helpfully pounded him on the back as he coughed, his eyes watering, while Alicia, Angeline and Simon-Simone scrambled for napkins to press into his hand.

He stared at Angeline, his dark eyes huge. "Are you

fucking *kidding* me?"

Everyone laughed, including Alicia, and Lionel said, "No, she's definitely not fucking kidding you."

Zeke coughed once more, then said, "Okay. Well. Well, then...that must have been exciting." He congratulated himself on being the king of understatement.

"Very!" Angeline said, grinning.

"She screamed again," Reuben said, deadpan. "Even louder."

"And that's why Reuben and I decided to get married. Not because I screamed again but because we figured luck like that had to be a sign that our marriage would also be lucky." She smiled fondly at Reuben before saying viciously, "Plus we'll now be able to tell our kids to like our marriage—or lump it."

Reuben nodded vigorously while Zeke raised a quizzical eyebrow.

"And that's when I came into the picture," Lionel said.

"To make arrangements for the wedding?" Zeke asked.

"Oh, sorry—no. To hand over the money. I own this casino."

Alicia gasped, her hand flying to cover her mouth.

Lionel grinned as he eyed her curiously. "You're new here, aren't you?"

"Ye-yes, sir," she replied, her eyes huge. "I started three weeks ago."

Lionel nodded. "I thought so. Anyway, I met Angeline, Reuben and Manny when we were doing the paperwork and the photos, etc., etc., etc." He waved his hand airily. "I was so charmed by their excitement and impulsive decision to get married that of course I offered the chapel to them free of charge. And Angeline was so excited because she could do so many more things while they were here, if she only knew what else there was to do, and Manny—"

Lionel looked at Manny and laughed affectionately. Manny squirmed a little uncomfortably under his grin.

"I rattled off about a dozen sights to see and activities

to do that didn't involve gambling," she muttered ruefully, her eyes on the drink in her hands. "You know me and my sightseeing."

Zeke nodded numbly. "Do I ever," he agreed but he didn't have the energy to say it with his usual sarcasm.

"Well," Lionel continued, "her enthusiasm was contagious and before I knew it, I committed Jack and I to trying out the Fremont Street zipline, and going on a bus trip to the Grand Canyon."

"A bus trip," Jack sighed, rolling his eyes. "With tourists! I couldn't believe it when he told me!" He gave Lionel an affectionately exasperated look. "If I didn't love him so much, I'd have told him to jump in the Bellagio fountain!"

"Anyway," Manny continued, "I met Simon-Simone while I was standing in line that evening to buy the tickets to the Grand Canyon."

Zeke turned to look at the woman in question.

"And that's a story all on its own," Simon-Simone told him with an apologetic glance at Manny. "I was overly sensitive and thought she was offended by me. We ended up bonding over my shoes. And then..." Simon-Simone's smile became slightly embarrassed. "Poor Manny! I sobbed my whole sad story out on her shoulder, right there in line. I told her all about how I'd finally decided to stop living a lie and how I'd hoped Vegas would be the best place for me to, well, practice being a woman, but it had all been a dismal failure, and how confused I still felt about–well, everything."

She shook her head. "I must have broken her heart because she brought me here, to Angeline and Reuben and Lionel and Jack. They all took me under their wings, gave me my new name, and took me with them to the Grand Canyon."

They smiled fondly at each other while Zeke simply stared, his eyes wide and disbelieving.

"This is some elaborate prank, isn't it?" he said finally,

turning to Manny. "You're playing with my head because I left you alone for the last few days."

Manny laughed and shook her head. "Trust me–I'm not that bright."

Zeke shook his head. "Okay, fine. So tell me, how did you meet those three over there?"

They looked over at two young women and a young man who were standing close together while they avidly watched a table full of poker players.

Manny said, "That's Cordelia, Alphonse and An-Li. We met them on the UFO watching tour."

"Total Area 51 geeks," Simon-Simone confided.

Lionel laughed his big booming laugh and said, "I thought they were going to get us shot!"

"I almost fainted when they started talking about disabling the cameras and making a run for the compound," Angeline said.

"Good thing Simon-Simone managed to talk them out of it," Jack added.

Simon-Simone nodded sagely, "Yeah, by pointing out that we were surrounded by soldiers with guns and they'd never make it past the fence."

Zeke shook his head in disbelief. "And those two?" he asked, indicating a man and a woman with matching bright green mohawks.

"Oh, God," Manny groaned, "that's Vic and Viki–they almost fell into the Grand Canyon!"

Angeline shuddered, "I was never so scared in my life– well, until the UFO tour." She turned to Zeke and Alicia and explained, "They started slipping off the donkeys on the way down to the bottom of the Grand Canyon."

"Good God!" Zeke blurted.

"That's what we said!" Jack agreed. "On the other hand, they've vowed they're never going to ride donkeys ever again."

"We met Perry when we went ziplining on Fremont Street," Simon-Simone said, pointing out the man in question. He was the dapper sixty-something man Zeke had noticed in the chapel.

Lionel nodded towards one purple-haired man, "Arturo was from the midnight helicopter ride."

Manny laughed, shaking her head, "He blew almost his entire budget just so he could say he'd flown in a helicopter."

Reuben said, pointing out each person as he named them, "Josh, Blonde-Josh and Ali were from the trip to Death Valley."

Lionel nodded and said, "Valeria, Ed and Tamara were gathered up at various casinos when we cruised the strip. And the rest," he looked around and shrugged.

"They're friends, or someone met them here in Vegas and brought them along," Manny explained. She shook her head and met Zeke's eyes with a small, slightly confused frown. "To tell the truth, I'm just as surprised and confused as you are," she assured him.

Zeke shook his head in silent amazement. A few minutes later, after Simon-Simone spirited Alicia away to the bar for refills, and Lionel and Jack went with Angeline and Reuben to one of the poker tables, Zeke stared around the room one more time then looked again at Manny.

"And here I've been feeling guilty for leaving you all alone and lonely," he said with a rueful grin.

Manny laughed. "No, you weren't."

Zeke gave her a wolfish grin. "No, I wasn't. I had other things on my mind."

Manny rolled her eyes and laughed again. "I'm sure. Well, I didn't come to Vegas to sit around."

"You've certainly proved that," Zeke agreed, and smiled, his eyes warm as he looked at her.

He could see Simon-Simone and Alicia returning, so he leaned closer and said, softly and quickly, "You've definitely surprised me."

Manny looked around the room and shook her head with a puzzled air. "I've definitely surprised myself," she admitted, and turned to take her drink from Simon-Simone with a smile.

Day 54

Rebecca bustled around the kitchen making breakfast while she spoke to Manny, the phone tucked between her shoulder and her ear. "It sounds like it was a great time," she said with a grin as she stirred the hash browns.

"It was awesome," Manny agreed with a huge yawn. "Sorry, Rebecca—it was a late night."

"What did Daisy think of it?"

"She wished she could have been there, if for no other reason than to see Zeke's face."

Rebecca laughed. "I have to admit—that must have been priceless."

"It really was—I didn't think anyone's eyes could get that big!"

Rebecca took a couple of eggs out of the fridge as she listened to Manny and exclaimed, "Damn!" as one of the eggs slipped out of her hand and smashed on the floor on her way back to the stove.

"What happened?" Manny asked, suddenly alert.

"Oh, nothing—I just dropped an egg. I'm making breakfast for me and Tris."

"Hmmm. How's that going? Have you talked to Jaime lately?"

"No," Rebecca sighed. "She's been calling Tris, but she hasn't spoken to me at all. And Tris isn't sharing. I have no idea if—"

Rebecca stopped abruptly as Tris shuffled into the kitchen, rubbing her eyes and yawning.

"Whoops—and here's Tris, looking for breakfast," she recovered quickly. She nodded at the broken egg on the floor and said, "Tris, could you please wipe up the mess I made? Thanks."

Tris shot Rebecca a dirty look, but dug out the paper towels to do as she'd been asked.

Rebecca frowned at Tris' back as she said to Manny, "I've got to go—talk to you tomorrow?"

"You bet. Say hi to Tris."

"I will."

Rebecca clicked the phone off and focused her attention on making omelets for breakfast. She continued to frown slightly as she watched Tris clean up the dropped egg then pour herself a glass of orange juice, all without quite looking her grandmother in the eye.

Rebecca said, carefully casual, "Morning, Tris. Manny says hi."

Tris shrugged carelessly as she sat down at the table.

"How'd you sleep?" Rebecca continued.

"Okay," Tris said without enthusiasm.

Rebecca sighed. "I know you're not thrilled to still be here, but I wish you'd at least pretend to be a little happier."

Tris slumped down in her chair, her arms crossed tightly across her chest, her bottom lip pouting out. "So you want me to lie?"

"No, but I do want you to make the best of a—a not-so-bad situation."

Tris snorted. "Oh, please! Since when have you ever sugar-coated anything for me?"

Rebecca paused, turning from the stove, the spatula still in her hand.

"I'm not sugar-coating anything. This *isn't* a bad situation—"

"Except both of my parents have dumped me here on your doorstep with barely a word."

"All right," Rebecca acknowledged calmly, "that is a bad situation, but not you staying here. And that still doesn't mean you shouldn't be trying to make the best of it."

"Why?" Tris demanded petulantly. "Mom and Dad just left everything, including me, behind. Why should I have to be the only one who needs to stick things out?"

Rebecca dished up their breakfasts, placed the plates on the table and took a seat across from Tris, all in thoughtful silence. Tris stared with distaste at the omelet and hash browns in front of her.

"Because somebody has to be the grown-up," Rebecca said finally. "And until your parents are ready to be that again, you're going to have to."

"What about you? Why aren't you being the grown-up?"

Rebecca raised one warning eyebrow. "And how am I not being a grown-up?"

"You complain about Mom and Dad and me all the time. Just because I'm in a different room doesn't mean I can't hear you!"

Rebecca blinked, suddenly scrambling to remember all the conversations she'd had on the phone or in person since Tris had arrived. She sincerely hoped Tris couldn't hear everything, especially some of the calls she'd had with Jackson.

She awkwardly cleared her throat.

"All right. That's a fair comment," she replied, pleased with how calm she sounded. "I'll try not to complain anymore. But other than that, am I treating you like it's your fault?"

"Isn't it?" Tris asked. She was trying for defiant but she instead sounded like the vulnerable ten-year-old she was.

"Are you nuts?" Rebecca blurted. "This situation is your parents' fault—and only your parents' fault. What they're going through and doing has absolutely nothing to do with you, or anything you have or haven't done."

Tris slammed her hands on the table, and yelled, "How can you say that? They left me! I must have done something to deserve it! Especially since you don't want me either!"

She violently pushed her chair away from the table and ran out of the room, leaving Rebecca staring disconsolately at the table.

Day 57

"Hey, Zeke," TJ said, putting the call on speaker.

"Hey, TJ. How're things?"

"Great," TJ said. "Never been better. You guys hitting the road again today?" Nothing in his tone revealed he was going to the hospital later in the day to undergo the last of the tests the doctor had ordered.

"Yeah. Manny and I are just standing here, waiting for somebody to pick up our luggage before we head out to some place in Nebraska."

"Nebraska?"

"Don't ask me—Manny's in charge of the itinerary. And she still hasn't learned the value of planning ahead. We have to be back in Los Angeles in a few weeks for some movie premiere thing she managed to score tickets for." Zeke deliberately raised his voice, "All this driving and being stuck in a van together is bound to make one of us homicidal sooner or later!"

TJ laughed as he heard Manny's faint reply of 'wimp' in the background, and he waited patiently while Zeke made arrangements to meet her at the van.

"What's in Nebraska?" TJ asked once Zeke was back on the line with him.

"Manny isn't saying. I think she just likes keeping me in the dark."

"Don't we all," TJ said drily. He glanced up as the door opened and Leah walked in. "Look I have to go," he said. "Leah's here to take me to—to another doctor's appointment."

"What—are you getting a *third* opinion?"

Leah raised an eyebrow at TJ as he hesitated for a split second before saying, "Yeah, a third opinion. Who knows? Maybe third time's the charm."

Zeke chuckled, then said, "Well, I hope this one turns out better than the last ones."

"Yeah, me too," TJ replied quietly.

"Is everything okay?" Zeke asked after a slight hesitation. "Between you and Leah, I mean."

Leah leaned forward. "Everything's just fine with us, Zeke."

"Whoops."

Leah laughed. "Sorry, I guess I should have said something when I walked in."

"Well, no harm done so long as you didn't overhear us talking about that hot blonde TJ met last night," Zeke teased.

"No worries. TJ and I will just have a little chat later; he'll tell me everything then."

TJ rolled his eyes. "Zeke, how is it you can still get me into trouble even when you're thousands of kilometres away?"

"It's a gift."

They laughed, then Leah said, "Thanks again for getting those articles done for me on such short notice. Especially when you were in Vegas! I feel bad about cutting into your partying time."

"Hey, considering you're bankrolling this trip, it was the least I could do."

"What story did you tell Manny?"

"Manny thinks I was tucked away with the hot blonde I really did meet the night we arrived. As far as she's concerned, I was far too distracted to bum around with her."

"She already knows your priorities well," TJ said drily.

"Was that a slam?" Zeke asked curiously.

"Just an observation."

"Anyway, wait until you get my next set of blogs. You're not going to believe what happened while I was busy getting that work done for you, Leah. I almost don't believe it myself. My readers are going to have a field day with this one."

"They've been having field days with all of your blogs so far, and traffic's increasing," Leah replied.

"Great! That's the whole reason behind this trip, after all–to help put *What Women Want* on the Internet map."

"What?" Leah gasped. "You mean it's not for you to maybe learn something?"

"How can I possibly learn anything when I already know it all? Hey, I've gotta go. Listen, TJ–good luck at the doc's. I hope third time really is the charm and you guys get better news this time around."

TJ grinned a little sadly, "Thanks, man. Drive carefully."

"Will do."

TJ stared at the phone in silence after he ended the call. He was very conscious of the weight of Leah's gaze on his bowed head.

"Why didn't you tell him what tests you're really having done?" she asked quietly.

TJ shrugged. "What can he do? Besides, these are just tests–we don't know anything yet. I'll tell him everything once we have some idea of what–if anything–we're dealing with." He lifted his eyes to Leah's. "Zeke may seem like a guy who doesn't give a shit about anything, but if he knew there was the slightest possibility of–of something being seriously wrong with me, he'd be back here in a shot."

Leah squeezed his shoulder. "I know he would. That's why I think you should tell him."

TJ covered her hand with his and shook his head. "Besides the fact that his blog is the most popular blog on your site, you know he'd just sit here, worrying and getting in your way. Which would drive you crazy. More importantly, he'd also be driving *me* crazy."

Leah lifted TJ's hand and pressed a kiss to his knuckles. "That's what I love about you the most, TJ. You're always thinking of me."

TJ stood with a weak imitation of his usual smile and took her in his arms. "I have my priorities," he agreed, "and my own sanity is number one on the list."

They kissed then he wrapped his arms around her and

squeezed tight, his face buried in her hair.

"Ready to go?" she asked, her voice muffled against his shoulder.

"No. But let's go anyway."

~~~~~

Manny and Zeke drove out of Vegas in relaxed, companionable silence. Manny sat behind the wheel with a smile tugging at the corners of her mouth.

"How many of the Misfit Toys were still in town today?" Zeke asked casually.

"None. I deliberately chose this morning because everyone would be on their way to their respective homes. Well, except Lionel and Jack, of course."

"Simon-Simone going to be okay?"

Manny pursed her lips as she considered the question. "I hope so. From the sound of it, she's not going back to the most supportive environment in the world. She may decide to continue being who her family expects her to be for the foreseeable future." She shook her head. "I just don't know."

"So, she was Simon when she got on the plane?"

"Had to. She's Simon on her ID."

Realization dawned. "Of course. That was a stupid question."

Manny shook her head with a smile. "I asked the same thing, except directly to her. Talk about feeling stupid."

"Ouch," Zeke laughed. "Now I don't feel so bad."

"She promised to let me know how she's doing."

"I suppose she can text you," Zeke said uncertainly.

"Or e-mail."

She indicated the back of the van. Zeke turned and saw a new laptop case nestled on the bed.

"You bought a new laptop?" he asked incredulously.

"I didn't have a choice," Manny replied drily. "Apparently the one I brought with me simply wasn't good enough. Angeline took me to the store and insisted on buying that thing for me. Complete with wireless and—I don't know—a travelling Internet or something."

Zeke laughed. "You're so technical!"

"Whatever. Anyway, my Misfit Toys as you call them insisted they'd friend me and I'm ordered—ordered!—to post regular status updates."

"How regular?" Zeke asked curiously.

"Preferably daily but no less than once a week." She shook her head. "I'm not sure what I'm supposed to post. I doubt anything else on this trip is going to be nearly as interesting as Vegas was."

"They probably just want to make sure I haven't finally snapped and left your body someplace."

Manny rolled her eyes. "Oh, please! You don't spend enough time with me to go crazy!"

Zeke raised his eyebrows.

"*How* many hours to Nebraska?" he drawled.

Manny shifted uncomfortably. "Good point," she muttered, and focused on her driving.

EPISODE SIX
Day 69

The sun hung low on the horizon, the late afternoon light glinting off the van where it sat on the side of the deserted dirt road, the engine ticking as it cooled. The hood was up, the smoke and steam still dissipating as Zeke and Manny stared with matching frowns from the exposed engine to the cell phones in their hands.

Zeke met Manny's eyes and slowly shook his head as he showed her his phone. "I've got nothing," he said.

"Same here," Manny sighed. "Please tell me you were a mechanic in a previous life."

"Sorry. You?"

"It turns on when I turn the key. That's all I need to know."

"We're fucked."

"Oh, yeah."

~~~~~

Zeke walked back to the van shaking his head.

"Still no signal," he called.

Manny groaned and hung her head.

"None from my side either," she said.

They stood and looked around them. All they could see was an endless expanse of gently rolling land, a tree or two, and the immense, slowly darkening sky. The sheer size of the land and sky pressed in on them, along with the profound silence of an empty countryside.

Zeke suddenly shuddered and said, "I don't see any lights coming on at all."

"Me neither."

Manny shook her head, then led the way back to the van, flung open the passenger side door and pulled a map out of the glove compartment.

"We're about a hundred miles from anywhere," Zeke reminded her as he squinted over her shoulder.

She frowned as she pinpointed their general location, pressing the map against the van as she began to trace their route, looking for the closest sign of life.

"No," she said slowly, "just a hundred miles from anywhere big."

Zeke squinted at the tiny circle Manny indicated.

"You have *got* to be kidding me."

She grinned at him. "It's better than nothing. And if I'm reading the map right, we should be able to get there by noon-ish, if we leave early enough."

He stared at her in consternation.

"You mean you want us to spend the night out here?"

"Well, if nobody drives by before then and gives us a ride."

"Why don't we start walking now? Three-four hours of walking–"

"More like five or six, if I'm reading the map right. It's also going to be dark soon, and even though we just have to follow the road, I'd still rather see where we're going. Besides," she glanced towards the west, "it's going to rain tonight."

He followed her gaze to see the dark clouds slowly building on the horizon. His shoulders slumped as he nodded glumly.

"It's going to be a long night," he muttered.

~~~~~

Time slowly ticked away.

Manny and Zeke threw blankets on the ground and sat in silence as the sun finished setting, staring at the gently rolling and completely deserted landscape, and watching the clouds on the western horizon.

"Remind me again whose idea it was to take the side roads?" Manny asked idly.

Zeke heaved a long-suffering sigh and hung his head.

Manny smirked as she added, "I believe the thought was we'd shave at least four hours off our time?"

"How was I supposed to know this piece of shit was going to give up the ghost in the middle of fucking nowhere?"

Manny laughed. "And in probably the only place left on this continent that doesn't have cell phone service."

Zeke groaned and slowly slid to the side until he was stretched out on the ground, his arms crossed over his eyes as he slowly shook his head.

"And we haven't seen another car since we got on this godforsaken road," he grumbled.

"Nope," Manny agreed simply.

They sat in silence for another moment, then Manny said briskly, "Well, it could be worse."

Zeke lowered his arms and turned his head to stare at her in disbelief.

"How?" he demanded.

"We didn't have an accident; the van just...quit working."

"There was smoke!"

"Well, yes, that was pretty scary," Manny agreed. "But," she glanced behind her at the vehicle in question, "it doesn't seem to be on fire anymore. I suspect it was really just steam."

"You mean you hope!"

Manny ignored the interruption. "Which means it should be safe to sleep in tonight."

Zeke groaned again and re-covered his eyes.

"We also have food, water, a bathroom—well, of a sort—and a relatively comfortable place to sleep," Manny continued. "I also have a couple decks of cards if you want to do something to pass the time."

Zeke heaved a long-suffering sigh, then, "Penny a point?"

"Depends on what we're playing," she countered. "I don't want to owe you my soul by the end of the evening."

He looked at her from beneath his arms and flashed his rakish grin.

"Glad to know you recognize my skill."

She rolled her eyes as she clambered to her feet.

"Yeah, and your ego," she said drily as she gathered up the blankets and led the way into the van.

~~~~~

Zeke threw his cards down in disgust as Manny once more made gin.

"Who was supposed to owe who?" he griped as he began to count his points.

Manny shrugged with a smirk. "You win some, you lose some."

"Well, I need to stand some," Zeke said. He rose stiffly to his feet, winced as he hit his head on the van roof, then headed towards the open back door of the van.

They both glanced upwards as thunder rumbled across the sky. The rain hadn't yet started, and the door was still open to allow the fresh, evening-cool air—along with, unfortunately, the evening bugs—into the van. Zeke stepped outside and stretched.

Manny shuffled the cards as she watched Zeke slowly turn in a circle, his eyes on the sky. He was dimly lit by the lanterns inside the van, his dark features half-hidden in the shadows, his hands planted firmly on his lean hips. He glanced at her over his shoulder and she blinked because he looked saturnine and dangerous and incredibly handsome with his dark eyes, messy black hair and five o'clock shadow.

Saturnine? **I don't think I've ever heard that word outside of a trashy romance novel. Are you sure you're using it correctly? Or do you mean something like satyr?**

Manny dropped her eyes to her suddenly shaking hands. Harvey sat beside her in the chair, looking between her and Zeke with bright interest shining in his dark eyes.

I was wondering where you were, she said drily.

Right here. Where I always am.

But blessedly silent for a change.

"You look like you're deep in thought," Zeke said, settling back at the table across from her.

She started and stared at him with wide eyes. He raised an inquisitive eyebrow and she flushed.

"Sorry," she said hurriedly, ignoring Harvey's smug albeit charming grin as she dealt the cards. "I was thinking about tomorrow. It's going to be a long walk."

"Twenty miles or so," Zeke nodded. He picked up his cards and frowned as he arranged them to his liking.

Manny did the same with her cards, leaning comfortably back in her chair.

"It's going to be a long day tomorrow," she muttered.

Zeke nodded. "And we can only hope the little hole-in-the-wall we're heading towards will have a garage."

"As long as it has a motel, I'll be happy," Manny said. She shook her head. "We should probably go to bed after this game is finished, especially if we want an early start tomorrow."

Zeke's gaze snapped to hers, his eyes wide.

She raised an eyebrow. "You do realize we're going to be sharing the bed, right?"

Zeke's dismayed expression would have amused her if it hadn't been so insulting.

"I can sleep in the front seat," he offered quickly.

Manny rolled her eyes in exasperation. "We can share the bed without it having anything to do with sex."

He blinked at her.

She frowned. "Haven't you ever shared a bed with

someone without having sex?" she asked slowly.

"Sure. But I've never shared a bed with someone I didn't end up having sex with at one point or another."

Now it was Manny's turn to blink at him.

"I'm...rather scared to ask if you ever shared a bed as a child, or at summer camp," she finally said.

Zeke laughed and shook his head. "I appreciate the offer to share the bed, but in case you haven't noticed, I'm a pretty big guy. I tend to take up the entire bed no matter how large it is—and that bed over there isn't exactly huge. I really don't have a problem with sleeping in the front seat."

"Thanks, but we have a long walk ahead of us tomorrow," she reminded him absently, frowning at the cards in her hand. "Trust me—you'll appreciate sleeping in a bed. And I'm out."

He gaped as she laid down her cards then glared at her. "Just for that, I will share the bed."

She gave him an innocent smile and shrugged. "That's the game, too, by the way." She tapped the paper with the scores. "According to this, you owe me at least two and a half beer."

He growled.

~~~~~

Manny rummaged her book out of her backpack and settled herself on the bed next to the wall while Zeke closed the door. The wind was starting to rise, the thunder was rumbling more often, and the smell of rain was getting stronger. As Zeke settled beside her, she glanced up as the first raindrops pattered then began to drum on the roof as the storm rolled in.

They glanced at each other, then Zeke checked his watch.

"Yeah, we would have been soaked," he said.

She nodded with a smile, then opened her book. Out of the corner of her eye, she watched him watching her. She looked curiously at him.

With a raised eyebrow he reached over and turned the book so he could see the cover.

She shrugged and blushed a little at his amused smile as he took in the lushly beautiful woman and surreally handsome man locked in a passionate embrace. The man's shirt was open to his waist while the woman's bodice was pushed halfway down her arms.

Are there pirates in this one?

Highwaymen.

Damn. Do I have to wear feathers in my hat?

That's a musketeer.

My mistake.

"Is it any good?" Zeke asked, amused.

"For a bodice ripper, it's not bad," Manny shrugged.

"Bodice ripper?" he asked, puzzled.

"Oh, come on—you've never heard of a bodice ripper?"

He shook his head.

"They're historical romances, usually with lots of sex. Didn't any of your girlfriends read these things?"

Zeke gave her a smug, arrogant smirk. "They didn't need anything like that—they had me."

"Oh, dear God," Manny groaned, shaking her head. She turned back to her book as Zeke laughed.

"Well," she huffed, "if you're bored and you're not ready to sleep yet, the books I've finished are in the bottom drawer of the cupboard over there."

~~~~~

Zeke tossed the book aside with a grimace.

"I can't believe you read this stuff," he grumbled.

Manny glanced up with a grin. "And yet you went through the whole thing," she pointed out.

"Well, at least it passed some time."

Manny nodded. She yawned as she dog-eared her place and tossed the book over Zeke and on to the floor. She adjusted her pillow and slid down under the covers, shifting to find a comfortable spot. Zeke did take up most of the bed and the fact they were both still in their jeans and t-shirts didn't make it any easier. But she finally settled on her side, her back to Zeke and facing the wall.

"Ready for lights out?" Zeke asked.

"Yep," she yawned again.

He flicked off the lantern.

"Zeke?"

"Yeah?"

"I snore."

Zeke froze, then breathed, "Wonderful."

Day 70

"You know, you really do snore."

It was eight in the morning and they'd already been walking for an hour. They each carried a backpack filled with the things they couldn't leave behind in the van along with their laptops and at least one change of clothes.

Manny snorted a laugh. "I warned you."

"Yeah, when it was too late to go sleep in the front," Zeke said drily.

"Like that would help. We were still in the same space."

"True."

"Did I wake you up?" Manny asked after a moment of silence.

Zeke glanced at her from the corner of his eye and grinned. "Just enough to roll you over. You stopped almost immediately after that."

"That's good."

They lapsed into companionable silence.

"So, do you want to play 'Ask Me Anything'?" Zeke asked idly.

Manny shrugged. "Why not? We haven't played for a while. And as promised, I won't ask you any questions about your personal life."

Zeke rolled his eyes. "You're too kind."

"I still feel a little guilty about beating you so badly at gin last night."

"As you should. I'll start. When was the last time you

had sex?"

Manny turned startled eyes towards him.

"You're asking me about my sex life?" she asked incredulously.

"Are you refusing to answer?" he teased with raised eyebrows.

"No! But I have to say I'm shocked. You usually can't even say the word to me, let alone actually ask me such a straightforward question about it! What's going on?"

Zeke shrugged, his eyes focused intently on his feet and the ground in front of them. "I'm just curious about how dangerous it really was to share a bed with you last night."

Manny smacked him hard on the shoulder. He rubbed the spot as he grinned at her.

"So platonically sharing a bed has eliminated the gag reflex when it comes to me and sex?"

"Maybe. I guess we'll find out. You haven't answered the question..."

Manny frowned, thinking. "A long, long time ago," she sighed.

"In a galaxy far, far away?" Zeke teased.

"It certainly feels like it." She mumbled to herself as she counted on her fingers.

"Six," she said finally, nodding decisively. "Yeah. Six."

Zeke frowned. "That's not so bad, I guess—six months."

"Years," Manny clarified, laughing. "Six *years*."

Zeke gaped at her. "Good grief! How can you possibly go so long without it? Are you a nun?"

Manny shrugged. "Maybe I should have been. Then again, you don't miss what you've never really had."

Zeke shook his head in disbelief. "Okay then—how many men have you slept with?"

"Two."

"Good God!" Zeke blurted.

"Hey, now," Manny objected, "I'll have you know I've slept with every man who's asked me!"

Zeke gaped at her. "Are you shitting me?" he demanded.

She wordlessly shook her head.

"That's...just..." he trailed off, at a loss for words.

Manny snapped, "It's not sad, or pathetic, or anything else, thank you very much. It just *is*."

Zeke blinked. "I wasn't thinking anything like that!"

"Yes, you were—I could see it in your face."

Zeke walked in silence for a long moment before he slowly said, "It's just—I don't think I've ever met anyone who's lived such a—a—"

"Celibate lifestyle?" she supplied in dangerously sweet tones.

He nodded.

"Then you don't get out much, do you?"

Zeke sighed. "Sorry I asked," he muttered. "Okay—your turn."

Manny pondered, then asked slowly, "Have you ever been in love? I mean, really in love?"

"I thought you said you weren't going to ask questions about my personal life!"

"I'm not asking if you're in love now or for any details! Besides," she shrugged, "I lied. The van needs to be fixed and I could use all the extra cash I can get."

He huffed a laugh as he shook his head.

"So?" she asked. "Have you ever been really in love?"

Zeke frowned, then snapped, "Yes."

Manny waited.

"That's it?" she finally asked.

He nodded tersely without looking at her. "Yes."

Manny sighed, "You know, considering this is your game, I don't think you really *get* the whole notion of sharing secrets."

"Says the woman who barely spoke to me for the first four days," he replied drily.

"And now I don't shut up."

"True."

"So, that's all you're going to say about that?"

"Yes."

Manny shook her head. "Okay, well, you did answer the question. Your turn."

"Have *you* ever been in love? Really in love?" There was a sharpness to his tone that had Manny curiously searching his frowning profile.

She shook her head. "No."

"What—never?"

"Never. And don't give me that look," she sighed, turning her face away from the shocked pity in his eyes.

Zeke flushed. "I'm sorry—but don't you—aren't you—aren't you lonely?"

Manny considered the question as they walked.

"Lonely?" she repeated slowly, thoughtfully. "Lonely." She shook her head. "No. But I do sometimes get tired of living without..." she hesitated, searching for words, "I sometimes get tired of living without strong emotion, of moving through the days in shades of grey." She laughed slightly. "But then I talk to Rebecca, or I hear about Daisy's or Jaime's failed marriages—and I count my blessings. Love is just too much like work."

"It's worth it, though," Zeke assured her sincerely.

"Is it? *You* won't even talk about it."

They walked in rather somber silence.

"I was twenty," Zeke said slowly. "She was...she was fascinating. A gleam in her eyes and a bounce in her step and she was just so...so hungry for life. She was adventurous and funny and smart and sexy and she...consumed me. She was all I thought about, all I wanted, all I needed. I would have done anything for her. I ended up defying my father for her—my friends—I walked away from everyone. For her."

Manny watched him, her eyes clear and curious.

"What happened?" she asked quietly.

Zeke shrugged, his eyes once more on the dirt road in front of his feet. "She—uh—she sent me back, like I was a child who'd run away from home. And I never saw her again. I was just a fling, you see, something to do while the husband she'd never mentioned was away, working for the summer. I was her summer boy toy—"

"Her boy toy?"

He nodded, flushing. "She was forty. She told me she loved me—until I actually showed up, bag and baggage on her doorstep." He shook his head, a rueful grimace on his face. "I was very young and very stupid and very deeply in love."

Manny's eyes were soft. "Oh, Zeke..."

He waved away her sympathy. "Anyway, that's why I don't talk about it."

Manny bit her lip before asking, "What happened when you went home? With your dad, I mean."

Zeke hesitated, slipping his hands into the pockets of his jeans. "I didn't go home. I haven't been home since."

"What—not once?" she demanded.

He shook his head, refusing to meet her eyes. "No, not once. Oh, we exchange stiff little notes every now and then, and a phone call every couple of months. He finally got a computer last year, so now we e-mail occasionally. God knows how long it takes him to type anything—" He stopped abruptly, pressing his lips tightly together and shaking his head.

"What about your mom?"

"My mom left when I was thirteen," he replied coldly, his voice clipped. "Last I heard she was in Auckland with a couple of kids I've never met."

Manny gaped at him. She opened her mouth to ask another question but he forestalled her.

"I don't want to talk about this anymore."

Manny looked at him sadly then nodded. "I think I'm done with this game for a while," she said quietly.

"Yeah. Me, too."

~~~~~

The sun was directly overhead by the time Manny and

Zeke made it to the centre of the small town they'd identified on the map. The town was like something out of the wild west, with dusty streets and wooden sidewalks. Main Street was all of two blocks long and jammed with small stores, most of which seemed closed for the noon hour. At the end of Main Street was a bar that had several pickup trucks parked diagonally in front of it. The bar sat next to what appeared to be a paved road and Manny felt unreasonably relieved at that small sign of modern civilization.

They trudged down the middle of the street, with only the sounds of insects chirping and their feet shuffling through the dirt to break the silence. Otherwise, there didn't seem to be anyone moving in the noonday sun. There wasn't even a dog barking.

"Did the world end and we just don't know it?" Zeke asked with a puzzled frown.

Manny simply shook her head.

They walked towards the small general store that at least had an open sign on the door although they couldn't tell if there was anyone actually inside.

Bells attached to ribbons jingled as Zeke pushed open the door. A twenty-something woman sitting behind the counter glanced up from her magazine and blinked at them. Her eyes widened as she took in their dusty, sweaty appearance and the naked relief on their faces.

"Good heavens!" she exclaimed.

~~~~~

"You guys ended up spending the night in the van?" Daisy said incredulously.

"Yeah," Manny sighed, sitting on the bed and gratefully toeing off her shoes. She fell back onto the mattress, dirt and sweat and all, with a blissful sigh.

"How was it?"

"Surprisingly comfortable."

"Manny! That's not what I'm talking about and you know it! Come on—spill!"

Manny laughed. "There's nothing to spill!"

"You didn't cop even one feel?"

"Daisy!"

"My God–you really are a nun!"

"Thanks."

"Well, did the thought at least cross your mind? I mean, even once?"

Manny bit her lip, then burst out, "Of course it did! He's freakin' gorgeous! And he just gets better looking the more time I spend with him! It's awful! But I promised him his virtue was safe with me. Plus, he still turns slightly green whenever we mention me and sex in the same sentence."

"Do you have a crush on him?" Daisy asked with real interest.

Manny thought about it, then said slowly, "No, I just like him. It's just too bad that if I were to get lucky on this trip, I'd never be able to tell him. If I did, he might actually woof his cookies."

"Ah, fuck 'im if he can't handle it."

"I can't do that–he'd *definitely* woof his cookies then!"

Daisy was startled into silence for a moment, then they both began to laugh so hard tears ran down their cheeks.

"Thanks, Manny," Daisy finally sniffled breathlessly, wiping her eyes and nose. "You have no idea how much I needed that."

"Well, I had a five-hour walk today and now I'm sitting in a rather dingy motel room across from a small-town bar. I needed the laugh, too!"

They chuckled, then, with a sigh, Manny said, "How are *you* doing, Daisy? Hub's moving out on Monday, isn't he?"

"Yes," Daisy said glumly.

"You sound like you wish you could change your mind."

"There's a part of me that does," Daisy sighed. "Twenty-one years of marriage, twenty-four years together–all of it down the tubes, because..."

Manny waited then gently prompted, "Because?"

"Because–I don't even know. Because neither of us cared enough to keep it going, I guess."

"Oh, Daisy," Manny sighed softly.

"The sad part is I never even knew we were in trouble."

"Never?" Manny asked skeptically.

"What do you mean by that?" Daisy said, slightly defensive.

"You were at the casino every night rather than be at home with Hub. That had to tell you something."

Manny listened to Daisy's thoughtful silence before Daisy softly said, "Yeah. Yeah, it told me something. I just didn't want to hear what it was."

"I'm sorry."

"I'll just be glad when he's in his own place. Right now, we're sort of in limbo and it's tense and awkward. It's...a strange atmosphere. Weird, you know? I'll be glad when we've moved on to the next step."

"Has he told you anything about the other woman?" Manny asked delicately.

"Not a word. Of course, I also haven't asked. I'm assuming the affair is still going strong."

"You haven't asked?"

"Hell, no! Right now, I'd simply end up screaming at him. And I just–don't feel like I can handle hearing about how it's all my fault and if I had only done *this* instead of *that* and blah, blah, blah. Not right now, anyway. Honestly? I don't think I'll *ever* want to know about it."

"Can't say I blame you," Manny sighed. "Some things are just better left unknown."

~~~~~

TJ laughed almost continuously at Zeke's description of the previous day and night.

"But you're safe and sound," he said comfortably once Zeke was finished.

"Oh, yeah, although I've definitely been in nicer motels."

"It's a tiny little town in the middle of nowhere—you're lucky there's anything like a motel or hotel at all!"

"Yeah, that's what Manny said, too. And it is spotlessly clean, just a little run down."

"And you have a bed to yourself," TJ added slyly.

"That, my friend, is an excellent point," Zeke agreed fervently.

"Did you get *any* sleep last night? I mean, it must have been pretty uncomfortable—for a lot of reasons."

Zeke hesitated, remembering the night before. He'd found it surprisingly comfortable, and he'd forgotten how good it felt just to sleep beside another human being. Even one who snored.

"Once I got her to move and she stopped snoring, I was out like a light," he said now to TJ.

He didn't mention how he'd carefully curled around her, to give her more room on the bed, before he, too, fell asleep. Or how he'd woken to find himself snuggled against her back while she'd apparently instinctively moved away from him and was almost plastered against the van's wall. But in that moment before he'd been fully awake, he'd felt an incredible sense of peace settle over him as he lay next to her.

He suspected it was because of that memory of how comfortable and safe he'd felt with her that he'd told her about his disastrous first love affair.

"Zeke?" TJ asked. "You fall asleep on me, man?"

Zeke started. "No—sorry. You're right, I wouldn't say I got a lot of sleep last night."

But he would say he was seriously confused by both his reaction to sleeping next to Manny and by his willingness to share his past with her.

"Listen, TJ—is Leah there?"

"Should I be jealous?" TJ teased.

"Why should you be any different than any other

man?"

TJ groaned then laughed. "Sorry, she's not here. She's off bonding with her friends."

"Drinking, you mean."

"You say potato..."

Zeke laughed. "Well, if you could leave a message for her. Just tell her that I won't be able to complete her latest assignment. There's no story."

"Will do. Can you share?"

"She wanted me to get more details about Manny's past, particularly her love life. I know my readers are really curious, so I took the opportunity this morning to dig for more information."

"Yeah? And there's no story? What? She wouldn't tell you anything?"

Zeke hesitated, feeling oddly protective. He shook his head, then remembered TJ couldn't see him.

"No," he told TJ slowly, "no, she didn't tell me anything."

They chatted for a few more minutes then disconnected the call. Zeke deliberately ignored the fact that that was the first time he'd ever lied to TJ.

~~~~~

That night, Zeke and Manny sat at a booth in the dim bar, cold beer in their hands as they waited for their meals to arrive. They looked around as the room slowly but steadily filled up. They received a lot of curious looks and more than one local walked over to strike up a conversation to get their story.

"They don't get a lot of strangers around here, huh?" Zeke observed drily, watching the latest curious local wander back to his cronies.

That particular local was a middle-aged farmer, the sleeves of his plaid shirt rolled up to his elbows. His eyes had been sharp and shrewdly curious, but kind. He'd been the third local to inform them that the only mechanic in town had gone to the city for the day, but would be back sometime in the evening. In the meantime, the van had been towed into town by another local and was now sitting at the garage, ready whenever the mechanic returned.

"Probably not," Manny agreed, taking a sip of her beer. She'd had a nap and was feeling comfortably mellow even if a little stiff and sore from the morning's long walk. She watched as the door to the bar opened again and another group of people wandered in and were met with loud greetings from the people at a table in the far corner of the bar.

"Looks like it's going to be a full house tonight," Zeke observed.

"It's Friday night in a small town," Manny shrugged. "Unless you go into the city, there's not much else to do but go to the bar."

Zeke shook his head and continued to observe the occupants of the bar while Manny frowned thoughtfully at her beer and began to pick at the label.

"You look like you have something on your mind," Zeke said casually, his eyes resting on a group of young women in snug blue jeans and tank tops sitting near the pool tables.

Manny shrugged glumly. "I was just thinking about life and the choices we make even when we don't realize we're making a choice at the time."

Zeke gave her his full attention.

She returned his stare with a puzzled frown. He raised his eyebrow in question.

"Do you ever second guess yourself?" she asked plaintively. "Do you ever have regrets?"

Zeke lounged back in his seat and took a quick swallow of his beer as he considered her question. He set the beer back on the table and shook his head.

"No."

"Never?" she asked skeptically, her gaze direct and unwavering.

"Never."

"You don't ever think about what you could have done differently with Dixie? You don't ever think about leaving your dad behind? You don't ever think about–others? You don't have any regrets?"

Zeke slowly shook his head. "What's done is done," he said simply. "I move on."

Manny puffed out her breath and dropped her gaze to her hands. She continued peeling the label from the bottle in front of her.

"Well, if you're not lying, then I envy you. Sometimes I think I've done nothing *but* second guess myself. I've spent the last fifteen years toeing the line, working hard, and doing my best. Giving everything I had to the job–so much so, I couldn't tell where the job ended and I began.

"But somewhere along the line, I lost my–my humanity. I lost my passion, my joy in life, my connection to other people. The colour had been leached out of my world and I...felt nothing. Which is why I'm on this trip.

"But I hadn't realized just how badly I'd lost that human touch until this afternoon, when I was talking to Daisy about Hub and the fact that their relationship is basically finished after twenty-four years. Oh, I said all the right things, but all I could think was: *thank God he's finally gone.*"

Manny shook her head and took a long swallow of her beer. She set it carefully down on the table with a tiny clink and met Zeke's eyes with a self-deprecating smile.

"What a sister, huh?"

Zeke met her eyes steadily, his face expressionless, his dark, hazel eyes unreadable.

"You didn't say that to her, though, did you." It wasn't a question.

She shook her head.

"You let her talk and made comforting noises, didn't you."

She nodded.

"Then I think...you were exactly the sister she needed

171

at that moment."

She stared, surprise in her blue eyes. Then she flushed as a smile tugged at the corners of her mouth.

"Thank you," she said softly.

They glanced up as the waitress arrived with their food. They smiled and thanked her as they leaned back to let her put the plates down in front of them.

Zeke shrugged as he unfolded the paper napkin and put it on his lap.

"I'm just speaking the truth," he said, picking up the ketchup bottle. "I don't think there's any law that says you have to actually like the guy your sister married. Not that I really know, of course. I've never met my sister."

He offered her the ketchup with a raised eyebrow and a smirk. He dipped one fry into the ketchup and lifted it to his mouth, then paused.

"Come to think of it," he mused, a thoughtful frown on his face, "I'm not sure my sister's even old enough to be married."

He popped the fry into his mouth and chewed rapidly.

"And don't look at me like that, Auntie Em," he said, his mouth full. "You said it yourself–you don't miss what you've never had."

Manny nodded awkwardly and dropped her gaze to her own food. She blinked rapidly, her lips pressed tightly together, and silently busied herself with the ketchup, salt and pepper.

~~~~~

An hour and a half later, Manny was at the bar watching Zeke play pool with the three young women who'd been sitting by the tables for most of the evening.

The bartender watched her with a sympathetic air, and Manny shook her head and said, "It's okay. We're just travelling together."

The bartender gave her a skeptical nod but said nothing.

She shook her head and turned back to watch the pool

game.

Zeke's pool partner was leaning comfortably against him as one of their opponents took their shot. His partner was tall, slender but curvy, with long chestnut hair. Manny had to admit she was quite stunningly beautiful, easily the most beautiful woman in the room. She certainly didn't look like a woman one would expect to find in such a small town.

Then again, Manny thought ruefully, she'd grown up with Rebecca who had also been quite stunningly beautiful and tucked away in a town even smaller than this one.

Good God—<u>again</u>?

Manny snorted into her beer. She turned a ruefully amused grin to Harvey, who was standing with a stunned expression beside her.

I guess he's just one of those guys who can't be alone on a Saturday night.

It's Friday.

Whatever.

She's quite something, I have to admit.

I was just thinking that.

He shot her an amused glance from dark eyes, his eyebrows raised. She groaned.

Forget I said that.

Done.

Harvey glanced around the bar. **Not much eye candy for you, though.**

Oh, I don't know. There are a few rather nice looking boys over there.

Harvey glanced at the table she'd indicated and studied the four rather stolid looking farm boys sitting there.

I think they're younger than Zeke, he mused.

I think you're right. They're definitely working boys, though. Look at those arms.

Harvey looked at their arms, then glanced down at himself.

I like you just the way you are, Manny assured him,

then frowned a small, puzzled frown.

He grinned at her then asked, **What?**

Nothing. It just seems like it's not as easy to change you anymore.

Don't worry about it, Harvey urged. **You're sitting alone at the bar while Zeke is over there and probably about to get laid–<u>again</u>, damn it. I also see there's going to be a band tonight,** he nodded towards the dance floor, **and when was the last time you watched a live band in a bar?**

Maybe once or twice since my groupie days, she replied thoughtfully, watching the bar staff and band members setting up.

Wonder what circuit this bar would be on? This town barely shows up on the map–how'd they manage to book a band?

Manny motioned the bartender over.

"Where's the band from?" she asked.

"They're local boys. They play every Friday night, mainly for beer on Saturday. But they're actually pretty good, and can play pretty much anything you can think to ask them to play."

"Beethoven's Fifth?" she asked.

The bartender grinned and he suddenly looked ten years younger than what Manny guessed to be his fifty-something. "If you'll dance to that, I'll buy you a beer."

She slowly smiled back. "Well, if they play it, I'll try it," she promised.

"All right," he said. "Let me talk to them."

He made to walk out from behind the bar and she stopped him, laughing, "Don't you dare! I was kidding!"

He winked and moved to serve a group of people further down the bar.

"Making another conquest I see."

Manny yelped and turned to face Zeke, a hand pressed to her chest.

She gasped for breath, then said, "I could say the same

for you."

She glanced significantly at the pool tables where the young woman was talking to her friends as she picked up her purse and beer. Manny raised an eyebrow as the woman swayed towards them.

I thought people only walked like that in the movies.
Hush.

Zeke leaned closer and murmured in her ear, "Come on, Auntie Em–look at her! Who would have thought a girl like her would be hiding in this little hole of a town? And her name is Babe–how appropriate is that?"

Manny shook her head ruefully, her eyes on the stage as the band members began to take their places and complete the sound check. She turned her attention to Zeke's pleading eyes and grimaced.

"Please," she groaned, "you're drooling in my beer. Go–have fun–play safe."

That sounds familiar.
Hush, I said.

Zeke grinned.

"Oh, I will," he said softly, his hazel eyes burning as Babe walked up beside him and slid an arm around his waist.

Manny briefly introduced herself to the other woman then watched them leave with their arms around each other.

She turned back to the bar when the door closed behind them and met the bartender's raised eyebrows and sympathetic eyes.

"Another?" he asked.

She checked her bottle and shrugged.

"Sure. Why the hell not?"

~~~~~

Babe kissed Zeke the second the bar door closed behind them and they stumbled across the paved road, laughing between deep, searching kisses, their hands fumbling at the other person's clothes.

They finally made it to Zeke's motel room and Babe pressed him against the door, devouring his mouth and then his neck as Zeke fumbled for his room key, which Babe seductively removed from his fingers and used to open the door, all without losing their grip on each other. Zeke stumbled backwards into the room, laughing as they almost fell to the floor.

Zeke retained enough presence of mind to remember to take the key from the lock as the door closed behind them.

It was the last rational thought he had for a while.

~~~~~

Manny nursed her beer for a half hour, listening to the band warm up and chatting idly with the bartender and the people on either side of her. She noticed people were still coming in and as far as she could tell, there were no longer any empty tables or chairs to be seen.

She regretfully swallowed the last of her beer and lowered it with a sigh. She began to fumble with her purse, motioning to the bartender for her tab.

"You can't leave now!" he protested loudly, and Manny froze, her eyes wide as everyone within earshot echoed his sentiments.

"Ladies and gentlemen!"

Manny twisted around to look at the stage as almost everyone else burst into loud, raucous cheers and whistles, stomping their feet and clapping.

Shit. Have we dropped into the middle of a Stephen King novel?

I sincerely hope not.

Let me tell you, I'll be seriously pissed if we have.

Manny swallowed.

The emcee waited for the noise to die down before he asked the crowd, "What night is it?"

Everyone roared, "Friday!"

"I can't hear you! *What night is it?*"

"*Friday!*"

176

"That's right! And you know what that means!"

The crowd burst into a cacophony of noise.

"That's right! It's time for–"

The entire crowd shouted, "*Last Dancer Standing!*"

The emcee waited for the cheers, whistles and applause to die down before he continued.

"All right, for those few of you who are new to our little town and our little bar–and I can see a couple of you–Last Dancer Standing is our Friday night dance contest. We sort everyone in the bar into twenty teams. Each member of the team then takes a turn in a line dance. Those who dance the best get to stay for the next round. Those who don't, are eliminated. We continue until we have the–" he pointed to the crowd.

"*Last Dancer Standing!*"

"Exactly! The team with the–"

"*Last Dancer Standing!*"

"–gets two free drinks for every member of the team, and an appetizer to share with their teammates. The next four teams get an appetizer to share with their teammates. Now, there are two things that new people need to know. Number one: the teams are randomly assigned. And number two: no one sits out this contest. *No one!* If you can wiggle a finger–hell, if you can wiggle your nose–you're in the contest! Now, at some point tonight, your bartender or waitress will have given you a little square coaster. On the back of it you'll find the name of your team; there's a matching centre-piece on one of the tables in this bar. When I say 'go'–find your teams!" He paused dramatically.

Manny could see Harvey from the corner of her eye. He was leaning against the bar beside her, munching popcorn. A huge grin split his face and his dark eyes were bright with interest.

Oh, <u>this</u> ought to be <u>fun</u>!

"*Go!*"

~~~~~

Zeke stared up at the ceiling, Babe's head pillowed on his bare chest. She was dozing lightly, her breath ghosting across his skin, one long, shapely leg draped over his. He frowned as he lightly stroked his fingers against her shoulder and back.

"She's fine," Babe said sleepily.

He started and met Babe's half-closed eyes.

"I thought you were sleeping," he murmured.

"Just dozing."

She smiled, leaned up and gave him a quick kiss, followed by a slower, deeper one. She dropped her head back to his shoulder.

"You were worrying about her, weren't you?" she continued sleepily, "your Auntie Em?"

"Well, I did leave her sitting alone in a bar in a strange town," Zeke muttered guiltily, shaking his head.

"This is Ringo," Babe laughed. "Trust me, she's probably safer in that bar than if she was sitting in her own living room."

Zeke huffed a chuckle. "Well, she was pretty tired. We'd walked a long way today. I suspect she left almost immediately after we did."

He paused, remembering their walk to the motel, and flushed a little.

"Well, hopefully not *immediately* after us," he amended.

Babe laughed huskily. "Too bad if she did—it's Friday night."

Zeke frowned down at the top of Babe's tousled head.

"Yeah?"

"It's Last Dancer Standing."

Zeke laughed. "Last Dancer—*what?*"

"Every Friday night. Everyone who's in the bar has to participate. Well, except staff, of course. Everyone's put on a team and has to take at least one turn line dancing. Trust me, it's a great time."

Zeke blinked at the thought of Manny sitting in a bar alone and having a dance contest—with mandatory participation–suddenly rear its ugly head. While she'd certainly proven herself open to new experiences and meeting new people, his mind boggled at the thought of Manny, with her tightly bound hair and prudish-maiden-aunt face actually unwinding enough to *dance*, line or otherwise.

He would have loved to have seen her expression when she realized what was going on, though.

"Zeke?"

"Hmmm? Oh–sorry. That sounds...cool," he said and tried to give her a sincere smile.

"It really is a great time and it gives everyone something to look forward to during the week." Babe lifted her head and looked at the bedside clock. "They should be getting to the top ten in about thirty minutes. Do you want to go watch?"

Zeke yawned and shifted into a more comfortable position. "I don't know...it's been a long day. And strenuous," he added with a wicked grin.

Babe smiled seductively and purred, "It'll help me get my second wind..."

"Let's go."

~~~~~

Zeke and Babe walked into the bar just as the emcee was introducing the top ten.

"This has been a great night! A record number of participants with lots of great–and not so great–dancing."

The emcee paused as the crowd laughed and everyone looked towards one table where one young man hid his face, then stood and gave the crowd a sweeping bow as they applauded.

Zeke glanced at Babe, one eyebrow raised.

"That's Mikey," she shouted into his ear above the noise. "He's always the worst dancer here, but he's always willing to try."

Mikey sat down, the crowd quieted and the emcee continued.

"And now we're down to the top ten! They've been given ten minutes to rehearse a line dance for their chosen song. When this dance is finished, we'll determine the top five who will then do one more dance after which there'll be the–" he pointed the microphone at the crowd.

"*Last Dancer Standing*!" the crowd yelled, including Babe.

Zeke grinned at Babe's enthusiasm. The crowd quieted as the band walked back on stage and picked up their instruments. They started playing a country song that wasn't familiar to Zeke but was apparently very popular with the ladies in the crowd, judging from their whistles, catcalls and laughter.

He crossed his arms and leaned casually against the wall, looking around the bar with interest. This was going to make a great story for his blog, he thought. He smiled indulgently at Babe who was moving to the music and singing the lyrics beside him. He blinked as the chorus began and the crowd erupted into even louder screams and applause and whistles. He looked at the dance floor and his grin widened as he watched the ten women gyrating suggestively to the music–at various levels of coordination and grace. If these were the ten best dancers in the bar, he thought, he would have hated to have seen the others.

His grin disappeared and he abruptly straightened when he realized the second woman on the left was Manny–with her hair hanging down, her shirt tied up and moving her shoulders and wiggling her ass like no prudish-maiden-aunt he'd ever seen.

He didn't like it.

He didn't like it one bit.

He watched, scowling furiously, as the dance finished to the cheers and hoots of the crowd and he watched grimly as Manny bounded off the dance floor towards two tables of people he assumed were her teammates judging from their cheers and pats on her back.

He met Babe's quizzical look and he quickly smoothed

his face into a smile.

"Manny's over there," he said tilting his head and taking Babe's hand. "Let's go say hi."

They threaded their way through the crowd and came to a stop behind Manny just as two waitresses delivered tequila shooters and small glasses of 7-Up to the group. Zeke watched with an unhappy frown as the drinks were distributed.

They all lifted their shot glasses, shouted "Slammers!", tapped the glasses twice on the table then drank the shot and chased it with 7-Up.

Zeke waited until Manny put her glass back on the table before he leaned forward and growled in her ear, "Isn't it past your bedtime, Auntie Em?"

She shrieked and spun around with a hand to her chest. She gaped at him, her eyes wide with shock, her cheeks flushed with exertion and tequila. Then she caught her breath and grinned.

"Zeke!" she cried expansively, spreading her arms wide and almost hitting the person on the other side of her. "*Hi!* Did you see me?"

Zeke smiled coldly. "Oh, I saw you."

"Wasn't it *awesome?* What a great idea for a contest! This has been so much fun!" She spun back to the table and staggered slightly.

Zeke quickly steadied her, his hands on her shoulders.

"Whoops," she said, laughing a little. She looked over her shoulder at him through her curtain of hair and grinned. She leaned slightly towards him and whispered conspiratorially, "Thanks—I've had a little bit to drink."

She turned her face back to the people at the table, leaned forward and cried, "Hey, everybody! This is Zeke! Remember I told you about him?"

Zeke was suddenly the focus of eight pairs of eyes and he hoped his face wasn't showing his growing anger with the situation, made even worse by the fact that Manny was definitely more than a little drunk. His Auntie Em who only ever drank one or two beer before primly calling it a night. Or the occasional glass of wine with dinner or, he conceded, at a wedding reception.

This Manny was shooting tequila like a pro and seemed perfectly comfortable with her shirt tied at her waist over low-slung jeans that left her tummy exposed, a tummy, he noticed, that poofed out a little above her waistband but was otherwise surprisingly flat, considering how plump she was.

He shook his head and quickly switched his attention to the other people at the table who were loudly greeting his and Babe's arrival.

Manny spun back to him and said, "I wasn't expecting you back tonight after you left with...um..." She blinked at Babe, her brows furrowed as she searched her memory.

"Babe," the woman in question offered with a gracious smile.

"Babe! Right, right, right."

"You've been having fun, I see," Zeke drawled, watching as the waitress delivered another round to the table.

"It's been a blast!" Manny nodded emphatically then quickly shushed him as the emcee called for the crowd's attention.

"We have the final five! The Margaritas! The Rummies! The Morgans! The Slammers! And the Martinis! Send up your dancers!"

Manny and her team burst into wild cheers when their team name was called. Manny was off her chair and bouncing with excitement. Her team clustered around her, patting her on the back, pulling her into group hugs, and high-fiving her before shooing her back to the dance floor.

Manny grinned at Zeke.

"Sorry, duty calls!" she said, then bounded back to the dance floor where she joined the other four dancers and the members of the band.

One of the women moved around the table to stand

next to Zeke while Babe chatted with some of the other members of the team.

"She's having so much fun," the woman chuckled, her attention on Manny, "it's just too cute."

She smiled at Zeke and held out her hand. "I'm Rosa."

Zeke shook her hand.

"Nice to meet you," he said, his scowl deepening as he watched Manny and the others confer with the band then head to the back and out of sight.

Babe turned to Zeke and Rosa and said, "See? Didn't I tell you it was a lot of fun?"

Zeke swallowed and nodded, and smoothed his expression with an effort.

"Pretty impressive," he agreed. He gave Babe a thoughtful look. "Do you win often?"

Babe shrugged, grinned and leaned into him. "So often, I'm not always allowed to compete."

Zeke raised an eyebrow. "Yes, you showed me your moves earlier."

They grinned at each other, then turned to the dance floor as the emcee began to introduce the final five.

This time they danced to a country-rock song that was more rock than country but the dance moves were just as, if not more, suggestive. Zeke struggled to keep his face smooth as he watched them. No one sitting at the table with him would understand why he was so angry with Manny, and, he conceded ruefully, Manny was in no condition at the moment to understand it either.

Tomorrow, he decided as the song ended and he joined the crowd in applauding the contestants, they'd have a long talk about the proper behaviour of prudish maiden aunts who are left on their own in a bar.

He started as Babe shifted even closer to him.

Rosa glanced at them then leaned over and asked curiously, "Is Manny really your aunt?"

"Hmmm?" Zeke turned his attention away from the five contestants waiting on the dance floor for a final decision. "No. No, we're just...um...friends, I suppose is as good a word as any. We're just travelling companions."

"Ah." Rosa gave the sound an odd significance.

Zeke frowned, then realization dawned. He emphatically shook his head. "Oh—no. No, no, no—nothing like that! She wanted to go on this huge road trip, she put out an ad, and I ended up along for the ride."

Both Rosa and Babe looked at him somewhat skeptically.

"So why do you call her Auntie Em?" Babe asked.

Zeke shrugged and gave her a wicked grin. "Because it annoys her."

Rosa and Babe laughed, and Babe shook her head as she said, "You're an evil, evil man."

"But I'm so good at it."

The emcee grabbed the microphone and said, "And the winner is...the Captain Morgans!"

Everyone in the bar cheered, with a few boos and catcalls from some of losing teams.

"Hey, hey, hey, now," the emcee said, "none of that. If you're all here next week, you'll get a chance for your team to win then. In the meantime, how about a big round of applause for our final five!"

The crowd cheered.

"And an extra big round of applause for our—" he pointed the mike at the crowd.

"*Last Dancer Standing!*"

The emcee put the mike back on its stand, then said as the dancers headed back to their respective tables, "The night's still young, folks, and the band's here 'til two. And now you know who can dance—and who can't!"

Everyone laughed, then the noise rose as people started talking again to their tablemates, and a reshuffling began as original groups slowly drifted back together, or merged into new groups.

Manny bounced back to the table, her shirt once more untied and demurely buttoned. She wiped her brow, then twisted her hair and held it off her neck as she laughed and talked with Rosa and the others trying to determine what appetizer to order as their prize.

Zeke realized she was in no hurry to leave, gritted his teeth and resigned himself to a long night.

He was right.

The bar was closing as he walked out with Manny, Babe and Rosa. He had an arm around Manny's waist although she seemed remarkably steady on her feet, considering the amount of tequila she'd downed. Zeke was reluctantly impressed. She'd also danced often during the night, and at the end she'd been sitting at a table with Mikey, listening intently to whatever long story he was telling her, her eyes never wavering from his face.

They walked Rosa home first, about a block from the bar, and stopped at her front gate.

Rosa said to Manny, "Call me when you wake up. I'll show you guys around town."

Manny nodded. "We will. Good night! We'll wait here until you get into the house."

Rosa laughed and shook her head while Babe stared at them with wide eyes.

"This is Ringo," Rosa assured them, "there's no need to wait!"

Zeke said quietly, "We'll wait until you get into the house."

Rosa and Babe exchanged amused glances, then Rosa shrugged, said good-night and headed into the house. They watched the lights go on before Zeke turned both Babe and Manny around and began the walk back to the motel.

Manny was beginning to crash, and Zeke kept a firm grip on her as she stumbled a little. He started when Manny slipped an arm around his waist, leaned her head against his shoulder, and closed her eyes as they walked.

He shook her a little, his other arm around Babe, and wondered just how ridiculous this looked. It was definitely a story for the blog, he thought ruefully. He could see the risqué comments now.

By the time they got to the motel, Manny was barely awake. Zeke sighed, then removed his arm from around Babe in order to dig out his room key.

"Here," he said, offering it to her. "I'll be along in a minute. I'm just going to toss her on the bed and find something she can use as a bucket in the morning."

Babe shook her head and laughed a little as she took the key. "I'll be waiting."

"Five minutes," he promised.

He watched Babe go into his room then turned to the task of waking Manny enough for her to find her room key.

She blinked sleepily then she slowly pulled herself upright and dug through her purse. She swayed as she tried to find the key slot, and he finally grabbed her and the key and opened the door. They stumbled inside, and they both laughed. Zeke shook his head as he remembered doing almost the same thing with Babe.

Manny said, "I'm okay. I can take it from here."

"I'm sure you can," Zeke assured her with a grin. "I'm just going to find something for you to puke into in the morning."

"I should be able to make the bathroom," she yawned on the last word as she watched Zeke pull back the covers on the bed.

"Should," he agreed, "but just in case."

She kicked off her shoes and laid down on the bed as he placed the trashcan by her head, then smiled sleepily at him as he pulled the covers over her.

"I'm not going to feel sorry for you in the morning," he warned her.

Manny snickered. "Considering who you have waiting for you in your room, I don't expect to see you in the morning," Manny mumbled, her eyes closing.

"Good point," he conceded.

He frowned down at her, oddly reluctant to leave her

alone.

She half-opened her eyes.

"G'night, Zeke," she said. She reached out and squeezed his hand. "Thanks."

She smiled at him.

"You'd be a good brother, you know," she murmured before slipping her hand away and snuggling under the covers. She was asleep almost instantly.

Zeke shook his head, and the last of his displeasure melted away.

Day 71

Manny became slowly and dimly aware that something was making noise somewhere nearby. Whatever it was, she wished it would stop. She snuggled deeper beneath the blankets, pulling them more fully over her head. She licked dry lips and tried to ignore her churning stomach, aching head, burning thirst, and all the fuzzy socks that seemed to be covering her teeth.

Sleep.

She needed more sleep.

She was sinking back towards oblivion when the noise began again and she frowned.

How much tequila did we drink last night? Harvey groaned beside her.

Too much.

I think we're going to be sick.

I think you're right–but not right now. I hope.

The noise stopped, then started again.

What the <u>hell</u> is that noise? Harvey groused.

I don't know but I wish it would shut the hell up.

...I think it's the phone.

Oh, God...

Manny reached out a hand and groped for the phone on the nightstand. She fumbled it to her ear.

"H'lo," she croaked.

"Aren't you awake yet?" Zeke cheerfully bellowed into

her ear.

She winced, mumbled, "Go 'way," and hung up.

The phone began to ring again almost immediately.

He's <u>such</u> a bastard.

"What. Do you. *Want?*" Manny all but whined into the receiver.

"Come on, rise and shine!"

"*Why?*"

"The mechanic's back in town."

~~~~~

Manny and Zeke stood listening to Billy, the mechanic, detail the repairs the van needed. Manny wondered if she looked as green as she felt and hoped this wouldn't take much longer. She longed to crawl back into bed and not come out for at least a day.

Maybe two.

With an effort, she focused on Billy and not on her churning stomach.

"...it'll take until at least Tuesday for us to get the part," he was saying, "but then we should have it ready to go by end of day Wednesday."

"Sounds great," Manny muttered.

Billy gave her a glimmer of a smile. "I know Ringo isn't much, but we're friendly enough. And I hear you both already made impressions at the bar."

Zeke raised an eyebrow while Manny just nodded owlishly but didn't trust herself to speak; she was too busy wondering if her face was as green as she felt.

"And if you really need to get somewhere bigger, there's a daily bus."

"I think we're okay here," Zeke said and glanced at Manny out of the corner of his eye, a smirk on his face.

"Especially today," Manny muttered.

Billy grinned. "Like I said, we're friendly enough and I'm sure you'll find things to do while you're here. Rosa asked me to remind you to call her today."

Manny swallowed. "It may not be until tomorrow."

Zeke laughed all the way back to the motel.

~~~~~

Daisy walked into the house feeling like a limp dishrag. The day had not been what she would consider successful. She was even too tired to go to the casino for a couple of hours.

As she divested herself of her coat, purse and shoes, she glanced at Hub sitting in the living room, some sports game she didn't even recognize blaring on the television set. Tonight was his second last night in the house, and to her surprise, the thought actually made her feel rather sad and surprisingly—disconcertingly—vulnerable.

Monday morning, she thought, twenty-four years of history would walk out the door. What would walk in was anybody's guess.

She suppressed a shudder.

Hub glanced at her as she padded slowly into the living room. He rose to his feet and headed to the bar with a frown. He fixed them each a drink and sauntered over to where she'd plopped down on the couch with a heavy sigh.

Daisy accepted the drink and made no objection when he settled beside her.

"Bad day?" he asked.

"The worst," she groaned. "So much for a quiet day in the office to get caught up on paperwork."

Hub waved his hand, urging her to go on.

She shook her head and shrugged. "An angry husband, busted by the usual evidence, tracked Max down. At the office."

"Good Lord!"

"Yeah, Max used more colourful words—some of which I'm almost positive were in a different language. Especially when the guy pulled a knife."

"Jesus!"

"That's much closer to what Max said at that point, too."

"Were you hurt?" Hub demanded, putting his drink

down and grabbing her hand, his eyes darting almost frantically as he tried to determine if she was injured.

"No, no—well, I hit my elbow on the door when Max pushed me into the inner office and blocked the door, the bastard."

Hub blinked. "The bastard?"

She rolled her eyes and explained patiently, "How am I supposed to help him if I'm stuck in a different room? I had to yell I was calling for help and dialling 9-1-1."

"I suspect Max can more than take care of himself," Hub replied drily.

Daisy waved his words away. "Yeah, yeah—Max has that big, bad, tough guy thing going on, shaved head and all, but he's not as young as he used to be, you know."

She shook her head, a worried frown wrinkling her forehead.

"So, what happened?" Hub urged when Daisy appeared content to sit, staring pensively into space.

Daisy started. "Oh—Max let me out in less than five minutes. The guy was out cold on the floor and Max didn't have a scratch on him."

"Impressive," Hub murmured sarcastically.

Daisy shrugged.

"That's never happened before," Hub added. "Max should—"

"No, no, it's happened before," Daisy corrected absently. "Although this is the first time I've had to call the cops. Max usually manages to defuse the situation before it gets that far."

"What?" Hub sputtered. "How could I not know about that?"

"You were never home," Daisy replied simply. There was no emotion in her voice; she was simply stating a fact.

Hub huffed a sigh and leaned forward, resting his arms on his knees.

"I—wasn't a very good husband to you, was I?" he asked softly, staring at the drink he cradled in his hands.

"I thought you were a normal husband," Daisy said gently, staring at her own glass.

She was too worn out to be angry, and she didn't have the heart at the moment to be cruel.

She continued, "You worked long hours to support us, especially when I was home with the kids. It's really only been the last couple of years–"

She grimaced.

"Probably when you started your affair, huh?"

Hub nodded tiredly, never looking away from the glass in his hands.

Daisy straightened and glanced in the direction of the bedrooms.

"Where're the kids?" she asked. "I don't really want to talk about this if they can overhear us."

"They're over at Rebecca's, staying the night with Tris."

"Oh, right," Daisy said, memory kicking in. "Big date with Jackson."

Hub shrugged. "Does she ever have small dates?" he asked.

Daisy shot him a fulminating look.

"Sorry," he sighed.

Daisy took a sip of her drink in silence.

Hub leaned back on the couch, and sighed again.

"I move out on Monday," he said quietly.

Daisy kept her eyes on the TV as she said, "I know."

He glanced around the living room.

"We've lived here for almost twenty years," he murmured.

Daisy nodded, her mouth tight, her eyes resolutely on the television.

"We bought it when we decided it was time to start trying for a baby," she agreed.

He gazed around the room in silence for a long moment, then asked fondly, "Remember the ugly colour in this room when we moved in?"

"Ha! Who could forget? Rebecca called it a cross

between projectile vomit and diarrhea."

"She was right."

"Manny's description of the colours in the bedrooms was even more brutal."

"With good reason," Hub groaned. "I thought that shit-green would never get covered by the primer. How many coats did we end up using, anyway?"

Daisy grinned. "That's tough to know for sure, especially after Manny took a pail and just threw the primer against the wall."

Hub chuckled. "Oh, lord, do I remember that! It didn't end well for Manny."

Daisy began to laugh. "N-n-no—she ended up covered in the primer herself."

"Because she got more primer on Rebecca than on the wall, and then Rebecca simply poured hers over Manny's head!"

Daisy howled with laughter. "Dear God—the *look* on her *face*!"

"M-Manny's or Rebecca's?"

"Either! Both!" Daisy gasped, clutching her stomach as she laughed, tears springing to her eyes.

"Then Rebecca—in the living room—"

"You mean when she started talking to the walls, begging them to just let the primer do its job?" Daisy asked.

Now they were both almost in tears, speaking in quick gasps.

"She swore the paint was possessed!" Hub hooted.

"She started c-calling on all the saints she could remember with every new roller of primer, and saying a little prayer—"

"Was that before or after she started bargaining with the walls? Trying to strike a deal with whatever paint gods might be listening?"

"No, that was Manny. I think she ended up vowing to dedicate her life to paint research if only the primer would cooperate and get rid of those awful colours. Of course, she had that primer in her hair for days afterwards, so maybe she did do a lot of paint research..."

They rocked on the couch, laughing so hard they couldn't catch their breath, tears rolling down their cheeks.

They finally sputtered into silence and smiled at each other, in perfect accord for the first time in weeks, warmed by shared memories and years of history.

Hub's face softened just before he leaned over and kissed her.

Daisy froze for a moment, a thousand thoughts flashing through her mind. How he shouldn't be doing this and there was still the other woman—and yet, he was also still her husband of twenty-one years, her lover for longer than that, and he was familiar and comfortable and—yes—safe.

Except all of that was over now, with an unfamiliar, uncomfortable and dangerous future looming ahead of her.

On Monday, they would begin the process of formally separating their lives.

Tonight—tonight, Daisy thought as she relaxed and began to kiss him back, was a chance to say good-bye to everything that had been good about their past together before saying hello to an uncertain and frightening future.

Besides, she thought as he pressed her back on the couch, what would it hurt?

~~~~~

It was dark when Rebecca opened her eyes and blinked at the unfamiliar wall. The hotel room was dimly illuminated by the light of the street lamps seeping through the curtains. Jackson stirred beside her, pressed warmly against her back, his arm resting comfortably over her waist. His breath lightly brushed against the skin of her neck and back, and she shivered.

He started awake, lifting his head and looking down at her in the shadows.

"What time is it?" he mumbled, his voice thick with sleep.

Rebecca glanced at the clock. "It's early. Only ten."

He lowered his head back to the pillow and nuzzled her shoulder, the stubble of his whiskers lightly rasping against her skin. She shivered again at the sensation.

"You know, if you'd agreed to come to my place, we wouldn't need to get out of bed at all tonight," he murmured into her ear, dropping a lingering kiss on the back of her shoulder.

"Oh?" Rebecca teased lightly. "Would you have been as creative if your kids were down the hall?"

"You'd be surprised," Jackson assured her.

Rebecca laughed softly and patted his hand. "I'll take your word for it," she said.

Jackson froze, and Rebecca knew he was suddenly fully awake, but not for any reason she was going to like. He lifted his head to look at her in the darkness of the hotel room. She bit her lip, and tensed, waiting for him to speak.

"Rebecca," he said slowly, "you have no intention of ever spending the night at my place or meeting my kids. Do you?"

"Jackson—it's just a bad time," she protested weakly. "I mean—Tris isn't handling her parents absence well, and two or three weeks ago, when I pushed Jaime about coming home, she ended up hanging up on me and I haven't talked to her since. Tris is barely speaking to me any more frequently. Her dad's gone off to a Buddhist monastery in France, of all places, and he calls once a week but he's not coming back any time soon, either. But he will at least talk to me on the phone! Honestly, Jackson, this is not the time to meet your kids or introduce anything new into the mix."

She rolled over and met his eyes.

"I'm sorry," she said softly.

"Are you?" he asked. He slowly cocked his head to one side, his dark eyes watchful and sad. "You don't really want anything to change, do you?"

Rebecca swallowed and forced herself to meet his gaze steadily.

"No," she replied simply. "I like things the way they are, at least for right now. And–I really am worried about Tris. I'm just not sure how to deal with her and her parents."

Jackson cupped her face and stroked his thumb over her cheek.

"You don't have to do this on your own," he murmured.

"I'm not. I have Daisy here, and Manny long distance, and unlike my daughter and son-in-law, Manny will come home if I ask her to."

Jackson heaved a heavy sigh and rolled onto his back, rubbing his hands wearily over his face.

"That's not exactly what I meant," he said ruefully.

Rebecca laughed as she slipped from the bed and stood with nothing but the shadows cloaking her body. She looked down at him.

"I appreciate the offer–I really do," she said. "But– really–I'm okay. Daisy and Manny will get Tris and me through this. They always do."

He gave her a sad half-smile before his gaze drifted down to her nude body.

"So, you really only need me for sex," he teased, not quite lightly.

She pulled off the covers, exposing him to her hungry eyes as she grinned wickedly.

"Not really," she replied. "I have some pretty impressive vibrators."

She climbed on to the bed and straddled him, not quite touching his body as she hovered over him. She leaned forward and braced herself with her hands on either side of his face. He put his hands on her waist, then slid one hand to her back as the other stroked up to fondle her breast.

"So what *am* I needed for?" he asked huskily.

Rebecca shrugged, and almost purred with pleasure as his hands continued their explorations.

"Well," she mused, "you do hold doors for me when my arms are full."

"I am nothing if not a gentleman."

"You've killed a spider or two in your day."

"Glad to help."

She slowly lowered herself on top of him.

"And you've fixed my car."

"Free car maintenance—that's always a plus."

She gave him a slow, sensuous kiss that he more than returned in kind.

She drew back slightly and said, "But the real reason, of course, is because without you, I'd still be wondering how to set up my DVR, not to mention my new phone."

He chuckled as he stroked his hands sensuously up her back.

"I always knew those IT classes would come in handy," he murmured.

She shrieked as he suddenly rolled her over and pinned her, laughing, beneath him.

"Well, I guess when you're second best, you just have to try harder," he said huskily and lowered his mouth to hers.

~~~~~

TJ glanced up as Leah padded quietly down the hallway and paused on the threshold of the living room.

"Hey," Leah said softly, her voice rough with sleep.

"Hey," he replied. "What are you doing up?"

"I was cold," she said simply, "and you weren't there to warm me up."

He gave her a half-smile and patted the couch beside him. She shuffled over and curled up beside him, his arms snug as he held her, her head on his shoulder. They sat in comfortable silence, TJ staring somberly at nothing.

"Worried?" Leah asked softly.

TJ squeezed her gently. "Sleep," he urged.

"I don't like sleeping without you," she mumbled, nuzzling closer.

"What would the feminists say?" he teased half-heartedly.

Leah pinched his arm without opening her eyes, and he chuckled.

"Sorry," he said.

She lifted her head and blinked sleepily at him in the dimness of the room.

"We should hear on Monday," she told him.

"Dr. Valesquez only said next week."

"I'm hoping for Monday."

"Me too."

They once more lapsed into silence.

"Are you going to worry about this every night until you know something?" Leah asked, her head once again resting against his shoulder.

"Are you?" TJ countered.

"Yes."

"Yeah."

TJ swallowed heavily.

"But staying up all night isn't going to help," Leah added.

"I know. But...I'm scared to sleep."

She quickly lifted her head to look at his face, hidden in the shadows.

He gave her a half-smile. "I only seem to be dreaming about the worst possible outcomes. And I dream about telling everyone—our friends, Zeke, work. I dream about...putting you through the hell of a long illness...about leaving you behind, leaving you alone."

Leah watched him somberly, digesting his words in silence.

"I've never made you a promise I couldn't keep, TJ," she said carefully, "and I've never lied to you. I'm not about to start now. So, I'm not going to say it's going to be all right—because it may not be all right. The only thing I will promise you is that no matter how hellish it may be, I'm not going anywhere. If—and it's a big 'if'—the worst should happen, I'll still be here, beside you. And I promise I'll be okay no matter what happens."

Leah leaned her head against his shoulder, and they sat in silence, listening to the dark.

Day 72

Daisy poured water into the coffee maker with a pensive frown on her face. She tensed as she heard the bedroom door open and Hub pad down the hall towards the kitchen. She didn't turn when he came into the room, keeping her eyes fixed on her hands as she continued through the motions of spooning coffee into the basket.

She stiffened when Hub slid his arms around her waist from behind and pressed a kiss to her neck.

He said, his breath whispering across her skin, "So, I guess I'll cancel my lease on that apartment today and get the furniture moved back as soon as I can arrange it."

Daisy froze, then she twisted out of his hold and turned to face him.

"What?" she asked incredulously. "No!"

Hub frowned. "What do you mean 'no'? We made love last night!"

"Yes we did, but that doesn't mean all is forgiven and we're back together. I'm sorry if you got the wrong idea, Hub. And honestly? If you think sex is all that's needed to solve our problems, you're sadly mistaken."

Hub glared at her, and now he was the same cold, disapproving man he'd been for the last few years.

"So, are you saying last night 'just happened'?" he sneered sarcastically.

Daisy rolled her eyes. "Of course not. We each had moments when we could have stopped, when we made a conscious decision to continue. But I meant it as a—a—good-bye, not as an 'all is forgiven'. I thought that was how you meant it, too."

Hub deliberately, scornfully, stepped away from her.

"So–last night was just–what? A farewell fuck before you pack me out the door?"

Daisy crossed her arms and glared back. "As I recall, you kissed me first. And considering you still have a *girlfriend*," venom dripped from the word, "I'm surprised you're so anxious to find some excuse to stay!"

"Does last night make you the other woman, then?" Hub snarled.

Daisy barked a laugh although there was no humour in it. "Maybe it does. Let me know how *she* likes it."

Hub snapped his mouth closed, his lips pressed tightly together. He turned and left the kitchen without another word.

~~~~~

Max raised an eyebrow at Daisy's focused and furious scowl as she viciously typed up his notes.

"Should I even ask why you're here on a Sunday morning?" he teased, his usual crooked smirk firmly in place.

"Not if you value your life," she growled without taking her eyes from the screen.

His eyebrows rose higher.

"What happened?" he asked in a worried tone, his smirk gone. "Are you still upset about what happened yesterday with Paolucci?"

Daisy very deliberately lifted her fingers from the keyboard, but kept her eyes fixed on the screen.

"I had sex with Hub last night. That's what I'm upset about."

Max blinked, his face expressionless.

"Well," he finally said slowly, "he is still your husband. Does–"

"I swear," she snarled viciously, finally looking at him, "if you ask if this means we're back together, I'll–I'll–I'll put salt in your coffee!"

"Whoa–whoa–whoa!" Max leaned away, his hands up.

Daisy sighed and deflated. She shook her head, rubbing her forehead.

"I'm sorry, Max. I'm just so angry at how *stupid* I was last night."

Max nodded cautiously. "Okay. Should I ask what happened?"

Daisy shrugged. "We were reminiscing and one thing led to another—and I thought...why not? A last good-bye to all our years together, you know?"

Max nodded. "Yeah. I know."

"I thought—what would it hurt? Then this morning Hub was all—'oh, I'll cancel my lease; no need to move out anymore; blah, blah, blah'. I had to set him straight. The sad part? The really sad part? I think he only slept with me because he thought it would save our marriage, and then he wouldn't have to leave the house and kids! Like all he had to do was give me sex, and I'd forget everything that's been wrong for the last few years! Hah! I don't think so!"

Max's eyes widened at every word.

"Casual sex with my soon-to-be-ex husband!" Daisy continued. "That can't be so unusual!"

"No," Max quickly agreed.

"All right, then."

"Okay."

"Fine."

"I...have things to do...somewhere else...I'm sure..."

"Good."

Max all but tiptoed into his inner office and very carefully sat behind his desk. He winced when Daisy once more began to viciously pound on the keyboard.

Several hours later, Max cautiously wandered out of his office because it seemed the amount of pressure Daisy was putting on the keys had finally eased. He handed Daisy a cup of steaming black coffee.

"No salt in the sugar bowl," he said. "I checked."

Daisy smiled and ruefully rubbed her forehead. "Thanks—and I'm sorry," she said as she took the cup.

Max led the way to the office's small waiting area and they each settled in to an armchair.

"Feeling a little calmer?" he asked.

Daisy sat back in her chair and stared at the cup cradled in her hands.

"Not really. Max...do you realize I've never lived alone?"

He frowned. "Never?"

Daisy shook her head. "Rebecca and I moved in together that first semester at university. I looked after Jaime when Rebecca was at work. Then, when Mom and Dad were killed that January, Rebecca and I dropped out of university and stayed home with Manny until she finished high school. We all lived together while we went to university. I met Hub when I was twenty-three, and we moved in together after I graduated. And, of course, we've been together ever since."

She lifted her eyes to his. "I've *never* lived alone."

"You're not really going to be living alone," Max pointed out gently, his green eyes soft. "You have the kids."

"I know—but it's not quite the same. They're kids, not fellow adults, you know? Plus they'll be moving out soon to start their own lives; that's what I've raised them to do. Anyway, I'm trying to say I don't actually know if I can live alone. The thought scares me. A little."

"Well, maybe when Manny gets back—" He stopped when he saw how vigorously Daisy was shaking her head.

"Manny has the opposite problem," Daisy said with a small smile. "She's been too long alone. We'd kill each other if we lived together now."

Max smirked. "At least you know that and won't make the mistake of trying."

"True."

Max stared intently at her. "You'll be fine," he assured her firmly.

"I hope you're right."

"Trust me. I am."

Daisy stared somberly at him. "I hope you're right," she repeated. "Because I don't want to take Hub back just so I won't be alone. That's not the person I want to be."

Max very gently touched her wrist.

"If you take Hub back, it'll be because you've truly forgiven him; that's the person you are."

Daisy blinked back sudden hot tears.

"Thank you," she managed.

Max leaned back and smirked, his not-quite-dimples on full display.

"Besides," he said lightly, "between me, Manny and Rebecca, we'll tell you if we think you're falling off the wagon. If you feel yourself weakening, you call one of us, and we'll talk sense into you."

Daisy laughed, a genuine laugh this time. She wagged her finger at him.

"You'll be sorry when I'm calling you at 3:00 a.m.!"

Max shrugged. "Why should you be any different than anybody else?"

~~~~~

Rebecca cautiously took a sip of her tea and watched Daisy systematically and viciously throw each couch cushion across the room.

"Not that," Rebecca warned calmly as Daisy took aim at a china cabinet filled with knick knacks. "That's from your parents."

Daisy paused, then she deflated and tossed the cushion back on the couch and followed it down. She pressed the balls of her hands against her eyes and groaned loudly.

"Are you done wrecking my living room?" Rebecca asked drily.

Daisy stared up at the ceiling. "Yeah," she sighed sadly.

"Okay, I know you feel like shit–and I don't blame you," Rebecca said. "On the other hand, you didn't go out and have sex with a complete stranger. Hub's still your husband–well. Sort of."

"I made him use a condom," Daisy whispered.

"You *had* one? How old was it?"

Daisy shook her head. "*He* had one."

Rebecca frowned and opened her mouth, then closed it again.

"Go ahead," Daisy sighed.

"You really did *decide* to go through with it," she said slowly.

Daisy nodded glumly.

"Did you ever think you did it to deliberately try to hurt him?"

Daisy opened her mouth, then closed it again with a snap, her eyes wide and thoughtful.

"Maybe I did," she said slowly. "Which would explain why I didn't really enjoy it that much."

"Oh, please!" Rebecca snorted. "I can't imagine Hub was ever that much fun in the sack!"

Daisy glared. "He used to be really fun. For a while, anyway."

Rebecca snorted skeptically. "You need to expand your horizons, Daisy. Honestly? I still find it hard to believe Hub would even have an affair! He just seems so...I don't know...bloodless and buttoned-down."

"Hey–I loved him!"

"Did you? Or did you just want to be safe?"

Daisy glared. "That's a shitty thing to say!"

Rebecca raised an eyebrow. "Come on. You lost your parents when you were nineteen and you met him just as we were running out of what little money they'd left us. Thank God it was enough to send all of us through university!"

"They didn't know they'd hit that black ice and..." Daisy trailed off. Even after all this time, the loss of her parents still ached.

Rebecca's voice gentled as she said, "I know, and I didn't mean that as a criticism in any way. They gave us things that are far more valuable than money."

Daisy nodded. "That they did."

She chewed her bottom lip, staring at nothing.

"I really loved him, you know," she finally said softly, sadly. "Once upon a time."

Rebecca moved to sit beside Daisy and leaned back on the couch, her head nestled on the cushions, her legs stretched out in front of her.

"I know you did," she said. "A part of you still does."

"Yeah? Which part?"

"The part of you that's always twenty-three, when you first fell in love. The part of you that's always twenty-six, when you walked down the aisle towards him. Those parts of you will likely love him forever."

Daisy thought about that for a moment, then she too slid down on the couch, her head level with Rebecca's, and asked, "Is there a part of you still in love with Devon?"

Rebecca slowly shook her head. "I was never in love with Devon. I never had the chance, really. And, of course, with adult hindsight, he had a lot of issues. Then again, so did I."

"Good point."

"Hey, now," Rebecca mock-protested.

Daisy glanced slyly at her and they both laughed.

"Feel better?" Rebecca asked.

"Not really."

They stared at the ceiling in silence.

"Could be worse," Rebecca finally said.

Daisy raised an eyebrow. "Oh?"

"Could have been a total stranger. Or your best friend's husband. Or your sister's husband."

"You and Manny aren't married."

"I do have Jackson."

Daisy brightened. "Ooh, Jackson! Never thought of him! He would definitely be tempting, especially with those puzzled puppy eyes."

Rebecca shook her head in mock disgust as she said, "Mental note: Keep Jackson far, far away from Daisy for a while."

They laughed.

"Okay," Daisy agreed, "a stranger or Jackson would have been worse."

"Or a good male friend."

"That would be worse?"

"If you're not both on the same page. And you know, once you cross that line, you can never go back."

"Speaking from experience?"

"Oh, yeah."

"So, an unsuspecting male friend would have been worse. Got it."

"Keep that in mind," Rebecca said, patting Daisy's knee and heaving herself to her feet. "Especially when you're working late with Max."

Daisy frowned. "I never work late with...oh."

Rebecca winked. "Come on—I think we need something stronger than tea."

"God, yes."

Rebecca pulled open the liquor cabinet and showed Daisy the tequila bottle, her brows raised in question.

Daisy nodded fervently and joined her at the bar.

Rebecca poured them each a shot, and they raised their glasses.

"Here's to forgiving ourselves for our mistakes," Rebecca said, "because we're going to make more of them in the future."

"Hear, hear," Daisy muttered and tossed back the drink.

Day 75

Zeke sat relaxed behind the wheel as they headed out of Ringo. He almost didn't even care they were heading to California—again. He glanced at Manny, who was slumped against the door, her eyes closed, her mouth slightly open.

Zeke shook his head, amused.

"Don't tell me you're still hungover from Saturday?" he

said, grinning.

"No," Manny groaned. "While you were—um—entertaining Babe last night, Rosa and the rest of Friday's Slammers took me out for a few—well, tequila slammers." She groaned. "Please try not to hit every damn pothole between here and L.A."

Zeke's grin abruptly disappeared.

"Was there dancing involved?" he asked with a frown.

"A little, yeah. Mikey was there, too. You know, he's actually not a bad dancer when he's doing the two-step."

Zeke's hands tightened on the wheel before he forced himself to relax and said, "You seem to be leaving a trail of friends behind you."

"That's a bit of an exaggeration," she mumbled, once more slumped against the door, her eyes closed.

"No? How many of them are going to friend you on Facebook?"

"All of them—but people friend on Facebook like I change my socks."

Zeke laughed. "Don't sell yourself short," he urged.

"Right now I just want my head to stop pounding."

"There's Tylenol in the glove compartment," Zeke reminded her.

"That's right," Manny groaned happily. "You're a good, good man, Zeke," she added as she scrabbled in the glove compartment, then downed two of the pills with her coffee.

"Go to sleep," Zeke smirked and chuckled quietly when she did just that.

~~~~~

TJ and Leah sat in Dr. Valesquez' office in tense silence, holding hands as they waited for the doctor to arrive. TJ stared off into the distance, his jaw set, his face carefully expressionless except for the muscles flexing in his jaw. Leah watched him worriedly as the silence quivered between them. Her grip on TJ's hand tightened and tightened again.

"Careful, or he'll have to fix my hand, too," TJ said suddenly, causing Leah to jump and squeak in surprise.

She looked down at where their hands were linked and laughed a little. "I'm sorry," she said and loosened her grip slightly.

TJ lifted her hand to his lips and half-smiled at her as the doctor strode in.

Valesquez pulled a chair close beside them and sat down. He put the folder he carried on his lap and calmly met their gazes.

"I'm sorry, TJ. We found a tumor in your colon."

EPISODE SEVEN
Day 83

Manny frowned as her phone trilled that she had received a text.

Again.

Zeke raised a questioning eyebrow as Manny pulled her phone out of her purse and they slowed to a stop out of the path of the crowd on the sidewalk behind them. They were in Los Angeles, taking in the sights, and Manny's phone had been buzzing with texts for most of the day.

Manny made a disgusted noise as she read the text.

"Trouble?" he asked.

Manny shook her head as she laboriously punched in a reply and hit send. She tucked the phone away again as they continued walking and said, "It's Roxie."

Zeke frowned, trying to remember which of the many people they'd met during the last few months was Roxie.

"She was my admin support," Manny explained, laughing slightly at his confused expression. "You know. At my job. My previous job, I mean."

"Ah," Zeke said as light dawned. "She's just saying hi?"

Manny shrugged. "Sort of. Apparently my old unit is having a hell of a time. Steph's basically set unachievable quotas, given their current state of technology and equipment. The unit has also been reorganized three times since I left, and they're living in complete chaos, which slows everyone down even more."

She shook her head, biting her lip with an anxious frown.

"They won't be able to meet their quarterly targets if this keeps up," she muttered.

"Manny," Zeke said firmly.

She glanced at him, still frowning.

"You don't work there anymore," he reminded her gently.

Manny's expression didn't change for a long moment, then she shook herself and nodded. "I know," she said, "I know. It's just...old habits are hard to break."

"You haven't mentioned them at all since we've been on the road."

Manny walked silently beside him then said, "I dreamt about work every night for about six weeks or so after I quit. It was my entire life for so long—both the work itself and the people there. I have absolutely no regrets about walking away, but that doesn't mean it was easy to turn my back on the people I left behind."

Zeke shrugged. "I wouldn't know," he said lightly. "For me, it's most often a case of 'out of sight, out of mind'."

Manny gave him such a long, thoughtful look he began to fidget slightly.

"What?" he finally demanded.

"I can't decide if you're telling the truth or if you're so used to putting on an act you honestly don't even realize you're doing it."

"Then it's not an act anymore, is it?" Zeke replied smoothly. "I think we're here—wherever 'here' is."

They stopped and looked at the sedate two-storey brick house. Manny pulled a piece of paper out of her pocket and checked it as she said, "A lady named Carina. She's a friend of Simon-Simone's, and she apparently has a vast collection of Cary Grant memorabilia. Simon-Simone said she'd talked to her and she was looking forward to showing it to us."

Zeke groaned. "You just love not telling me anything until it's too late, don't you? Then I'm stuck!"

Manny laughed up at him. "You love it," she assured him.

Zeke shook his head as he opened the gate and bowed her towards the front door.

~~~~~

"You enjoyed it in spite of yourself, huh?" Leah said absently.

"Carina was very charming," Zeke admitted grudgingly, "and Manny's love for all things Cary Grant seems never-ending."

"We all have our little obsessions."

Zeke paused, frowning. "Are you all right?" he asked.

"What? Yes! Why?"

"You seem distracted. Are you and TJ running into more problems? With having a baby, I mean."

Leah paused. "We've...decided to put that on hold for a little while," she said carefully.

Zeke's frown deepened. "Okay," he said slowly. "That...doesn't sound good. Is there something going on I should know about?"

"I think you should talk to TJ about that," Leah said.

Zeke hesitated, nonplussed. "You're worrying me, Leah," he said sharply.

"I'm sorry—I don't mean to worry you. Listen, Zeke, I have to go. Send me the text for your next three blogs and I'll review them tonight. Okay?"

"Okay," Zeke agreed grudgingly and thoughtfully disconnected the call.

~~~~~

"Hey, Zeke," TJ said cheerfully.

"Okay, you sound better than Leah," Zeke said.

"Leah? What?"

"Leah said you guys were putting having a baby on

hold right now?" Zeke couldn't hide the concern in his voice.

TJ chuckled. "Okay, I have to say I never in a million years thought you'd be concerned because someone *wasn't* having a baby."

"You're avoiding the question," Zeke snapped.

"Yes, we've decided to put things on hold for a little while. *What Women Want* is starting to get some really great buzz on the Internet, thanks in large part to your blog. Not to mention my company's in the middle of negotiating a multi-million dollar project, and that's going to take up a lot of time for the next few weeks."

Zeke's frown didn't lighten. "Why do I get the impression there's something you're not telling me?"

"I don't know, Zeke," TJ said patiently, "I'm not living in your head. Thank God."

"Hey!"

TJ chuckled. "Don't worry. Have fun and keep writing those blogs! The traffic is increasing daily, you know."

"I know." Zeke paused. "You'd tell me if you and Leah were having problems, right? You wouldn't hide anything from me just because I work for her, would you?"

TJ paused, then said, "I'm sorry if we're worrying you, Zeke. Really. Everything between me and Leah is fine. Better than fine. We just decided that, with everything else that's currently going on in our lives, we just don't have the time to focus on having a baby. But we're more solid than ever. I wouldn't lie to you about that, Zeke."

Zeke let out a long breath. "All right," he said. "Sorry if I came across rather strong. It must be all this time I've spent with Manny."

"She's a worry-wart, is she?"

Zeke laughed. "Sometimes. Other times, not so much. Okay. I just wanted to make sure things were okay with you and Leah. I'd better go; I have blogs to write."

"Sounds good," TJ said cheerfully.

Zeke's frown was even more thoughtful as he

disconnected the call.

~~~~~

Leah walked into the house and tossed her keys on the table beside the door. She wandered into the living room.

"Hey," she greeted TJ, who was sitting on the couch working on his laptop.

"Hey," TJ gave her a fleeting smile before he refocused his attention on the computer.

She dropped a kiss on the top of his head, then flung herself on the couch beside him. She idly watched the screen as TJ typed rapidly.

"Zeke call you today?" she asked.

"Yeah."

She waited, but when TJ didn't offer anything more, she said, "You need to tell him."

"After the surgery," TJ said firmly. "There's no point having him come back any sooner. Dr. Valesquez said it might be benign, so until we know for sure–"

"You've been using that excuse ever since we first found out there may be a problem," Leah said sharply. "What are you worried about?"

TJ sighed, set his laptop on the coffee table and turned to Leah. He looked steadily at her.

"I'm worried about making it real," he said softly. "Saying it's cancer before we know for sure just feels like...we're giving up before we've even begun."

Leah threw her arms around him and hugged tightly.

"My surgery is scheduled eleven days from now," TJ whispered into her neck. "We'll have the results of the biopsy within two days after that. Then we'll tell Zeke everything. Even if the news is bad. Okay?"

Leah sighed. "He'll be pissed when he finds out we kept this from him."

"He'll get over it."

"He'll make us pay," Leah warned.

TJ chuckled slightly. "I'd be disappointed if he didn't."

"I'll remind you of that when you're complaining to

me," Leah said drily.

"I'd be disappointed if you didn't," TJ grinned and kissed her soundly.

Day 84

Manny stepped out of the shower and wrapped a towel around her body then another around her hair. She opened the door and padded towards the small table where the coffee pot was located. She caught a glimpse of herself in the hotel room's full-length mirror and grimaced at the sight.

You should stop doing that.

Doing what?

Hating what you look like.

Just in a mirror. I swear I'm prettier and skinnier than that!

Manny.

Harvey.

Harvey sighed. **It's one of those kind of days, is it?**

I need coffee, okay? Let me at least have coffee in my hands before we start arguing. I mean, before I start arguing with myself.

Harvey shook his head, his arms crossed as he stood between the beds, tapping his bare foot.

Manny took a sip of the coffee and sighed gratefully. She turned and looked at him.

Okay. What's going on?

All I wanted to say was if you don't like how you look, there are things you can change. We are in Los Angeles.

I am not getting plastic surgery!

Harvey laughed. **I was thinking more about a makeover. Nothing so drastic as plastic surgery.**

A makeover?

You have heard of those things, right? You know, change your haircut, put on some makeup, buy some different clothes—

I know what they are! I just hadn't thought about doing it before.

Manny slowly sipped her coffee, deep in thought. Her phone buzzed with Zeke's ringtone and she started.

"Hello," she answered cheerfully.

"Hey. What do you have planned for the day?"

"Nothing so far. Why?"

"I've got some work to do; an old client needs some development work done ASAP. I should be finished today, but it may take most of tomorrow, too."

"Okay. I think I'm going to just wander around then. See what I can find."

"Oh, God. *Please* don't bring back half the city as your new friends!"

"I was only planning on bringing back—at most—a quarter of it," Manny replied primly, then laughed at Zeke's dramatic groan.

She padded back into the bathroom, towel-dried her hair and began to comb out the tangles. She realized she was avoiding her reflection and forced herself to look in the mirror as she dealt with her hair. She paused in her task and frowned thoughtfully, slowly cocking her head to one side.

It'd be fun, Harvey urged.

Yeah. Yeah, I think it would.

~~~~~

Manny chatted rather nervously with the pretty young woman, Olive, who was cutting her hair. She forced herself to sit still, but she could feel herself vibrating like a taut wire. Her back was to the mirror and she hadn't seen the results yet, although she had seen the long ponytail which had been Olive's first cut. Manny had promised to leave everything up to Olive, but as the minutes ticked by and the scissors kept snipping, she was getting more and more nervous.

"Relax," Olive said, "you're going to look great!"

Manny gave her an uncertain smile.

"You know," Olive said, "if you want...my boyfriend's a photographer. I could give him a call, see if he could do some glamor pics for you."

Manny's eyes widened.

"Glamor pics?"

"Yeah. Full makeup and outfits and everything. He does head shots for aspiring actors, so he knows how to make people look really good."

Manny hummed as she considered it. "Where's he located?"

"Just down the block. And he's pretty reasonable when it comes to the price."

Manny grinned. "You know, it does sound like fun, actually. Assuming I like what you've done to me."

Olive grinned back. "Trust me–you'll love it! I'll call once we're done here. I know he didn't have any appointments when he left this morning, but you never know what the day might bring."

"Especially with his girlfriend sending him work."

Olive shrugged sheepishly. "I don't send everybody."

Manny laughed. "Give him a call. I've never had a professional picture of me–just me, I mean."

"Super! Now, are you ready to see the new you?"

Manny gulped, then took a deep breath and nodded.

Olive spun her chair with a flourish and Manny stared at the woman in the mirror.

Her long hair was gone, replaced by a tousled cap that framed her face, gently curled around her jawline and left her neck bare.

Manny tentatively touched the ends of her hair. She gave her head an experimental shake, feeling oddly light without the long-familiar weight of her hair. She blinked as she realized her hair colour, while still not-quite-blonde-not-quite-brown looked...almost...pretty.

Too bad she still had the same plain face, the same thirty extra pounds–and she still felt the same. Dull, old and plodding, and no amount of gambling, drinking, dancing—or superficial makeovers—was going to change *that*.

She glanced at Harvey to find him giving her a sarcastically sympathetic look as he mimed playing a violin.

Get away from me.

Just—<u>enjoy</u> yourself! Don't you ever get tired of keeping yourself down?

She deliberately turned and smiled at Olive.

"It's lovely. What's next?"

"Let me call my boyfriend."

~~~~~

Manny walked into the hotel restaurant and rather nervously looked around. She saw Zeke sitting at a table engrossed in the menu. She thanked the hostess, took a deep breath, and briskly walked towards him.

Manny was somewhat gratified by his double-take and the way his eyes widened when he caught sight of her. She was slightly taken aback when his eyes narrowed, his brows lowered and he began to scowl.

When she got to the table she ignored the scowl and said, "So? What do you think?"

She turned her head from side to side, showing off the new haircut from several angles.

"What did you do?" Zeke demanded incredulously.

"Well, if you don't know what a haircut looks like..." Manny said drily as she slid into the chair opposite him.

He stared unblinkingly at her. "Why would you cut your hair?" he asked.

"It was time for a change," she said, picking up the menu and frowning as she read it.

"But—but—"

Manny glanced at Zeke and raised an eyebrow in challenge. "But—what?"

"Why are you trying to—to turn back the clock?"

"I'm not trying to turn back the clock," Manny protested mildly.

"Look at you!" he said, gesturing vaguely at her.

"You've cut your hair!"

"I think we've already established that," Manny drawled.

Zeke was shaking his head, wide-eyed. "It's not...not *you*!" he blurted.

Manny laughed then. "Sure it is. I've had it this short before–I liked it then, I like it now. I was tempted to colour it, too, but Olive–the girl who cut my hair–convinced me it looked good like this."

"Well, I'm not sure I like it!" Zeke huffed, leaning back in his chair and crossing his arms.

Manny froze then very precisely laid down the menu and leaned over the table, glaring at him through narrowed eyes.

"You don't *have* to like it, Zeke," she hissed quietly, trying to keep her voice down in the crowded restaurant, "I didn't do this for you! And it's just a damn haircut! What are you so angry about?"

Now it was Zeke's turn to lean over the table, his own eyes hard and coldly angry. "You won't stay where I put you," he growled.

Manny frowned. "I don't even know what that means," she snapped.

"I *mean*, you keep *changing*–"

"That's the whole point!"

Zeke plowed on like she hadn't said a word, "–doing things I never expected you to do or even think of doing! From the Misfit Toys to raucous card games to wiggling your ass like–like–"

"Like what, Zeke?" Manny asked, her voice dangerously quiet when Zeke stammered to a stop.

Zeke shook his head and waved it away. "Never mind," he said. "The point is, you're supposed to be demure, retiring, repre-e-e--buttoned-up–buttoned-down...*Auntie Em*! Not–" he gestured angrily, encompassing everything from her haircut to her shoes, "*this*!"

"Supposed to be? *Supposed* to be? As far as I know, I

have no obligation to fit any of your pre-conceived and petrified notions of who and what I should be! And you have no right to expect me to!"

"Um...are you ready to order?"

Their heads snapped towards the waitress who was standing rather timidly beside their table.

"You know what," Manny said, abruptly rising to her feet, "I'm not hungry anymore. I think I'm just going to go back to my room. See if I can get my appetite back."

Zeke made no effort to stop her from leaving.

~~~~~

"...I guess I won't tell him about the pictures then," Manny sighed, laying back on the bed and scowling at the ceiling.

On the other end of the phone, Daisy paused before she tentatively asked, "Pictures? What pictures?

"Well, Olive's boyfriend is a photographer—you know, head shots for aspiring actors? Well, I got some glam shots and some...you know...sexy lingerie pictures done."

Daisy paused before she slowly said, "You posed for...sexy lingerie pictures? *Really?*" Her voice squeaked on the last word.

"Really. I'm going to get the prints tomorrow."

"I am blown away. Manny. I don't even..."

Manny sighed. "Don't you start!"

"I think that's *awesome*! That's something I've always wanted to do and I've never had the guts!"

"Hey, if you like them, would you like to come down? Rebecca, too, if she can get away. You guys are only four hours away by plane; we could get more pictures done together."

"Sexy lingerie pictures? *Together?*"

Manny laughed at Daisy's scandalized tone. "I was thinking more about the glam shots, but if you want to do the lingerie ones, go for it! Without me with you, though, because that would just be sick!"

Daisy laughed. "I'd love to—even if I don't like the

pictures. But I'm not sure I can get away...tell you what? Let me talk to Max tomorrow and get back to you."

Manny sighed. "I hope it works out. I really miss you."

"I miss you, too," Daisy said softly. "I'll let you know tomorrow."

They said their good-byes, and Manny tossed the phone aside then wearily pressed the heels of her palms against her eyes.

Day 85

Manny stared at her reflection in horror.

This looked much better in the store.

She gulped as she turned sideways to check out her butt.

Damn. I don't think that much flesh is supposed to be stuffed into such a little bitty piece of spandex.

She turned back to fully face the mirror.

And these–she cupped and raised her breasts–*should be somewhere up around here.*

She released her breasts and covered her face with her hands.

What was I thinking? I can't go out to the pool in this! I'll cause a riot and not in a good way! Jesus H Fucking Christ...when did I get old?

Are you done?

Manny shook her head and refused to remove her hands from her face.

I was wondering when you were going to show up.

I've been here all along. Harvey stood looking impossibly handsome in a white polo shirt that contrasted sharply with his salt-and-pepper-but-still-mostly-pepper hair, his dark eyes watching her with an odd mixture of mockery and sympathy. **Look. It's not that bad.**

It's bad enough! I didn't even mention the cellulite! Or the thunder thighs! The paunch! Look at that stomach! Oh, God–I need mind bleach! She turned her back on the mirror and fumbled with the clasp of the bikini top. *Thank God I can get undressed with my eyes closed.*

Chicken.

Her fingers froze.

What?

The whole point of this trip is to try new things; get out of your comfort zone. Look at you—after everything else you've done so far, from ziplining to line dancing, you're having a meltdown about wearing a bikini?

In public!

You're not in public now! And honestly—okay, yes, you sag more than you used to do; you may have a bit more ass than bikini bottom—but have you seen the others at the pool? You're no worse than they are and in some cases, you're better.

We're in Los Angeles! They're all beautiful here!

Harvey laughed. **That's just a myth.**

They'll all laugh at me, Manny whined.

Manny. Look at me.

She reluctantly raised her eyes to meet his.

You and I both know—they—whoever 'they' are—won't even look at you. They're not going to laugh at you because they're not even going to see you.

Manny blinked at him, feeling battered and bruised and wanting nothing more than to crawl into bed and have a good cry.

I thought you were supposed to make me feel better.

No. I'm supposed to make you feel the truth.

...since when?

Since you stopped having me rescue you from pirates and started talking to me instead.

Damn. My fault again.

Indeed.

Manny took a deep breath as she forced herself to turn around and look into the mirror again.

Good girl.

Shut up. I still haven't decided if I'm going to wear this outside this hotel room!

Why? Are you afraid Zeke's going to see you in it, and get even angrier with you? Or worse: laugh until he pukes?

What? No!

Sure? I suspect you bought this bikini this morning in order to rub his nose in his opinion that you're demure, retiring and repressed, and now you don't even have the guts to go through with it.

...he didn't say I was repressed.

Only because he caught himself at the last minute.

Manny sighed and hung her head.

Zeke had nothing to do with why I wanted to wear a bikini to the pool.

No? Then why did you want to?

...to feel...sexy. And I did feel sexy in the store. But they must use trick mirrors or something, because I thought I looked pretty good, for my age. Now I just look like another pathetic middle-aged woman trying to recapture her lost youth. Just like Zeke said.

Well, you can let yourself worry you're as pathetic as Zeke seems to think—and become just as demure, retiring and repressed as he says you already are...or you could just say fuck it, I feel great in this bikini, and anyone who judges me can bite my luscious ass. What's it gonna be?

~~~~~

Manny yawned and let her book droop down into her lap. She lifted her face to the sun, closed her eyes and concentrated on the feel of the sun on her face and shoulders, her exposed stomach and legs. She felt soft and warm, and—oddly—snuggly.

Snuggly?

Cuddly?

From his position on the lounger beside her, Harvey laughed his low, seductive laugh, his expressive dark eyes hidden behind sunglasses, his bare chest gleaming in the sun.

Gleaming in the sun? That's almost as bad as

saturnine. You have <u>got</u> to stop reading all those romance novels; I'm really beginning to worry about you.

Manny grimaced. ***Oh, shut up.***

"Wow—I expected to find you looking happier than this!"

Manny's eyes popped open and she gaped at Daisy and Rebecca standing by her lounger with huge grins on their faces. She screamed and jumped to her feet, throwing her arms around first Daisy and then Rebecca, all three of them laughing, squealing and bouncing with excitement.

"I have to say, I'm a little freaked out right now about being hugged by a broad in a bikini," Rebecca laughed.

"Ah, you love it!" She turned to Daisy. "You sneak! You planned this all along!"

Daisy nodded rapidly, grinning. "Of course! Did you honestly think I'd pass up a chance to attend a real, live red carpet Hollywood premiere of the latest Robert Downey Jr. movie, plus sit in the California sun for a week? Are you *nuts?*"

Rebecca said, "We have a list of things to do that's as long as your arm. Some of them would be more fun in the presence of the delicious Mr. Powell. That is, if you're talking to him again."

"I haven't seen him today; we spoke briefly on the phone this morning, but it was mostly words of one syllable. Besides, he's been working the last couple of days."

"But you are talking to him again?" Rebecca pressed.

Manny sighed. "Probably," she muttered. "Like I have a choice."

"Good," Rebecca said, ignoring the last part of Manny's comment. "Let's find out if he's done working, so we can go shopping—"

"Shopping?" Manny blurted, her eyes suddenly wide.

Rebecca nodded decisively. "Shopping. And I don't know about Daisy, but the first place I want to go is wherever you got this bikini. It's gorgeous! And you look great!"

Manny flushed, then grinned. "Even though I have more ass than suit?"

Rebecca airily waved away her comment. "*Everyone* has more ass than suit–it's the way they're designing the things nowadays. Now pack up and let's go."

Manny laughed as she quickly slipped her sandals on and got into her cover-up.

"Say, do you guys want to share my room?" she asked as they headed back into the hotel. "It'd be just like a pajama party!"

"We're already there," Daisy replied.

"Say what?"

"Good thing your buddy Lionel owns the hotel. He made all the arrangements for us."

Manny groaned, then laughed and shook her head as she led the way back to their room.

~~~~~

Zeke kept a neutral expression on his face as he opened his door. He was grateful Manny had called first to see if he had time to see her. He'd been in the midst of writing a scathing blog about her ill-advised decision to change her look and style, and he'd wanted to finish and send it off to Leah before he saw Manny again. He hoped writing the blog would help him calm down; he had to admit he did feel a little better, but he was wary about what stunt she was going to pull next.

"Hi, Zeke–remember us?" Daisy said brightly, a grin very much like her sister's on her face.

Zeke's jaw dropped. "Daisy! Rebecca! What–when–? Wow! You guys look great!"

"Sure," Rebecca said as she moved past him into the room, "*we* look great. Manny gets a lecture!"

Zeke flushed as Daisy followed after Rebecca, nodding in agreement. Manny was last, a rueful look on her face.

"Do you tell them everything?" he growled at her.

"Pretty much, yeah."

"Look at her! She looks great!" Daisy insisted. "I have no idea how you could have objected to this! She looks at least twenty years younger!"

Manny sputtered a laugh. "You're such a liar," she grinned, "but thanks."

There was a moment of awkward silence.

"So...?" Rebecca drawled.

"So?" Zeke asked.

"Are you going to kiss and make up with Manny—and therefore, by extension, us? Or do we have to inflict ourselves on this poor city without you?"

"Kiss and make up?" he squeaked.

"It's a figure of speech," Manny sighed. "Asshole."

"With the three of you, it never hurts to be sure," Zeke fired back.

"He has a point," Daisy said thoughtfully.

"That he does," Rebecca agreed.

"So, hop to it, Mr. Powell," Daisy said firmly. "Apologize to the lady and let's get the hell out of here. We have things to do and places to see."

Zeke stared wide-eyed at the two women standing firmly in front of him. They were like forces of nature, he thought, amused and bemused, and about as difficult to resist. He turned his attention to Manny. She'd been out in the sun, he noticed. It was still unsettling to see her with short, breeze-tousled hair rather than with her sleek bun or long, straight curtain of hair hanging down her back. This new haircut made her face look rounder, softer somehow— and Zeke realized Daisy hadn't been exaggerating very much: Manny really did look years younger.

"Before I do anything—" he paused as all three women groaned loudly, "I just want to know what you ladies have planned. Maybe I should stay behind in case you need bail money."

Rebecca raised an eyebrow. "Quick learner, this boy," she murmured to Manny.

"Not always," Manny replied drily.

"Good point. Zeke, come on. You were a dumbass, and you know it."

Zeke straightened to his full height and glowered at Rebecca. "I had an honest reaction. What was she thinking?"

"I'm standing right here," Manny snapped, "and I was thinking it would be fun to have a makeover."

Zeke turned his glower on her.

She glowered back.

He threw up his hands. "All right! Fine! You're right! I'm sorry, I over-reacted. The haircut is...fine."

Manny rolled her eyes. "Fine as in looks good, or fine as in you approve?"

Zeke hesitated. "Fine as in looks good," he said, reluctant to give in but knowing Leah would skin him alive if he let the three women go off on their own and he didn't get at least a couple of blogs out of the experience.

The three women glanced at each other.

"Good enough?" Daisy asked.

Rebecca shrugged as she waggled her hand. "It lacked a certain amount of sincerity."

"It lacked any sincerity, you mean," Manny said drily.

Zeke closed his eyes and prayed for patience.

"I'm sorry, Manny," he said. "Really. I had no right to react the way I did, or say the things I said." He opened his eyes and steadily met her gaze. To his surprise, he actually meant what he'd just said. "I am sorry."

Manny considered him thoughtfully, then nodded. "Thank you."

Daisy and Rebecca exchanged glances, then turned their attention back to Zeke.

"Well," Daisy said briskly, "now that that's taken care of, let's get out of here."

Zeke shrugged. "Okay. Where are we going?"

"Shopping!" all three women cried.

Zeke's eyes widened with horror. "Shit!"

Day 88

Zeke was the first to arrive in the hotel lobby, looking dapper in black slacks, crisp, white button down shirt and a black suit jacket that emphasized his broad shoulders and dark good looks. He had a tie tucked in his jacket pocket in case they decided to go somewhere where a tie was required.

As he found a place to sit where he could see both the elevators and the stairs, he thought ruefully that unless they'd made reservations, the only place they'd be able to get into would be a fast food joint. This *was* Los Angeles after all.

Zeke relaxed into his armchair with a grateful sigh. The three women had been keeping him on the run. If they weren't shopping, they were sight-seeing, and if they weren't sight-seeing, they were off on secret missions that none of them could be charmed into talking about. He could see that Manny came by her tourist tendencies honestly. But, he grudgingly and rather fondly admitted, he was enjoying himself.

A lot, if he was really honest with himself. Daisy, Rebecca and Manny were funny, witty and kind, and Zeke found himself caught up in the centre of their whirlwind and treated as if he'd always been there. That didn't mean, though, he wasn't glad for a few minutes respite after three days of being almost constantly in their presence. On the up side, he'd gotten used to Manny's new hairstyle.

Finally.

Zeke settled more comfortably into the deep plush of the one armchair that was perfectly situated for him to watch both the elevators and the bottom half of the long, sweeping staircase that dominated the hotel lobby. He glanced at his watch and saw he had a few minutes before he could reasonably expect the others to arrive. He relaxed and proceeded to people watch, wondering what the couple in the corner was discussing so intently, and whether the other couple checking in were actually married to each other.

His idly roving attention was caught by a pair of killer high-heels and shapely legs carefully descending the staircase. The woman paused on the stairs, and Zeke hoped Daisy, Manny and Rebecca wouldn't show up for another few minutes. If the face and the rest of the body lived up to the promise of those legs, he wanted to be able to enjoy the view without being teased unmercifully.

The feet took another step, then paused again and the woman half-turned to speak to someone coming down the stairs behind her. But that one extra step showed legs that went all the way up to a lusciously curvaceous ass covered in a vibrant blue skirt that hugged the curves of her hips and thighs until it flared into a flirtatious frill on the bottom of a skirt that brushed the tops of her knees.

The woman on the stairs was joined by a man, and they both continued their descent down the stairs just as an elevator arrived. Zeke glanced over and smiled in greeting as Daisy and Rebecca walked towards him with welcoming smiles, looking cool and elegant. He smiled back, then glanced back at the staircase to find the legs had morphed into Manny, listening intently to the man beside her as they came to the bottom of the stairs.

Zeke felt his mouth sag open. He was dimly aware of Daisy and Rebecca coming to a stop beside him, chatting about how they'd known that dress would bring out the colour of Manny's eyes, and how glad they were to see her wearing something other than all that boring grey.

Zeke felt like he was watching from a great distance as Manny parted from the man who had joined her on the stairs and walked up to them, frowning. He blinked and realized she'd asked him something.

He shook his head, "I'm sorry—what?"

"Are you okay?" Manny repeated, her frown deepening.

Daisy and Rebecca looked at him with sudden, sharp

interest.

Rebecca said, "Manny's right. You look like you've just been hit between the eyes. Are you all right?"

Zeke continued to stare off into space, but he said faintly, "Yeah. Yeah, I'm good." He shook his head again and looked wide-eyed at the three women. "I was just...surprised by something. That's all."

Manny's frown didn't ease. "Do you need a few minutes?" she asked, concerned.

"No–no." With an effort, he forced a smile at the suddenly, profoundly unfamiliar woman standing in front of him. "I'm ready to go, Auntie Em." He almost stumbled over the teasing nickname.

She rolled her eyes and tsk'd, then turned to lead the way out of the hotel. Zeke found his eyes involuntarily dropping to watch the sway of her ass as she walked in front of him. He pulled his eyes away, appalled.

She's *Auntie Em*, he told himself in horror. She's not even supposed to *have* an ass!

His eyes met Rebecca's, who was walking beside him with an amused and all-too-knowing smile.

"She cleans up nice, doesn't she?" Rebecca murmured softly.

He stared at her for a moment, then quickly looked away.

Rebecca laughed a low, husky laugh but to his relief she let the subject drop.

~~~~~

Zeke gradually regained his equilibrium during dinner, although everything still had a touch of the surreal to it. But the ladies were in fine form, and uncharacteristically ignored his quiet aloofness while they ate. Zeke kept stealing glances at Manny, who looked and acted exactly the same as she always did.

He couldn't understand why he had this sudden physical awareness of her.

It made no sense.

Zeke felt much more himself after they left the restaurant and wandered to the neighbourhood bar they'd discovered on Daisy and Rebecca's first night in town. He was greatly relieved to discover that Manny, while still looking very nice in her blue dress, was no longer the sexy creature he'd seen back at the hotel. His first shot of whiskey burned away the last of the cobwebs, and when he let Rebecca out of the booth to go the bathroom, he was finally ready to take part in the conversation that had been going on without him.

His ears perked up when he realized Manny and Daisy were speaking more freely than they had up to this point in his presence. Perhaps, he thought, it paid to be distracted.

"Let's face it, Manny," Daisy was saying, her words slightly slurred, "you're not known for your great relationship decisions. Who was that guy in university? B-B-"

"Bosco," Manny sighed.

"Bosco. Who has a name like *Bosco*!"

"He was nice!"

"He tried to emotionally blackmail you!"

"He didn't succeed!"

"Because you didn't know what he was doing!" Daisy turned to Zeke. "Get this—"

"Daisy," Manny warned. Daisy waved her off and continued.

"*Bosco*," she stressed sarcastically, "starts dropping little snide hints about women who always let him pay for everything and never put out. Little Miss Genius here is all sympathy and understanding—and until he stopped calling, never figured out the 'women' he was talking about was *her*!"

"I never *thought* of him like that," Manny groaned and covered her face with her hands. "I thought he was just being friendly."

"Yeah—*friendly*." Daisy shook her head and took another sip of her beer. She shared a rueful look with

Zeke. They glanced up as Rebecca rejoined them, and Zeke let her back into the booth.

"What'd I miss? Why is Manny hiding her face?" She turned a stern look on Daisy. "Have you been telling tales out of school again?"

Zeke leaned over and said, "Bosco."

"Oh–*him*."

Manny dropped her hands, shaking her head. She grabbed her beer and took a big gulp. "How the hell people figure that stuff out I'll never know."

"You stopped trying," Daisy scolded.

"Do you blame me?" Manny retorted.

Rebecca shook her head. "One not-so-good experience–"

"Three, actually," Manny muttered.

Rebecca leaned over and conspiratorially pressed her shoulder against Zeke's as she said, "That's true–there *were* three."

Zeke took a sip of his beer hiding a wicked grin. "Tell me more," he invited and Manny glared at the laughter in his voice.

"Look," Manny said, "they were barely blips on the radar of my life. The time it would take to tell the stories would be longer than they were around."

"Oh, come on–" Daisy said.

"Do you want me to tell him *your* stories?" Manny snapped.

"I have no stories," Daisy protested. She straightened, put a hand to her chest and swayed slightly. She giggled as she caught herself and refocused on the conversation. "I was as pure as the driven snow–" She stopped abruptly as Rebecca and Manny hooted with gales of laughter. She rolled her eyes at Zeke. "It's true," she insisted. "I married Hub at the tender age of twenty-six after dating for a year and living together for two."

"Off and on," Manny said sarcastically.

"Please–don't put that image in my head," Rebecca

groaned.

Manny stared blankly then realized what she'd said. "Ewwwww."

"I've been with Hub for twenty-four years," Daisy said with dignity, then drooped slightly, her mouth turning down at the corners. "Twenty-four years," she repeated sadly.

After a moment of silence, Rebecca said briskly, "Well, maybe you'll be able to eventually work things out."

Manny nodded and took another gulp of beer.

Daisy gaped at Rebecca. "You hate Hub," Daisy said, shaking her head. "You, too, Manny."

"But you love him," Manny said gently, "and he treated you well enough..." she shrugged her shoulders, "relatively speaking, for most of your marriage. If he makes you happy..." she trailed off into silence.

Zeke shifted uncomfortably then said, "I've gotta ask."

The three women refocused their attention on him, raising eyebrows in question.

"What's your husband's name," Zeke asked curiously, "and doesn't he object to just being called Hub?"

To Zeke's confusion, the three women burst out laughing.

Finally, Daisy grinned, and said, "His name is Hubbard. *Percy* Hubbard. The poor man didn't really have a choice."

Zeke slowly grinned. "I guess not," he agreed, and joined in their laughter. His eyes met Manny's and he blinked as another jolt of awareness shot through him. He quickly glanced away, studiously ignoring the sensation.

Things would be back to normal in the morning, he assured himself, and settled in to enjoy the rest of the evening.

Day 89

Manny moaned at the loud knocking on her hotel door. She covered her head with the blanket as Rebecca stumbled out of bed.

"This had better be good," Rebecca growled as she yanked open the door.

"Well, it *is* lunch time," Zeke said cheerfully as he walked into the hotel room.

"Who cares?" Daisy muttered from her place beside Manny, only the top of her tousled blonde head visible from beneath the covers.

"My stomach, for one," Zeke said drily as he opened the curtains. He walked back to the bed, lifted the edge of the blanket and tickled Manny's foot. Manny sat up, shrieking in protest, then quickly covered her eyes.

"Mother of God, it's bright!" she groaned.

Zeke laughed at her, his eyes warm and dancing as he took in her tousled hair and sleep-flushed face. But thankfully, he thought, he felt only an amused affection. Those disconcerting moments of *awareness* he'd experienced the night before were gone.

Like they had never been.

The world was back on its axis, Zeke thought smugly, and Manny was firmly back in the place he'd put her.

He glanced at Daisy, who was still stubbornly hiding beneath the blankets, and then at Rebecca, who had just returned from the bathroom and was now standing with her hands on her hips, mock-glaring at him.

Rebecca looked stunningly beautiful in her silk pajamas, her red hair framing her heart-shaped face. Zeke grinned appreciatively at her.

"Don't give me that come hither look, young man," Rebecca snapped. "I could use another couple hours of beauty sleep."

"Oh, please," Manny groaned, laughing, "like you're not beautiful enough already!"

"Well," Rebecca pouted, "the extra sleep doesn't hurt."

Manny laughed again, threw back the covers and stood with another groan. She closed her eyes, put her hands in the small of her back and arched backwards, stretching, before she straightened the t-shirt and boxer shorts she used as pajamas and sleepily shuffled past Zeke to the bathroom.

"We'll just make Zeke pay for lunch as punishment," she said and grinned at him as she closed the door.

Zeke barely heard her; he was too busy trying to catch his breath and desperately trying not to think how her legs seemed even more beautiful than they had in those shoes; how her ass seemed even curvier and sexier than the way it had looked in that blue dress.

But she was still *just Manny*, he told himself, stunned. She was still a bit too plump, a bit too plain, a bit too dull–Zeke couldn't figure out where these *moments* were coming from–or why.

The only thing he knew for sure was that these moments had to stop. And stop *now*.

She was his Auntie Em–and by God, his Auntie Em she would stay.

Day 91

Manny watched Zeke with a puzzled frown. She wasn't sure what, exactly, was going on in his head. He seemed to flip-flop more quickly between his normal, teasing, slightly aloof self, to darkly brooding, his black eyebrows lowered thunderously over his hazel eyes as he scowled at–as far as she could tell–nothing at all.

It worried her, and as Daisy and Rebecca's week sped to an end, Manny was beginning to wonder if Zeke was going to go back with them. She wondered if his mood changes were because he didn't know how to tell her he wanted to cut his trip short. They were having fun, joking and laughing, but Manny could still feel a lingering tension between her and Zeke, and she didn't like it. She wanted their easy-going relationship back; she didn't want to believe it could be gone forever simply because she'd cut her hair.

If she'd known he'd react like this...

Oh, what? You wouldn't have cut your hair? Really?

Well...I might have waited until I got home.
Seriously.
...maybe.

Harvey huffed a sigh and shook his head. Manny heaved a sigh as well, then looked at him in the bathroom mirror as she finished buttoning her shirt.

It doesn't matter what I might or might not have done; I didn't know, and I did cut my hair. I just...he's been so moody—and tonight's the premiere. I just want all of us to have fun.

And we will. Zeke's moods aren't your responsibility.
...I know.

And you didn't do anything wrong. Even if you were lovers, he'd have no right to dictate what you do or don't do.

I know. I know! I just wish I knew what was bothering him...

Well, when Daisy and Rebecca go back, you can ask him.

If he's still here.
He'll be here.

"Hey—what the hell are you doing in there?" Daisy yelled, pounding on the bathroom door. "There's a red carpet to watch, and Robert Downey Jr. to see! Let's move it!"

Harvey grinned at Manny, his eyes warm. **You heard the lady—get a move on!**

She grinned back.

"Hold your horses—I'm coming!" she called, and opened the bathroom door.

Day 92

"We made eye contact," Daisy insisted, "there was a connection."

"Daisy," Rebecca said, laughing, "there were at least three rows of people in front of us. We barely saw him!"

"But what we saw..." she sighed dreamily.

"Down, girl," Manny grinned, "I think you're actually drooling."

Daisy made a show of wiping her chin. "I think you're right."

Zeke watched them, fascinated.

"All this because you caught a glimpse of Robert Downey Jr.? Really?" he asked skeptically.

"If you were gay, you'd understand," Rebecca sighed dreamily.

Zeke snorted a laugh. "No doubt."

"I never thought I'd ever even be in the same general area as him," Daisy explained, "so, yes, I'm still very excited. I don't care that I had to look over four rows of heads, and all I really saw was a quarter of his profile–it was *still* awesome! I'm so, *so* glad you met Lionel in Vegas, Manny."

Manny nodded fervently. "Me, too."

Zeke ruefully shook his head as the three women began again to chatter excitedly about the red carpet event and the subsequent movie, sounding more like twenty-somethings than forty-somethings. He couldn't wait to write his blog about *this*.

~~~~~

TJ and Leah looked up as the doctor walked into TJ's hospital room.

"Hey, doc," TJ greeted cheerfully.

"Hi, TJ. How are you feeling today?"

TJ shrugged. "Just fine. If you weren't so sure there's something wrong with me, I'd think I was perfectly healthy."

The doctor smiled thinly. "Well, hopefully that means we've caught it early."

"Caught it early?" Leah pounced. "I thought you weren't sure what it was. That makes it sound like–like you *do* know. For sure."

The doctor's smile faded and his face softened sympathetically as he looked from Leah's wide, accusing eyes to TJ's worried ones.

"There's a chance the tumor is benign–but it's a very slim chance. All the test results show me it's cancerous–the only real question is how far along it is. There's no evidence it's anywhere other than the colon–which is a good sign. A very good sign. But–it's still most likely cancer. And that means you may have a tough fight ahead of you."

The doctor hesitated.

"I'm sorry," he said. "I didn't intend to give you false hope."

TJ shook his head, his face drawn and white. "Any false hope was my own fault, doc," TJ said, "not yours."

The doctor pulled up a chair beside the bed. "Well, let me tell you what's going to happen between now and the day after tomorrow, when you'll have your surgery."

TJ tightly gripped Leah's hand and focused his attention on what the doctor was saying.

Day 93

Leah nervously drummed her fingers on her desk. She reached for the phone, then hesitated and pulled back. She drummed her fingers even harder. Faster.

Finally she slapped her palm onto her desk, and grabbed the phone. She hit speed dial and waited.

"Zeke?" she said. "Sorry to wake you–but there's something I have to tell you."

~~~~~

Manny stared at Zeke, sitting beside her on the couch. He leaned forward, his forearms resting on his legs, his hands clasped tightly in front of him.

"When's the surgery?" she asked, her eyes soft with sympathy.

"Tomorrow," he said quietly, staring at his hands.

Manny put a tentative hand on his shoulder, and felt him tense beneath her touch. She swallowed. "Go home."

His head shot up and he blinked at her. "What?"

"Go home," Manny repeated firmly. "Be with your friends; it's where you're most needed. Once you know more, you can always meet me at one of my stops. If you want, of course. And if...if...Well. You know."

"If TJ's okay, you mean."

"Yes."

Zeke stared at her, an unreadable expression on his face. "I think I'll take you up on that," he said slowly.

She frowned, slightly puzzled even as she nodded. "Good."

A faint smile curved his lips. "Thank you."

Manny waved away his thanks. "I just...really hope your friend will be okay."

Zeke's faint smile deepened. He rose to his feet and headed towards the door. "Thank you. I hope so, too."

Manny watched him go, her puzzled frown deepening. "Zeke!"

He paused and turned, his hand on the door handle. He raised his eyebrow in question.

"You—something's been bothering you the last few days. Maybe...maybe this is a chance to take care of whatever it is?"

Zeke's expression didn't change as he considered her words, then he slowly nodded.

"Maybe it is," he agreed. "Maybe it is."

~~~~~

Manny hugged Daisy, then Rebecca.

"This was fun," she said.

"It was," Daisy agreed.

"Call as soon as you get home, no matter the time."

"We will," Rebecca assured her.

They paused, all of them blinking back tears, then they hugged again before Manny turned to Zeke, standing tall, anxious and silent beside them, frowning furiously.

"Take care, Zeke," Manny said quietly. "I'll be hoping for your friend."

He blinked and scowled, then his face softened.

"Thank you," he said. "That...means a lot to me."

She smiled hesitantly, then held out her hand. He stared at it unblinkingly for a long moment before he slowly, almost cautiously, reached out and gently grasped it.

"I'll call you," he said, his voice thick with emotion, before he abruptly dropped her hand and walked away to stand in line to go through the security gates.

Daisy and Rebecca raised their eyebrows, said good-bye once more to Manny, and left to take their own places in line.

Once through security, and with almost two hours to fill, the three of them wandered into one of the licensed restaurants and took their places at the bar.

Zeke ordered whiskey, on the rocks, and ignored the looks Daisy and Rebecca exchanged across him.

"This seems to be more than just worry about your friend," Daisy said carefully once they had their drinks. "Do you have a fear of flying?"

Zeke drained his glass, then shook his head as he viciously crunched an ice cube between his teeth.

"Flying?" he muttered, and called for another drink. "No. But I do have a fear of falling."

EPISODE EIGHT
Day 94

Zeke sat in the darkened hospital room, Leah sleeping in the chair beside him, her head resting on his shoulder. He couldn't sleep. He watched the man in the bed; watched his chest rise and fall in a steady rhythm.

TJ'd had his surgery first thing in the morning, and had come through with flying colours. He'd still been in surgery when Zeke arrived, had been woken briefly by the hospital staff once he was in his room, and had promptly gone back to sleep after seeing and speaking groggily to Leah. He was still sleeping peacefully as evening fell and Zeke and Leah waited.

Zeke sat still, his shoulder and arm numb under the weight of Leah's head. He deliberately kept his mind blank, shying away from any thought of cancer and what that meant for the man sleeping so peacefully on the bed. He deliberately refused to think about what it meant for the woman sleeping on his shoulder. He deliberately refused to think about what it told him about his own mortality. He was here, and TJ had come through the surgery without any issues, and that was enough. For now.

A distant part of his mind wondered where Manny was right now and what she was doing. He reluctantly grinned.

Considering her penchant for picking up misfit toys wherever she went, she was probably already knee deep in people, wherever she was.

His smile faded as he once more focused on watching TJ breathe and waited for the dawn.

Day 95

A nurse quietly bustled into the hospital room and Leah startled awake, sitting up with a snuffling gasp. She blinked hazily at Zeke, frowning, before memory returned and she quickly turned her attention to TJ.

"I'm just going to wake TJ for a moment, and check his incision," the nurse explained kindly. "We'll be getting him out of bed later today, too, but right now we just need to check on him, and then we'll let him go back to sleep."

Leah nodded as the nurse gently roused TJ, who groggily responded to her questions in a dry, raspy voice. She smiled encouragingly and promised him some ice chips, then proceeded to check the machines surrounding him, pull a small blood sample, and make notations on his chart.

"You're looking good, TJ," she said cheerfully. "You came through with flying colours. I'm going to get you those ice chips, and let you talk to your visitors, then you should probably get some more rest. We'll get you out of bed around mid-morning, and the doctor will be by to see you sometime this afternoon."

"Visitors?" TJ rasped and the nurse nodded in Leah and Zeke's direction. He turned his head, frowning, although his face softened when he saw Leah. His eyes widened when he saw Zeke. "Aw, man–" he groaned hoarsely as the nurse bustled out the door.

Zeke smirked. "I couldn't miss this," he said lightly.

"I told Leah not to tell you anything," TJ croaked as the nurse returned. She placed an ice chip in his mouth and put the cup on the table beside his bed then wished them all a good morning and left to continue her rounds.

Zeke smirked, "Yeah, but you're not the brightest bulb in the light socket, so she decided to ignore you." He sobered. "I'm glad she did. The two of you didn't need to go through this alone, you know."

TJ wearily closed his eyes. "Just until we knew for sure," he sighed.

Zeke shook his head.

"We both appreciate you being here, Zeke." Leah said. "Thank you."

"Anytime. And I'm sticking around until we know the prognosis."

"...refuse to have cancer," TJ mumbled sleepily.

Leah snorted. "Yeah, because you have that much power." She turned to Zeke. "We're glad you're here, Zeke. Really." She flashed a smile at TJ. "Maybe you're right—maybe he wouldn't be such a bad dad for our kid after all."

Zeke's eyes snapped to Leah's.

"Say *what*?"

Day 96

Rebecca glanced up as Tris walked into the house.

"Hi, Tris," she called cheerfully. "How was your day?"

"Fine," Tris grunted, walked down the hall into her bedroom and closed the door with a sharp snap.

Rebecca's lips tightened as she rose from the couch. She shook her head as she walked down the hall and knocked on Tris' bedroom door.

"Go away, Gramma," Tris yelled.

Rebecca opened the door, and leaned against the door jamb, her arms tightly crossed.

"Tris, this can't go on," Rebecca said firmly.

Tris sighed dramatically and rolled her eyes.

"*What*, Gramma?" she asked impatiently.

"Your attitude, for one," Rebecca snapped. "You may not like me much, but I am *still* your grandmother!"

A look of guilt flitted across Tris' face. It gave Rebecca

a tiny spark of satisfaction. She didn't think she'd ever seen guilt on Jaime's face.

Then Tris' mouth set in an all-too-familiar stubborn line as she said, "Well, so what? You don't want me here any more than I want to be here! You should send me to be with my mom!"

Rebecca felt her heart squeeze tight.

"Tris—"

"You don't like me! You don't want me! So why should I have to stay where I'm not wanted?"

Rebecca stared at Tris in horror and sorrow.

"Okay," Rebecca said, moving further into the room. She struggled to keep calm, and to not retreat from the confrontation. "Okay," she said more firmly and moved to sit on the bed.

"Get out, Gramma—I don't want you in here."

Rebecca hesitated. "Tris, this can't go on! We need to work this out," she said and sat down on the bed.

"*See?* You won't even let me have my own room! *Get out!*" Tris screamed, and Rebecca flinched at the shrill words, even as she felt a rising tide of anger begin to drown out her guilt.

"This is the first time in your life that I've come into this room without being invited," Rebecca snapped, "and I'll leave once I've had my say. Regardless of what you may think, I *do* want you here. You're my granddaughter and I love you. But I will no longer tolerate your attitude. Right now, Jakob and Janika have free rein to take you anywhere you'd like to go when they're looking after you. I can just as easily take those privileges away. I'm not asking for much, Tris. A civil tone, and coming out of this damn room for more than meals! Perhaps even a 'hi, Gramma, how are you?' once in a while—asked without that sarcastic, contemptuous tone. I don't know how long your parents will be away, and your other grandparents are on the ocean somewhere, so you need to make the best of an unfortunate situation."

Rebecca stared hard at Tris, noticing how her mouth turned down and her bottom lip pouted out.

"And pouting about it isn't going to change anything," Rebecca added firmly. She stood. "Now I'm going to leave your room, just as you...asked. Supper will be ready in an hour."

She very carefully closed the door behind her.

Rebecca returned to the living room, poured herself a small shot of tequila and swiftly tossed it back. She hated confrontations with the people she loved. That wasn't quite true, she admitted as she set the shot glass down and grimaced at the taste and burn of the tequila. The only confrontations she couldn't seem to handle were those with Jaime and now Tris. She could handle the occasional arguments with Manny and Daisy just fine. Then again, she knew Manny and Daisy would never leave her.

She shook her head as she put the tequila away and carried the shot glass into the kitchen to put in the dishwasher. It was time to decide what to make for supper.

Day 97

Zeke winced at the sleepy way Manny answered the phone.

"I'm sorry–I didn't mean to wake you."

"S'okay," she assured him sleepily. "What did the doctors say today?"

"That there's a really good chance they caught the thing early enough that he'll be fine. Maybe won't even need chemo–if he's lucky."

"That's wonderful!"

"Not for sure, yet, though. We'll find out more when he goes back for his six week check-up."

"I'm glad, Zeke. Really, really glad. Cancer is...a horrible way to die."

"Yeah..." He sat in brooding silence for a moment then shook his head. "So, where are you off to next?"

"Memphis, then Nashville."

"Have you made any more new friends since I've been gone?" Zeke teased.

"Only about a hundred and fifty. I'm slowing down," Manny replied and chuckled. Zeke felt the husky sound slide across his nerve endings, and his body tightened. Had her laugh always sounded like that, he wondered, as his stomach filled with slow fireworks, warming him. He shook his head, and ignored the feeling with an effort.

"Seriously," he said, "you've been okay alone? You haven't really been talking to strangers, have you?"

"No more than usual," she assured him. "Besides, talking to strangers is the whole point, remember?"

"Are you at least leaving them behind, or am I going to meet you and find you're now leading a convoy?"

Manny chuckled again. "You'll have to wait and find out for yourself," she teased. "You know how much I like to surprise you."

Zeke chuckled too. He felt the tension lifting from his chest, his shoulders relaxing. When he'd started this trip a little more than three months earlier, he never would have predicted he'd miss Manny's voice and sense of humor and—yes—her new-found penchant for talking to everybody and their dog. He wondered what he'd missed the last few days, what characters she'd met and befriended because—because that was simply what she did.

"Zeke?"

"Yeah—I'm here. Sorry."

"Didn't mean to bore you."

"You didn't—I'm not—" Zeke sighed. "Sorry, Manny. I was thinking of something else."

"Dixie?"

"Wha—*Dixie*? Where did *that* come from?"

"Well, something was bothering you for days before you left, and I've been wondering what it was. I thought...you know, maybe you were thinking of Dixie, and how things ended with her. This could be a chance for you to—to...mend fences. Or something."

"I thought I told you that when I leave, I leave. I don't look back."

"Oh. Well. It was just a thought."

Zeke frowned, his dark brows lowering over his stormy eyes. He wondered what Manny would say or do if he told her he'd been moody because he'd been knocked off-balance by a sudden sexual awareness of *her*. A sexual awareness that still seemed to sneak up on him when he least expected it, as evidenced by his reaction to her laugh.

"Interesting thought," he murmured, then frowned as he realized he *should* tell Dixie about TJ. TJ and Leah hadn't been especially close to her, but they'd liked her, and they'd struck up a casual friendship. Just because Zeke's romantic relationship with her hadn't worked out was no reason to pretend her connection to TJ and Leah had never existed.

As Zeke continued his gentle, undemanding conversation with Manny, he decided he'd go see Dixie in the morning.

Day 98

Zeke rang the doorbell then nervously rubbed his hands on his pants as he waited for the door to open. He was almost amused by the level of surprise on Dixie's face when she recognized him.

"Zeke!" she finally managed. "What—what are you doing here?" She automatically stood aside to let him into the house, and Zeke suspected she didn't even realize what she was doing.

"I'm in town for a few days—thought I'd drop by to—"

"You've been out of town?" she asked sharply.

Zeke chuckled. "I forgot you don't follow my blog. Yeah. I've been on a road trip..."

Zeke trailed off as his attention was caught by a picture on the mantle. It showed Dixie snuggled up to a handsome older man; they both smiled happily at the camera as balloons and streamers drifted around them. Zeke frowned, his eyes beneath his lowered brows drifting slowly across the other pictures on display. They all showed Dixie and the stranger in similar poses at a variety of locations.

He turned and looked thoughtfully at her. "I see you've already replaced me," he said mildly.

Dixie frowned, her eyes narrowing. "Did I ever really *have* you?" she challenged.

Zeke looked at her, feeling suddenly lonely and tired. "Yeah," he replied softly, "yeah, you really did. Anyway, I–I–I didn't come here to hash over what happened between us. I came to tell you TJ's in the hospital. He had surgery four days ago."

Dixie frowned. "Surgery? For what?"

"Colon cancer. They think they caught it in time, but should have a more definitive prognosis when he has his six week checkup."

"Well," Dixie said faintly, "that's a good sign, then, if they can wait that long."

"Yeah," Zeke replied absently. His attention was once again focused on the picture with the balloons and streamers. He peered more closely at it. Behind the happy couple was a banner; a banner that welcomed in the new year. The new year that was still the *current* year.

He stepped back, and heard Dixie's sharp intake of breath.

"I see," he muttered slowly.

"What do you see?" Dixie demanded, and under other circumstances her defiant contempt would have amused him as the last ditch effort to shift the blame onto his shoulders that it was.

He turned and smiled a slightly bitter smile. "That I never actually had *you*, did I?"

Dixie rolled her eyes, her arms crossed tightly in front of her as her eyes darted everywhere but at him.

Zeke forced an insincere smile. "Anyway. I just wanted to tell you about TJ. He's at the Cross if you want to visit."

Zeke brushed past her and headed for the door.

"That's it?" Dixie demanded behind him. "That's all you have to say?"

Zeke stopped and slowly turned to face her. He carefully pondered the question.

"Thanks for kicking me out," he said finally. "It was the best thing you could have done for me."

Dixie threw up her hands. "You—you—you! All about you! Maybe I did it for me!"

Zeke laughed, a harsh bark of sound that betrayed the anger and hurt he was desperately controlling. "Yeah, you did it for yourself—but considering you had this guy for—how long?—while we were still together, I'm not feeling all that bad about getting something out of it. You never trusted me—and now I see why. Were you cheating the whole—you know what? It doesn't matter! It's over and done, and I—stupid me—wanted to do you the courtesy of telling you about TJ. Now—well, I suppose that was all a lie, too."

Dixie shook her head, her arms crossed even more tightly across her stomach. "No, I...I like TJ. And Leah."

"Well, I'm not sure if they're going to like you that much, after this."

Her eyes flew to his. "Why would you tell them?" she demanded angrily.

Zeke laughed harshly. "Why should I continue to shoulder all the blame for the end of our relationship? And why would I lie to them about it?" He shook his head. "They won't throw you out if you visit, but they're not going to be singing your praises, either."

Zeke shook his head and headed for the door again. "Good-bye, Dixie," he said, and gently closed the door behind him.

~~~~~

"Did you go to see her?" Manny asked.

Zeke hesitated.

"You did, didn't you? What happened? How did it go?"

"Yeah, I went to see her–and I'll tell you about it when I see you, okay? Not over the phone."

"Oh." The disappointment in her voice was palpable. "It didn't go well, huh?"

"To say the least. Of course, it could have been worse."

"Oh?"

"I could be talking to you from jail."

Manny laughed. "How can I be sure you're not?"

"I guess you'll just have to trust me."

"I do."

Even though the words were teasing, they set off an explosion in Zeke's chest he wasn't expecting. A mix of pleasure and happiness, and guilt, because he was still writing his blog and still using her journey of self-discovery for his own personal gain. It somehow made him feel...dirty. Not even acknowledging how his own behaviour had doomed his relationships with women, including, yes, Dixie, made him feel as bad as he did right now, sitting here on the phone listening to Manny tease him with her voice husky with sleep, knowing he hadn't told her the whole truth.

Good God, he was getting a *crush* on her, he realized suddenly, stunned. On *Auntie Em*!

"I've got to go," he said abruptly.

"Oh–okay," she said. She sounded startled, but not hurt. "Talk to you later."

"Yeah. Good night."

"Night."

~~~~~

Manny thoughtfully hung up the phone.

That was odd, Harvey mused.

Whatever. Somebody probably walked in.

Manny yawned, snuggled deeper into her blankets and drifted back to sleep.

Day 104

Rebecca absently answered her phone, her attention

focused on the paperwork in front of her.

"Mom?"

Rebecca's head snapped up, paperwork forgotten.

"Jaime!" she said, relief palpable in her voice. "Where—what's going on! It's been weeks!"

"Yeah, don't nag," Jaime sighed.

Rebecca closed her eyes and prayed for patience. "I'm sorry, sweetheart. I've just been worried about you. How are you?"

"I'm fine—and you weren't so worried you didn't go to Los Angeles for a week."

Rebecca pinched the bridge of her nose, her eyes closing in frustration. "Well, I didn't see a point in waiting by the phone on the off-chance you'd decide to call," she snapped. "Besides, I had my cell phone with me if you did. Now, Jaime. What's going on?"

Jaime heaved a long-suffering sigh. "I met my dad. A few weeks ago, actually. He's wonderful! I don't know why you kept me away from him all this time!"

"I didn't—" Rebecca began then stopped herself. There was a hollow feeling in the pit of her stomach. She was never going to convince Jaime about...anything.

"Anyway," Jaime continued as though Rebecca hadn't spoken, "he's asked me to stay for a while longer. He wants me to get to know him; he wants to get to know me. And, when the time is right, he'll introduce me to his family, including his wife and kids."

"Sounds familiar," Rebecca muttered bitterly.

"*Mom. Please.*"

"Hey—weren't you the one who said I was too perfect about all this?"

"Just—let me have this. All right?"

"Fine. Fine." Rebecca took in a deep, calming breath. "I'm happy for you, Jaime. I hope—I hope you find everything you're looking for. When do you want Tris to join you? School's out for a week next month—"

"I haven't told him about Tris yet."

Rebecca paused, blinking. "What? Why?"

"Because this is about me right now," Jaime snapped. "Me and my dad, getting to know each other. I'll tell him about Tris soon—but I want to get to know him first as just *my* dad before I have to share with him anybody else."

Rebecca swallowed all the words she wanted to say, reminding herself that Jaime was a grown woman.

"All right," Rebecca said faintly. "Do you want me to tell Tris to call you when she gets in?"

"No, I'll call her later. Dad's going to be here any minute. He's going to take me out to the old homestead."

The old homestead? Rebecca thought dazedly. There'd been nothing old about it thirty years ago, and 'homestead' was far too simple a word for the sprawling house and land Devon's family had called home. "Okay," she said quietly. "Have fun."

"I will," Jaime said happily and ended the call.

~~~~~

Rebecca growled, "How I managed to raise such a self-centred child..."

Manny said weakly, "She's...just...trying to discover who she is. Connect with that part of her heritage she's never known."

Rebecca snorted. "That doesn't bother me. But to not tell her new family about Tris? Really? That I don't understand."

"I'm sorry, Rebecca. I wish I knew what to say, but—I don't. This is one of the reasons why I never wanted children—trying to understand their motivations after you've done your best to raise them."

Rebecca laughed, but there was no humour in it. "I used to envy you, you know."

"Envy *me*?" Manny blurted. "What on earth for?"

"Not just you—you and Daisy. Because you were young and having fun while I was tied down with a child. I—I hate to admit it, but I resented Jaime on more than one occasion. When you and Daisy were going out with your college buds, drinking all night, dancing..." Rebecca stared off into space, her lips twisted ruefully. "Playing with boys–"

"That would have been Daisy," Manny objected.

Rebecca huffed a laugh. "Didn't matter which one of you it was–it wasn't me. One stupid mistake and I paid with my youth. Maybe–maybe that's why Jaime is the way she is. She picked up on that...envy and resentment when she was a baby and never forgot it."

Manny decided to ignore that last thought for the moment, but made a mental note to make sure Daisy called Rebecca that night.

"I always thought you enjoyed your life?" Manny said instead.

"I did. Eventually. But you know how hard those first few years were–how hard your parents tried to get me to stop my self-destructive behaviour right after Jaime was born. After they died, well, it took the wind out of my sails." Rebecca bit her lip as she realized what she'd said, and who she was talking to. "Out of all of our sails," she amended, "and when you and Daisy came back to the land of the living and started going out and making other friends–I felt...left out. You know. The only one with a kid at that age, and working, and I couldn't play as much as you guys could." She shook her head.

"I'm sorry," Manny said softly.

"It's nobody's fault–well, except my own, I suppose." Rebecca laughed slightly. "I did a lot of things that first year or so after Jaime was born. A lot of things...I'm not very proud about. I've done a lot of things since. I've been...quite sexually active in my time. But I've never fallen in love, and I've never allowed any of my lovers to meet Jaime or Tris, and the men have been...you know, just as anxious to keep things light and–and–on the surface, you know what I mean?"

"Yes."

"And now there's Jackson." Rebecca heaved a heavy

sigh. "He wants...he wants a real relationship! He's in love and I just don't know how to deal with that."

"At least he's in love with you."

Rebecca barked out a sharp laugh. "That's the bad part," she said. "He's got young kids—a little older than Tris—and I just...I just don't want to deal with kids anymore. Especially not when I look at Jaime and realize just how much I must have sucked as a mother."

"You didn't—and don't—suck as a mother," Manny replied firmly. "You can't be blamed for Jaime losing her mind."

Rebecca shrugged, and blinked back tears. "Maybe I should have told her more about her father. Tried to find him when she was a teenager and she started asking questions, asking to meet him. Maybe I should have tried to forge a relationship later on with his parents."

"And yours?"

Rebecca laughed bitterly. "You know my father—he'd never change his mind."

"It's been thirty years, Rebecca. Maybe—"

"Enough." Her cold tones left no room for debate. "Besides," Rebecca continued after a moment of tense silence, "Jaime isn't interested in my side of the family. She's never once asked about my parents. She's only interested in her father and his family."

"Does she know your parents are still alive?"

"She's been in our home town for months. She has to know by now." Rebecca snorted a bitter laugh. "Just something else for her to be angry about."

"Rebecca..." Manny hesitated.

Rebecca frowned before realization dawned. "No."

"Maybe—"

"No. No, no, no! I'm not going back there! I'm not going to let them take another shot at me!"

"You're not sixteen anymore! You're a beautiful, successful woman who raised her daughter on her own. You have a beautiful granddaughter—friends—a career—a handsome, successful man—a life! You're strong and a survivor, and there's nothing they can do to you anymore! And after thirty years—maybe they're ready to admit their mistake. With Jaime wandering around with her dad, maybe they even feel some regret over everything they threw away."

Rebecca pressed her lips tightly together. "It's not worth it. They threw me out. Told me never to darken their door again. Jesus, Manny—they would cross the street when they saw me coming! Your own parents tried to make them see reason, and they refused."

"I'm not saying you should forget what they did," Manny said softly. "But it's been thirty years. Maybe it's time to *forgive*."

"Yeah? What for?"

"So you can feel like you deserve what Jackson's offering you. If you love him—"

"I never said I loved him. I said he loved me."

Manny hesitated, trying to decide how to bridge the suddenly tense silence between them. "Okay. Okay. Well. I...guess I'll...get something to eat..."

"You do that," Rebecca said coldly, and disconnected the call.

~~~~~

Rebecca knocked on Tris' door and waited for the usual 'go away'. To her surprise, Tris grudgingly told her to come in.

She cautiously entered the bedroom then gingerly sat on the edge of the bed while Tris studiously focused on the homework she had propped up on her lap.

"I spoke with your mother today," Rebecca said.

"I know," Tris said coldly, but Rebecca could see her eyelids fluttering rapidly.

"She's not planning on coming back for...a while."

"I know," Tris repeated, only this time she couldn't hide the tremble in her voice.

Rebecca sat very still, her only movement the slow rub

253

of her trembling hands down her thighs.

"I know this hasn't been...good for you," Rebecca said softly, her eyes on her hands rather than her granddaughter. "I know you don't like me very much, and I...don't know how to change that. I also know I haven't been the most...affectionate, or—or nurturing of grandmothers, either. But that's something I *can* change."

"You don't have to," Tris said in a tiny voice. "You're not the only one who doesn't want me. Mom and Dad don't want me with *them*. Gran and Pappy don't want me either—"

"Now, you know none of that is true," Rebecca said firmly. "I've told you I do want you here. Your parents love you; they're just...going through some tough times right now. And as for Gran and Pappy—we just don't know where they are, or how to get in touch with them."

"We could if it was an emergency," Tris muttered.

"Yes. But is this really an emergency? Whether you like me or not, and whether you believe it or not, you *do* have a home here. I *do* want you here. You are my daughter's daughter. My blood. My family. And I love you. Very much."

"But you don't like me very much, either," Tris challenged.

"Love for your family is automatic, Tris. *Liking*, though, is something that's earned, and it may never happen. I think...we could both grow to like each other, if we stopped..."

Rebecca stared at her hands then glanced over at Tris. Tris had stopped pretending to focus on her homework and was staring at her. Her eyes were red-rimmed and vulnerable, the dark chocolate brown in sharp contrast to her straw-coloured hair. Her father's hair; her mother's face; her grandfather's eyes, Rebecca thought, and her heart twisted with love and regret.

"If we stopped acting like enemies, maybe we wouldn't *be* enemies," Rebecca continued softly.

Tris blinked and looked down, her hair falling in soft curtains to hide her face.

"I'm never going to be the kind of mom you see on TV or in old movies," Rebecca said quietly. "I'm never going to be that kind of grandmother, either. I have a job, and I have a lo—life. But how about this? I'll make sure I'm home when you get home from school. We'll eat supper together—at the table—and we'll spend an hour after supper together. No TVs, no phones, no computers, no one else. Just us. We can talk, or play cards, or...we can stare at everything but each other."

She hesitantly patted Tris' knee.

"We may never learn to like each other," she added softly, "but we have to start somewhere. Okay?" She looked steadily at Tris. "So, what do you say? Do we have a deal?"

Tris hesitated, then nodded and gave her a fleeting smile, and for the first time, Rebecca felt a small sliver of hope.

Day 107

A few days after TJ was comfortably ensconced back in his own bed in his own home, Zeke finally asked the question that had lain dormant in the back of his mind: what had Leah meant by saying he'd be a good father for their baby after all?

Leah and TJ shared rueful and somewhat guilty looks, then explained their initial plans for trying to have a baby before the doctors had found the tumor, including their discussion of Zeke as a potential donor if their other options failed. Zeke listened carefully, his brows lowered darkly over his disbelieving hazel eyes.

They stared at him with wide-eyed trepidation once they finished their story.

"So..." Zeke finally said slowly, "you're holding me in reserve? So to speak."

"If you're willing, of course," TJ said. "If we have to

use a donor, we'd like him to be someone we know. Someone we trust. But it's a big step that stretches the bounds of friendship, and if you don't feel comfortable with it, you can always say no. I mean, we get why you'd refuse."

Zeke nodded, frowning as he tried to wrap his head around fathering a child for his best friend, the brother of his heart if not his blood.

"There's lots of time to think about it," Leah assured him. "We're not going to pursue anything until we know what's going on with TJ, and then it's only after we've exhausted all possibilities of him being the father."

She frowned as her cell phone vibrated in her hand. She glanced at it, sent it to voice mail, and gave TJ a smile. "TJ's still Plan A."

Zeke frowned. "I thought he couldn't–that he didn't have enough–"

"All you need is one," TJ grinned. "We thought of you for Plan B–if you agree."

Zeke hesitated.

"You don't need to decide anything right now," TJ assured him again.

Zeke's frown deepened as he had a sudden flash of Manny telling him about what happened after her parents had died; about Daisy and Rebecca and Jaime; about family and friends. He refocused on TJ.

"I would do anything for you, TJ," he said firmly, "you know that. If you need me to do this, then I will. You just let me know what I have to do and we'll work it out."

"Assuming, of course, that *your* sperm count is normal," Leah said briskly, frowning as her phone vibrated; she once again sent it to voice mail.

"Look at me," Zeke teased, "could there possibly be any doubt?"

Leah rolled her eyes. "I'm sure you impregnate women just by looking at them," she assured him drily.

"God, I hope not," Zeke groaned. "I've looked at a lot

of women. It could make things very awkward once all those kids are old enough to date."

Leah laughed, shaking her head, then cursed as her phone vibrated yet again.

"I'd better check in with the office," she sighed, "that's the third time they've called. I'm going downstairs to the study, in case I need the computer." She dropped a quick kiss on TJ's lips. "Please don't plot revolution while I'm gone."

"I can barely get out of bed without help!" TJ protested.

"Maybe," Leah said as she walked towards the door, "but you do have Zeke right now to do your bidding."

"Hey!"

"*You're* the one who called him!" TJ called after her. She airily waved away his comment as she left the room.

TJ turned to Zeke, the special smile he seemed to save only for Leah curving his lips.

"How'd you know?" Zeke blurted.

TJ blinked. "That she called you? You told me, remember?"

"What? No! How did you know you could trust her? How did you know it was safe to love her?"

TJ frowned as he took in the look in Zeke's eyes.

"I didn't," TJ said finally, gently, "but I couldn't live with the thought of not even trying with her. Besides, who says love is safe? It *isn't* safe—it's hard work, and a daily decision."

Zeke stared unblinkingly at him.

"...and unlike what whatshisname said, love is all about saying you're sorry," TJ added.

Zeke frowned. "Ryan O'Neal?"

"I was actually thinking about the guy who wrote the book."

"You read the book?"

"You saw the movie?"

They were still laughing, TJ's interspersed with small

yelps of pain, when Leah burst back into the bedroom, flushed and wild-eyed.

"Our servers are overloading!" she blurted.

"Say what?" TJ asked, still grinning.

Leah shook her head, waving her hands excitedly. "Someone—we're still checking—profiled the site sometime, probably late in the day, yesterday—specifically your blog, Zeke. We've had over half-a-million hits since midnight! And they're still coming!" She rushed to Zeke, grabbed his shoulders, and excitedly shook him. "We've gone viral!" she cried, then threw her arms around him in a bone-crushing hug.

Zeke grunted, staggering under the onslaught, as TJ pulled himself up in the bed and said, "That's wonder—ow..."

Leah spun and pointed a finger at him. "You. Be careful. Make sure Zeke helps you out of bed—"

"The nurse said—"

"I don't give a shit what the nurse said—you're still sore and I don't want you pulling your incision. I've got to get to the office; make some emergency purchases—" she spun back to Zeke. "I knew that blog was going to put us on the map!" She spun towards TJ, and dropped a quick, hard kiss on his lips. "I've got to go—" she spun again and rushed out the door.

TJ and Zeke blinked in the sudden shock of silence.

"Hurricane Leah," Zeke murmured softly.

"Yeah..." TJ breathed.

"Viral, huh?"

"Yeah. Congratulations."

"Yeah. Thanks."

"You don't sound too happy about it," TJ said shrewdly.

Zeke sighed. "I was hoping to stay home even after you were back on your feet."

TJ stared. "You were? Why? I thought you were having a good time?"

Zeke sighed again. "It's complicated."

"Well, let's get me out of this bed and down to the living room, and you can tell me all about it."

"Yeah," Zeke said, moving to help him, "yeah, I think that might help."

~~~~~

Leah sat behind her desk and listened to Zeke's carefully worded explanation with a raised eyebrow and, at some points, an amused smirk.

"I think it would be best for everyone if I were to make some excuse to her, and cut this trip short," Zeke finished, leaning back in his chair.

"Why?" Leah asked bluntly.

"I just told you why."

"No. You gave me what you thought would be an acceptable reason why. Now give me the real reason."

Zeke huffed out an exasperated breath. "Have you been talking to TJ?"

"TJ isn't your only friend, you know. I can tell when you're trying to hide something from me."

Zeke glowered at her. "I think I'm falling in love with her," he grated out.

Leah burst out laughing. "With *Manny?*" Her eyes widened as she took in his expression. "Holy shit, you're serious."

"Yeah, I'm serious. And this latest fiasco with Dixie just reminded me why I don't believe in love in the first place."

Leah frowned. "Why do you think you're falling in love with her, then? Especially if you don't believe in it?"

"Because I don't know what else to call it! I care about her feelings—I'm even feeling guilty about the last few blogs, since I wrote them when I was really pissed at her, and they're particularly cruel and she doesn't deserve that. And now the fucking thing has gone viral—how long before she finds out about it from one of the thousand-and-one Misfit Toys she's picked up along the way? I don't want her hurt! And then—in L.A.—she had on this *dress*, and these *shoes*, and I thought it was just because she took me by surprise, but then she was wearing those *boxers* and she was still sexy, only she's not—not really—she's still just a middle-aged, plain, dumpy woman only now she also has an ass that just won't quit!"

Zeke paused, out of breath, and glared at Leah. She stared back at him, her eyes wide and her mouth hanging open before she closed it with a snap.

"So, this is why you think you're falling in love with her," Leah said, "instead of maybe just falling in lust with her? Which—sorry, Zeke—that's what it sounds like."

"It's more than lust! Or..." he paused, thinking. "I mean, I wouldn't even call it *lust*, exactly. It's just...she's...*nice*. And she's smart, and funny, and she—she attracts people, because she makes them feel welcomed and accepted and *acceptable*, and I don't think she even realizes what she's doing because she always seems surprised that people want to keep in touch with her after we move on. And—I like her."

Leah shrugged and shook her head with a laugh. "I'm sorry, but I think you're blowing everything way out of proportion. Of course you're fond of her—you've spent the last three months—more—spending almost every single day with her. That doesn't mean you're getting a crush on her—not a *crush* crush—"

"A crush crush? I can see you make your living with the written word."

"Oh, ha ha, funny man. You know what I'm talking about. You *like* her—you may even—as you think—love her a little bit. That doesn't mean you're *in* love with her—and in fact you probably aren't." Leah leaned forward with a serious expression. "Zeke, this is what's known as friendship. You just happen to be feeling this friendship with a member of the opposite sex."

"I've been friends with women before, Leah."

"Oh, yeah? Besides me, name one other female friend

you have—or had. A *real* one."

Zeke opened his mouth—and hesitated. He closed his mouth and frowned, thinking.

"Hah! Knew it! No wonder you're freaking out!" Leah smiled fondly at him. "You're just making a friend, Zeke. Nothing to be afraid of."

Zeke rolled his eyes. "I'm not sure if you're helping or not," he said sarcastically, "and I certainly don't remember suddenly becoming sexually aware of you!"

Now it was Leah's turn to roll her eyes. "You thought I was sexy from the beginning, moron. It didn't come as a surprise to you!"

"But that's not what I'm talking about!"

"Of course it is! The only difference is you had convinced yourself that Manny was this...well, non-entity. Rather, this non-sexual entity. Which—seriously, Zeke—was pretty naïve of you. Anyway, you're suddenly seeing her as she really is, not as you want her to be."

Zeke's frown deepened as he shifted uncomfortably in his chair. "So, what are you saying?"

Leah shrugged, leaning back. "You're not falling in love, okay? Don't worry about it."

Zeke's frown didn't ease as he struggled for a long moment to determine what to say next. "If I go back, I want to tell her the truth about me. About the blog."

"Why?"

"Because I feel like a fraud! She's been nothing but honest with me, and I'm...I'm travelling with her under false pretenses. Even if the blog hadn't gone viral, she deserves the truth."

"No."

Zeke blinked. "No, she doesn't deserve the truth?"

"No, I mean, yes, of course she deserves the truth—but not until the trip is over." Leah leaned forward again, her eyes intent on his. "Zeke, your blog readership is going through the roof. The *roof!* People are loving the story of Manny's mid-life crisis and your reactions to it. You can't pull the plug now! They want to know how the story's going to end! And if she knows who you are and what you're doing, you know things are going to change. She's not going to share as much with you, or be as honest and open with you. You need to keep her in the dark until the trip is over. Your readers are absolutely dying—"

She stopped abruptly, blinking rapidly, and Zeke knew she'd been forcefully reminded of TJ and his health crisis. She shook her head.

"Sorry—your readers are absolutely salivating to find out what happens next. Who she's going to meet—what she's going to do—and how you're going to react to it." Leah cocked her head to one side and considered him thoughtfully. "You know all this. You keep up with the comments—you've read a lot of this latest onslaught of commentary."

"I do know." He sighed and leaned back in his chair, stretching his long legs out in front of him. "She's going to be really hurt when I tell her the truth."

"Zeke," Leah reminded him gently, "you'll never have to see her again when the trip is over."

"So much for friendship," he snapped.

Leah shrugged. "Let's be honest, here. You've been in an unusually intense situation with her. When you're both back in the real world maybe your friendship will last. Maybe it won't."

Zeke glared but couldn't argue against her logic. Besides, he also knew what she didn't say: based on his past history, his friendship with Manny *wouldn't* last.

The thought saddened him even though he couldn't dispute the truth of it.

"Where are you supposed to meet her?" Leah asked.

"We haven't made any firm plans yet," Zeke sighed. "She's heading to some obscure park in the middle of nowhere this week. She heard about it from some guy she met in Nashville."

"Well, things are pretty stable with TJ right now. I'll

talk to him tonight, but I think you can meet her there."
She grinned at him. "We need even more blogs, more
often. We have a huge audience to keep entertained now."

Zeke sighed and reluctantly nodded.

Day 108

Manny pulled into the main entrance to the
campground. She could see signs pointing the way to
campsites, but she also saw several cabins nestled in the
trees around an open, well-maintained common area.
Manny briefly considered camping in the van, but the
thought of the possibility of a private shower—and not
having to empty out the van's toilet—made her mind up for
her.

She pulled up to the cabin that had an 'Office' sign in
the window. She walked in and glanced around, brushing
her hair out of her face. Even now she still found it strange
to have short hair.

A young man in a park ranger uniform came out of the
back room and came to a stop behind the front desk.

Whoa.

I'll say.

The young man gave her a slow, sexy grin. He was
blonde, broad-shouldered, lean and muscled, and he
looked to be about twenty-five.

"May I help you?" he asked in a low, husky purr of a
voice, and Manny's eyes widened even more.

Guh.

**Whoa. Those are an awful lot of hormones all of a
sudden.**

Guh-uh.

Well...shit.

EPISODE NINE
Day 109

Manny dreamily brushed her teeth and revelled in her memories of the day. Brett–the blonde park ranger who'd been at the front desk when she arrived–had taken her for a hike, teasing and flirting the entire time. Manny learned he was older than he looked–thirty. She also learned that he loved his job, was very good at it, and he especially loved the women he met during the season. The way he looked at her, casually brushing his hand against her arm or shoulder or back, told her he'd definitely love to get to know her better, too.

You do know it's because you're the only woman here right now, Harvey said drily.

Manny rolled her eyes as she rinsed her mouth and toothbrush.

Uh, yeah. I'm not an idiot.

She glanced at Harvey, looking as perfectly handsome as ever in his boxers and t-shirt.

Should I be jealous?

Considering you're a figment of my imagination, I'd say no. Especially since I'd be jealous of...myself?

Whatever. You're awfully twitter-pated. Don't do anything you might regret.

What's this? You're the one who's usually pushing me to do the things I end up regretting!

That may be. But Zeke isn't here to watch out for you–

Oh, please! Since when has Zeke been watching out for me? He's the one who keeps ditching me whenever a good-looking woman looks at him sideways. Besides, do you really think I'd tell Zeke about this if he were here? He gets grossed out at the thought of me getting naked when I shower. He'd probably puke if he thought I might actually have sex with somebody! Somebody real, I mean. No offense.

None taken.

Manny sighed as she pulled back the covers and crawled into bed beside Harvey.

Besides, it's not like anything's going to happen anyway.

No?

No. Like you said, I'm the only woman here right now, and he's just killing time. This is all very nice, but I'm really not stupid enough to think he's overwhelmed with lust for me.

Don't sell yourself short. You're pretty cute...for your age. You're not too fat and in the dark, he'll never notice the wrinkles.

Manny snorted pained laughter, rubbing her face. *My ego is overwhelming. Anyway, it doesn't matter. I'm sure a prettier and/or younger woman will arrive tomorrow and that will be the end of it. But man,* she added wistfully, *it's been fun while it lasted.*

Day 110

But a younger or prettier woman never arrived, and Brett spent the day with Manny, showing her an obscure trail and hiking with her for most of the day. As he walked her back to her cabin, he smoothly asked her to dinner, and even Manny, as rusty as she was, was left in no doubt

265

he didn't just have food in mind.

She stared at him like he had a third eye.

"I'm sorry?" she blurted.

Dear God, don't look behind you!

She looked behind her, positive he was talking to somebody else.

Harvey groaned and put his hand over his eyes as Brett said, "I asked if you'd like to have dinner with me."

She blinked owlishly.

"Um...okay," she said. "Where?"

"How about my place?" Brett leaned closer. "I make a spaghetti sauce that's positively sinful," he practically purred in her ear.

She shivered, both at his tone and the feel of his breath against her skin.

Harvey rolled his eyes.

"That sounds...nice," Manny said, her voice faint.

"Good," Brett said, straightening. "I'll expect you at seven?"

"Okay," she nodded, like a puppet on a string.

Don't drink anything he pours you, Harvey warned.

Oh, please!

That boy's on the make—and you need to be <u>careful</u>. Zeke's not here to come looking for you.

You don't think I know that? I'm horny, not stupid! Come on—Brett seems harmless enough, and <u>look</u> at him! The last time a guy that good-looking gave me that kind of come-hither look was...what? Ten years ago? More?

Yeah...well...just be careful.

I'll be careful.

~~~~~

Manny took a deep breath and knocked on Brett's door at seven on the dot. She wiped her hands nervously on the seat of her jeans and hoped she didn't look as wide-eyed excited as she felt.

Or as terrified.

<u>You</u> can stay outside, she said to Harvey.

Where you go—I go.
Not this time.

She smiled nervously as Brett opened the door with a knowing, confident grin. For a moment, Manny felt like turning tail and running, and not stopping until she was safely behind the locked door of her cabin.

Then she straightened her shoulders, smiled and stepped over the threshold.

~~~~~

Brett handed her a glass of wine and settled on the couch beside her.

"Relax," he coaxed. "I don't bite—unless I'm asked to, of course."

He winked.

Manny was glad she'd banished Harvey for the duration.

She took the offered wine and took a small sip. She'd relaxed during dinner—the spaghetti sauce really was almost sinful—but she'd tensed up again when they moved to the couch in front of the fireplace.

Brett deliberately took her wine glass and placed it on the coffee table. Then he put an arm around her. Her entire body stiffened in a combination of terror and anticipation. As he smiled at her, she deliberately ignored the fleeting disappointment that he was so...well, smarmy—followed by the thought he was at least a *gorgeous* smarmy.

Brett leaned forward, angling his head as he lowered his mouth towards hers.

Manny instinctively turned her face away and blurted, "I'm no good at this."

Brett leaned back, blinking at her in surprise. He searched her eyes and face, a look of concern flitting across his features. It was probably the most honest expression she'd seen on his face since she'd met him.

"That's okay," he said soothingly, "I am."

Brett leaned forward again, and this time Manny forced herself to allow him to kiss her. She sat, rigid and nervous and awkward beneath his lips, and tried to relax. She opened her mouth for him, tentatively kissed him back and stroked her tongue over his as he explored her mouth.

Brett nibbled gently at her lips as he said, "See? That wasn't so bad."

She stared at him, her eyes huge. "No," she murmured slowly, shaking her head, "no, it wasn't."

Manny tensed as Brett once more pressed his lips gently but confidently against hers, her muscles tight and stiff as he gathered her closer.

"Relax," he murmured, his voice soft as velvet, luring her into its depths.

She forced herself to stay still, but gasped sharply as he skimmed a firmly possessive hand down her bare arm then flinched as he moved his mouth from her lips to her neck and began to suckle.

"Yeah, baby—you like that?" he asked hoarsely then began to kiss, lick and suckle on her neck in earnest.

She *tried.*

She tried to relax, to enjoy the touch of his hands, the feel of his mouth, the heat of his body.

But she'd been untouched for too long. Her skin was too sensitive; his fingers and lips leaving trails of sharp, biting electric sparks that shocked rather than aroused and only made her even more tense.

In her dim memories of sex, she knew she'd enjoyed it. Perhaps not to the extent described by every romance novel she'd ever read, but she'd enjoyed it well enough. But right now...right now, she was shaking in a mixture of arousal and—dear God, she was *still* terrified. She couldn't make herself relax, she couldn't stop shaking, and Brett just kept *talking*, trying to encourage her, she supposed.

Except he never once used her name, and kept calling her babe and baby.

Out of all the pet names he could have chosen, she thought in growing panic and irritation, he had to choose that one.

Harvey was obstinately silent, probably sulking somewhere.

Manny tried to refocus, to shut off her mind, to stop shaking, to relax, to enjoy the moment, to let nature take its course, to enjoy being kissed and caressed, to be grateful for the fact that *somebody* was attracted enough to want to have sex with her, no matter the reasons. She shook from warring emotions and spiralling thoughts.

She could do this, she told herself grimly. She could *do* this—

Then Brett burrowed a hand beneath her shirt and cupped her breast, and she shoved him away without thinking.

"I can't—I can't do this," she blurted desperately.

Brett frowned, blinking, confused. "What? Why?"

"Because—because—because I just can't!" Manny wailed, almost in tears. "I'm so, so sorry! I didn't mean—I thought—but this is just—"

Brett's eyes widened. "It's okay, it's okay," he hastened to assure her as he awkwardly patted the back of her hand, "I'm sorry, too. I thought you wanted this as much as I did."

Brett's look of confused consternation would have been funny under other circumstances, Manny thought as she sniffed tearfully. Her shoulders slumped in defeat, and she realized there was no way she could begin to explain this when she didn't fully understand it herself.

"You should probably go," she muttered, unable to meet his eyes.

"This is my cabin," Brett reminded her blankly.

Her eyes flew to his, her face turning bright red. She yanked her hand out of his.

"Oh! Oh, right. Right. Then...I should go."

She surged to her feet, fumbling for her purse and scrambling to put on her shoes, her entire body burning fiercely with humiliation. Her eyes kept sliding past him, never quite landing on his face.

Brett leaned against the wall by the door and watched her, his arms tightly crossed, as she finally got her shoes on and straightened. She forced herself to meet his eyes.

"I'm sorry," she said again. "I should have known better."

"You win some, you lose some," Brett shrugged ruefully. "I'll see you around."

She nodded jerkily, muttered, "Good-night," and bolted.

Day 111

Manny paced her room, fidgeting, her hands twisting together as she shook her head.

"Stupid, stupid, stupid," she muttered with each step.

She was flushed with humiliation and self-loathing, her heart beating rapidly, breath coming more quickly.

She wrung her hands and thought she needed to leave without seeing Brett again. Of course, she thought bitterly, the sick heat of embarrassment suffusing her again, that wouldn't be difficult. Brett was already pursuing two twenty-somethings who had arrived that morning before Manny had gathered enough courage to creep out of her cabin. Manny had expected him to not have time for her, especially when she'd noticed the two young women in one of the neighbouring cabins, but it was the way he'd looked right through her that had sent her scurrying back to her cabin, calling herself every name she could think of.

The sudden rapid knocking on her door made her jump and give an involuntary yelp. She pressed a hand to her chest and tried to catch her breath. She walked cautiously to the door, her eyes wide, wondering who could be there, until she remembered that she'd promised the couple two cabins over that she'd go hiking with them today.

Manny plastered a smile on her face as she opened the door, then gaped at a grinning Zeke.

His grin faltered as he took in the look on her face. He

gently urged her back into the cabin and stared searchingly at her. She knew she was blushing furiously and began to curse herself even more intensely.

Calm down! Harvey commanded. **You haven't done anything wrong!**

It's embarrassing! No, <u>humiliating</u>! That's what it is!

You made out with a guy who's now ignoring you for somebody younger and prettier–

Thanks.

You still didn't do anything <u>wrong</u>!

"Manny?" Zeke demanded sharply. "What's the matter? What's wro–Oh. My. God! Is that a *hickey* on your neck?"

Manny winced as his voice rose in both volume and pitch, then stared at him in horror as his words sunk in.

"What?" she screeched and rushed to the nearest mirror. "Shit!" How on earth had she managed to shower and dress without noticing *that*?

Zeke gaped at her, and in the corner Harvey was watching, his arms crossed, an unholy grin on his face.

This ought to be good, he chortled.

Oh, sweet Jesus, <u>shut up</u>!

Zeke's expression changed from shocked and appalled, to concerned, to terrified–to enraged.

"Did somebody–? Who was it? Where is he? I'll *murder* the son-of-a-bitch!"

Manny gaped at him again.

What?

"What? *No!* No, no–he didn't do anything I didn't allow him to do."

Now it was Zeke's turn to gape at her. When he realized she was telling the truth he shut his jaw with an audible snap.

"Jesus, Manny! I've only been gone–what? Two weeks? And you're off getting laid the first time I leave you alone?"

What! Harvey yelled.

"What?" Manny screeched again.

Zeke's expression flashed regret before his face hardened again.

"You heard me! What kind of woman are you?"

What? Harvey howled.

"*What?*" Manny screeched for the third time. "Are you calling me a *slut? You?*"

"What the fuck do you mean by that?" Zeke snarled.

"I mean," Manny growled, stalking towards him, "I *mean* it wasn't *me* who buggered off in San Francisco or Las Vegas *or* Ringo! And you have the gall–the *gall*–to *judge* me?"

By this point, she was poking him in the chest with every word and had him backed up against the wall as she rose onto her toes to yell in his face.

They glared at each other.

"I only slept with Babe," Zeke snapped.

Manny frowned, blinking. She shook her head in confusion, momentarily distracted from her justifiable rage.

"What?" she finally managed.

"Luciana and I just hung out. Alicia was a cover because I needed to work on–something, and–and I needed a break from your sightseeing. Babe's the only one I actually slept with."

Manny, still frowning furiously, eased down off her toes, one hand unconsciously on Zeke's chest in order to keep her balance.

"Well, I didn't have sex with Brett," she finally said. "I chickened out."

Zeke blinked.

"Oh," he said.

"Yeah. Oh," Manny agreed and stepped away from him.

"So–who is this...Brett guy? And where is he now?"

Manny shrugged. "He's the park ranger here, and he's moved on to the two twenty-year-olds who arrived this morning." She turned away. "No harm done," she added flatly.

"Except to us," Zeke said.

Manny bowed her head, but kept her back turned. "That's not Brett's fault, is it?" she said coldly.

Zeke hissed in a sharp breath. "No," he admitted. "No, it isn't. Would it help if I told you I–I'm sorry?"

"You're always sorry, Zeke," Manny sighed.

Zeke shifted uncomfortably. "That's because I'm always wrong," he said softly. "Do you want me to go back home?"

Manny hesitated. "I'll let you know," she muttered.

~~~~~

"Are you...okay?" Daisy asked delicately.

"Yeah, I'm fine," Manny sighed dully. "I just have to accept the fact that I'm never going to have sex again."

"Manny–"

"If I'd known that was all I was going to get, I would have paid more attention."

Daisy tried to stifle her chuckle. "Don't give up. You never know what might happen tomorrow. You'll meet that guy and it'll just...happen."

"If I couldn't let it happen with Brett, then it ain't ever gonna happen," Manny replied. "Young–cute as the day is long–built like a brick shithouse and willing to fuck me like a rabbit."

Daisy paused, considering. "...rapidly?" she finally asked.

"I was thinking repeatedly."

"Which then translates to rapidly. Ooh, I think you made the right decision there, Manny."

Manny opened and closed her mouth several times, a small squeaking noise coming out whenever she tried to speak.

"Quality, baby, not quantity!" Daisy hooted.

Manny shuddered. "Ugh! Don't call me baby! Brett was calling me that every five seconds."

"So?"

"It felt like something out of a porno...and like he couldn't remember my name." She shuddered again.

"Okay–first of all, just how many pornos have you seen? And now I know you *definitely* made the right choice!"

"Thanks," Manny replied drily. "Zeke agrees with you, by the way."

"Zeke?" Daisy asked sharply.

"Yeah–he arrived this morning. God knows when he left home in order to get here that early."

"Good Lord. How–you *told* him?"

"Not–I wasn't going to, but I have this huge-ass hickey on my neck. Zeke assumed the worst, so I had to tell him the truth, otherwise I think we'd be hiding body parts in the woods right now."

"Awww. That's actually rather sweet!"

"Sure. Until he accused me of being a slut."

"Say *what* now?"

Manny winced as she jerked the phone away from her ear, then carefully replaced it.

"I set him straight pretty damn fast, let me tell you! He won't be making that mistake again!"

"I should hope not!"

"Anyway. Brett's already putting the moves on a couple of twenty-year-olds, and I'm...really looking forward to leaving for our next destination. This...everything is just so stupid on so many levels."

"Could have been worse," Daisy said brightly.

"How?"

"You and Zeke could be hiding body parts in the woods."

"True."

Daisy's voice became very serious. "Brett could have reacted badly to you suddenly putting on the brakes. *Very* badly."

"I know," Manny said soberly. "I'm always grateful for

the kindness of most strangers."

"Just—be careful. Okay?"

"I will. Now I just have to decide if I'm going to forgive Zeke. Again."

Daisy hummed.

"What?" Manny demanded.

"I'd prefer it if you did forgive him. Or at least decide to tolerate him for a while longer. He may be a moronic asshole, but—and I realize this sounds strange—I trust him. To keep you safe, I mean."

"Yeah, when he decides to stick around," Manny said bitterly.

"Well, maybe it's time for you to set down different ground rules. Tell that if you let him stay on the trip, he at least tries to think before he speaks. Give him royal shit for his double standards, and—I don't know—say he can't get laid if you don't get laid."

Manny was once more reduced to squeaking noises.

When Daisy finally stopped laughing she said, "And dear God, tell me what he says! Take a picture of his face, if you can."

"I'll see what I can do," Manny replied drily. "Thanks for your help."

"I'm always here for you," Daisy said airily.

Day 112

Zeke saw the tall blonde man walk into the office ahead of him. The blonde's uniform was crisply pressed, and Zeke supposed he could understand why women would find him attractive.

He'd surreptitiously watched Brett, waiting for the perfect moment to pounce. Research for his blog, he assured himself, and had absolutely nothing to do with his own confused feelings of anger, guilt and remorse. He'd planned to tell Manny the truth about the blog even though Leah wanted him to still keep it secret, but their argument yesterday morning, and the revelation that

Manny had taken the first–okay, the second...possibly even the third–chance she got to try and get laid–well, it had shocked him. But that was no excuse for his reaction, and even now, he wasn't sure what had been driving him to insult her the way he had. He didn't like what it told him about himself.

However, none of that changed the fact that her behaviour was completely out of character and he didn't understand *that*, either.

Until now, looking at Brett.

A handsome thirty-year-old–what the hell was he doing with Manny, Zeke fumed as he pushed open the door and entered the office.

The blonde man looked up with a smile, and Zeke gritted his teeth as he got a good look at the high cheekbones, clear blue eyes, and square chin.

"May I help you?" Brett asked.

"Just trying to get the lay of the land," Zeke replied lightly and winced inwardly at his unfortunate choice of words. "Manny told me you had some maps of the park? I forgot to get some from the girl who was here yesterday."

Brett's eyes widened, and Zeke was pleased to see him swallow as his smile faded.

"*You're* Manny's travelling companion? The one she was meeting here?"

Zeke grinned, a hard, predatory gleam in his hazel eyes as he walked to the desk. He was inordinately pleased to realize he had a couple of inches in height and breadth on the younger man.

"The one and only," he agreed mildly enough.

"And...she told you to come talk to me?"

Zeke shrugged. "Of course. You're the park ranger, aren't you?"

"Yes. Yes, I am."

"Great! We're looking for a nice hike, not too strenuous, but which will give us some great views of the park."

"Oh! Yes, of course." Brett pulled out a map and proceeded to unfold a map and point out a couple of trails that would meet those requirements.

Zeke thanked him and as he refolded the map he casually added, "By the way, if you come near Manny again, I'll break both your legs."

Brett reared back. "What?" he sputtered.

"She told me you didn't do anything she didn't allow, but I've been watching you in action. I suspect you were amazingly persistent, and you dazzled her with flattery and charm and attention. She's not like a lot of other women— she would have thought you were sincere. And then yesterday and today, you're sniffing around the two youngsters who've just arrived."

He steadily met Brett's eyes.

"I don't like anyone hurting my friend. So, I'd appreciate you staying as far away from her as possible for the rest of our stay. Got it?"

Brett's mouth opened and closed like a fish, but he couldn't find anything to say until Zeke was at the door.

"If she's sleeping with you, why was she in my cabin the other night?"

"She's not sleeping with me," Zeke said without turning.

"Then what's it to you?"

"She's my friend, and she's like—" he chuckled, "a babe in the woods when it comes to men." Zeke turned, and now he looked dark and dangerous as he stared hard at Brett. "I don't want her hurt any more than she already has been. Do we have a deal?"

Brett gulped and nodded, his blue eyes wide.

Zeke very gently closed the door on his way out.

~~~~~

"Are you trying to kill me?" Manny moaned as she almost fell into her cabin. She hobbled to the couch and flung herself down. "My feet feel like they're on fire."

Zeke shrugged sheepishly. "I think I zigged us when we

should have zagged."

Manny groaned as she eased off her sneakers and blissfully wiggled her toes.

"My own fault," she sighed, "I should have called a halt after I realized we were going straight up."

"It wasn't *straight* up," he tsk'd as he sat beside her on the couch. "A sixty degree angle–tops." He motioned for her to put her feet up on his lap.

"Are you nuts?" she exclaimed in horror. "You can't– my feet stink! And they're hot and sweaty and–" she ended with a yelp as he reached down with an exasperated sigh, grabbed her feet and plopped them on his thigh.

"I'll wash my hands later, Auntie Em," he assured her impatiently and began to rub her right foot.

Any additional words of protest died on her lips as her eyes closed, her head fell back and she groaned in a mixture of pleasure and pain.

"You're right–your feet *are* stinky and sweaty," he teased.

"I'd kick you, but that would mean I'd have to take my foot away." She didn't even open her eyes as she spoke.

"And ruin any chances for the other foot to be rubbed, too?" he asked drily.

"That, too," she nodded as she flung one arm across her eyes. Her shirt rode up slightly to expose a thin band of pale skin above the waistband of her low-slung jeans.

Zeke, to his immense relief, had no reaction at all to her almost wanton posture. Leah was right, he mused as he moved his hands to Manny's other foot. He'd been simply over-reacting to the fact that he really liked her. He'd confused it with falling in love because–as Leah had so accurately noted–he didn't have many female friends. He simply hadn't known how to define what he was feeling especially since, until Manny, he could count his female friends on one finger. He simply hadn't recognized his purely platonic affection as, well, purely platonic affection.

He considered her from under lowered brows and half-lowered eyelids. The more he looked at her, the more he realized Leah was right: when it came to sex and romance, Manny was *definitely* not his type.

Besides the age difference, she wasn't exactly beautiful. Not the beautiful he preferred, anyway. She'd lost a little bit of weight on this trip but she was still plump. He'd just been thrown for a loop by her makeover, such as it was, and then the news about TJ had really knocked him off-balance. That was all. He'd just confused his natural liking for her as something...more.

Yeah.

Leah was right. To his relief.

"You look very focused."

Zeke glanced at Manny, startled.

"And pissed," Manny added.

"I'm not pissed at all," he assured her.

"Good to know," she yawned and stretched, then winced. "Shit, I'm sore. You seemed to be a man on a mission on that hike. Were you hoping I'd fall off a cliff somewhere? Just so you know—you're not in my will."

He pressed tighter against her foot and she yelped, jerking her foot out of his hands and off his lap. She glowered as she heaved herself into a sitting position.

"Did I hit a nerve so you had to return the favour?" she snapped as she stripped off her socks and dug her toes into the carpet, sighing with pleasure.

"No," Zeke said shortly.

"No? That's it? You just felt the urge to walk my feet down to the bone?" She looked at him steadily. "You seemed pretty focused. Are you worried about TJ?"

"I'm a little worried, yeah—he's come down with a cold now."

"A *cold?*"

"Yeah, the guy can't seem to catch a break. But that's not what I was thinking about."

"Oh? Then what's on your mind?"

Zeke sighed, leaning back and stretching his long legs

out in front of him.

"*You're* on my mind," he admitted.

"Me? What? Our fight yesterday?" Surprise and confusion was vivid in her voice. "I thought we settled all that this morning."

"We did–although I didn't appreciate you snapping that picture of me right as you told me no sex for me if you don't get any!"

Manny laughed. "I had to; I'd promised Daisy."

"Thank you so much. Anyway, I wasn't thinking about any of that. I was thinking about your...um...*unusual* behaviour with Brett."

Manny's eyes dropped from his and she shifted uncomfortably.

"I made a mistake," she muttered.

"You took a chance," he corrected gently, "but what I don't understand is why. What was it about Brett that drew you so far away from your normal behaviour?"

Manny flexed her toes in the carpet, her eyes riveted on her bare digits.

"You haven't had sex in six years," Zeke reminded her quietly. "Why Brett? He's so–so–"

"Smarmy?" she asked with a slight smirk.

"Yes! And completely phony. You know you would have been just another anonymous notch on his bed post."

"Like you and Babe?"

Zeke opened his mouth, then slowly closed it.

"You're not me. Or Babe," he said.

"I know. And I wasn't trying to be like you. Brett is smarmy, yes, but–it was flattering, to be pursued so–well, not ardently, but–oh, hell," she groaned and buried her face in her hands. "It was flattering to be pursued, no matter how fake it was."

She lifted her head and leaned her chin on her hand with a rueful grimace.

"I would have preferred someone a little less fake, but you know, it's been a long time since sex was even a remote possibility. I thought I'd take a chance."

"And yet you couldn't go through with it. Why not?"

Manny shrugged. "I don't really know. Maybe because I've never liked sex without emotion. Maybe because he *was* so fake." She frowned, staring off into space before she firmly shook her head and rose to her feet with a groan. "Anyway, it's not important. I'm going to go soak in the bathtub. Hopefully I won't seize up and drown, thanks to you."

Zeke also got to his feet.

"Okay," he said. "I'll see you in the morning."

"Not too early, though," she said hobbling to the bathroom door, "I need some time to recover. And plan my revenge."

Zeke laughed as he let himself out of Manny's cabin and headed towards his own.

He was grateful to Leah for setting him straight about his feelings. His next blog would now be a clear re-telling of this tale, not one clouded by misunderstood feelings.

He strode off, feeling at peace with himself for the first time since L.A.

Day 113

Manny heard the door open behind her as she smiled, thanked the girl behind the counter and accepted the receipts for the cabin rentals. She was folding them to put in her purse as she turned, and met Brett's uncomfortable gaze. She froze and flushed guiltily.

He hesitated, then smiled tentatively at her.

She shifted uncomfortably, then bit her lip, lifted her head, and smiled back.

He hesitated again, then made his way to her.

"Hi," he said sheepishly.

"Hi."

They stood in awkward silence, Manny acutely aware of the girl's avid interest behind her.

"Listen—" they both started, then stopped and laughed.

In silent accord they went outside, where they fidgeted before Manny finally said with a grimace, "I wanted to say I'm sorry for–for–"

Brett shook his head. "You changed your mind. That's allowed. You have no need to apologize for that."

Manny smiled ruefully. "I know, but I feel better now."

He shrugged. "I was disappointed, but hey. Shit happens.

"No hard feelings?" she asked.

"Of course not. And–uh–I know you saw me working those new girls." Brett looked down, scratching at his ear, and he had the grace to look slightly embarrassed. "This is what I do," he muttered, shrugging. "I win some; I lose some."

"They shot you down, huh?" Manny said sympathetically.

"Pretty brutally," he sighed.

She bit her lip then laughed.

"You at least were nice enough about it," he told her.

Manny shrugged. "I try to be nice," she agreed.

"So–no hard feelings?"

"No hard feelings."

He smiled, a genuine smile and not the smarmily fake one he'd previously plied her with.

"Let me walk you to your van," he offered.

She smiled and nodded. "I'd like that."

They ambled from the office to the parking lot in companionable silence interspersed with the occasional comment about the weather, the scenery and the next stop for Manny and Zeke.

Manny glanced up and bit her lip when she saw Zeke leaning against the driver's door of the van, his arms crossed, sending them a fulminating glare from beneath dark brows lowered over thunderous eyes.

"You know, that man glowers all the time," Brett murmured to Manny, his blue eyes wide and cautious.

That surprised a laugh out of her. "I'm used to it by

now."

"Tell me–is he any fun at all?"

"Lots, actually–when he decides to just relax and enjoy himself."

Brett shook his head in wonder. "Hard to believe, but if you say so." He looked at Zeke again and slowed his steps.

"You know, on second thought, I should say good-bye to you here."

Manny frowned. "Are you scared of him?" she asked with interest.

"Well, he did threaten to break both my legs if I came near you again."

Her jaw dropped and she flushed. "He did?" she squeaked.

Brett nodded vigorously. "I'm almost positive he was serious."

Manny glanced at Zeke from the corner of her eye. "Judging from the way he's glaring at you right now, I'm thinking you might be right." She bit her lip and tried to hide her amusement. "Nice to know he looks out for his poor old Auntie Em," she muttered.

Brett looked quizzically at her but she shook her head.

"A long story," she said, "and we don't have the time."

Brett nodded and they stared at each other for a long, suspended moment before Brett slowly smiled at her. It was, once again, a genuine smile, and Manny smiled back.

"I'm sorry to see you go," he said, "and I sincerely mean that."

"Thank you," Manny said. "I've enjoyed my time here."

Now Brett's grin turned devilish as he said, "You could have enjoyed it a lot more..."

Manny laughed and shook her head. "I'll just take your word for it."

Brett shrugged in rueful defeat, and opened his arms. Manny hesitated, then stepped forward and hugged him warmly.

Manny murmured against his shoulder, "I did appreciate the pursuit." They moved apart as she added, "And that spaghetti sauce really was sinful."

Brett shrugged. "I get it from an old Italian guy in town."

She gaped, then threw back her head and laughed, shaking her head. "You are *such* a bastard," she said.

He laughed and nodded. "This is what I do."

"I know."

They grinned at each other then both looked over as Zeke called out an irritated, "Okay, okay—break it up—we've got a long way to go today!"

Brett and Manny exchanged ruefully amused looks.

"Take care of yourself," Manny said.

"You, too."

Manny noticed that Brett stood in the parking lot and watched as they drove away. She thought it was a good thing he couldn't see Zeke's dark glare, his gritted teeth, or the death grip he had on the steering wheel.

That night, Zeke pounded furiously on his laptop's keyboard as he wrote his latest blog. He scowled and swore softly as he sent it off to Leah.

Day 114

"*Women of a Certain Age should be smart enough not to fall for the smooth line of the first Lothario who shows up,*" Leah read aloud.

TJ's eyebrows rose even higher than they'd already been raised as she continued, "*God save us all from cougars who are still only kittens at heart and in experience. They'll fall prey to any prowling wolf, wily coyote or pouncing fox they stumble upon. Even cougars need to be protected when they're still just clueless babes in the woods.*"

TJ sat in thoughtful silence once Leah finished and carefully refolded the paper in her hands.

"You may have been too hasty in dismissing his feelings," he rasped slowly.

Leah tapped the folded paper against her lips as she stared into space.

"You may be right," she agreed. She gave him a slow grin. "I guess we'll just have to wait and see what happens next."

EPISODE TEN
Day 117

"You're where?"

"Some pissant little town in Florida," Zeke sighed. "Manny thought it looked pretty, so we're here for a few days. Personally, I think it's only because she can probably meet the whole damn town in two days."

TJ laughed a raspy laugh that turned into a dry, wracking cough.

"Jesus, buddy–you okay?" Zeke asked when TJ came back on the line.

"Yeah, I'll be fine. I just can't seem to shake the last of this cold. And the more I cough, the more I pull my incision, so I'm still really tender, too."

"What does the nurse say?"

"Not much, except to say it's not that bad, and to get out of bed."

"Sorry?"

"Yeah, Leah's beyond pissed. But she's been so swamped at work–your blog, man, shows no sign of slowing down!–she hasn't had a chance to phone the agency and ask for a new nurse, or a second opinion, or whatever."

"Do you want me to do it?"

TJ paused. "Wow–Manny's rubbing off on you. That's really nice, Zeke–but really not necessary. I like this nurse; she's a bit brusque, but tough love may be exactly what I need. To a point, anyway."

"Well, what does the doctor say?"

"Nothing. I haven't seen him."

"TJ!"

"Hey–I have three weeks to go before my six week check-up. That's soon enough."

Zeke growled in frustration. TJ laughed, then coughed again.

"I'm okay, Zeke. Really. Go have fun in Florida."

"It's a tough life," Zeke sighed dramatically.

"Fuck off," TJ said. "Wait until I'm all healed up; I'll take Leah on a long holiday to a tropical island during the depths of winter, and leave you here, freezing your ass off."

"What's new about that?" Zeke asked drily, and they both laughed as they ended the call.

Day 118

Manny smiled at her hostess' sixteen-year-old son as she walked into the dining room. He ducked his head and mumbled hello, hiding his face behind a shock of stringy brown hair. Manny mentally shrugged.

Ted had been pretty shy with her and Zeke the last two days, and she suspected he'd gladly hide in his room if his mother, Cora, didn't insist on his presence. Manny thought he seemed like a typically awkward teenager, going through that stage where they simply didn't know how to act in certain situations. The few times she and Zeke or another guest had coaxed actual conversation out of him, he'd been bright, well-spoken, and remarkably well-informed. Of course, as Cora noted drily, he was almost constantly online.

Manny saw he was focused on his phone as she sat down at the table with her plate of food. She glanced up as

Zeke walked in and greeted everyone.

"More coffee?" Zeke asked as he filled up his plate from the small buffet table.

Manny nodded. "Please."

Cora bustled in. "I'll do that, Zeke. Go sit down."

Zeke thanked her, then said as he made his way to the table, "So, how many Misfit Toys have you gathered this time around?"

There was a loud clatter as Cora knocked a cup off the buffet table and it shattered on the floor.

"Oh!" Manny exclaimed, rising to her feet.

"No, no, no," Cora said, her face bright red with embarrassment, "I was clumsy–it's okay. Teddy," Manny glanced at Ted, who was staring wide-eyed at his mother, "come with me to the kitchen–there's a new pot of coffee that's just finished brewing."

"But that pot's half-full," Manny protested mildly, "I can–"

"No, no, no–come on, Teddy."

Ted nodded and hastily stood. They picked up the shards of the broken coffee cup, and hurried into the kitchen as Manny returned to her seat and Zeke finally sat at the table.

She glanced ruefully at him. "Anyway, I met two Misfit Toys yesterday."

"Only two?" he asked drily as Cora and Ted returned to the dining room.

"Well, while you were holed up working, I was busy looking for a beach that wasn't wall-to-wall people."

"You didn't want to meet people?" Zeke asked in mock disbelief.

"Well, not while I'm wearing a bikini," Manny replied, then stared in horror at Ted. "Sorry, Ted–didn't mean to put that image in your head."

Ted blushed and ducked his head, peeking out from behind his hair.

Manny made a mental note to ask Daisy if Jakob had

ever gone through this shy, awkward stage.

Cora, on the other hand, seemed rattled and excited as she filled Manny's coffee cup, then sat chatting too-brightly with them, her eyes darting from Manny to Zeke and back again.

Manny mentally raised her eyebrows.

"Are you guys okay?" she finally asked.

Cora started. "Oh–oh! Yes. Just...some exciting news. On a personal level. That's all."

She beamed at them both.

Manny and Zeke stared blankly back.

"Good to hear," Zeke finally said slowly, and carefully neutral. He glanced at Manny from the corner of his eye. "So, what's the agenda for today?"

"Exploring the town," Manny said promptly. "Meeting the locals."

Zeke heaved an exaggerated sigh and ruefully shook his head.

Day 119

Zeke trudged over the slight hill and saw the expanse of water and the soft, sandy beach come into view. He glanced to his left and saw the back of Manny's head peeking over the edge of her lounge chair. Zeke headed in her direction.

"Hey," he called, "there you are! Ted told me–"

He stopped in his tracks as Manny shrieked, sat up and grabbed the towel she'd been sitting on to cover her chest, toppling off the lounger as she did so. Zeke caught a flash of pale breasts, yelled, "Holy–you're *naked*!" and abruptly turned his back.

"Just topless!" Manny cried, and Zeke could hear her struggling to her feet behind him. "I didn't expect you to find me!"

"Oh, so who were you expecting?" Zeke snapped, trying to banish that brief glimpse of her body from his memory.

"I wasn't expecting anybody! Ted said this was a private beach, and I could sunbathe nude if I wanted!"

"Why would you want to?" Zeke demanded.

Manny sighed. "What do you *want*?"

"Are you decent?" Zeke asked.

"A little too late for that now."

Both Zeke and Manny spun around to gape at the police officer who had approached from Manny's other side. Manny stared, her eyes huge, then she groaned and hung her head.

~~~~~

Daisy took a deep breath and opened the door. She smiled tightly as Hub stepped over the threshold. He smiled just as tightly in response and held up the manila envelope in his hand.

"I'm glad you agreed to meet without the lawyers to go over the draft settlement," he said.

Daisy shrugged. "As angry as I am with you, Hub, you do still love your kids, even if you don't show it all that often." She raised a placating hand. "I'm stating my opinion, not a proven fact or even a judgement. Okay?"

Hub gave her a sullen nod as he settled on the couch.

"Besides, the settlement isn't complicated. I'm not asking for alimony," Daisy continued, sitting down beside him, "only child support–and you can pay that directly to the kids. Whatever cash or investments we have can be split down the middle, and then I'll pay you half whatever the house is worth out of that. It's pretty simple."

Hub nodded. "Surprisingly simple, considering we were together for twenty-four years."

Daisy smiled briefly. "It's not like we lived an extravagant lifestyle," she said drily. "Let's face it, we were pretty conservative...once we started living together."

Hub paused frowning, then he grinned, and the years dropped from his face. Daisy blinked as, for a moment, the man she'd fallen in love with looked back at her.

"We had some good times though, didn't we?" Hub

said almost wistfully, his grin dimming.

Daisy nodded. "We had a lot of good times." She looked at the small bar nestled in the corner of the living room. She laughed. "Remember the time we crashed that wine and cheese party at the university art gallery?"

Hub frowned before remembrance dawned. "And we each stuck two bottles of wine under our coats to smuggle them back home?"

"And one of yours fell out? Right in front of the security guard!"

Daisy laughed as Hub chuckled and shook his head.

"Good thing you and Manny knew him."

"Although I would have enjoyed watching the strip search he threatened to do to you."

Hub groaned. "He laughed at me every time he saw me after that."

"Hey, at least he didn't catch us in the storage room that time."

"No, that was a different security guard–which, of course, made it all better!" Hub said drily, rolling his eyes. His expression softened. "It was a good time," he agreed.

Daisy shifted uncomfortably, dropping her eyes to the manila envelope in her hand. "Well, that's all in the past now," she sighed.

"When did it start to go wrong?" Hub asked sadly.

Daisy shot him a suddenly annoyed look. "I don't know–you tell me. I'm not the one who had an affair! *Why* did you do that?"

Hub shrugged helplessly. "I don't know. I guess I was feeling...old. And she was young and pretty and interested–in me and everything I did." He sighed and looked at his hands. "You haven't been interested in me or anything about me for..." he shrugged again, "ever, it seems."

Daisy reared back. "That's not true!"

Hub raised his hands. "I'm not accusing you–I'm trying to tell you what I felt. And I felt like you didn't care anymore, and she was..." he shrugged helplessly.

"There?" Daisy asked drily.

"Yes—in a way."

Daisy sat in thoughtful silence then said, "I almost feel sorry for her."

Hub glanced at her. "It's over, you know. Me and her."

"No, I didn't know," Daisy replied quietly.

"Daisy—"

The shrill ring of Daisy's phone interrupted him. Daisy glanced at it, then frowned as she answered it.

"Hello? Manny? You're *where*?"

Day 120

Manny heard Daisy and Rebecca long before they rushed into the holding cells area. They hurried to the bars of Manny's cell with a hasty glance at Zeke in the adjoining one. Zeke and Manny rose to their feet and moved to the bars.

"Hey, guys," Manny said.

Daisy grabbed the bars with a death grip. "Don't 'hey guys' me! I can *not* believe you ended up in jail!"

Rebecca leaned in. "What's the story? The cop at the front desk was pretty pissed."

Manny rolled her eyes and glanced at Zeke. "That was Zeke. We didn't do anything really bad, and if Zeke hadn't pissed him off I'm almost positive he would have let us off with a warning."

Zeke said, "I would like to say—for the record—that this is all her fault."

Manny rolled her eyes again and shook her head at him. "Thanks," she said drily.

Daisy levelled a death glare in Zeke's direction. "I don't care what you say—I'm blaming you anyway!"

"Hey!" Zeke protested.

Rebecca lowered her voice with a grin, "Come on, Manny—spill!"

Manny ignored her. "Are you gonna be able to get us out of here?" she asked Daisy.

"That depends on what you've done!" Daisy snapped.

"Well, we didn't kill anybody!"

"What's this 'we' business?" Zeke protested. "I'm an innocent bystander!"

"Oh, please!" Manny said. "You drove the getaway car!"

"We didn't get away, remember?" Zeke snapped. "We didn't even get to the car!"

Rebecca gasped, her eyes wide. "Oh, my God—you robbed a bank?"

Daisy's eyes widened, too. "That—that—that's a lot of time..."

"Oh, for—we didn't rob a bank!" Manny sighed.

"I didn't do anything!" Zeke said loudly. "I wasn't there!"

All three women yelled, "Shut up!"

"Well, I wasn't..." Zeke pouted.

"It was indecent exposure," Manny said loudly, "and Zeke wouldn't have been arrested at all if he hadn't mouthed off to the cop!"

"I think it was my question about what I had to do to get him to let us off with a warning," Zeke muttered.

"Yeah," Manny said drily, "he apparently took it the wrong way—as in, an offer of a bribe. Of...one kind or another."

Rebecca and Daisy ooh'd, then Rebecca said, "Indecent exposure? Manny..." she sniffed, feigning tears, "I'm so proud!"

"Stop encouraging her!" Zeke snapped. "Honestly!"

Daisy shook her head. "On the one hand, I'm with Rebecca. On the other hand, I agree with Zeke—and that can never be good."

"Hey!"

"I heard about your reaction to Brett," Daisy said, her index finger raised in warning.

Rebecca laughed and winked at him. "You should see us when we don't like you. Which brings us to this...Ted...he deliberately set you up?"

"It appears that way," Manny sighed. "But he's only sixteen. I think it was just a prank that got out of hand."

"Yeah," Daisy said grimly, "a prank that put you in jail and separated you from your belongings for a least forty-eight hours."

"This seems pretty elaborate just to steal some petty cash," Zeke said skeptically.

"Or maybe he's running another type of scam," Rebecca said. "Now. Where do we pay the bail money?"

"Probably the cop at the front desk," Manny sighed. "I'll never get a job again," she groaned, leaning her forehead against the bars, "especially with a conviction for indecent exposure!"

"Don't sweat it," Rebecca assured her, "you can always sell real estate."

Daisy waved away their comments. "We'll worry about all that later. First we have to get you out of jail. Then we find out what the scam is—and *then* we show Zeke how we treat the people we *don't* like."

~~~~~

The four them walked into the hotel room, and Rebecca tossed her purse and overnight bag heavily on one of the beds.

"All right," she said, planting her hands firmly on her hips, "now that we have some privacy, let's talk about how we're going to make this Ted pay."

"And how we can find out what the little worm was up to while you were in jail," Daisy added, dropping her own purse and overnight bag on the second bed.

"Did you bring your laptop?" Manny asked Daisy. Daisy gestured at her overnight bag and Manny dug it out as the others settled on the beds and continued talking.

"I'll call Jackson in about an hour," Rebecca said. "He'll be finished with his meetings by then. He can tell us how to tell if your laptops have been tampered with."

Daisy nodded. "I'll call Max; he can find out if your

credit cards have been used at all."

"I can check online–" Zeke protested.

"Yeah, but charges don't always show up right away," Daisy said.

"True."

Rebecca said, "And then there's whether your ID has been used online for other purposes. Jackson can help us there, too. Like if something malicious was done to somebody else, using your ID."

"Well, I think that's definitely part of it," Manny said in a high, strained voice.

The others looked over at her. She was pale, with bright spots of red on her cheeks, her eyes wide as she stared at the computer screen.

Zeke frowned. "What do you mean?"

"Ted sent a link to all my friends on Facebook, telling them to check out a certain website," Manny said slowly, her voice brittle with rage, "but I'm not sure Ted is the one being vindictive."

Manny turned the laptop around to show everyone the screen. Zeke's jaw dropped as he recognized the *What Women Want* website–and his blog.

~~~~~

Ted glanced up from his comic book and flushed a dark red as Manny walked into the dining room of the bed and breakfast and headed in his direction. She paused on the opposite side of the table and considered him expressionlessly.

Ted brushed his long hair back and nervously met her eyes.

She considered him silently, then nodded at the table.

"May I sit?" she asked gently.

Ted hesitated, then jerked a nod. Manny sat down, then leaned forward, her hands clasped loosely on the table in front of her.

"You...uh...you set me up," she said.

Ted did a combination of a shrug and a nod. "Yeah. I

arranged for you to be arrested."

"How?"

"Ira's been wanting me to do a favour for him for the last few months. So, I sent you to that beach, and then Zeke, and asked Ira to 'arrest' the two of you–trespassing, if nothing else–and to keep you in prison for a couple of days."

Manny frowned. "*Why?*"

"Because I needed some time to figure out if you two were who I thought you were."

Manny nodded without surprise. "The people in the *In Praise of Older Women* blog."

"Yeah. I mean, I was pretty sure, but...I wanted to be sure before telling you. Zeep–the screen name for the author of the blogs–was pretty clear his travelling companion had no idea he was writing about her. If it was you...I just thought you should know."

"Why?" Manny asked again.

"Because...because Zeep's sometimes not very nice–and now that I've met you, I know you are, and you're just trying to have fun. Zeke's nice too, but...well, if Zeke and Zeep are one and the same, then you should know. You should know what's *really* in it for him."

Manny swallowed with difficulty, her eyes on her hands. "I'd...wondered. I read a couple of the early blogs–he was...pretty brutal."

"Yeah," Ted said, "his 'thing' is snarky coolness, but he's been, well...mellowing isn't the right word, exactly, but giving you some grudging respect. And genuine liking. He defends you a lot in the comments, but he also needs to keep his readership, and most people are reading to find out how he's going to react to whatever you do next. His latest blog was posted yesterday morning–and it just confirmed that Zeep and Zeke are one and the same."

Manny shook her head. "The blog's pretty popular, huh?"

"It went viral a few weeks ago, yeah."

"You sound...mixed. Like you dislike him and admire him at the same time."

Ted shrugged again. "Hey–he's making money on the Internet–that's impressive. And I enjoy–enjoyed–his blogs. At least until I actually met you. He's a good writer, and funny. But–you–you're not clueless, or an object of fun, or pity. And you deserve to know who you're travelling with."

Manny sighed. "I could have done without the couple days in jail. Or having my sister and friend cough up bail money! You could have just told me."

"I had no proof. I had to get my hands on Zeke's laptop–uninterrupted–to find evidence."

"Instead of–I don't know–just sending me a link?"

"Would you have clicked it?"

"If I'd known it was from you, yeah. Probably."

"When?"

Manny opened her mouth, then slowly closed it. "Well, what's done is done. Although the bail money thing is still an issue."

Ted shrugged. "Ira'll return the money as soon as I call him."

Manny huffed. "So...we weren't really under arrest, were we?"

Ted chuckled. "No. Like I said, Ira wanted me to do a favour for him."

Manny frowned. "But he–?"

"Well, I asked for something first; now I'll have to come through for him."

"What could he possibly want that would be worth risking his job?"

"He likes my mom."

Manny gaped at him. "You pimped out your *mother*?"

Ted grinned. "It's okay; she likes Ira, too, but she's too scared to do anything about it. This just gives me a reason to force the issue. And if I help her make progress with Ira, maybe she won't be quite so pissed with me."

"Well–you *have* cost her two paying customers," Manny

reminded him.

"Oh, not just that! She reads Zeep's blog, too. She wanted his autograph."

~~~~~

Cora caught Manny as she left the dining room.

"I'm sorry you found out this way," she said, wringing her hands.

Manny forced a smile. "So am I. It...wasn't what I was expecting."

Cora bit her lip. "Listen–I've been reading Zeep's blog since it started–and I have to tell you, I think you've done a number on him."

"Not yet," Manny said drily, "but when I get through with him–"

Cora chuckled, shaking her head. "No, no–I mean...he sounds...I mean, his writing–it's like you've befuddled him. He can't seem to figure you out, and he's–well. You should read it. All of it, I mean, not just the first blog or two."

Manny smiled thinly and said, "Maybe someday. But not today."

~~~~~

Manny, Rebecca and Daisy were flat on their backs on one of the beds, staring silently at the ceiling until Rebecca muttered, "I'm just...heartbroken. I really liked him."

"Me, too," Daisy sighed.

"But his blog," Rebecca continued. "He seems to have some pretty harsh opinions of...of..."

"'Old' women," Daisy bit out. "He needs to be careful. He's not that far away from forty himself. The son-of-a-bitch."

"Well," Rebecca said grimly, "when I get over the shock, I'm going to make him sorry he ever crossed our paths."

"And I'll help you," Daisy said, equally grim. "With pleasure."

Rebecca and Daisy fell silent and they glanced at Manny, lying stiff and silent between them, staring fixedly at the ceiling. They shared a worried look. Daisy opened her mouth just as Manny's cell phone rang. Rebecca and Daisy jerked in surprise; Manny didn't react at all.

They lay in tense silence as the cell phone rang until it went to voice mail. A few moments later, the phone began ringing again. Manny frowned slightly, but otherwise refused to react.

Daisy sighed, heaved herself out of bed and grabbed the phone.

"Manny's phone...This is her sister Daisy...um...she doesn't want to speak to anyone right now...Who is this again?...Hang on." Daisy pulled the phone away from her ear and frowned at it. "Is there a speaker on this thing?"

Manny heaved an irritated sigh as she sat up, pressed a button on the proffered phone, then got off the bed.

"I'm not in the mood for anybody," she snapped.

"Manny?" a feminine voice said through the speaker. "I'm Leah Huxley. Zeke works for me."

Manny froze, then said loudly, "I'm *really* not in the mood for this!"

Leah said, "Please–I'd like to talk–maybe explain–and ask you to give Zeke a second chance."

"Why? So he can keep writing his precious blog at my expense?"

"Because your friendship has been the best thing to ever happen to him. Well, since he met TJ–my husband–anyway. And, of course, me."

"At this moment, I don't give a damn." Manny glanced at Daisy. "Shut it off."

"Wait–"

Daisy ended the call and tossed the phone back on the second bed.

Manny restlessly paced the room, then turned abruptly to face Daisy and Rebecca. "I'd like to be alone for a while," she said.

Rebecca stood and hesitantly put a hand on Manny's shoulder. "Are you sure? I'm not–you don't have to go through this alone, you know. We're here for you."

Manny forced a smile that was a dim copy of her usual grin. "I know," she said, "and it's not forever–just–give me a little time to...process, you know? Just an hour. Okay?"

"But–"

"Okay, okay," Daisy interrupted. "Come on, Rebecca. Let's give her some time. Call if you need us."

Manny shrugged. "Come back in an hour. I'm gonna take a bath–try to relax, get some perspective. And then..."

"And then?" Daisy asked carefully.

"And then I'm gonna murder the son-of-a-bitch, and I'll need your help to hide the body."

"Sold," Rebecca said with a decisive nod. "See you in an hour."

~~~~~

Manny leaned her head back, closed her eyes, and sighed. She deliberately relaxed her shoulders in the hot, soapy water, but stubbornly refused to let out the tears that burned behind her closed lids.

Are you gonna be okay? Harvey asked.

Aren't I always? Manny winced at her bitter tone. She opened her eyes and glanced at Harvey. His eyes were warm with sympathy.

It's gonna take a while, she sighed, *and I need to figure out...*

Was any of it real? The friendship?

Exactly. Or was everything as real as you are?

I don't know what to tell you–

Of course not–you're a figment of my imagination after all.

–except you need to talk to him, and then cut your losses.

Or cut him?

Harvey slowly grinned. **If I was real, I'd kill him for you. But you know you don't really want him dead. Although Rebecca might do it.**

Manny reluctantly grinned back. *Maybe. Probably.*

Most likely. She shook her head. *Anyway. Cut my losses.*

Send him home with Rebecca and Daisy. Continue on your own. You don't really <u>need</u> him, you know.

Because I have you?

Because you have yourself.

~~~~~

Manny shifted slightly, her eyes firmly on her coffee cup rather than Zeke, who was sitting across from her, his hazel eyes never wavering from her face, his hands tight around his own cup. With an effort, Manny unhunched her shoulders and straightened. With a slow, deep breath she met his gaze.

"We've been here before," she murmured.

Zeke frowned.

"Sitting awkwardly in a coffee shop," she clarified.

A small smile curved Zeke's lips. "I remember."

"Are you going to apologize?" Manny asked, an ironic lilt to her voice.

"No."

Manny blinked, her eyes widening. "That's it?" she demanded incredulously. "This is going to be a short coffee."

"I'm not going to apologize," Zeke said. "This is what I do for a living."

"What? Travelling with pathetic middle-aged women in search of their lost youth? I believe that was the phrase? Where I come from, there's a word for guys like you."

Zeke's eyes narrowed, the faint smile gone now from his lips. "Blogging. Sharing my opinion about things and being a bastard about it. My role—especially on that site—is to stir up controversy. To get people talking and, more importantly, coming back."

"But you don't think you should apologize for making my...my intensely personal journey a subject of public mockery? Without my knowledge or consent, by the way!"

"No. I'm...more sorry than I can say that you were hurt by it—but no. And you should read all the blogs before you

301

judge."

Manny barked out a hard strident sound that was almost laughter. "Oh, because it gets so much better!"

"You should read them," Zeke repeated. "All of them. And then we'll talk."

Manny stared incredulously at him. "You are such a fucking jerk! I'm angry here! And hurt!"

"This is you hurt and angry? You showed more emotion after I found out about Brett!"

"Because you called me a slut!"

The other patrons in the small store turned and stared. Manny flushed and met the eyes of one of the young women sitting at the table next to them, and who had been sliding appreciative glances Zeke's way.

"Trust me," Manny snapped at her, "you *don't* want what I'm having!"

"Jesus, Manny!"

She turned her glare on him. "Angry enough for you?" she asked coldly.

Zeke raked a hand through his hair. "This still isn't angry! You're so repressed–no wonder you needed to run away in order to find yourself!"

Manny gasped. "Fuck you! You have no idea what the hell you're talking about–and you need to leave!"

Zeke stood up, his chair scraping loudly across the floor. "Fine. We'll talk about this later."

"No, you idiot!" Manny snarled, standing up just as violently. "I mean you need to leave me alone! You can go back with Daisy and Rebecca, or you can get back on your own, or you can go to hell–but we're done! You can find somebody else to use as the butt of your blogs!"

Zeke stared, his face stark as she stalked away.

~~~~~

"So, that's it, huh?" Leah asked sadly.

"Apparently," Zeke bit out.

TJ began to cough, but managed to say, "What flight will you be on?"

"That sounds really bad, TJ," Zeke said.

"Ignore me," TJ rasped, still coughing. "What flight will you be on?" He took a sip of water, then leaned back on his pillows to catch his breath.

"Leah? How bad is he?"

Leah shot a look at TJ, who shook his head.

"Bad," Leah said, and stuck her tongue out at TJ, "but he's holding his own. We have a new nurse coming at the end of the week. I'm hoping whoever it is will make him see sense."

"I'm fine; it's just a bad cold," TJ rasped.

Leah rolled her eyes, then said, "What flight are you on, Zeke?"

"I haven't booked anything yet. I'll let you know."

TJ said, "I'm sorry, Zeke. But you know—I didn't expect you to actually grow to like the woman."

"Hey," Zeke said with patently false cheer, "I like her, yeah. The Old Maiden Aunt thing, you know? But you know what? Screw her if she can't take a joke."

"This is all my fault," Leah sighed. "I should have let you tell her the truth when you wanted to. Or tell the truth right from the start."

"No, you were right. She would have been self-conscious—and she never would have shared the things she did with me. Knowing she was being observed—recorded? You know what I mean—it would have changed everything."

"But it changed everything anyway," TJ said.

Zeke swallowed, then said lightly, "Well. Too late now. I've gotta go. I need to get the rest of my stuff from the van and book a flight home—all without getting pulverized by Daisy or Rebecca."

"Not Manny?" Leah asked.

"She's made it clear she doesn't want to see me again."

"Zeke—" Leah began.

"Gotta go," Zeke said, and disconnected the call. He tossed the phone down on the table and roughly rubbed his hands over his face.

Day 121

Zeke was almost relieved to see just Rebecca waiting for him by the van, but then he frowned as he glanced around the rather seedy parking lot. At least it was above ground he thought.

"You haven't been waiting out here by yourself, have you?" he demanded as he walked up to her.

Rebecca rolled her eyes. "It's broad daylight, Zeke! Plus you called me five minutes ago, to let me know you were on your way. Besides, there's what? Fifty people in this town? I think I'm pretty safe hanging out in this open air parking lot."

Zeke scowled. "Regardless. Daisy should have waited with you," he muttered.

Rebecca cocked her head to one side and considered him thoughtfully. "You know, I just can't figure you out."

Zeke raised an eyebrow.

"How such a sweet man can be such an asshole," she clarified.

"Hey!"

"I'm serious, Zeke. You're this bizarre mix of–of casual...cruelty is too harsh a word..." Rebecca paused, frowning furiously. Zeke shifted uncomfortably under her intense stare. She shook her head. "You're sometimes so oblivious to just how much your words and actions can hurt someone–and yet you're also such a good guy." She tossed him the keys to the van. "I'm almost sorry you're not going to be continuing on with Manny."

"Continuing on?" he asked sharply.

Rebecca shrugged and nodded. "She says she still has to see Disney World, the Kennedy Space Centre and Key West before she starts to meander home."

"*Meander?*" Zeke asked as he yanked the van door open and clambered inside.

Rebecca followed.

"Manny says she's not going to let this slow her down, or shorten her trip."

Zeke's frown deepened as he began to search the van for any stray possessions he may have left there.

"Good God," he muttered, "the last time I left her alone for any length of time she almost jumped the first half-good-looking guy who smiled at her! I assumed she'd be going home with you and Daisy."

"She still has the van," Rebecca reminded him mildly, "and honestly–why shouldn't she jump the first half-good-looking guy who smiles at her? She's free, female and over the age of twenty-one, and it's not like she has some other guy waiting for her. And contrary to your blogs, she isn't some dried up old maid whose only purpose is to sit and watch the world go by."

"I never–" he stopped abruptly.

Rebecca nodded. "Yeah. Better stop while you're still only half a mile behind."

Zeke shook his head. "I'm amazed you haven't knocked me over the head and used the van to hide my body somewhere."

"It crossed my mind. Believe me. But Manny needs the van, and clean-up would be a bitch."

Zeke reluctantly grinned then sobered. "I never meant to hurt her, Rebecca. I actually intended to tell her when I joined her at the park a few weeks ago–but there was Brett, and...well, it just didn't seem to matter that much."

"So–what? You thought she'd never find out about the blog?" Rebecca asked skeptically.

"I honestly thought she'd never find out. Or by the time she did, it'd be long after we got back home and gone our separate ways."

Rebecca sighed sadly and shook her head. "That was just stupid."

Zeke shrugged, not quite meeting her eyes. "I guess." He glanced slowly around the van. "So, are you and/or Daisy going to travel with Manny now?"

Rebecca snorted a laugh. "No. Neither of us can get away. Daisy's in the middle of finalizing her divorce and has a meeting with her lawyer and the bank the day after we get back. I have my granddaughter staying with me, and I can't take her out of school."

Zeke frowned again. "So Manny's really continuing on alone?"

"Yeah."

He slid a sideways glance towards her. "You actually don't sound like you're pleased about it."

"I'm not. She'll end up bringing home every stray she finds."

Zeke smiled slightly. "True. How did she end up the way she did? I mean, how did she end up with just you and Daisy and her job as her life?"

Rebecca narrowed her eyes. "Are you asking for your blog, or are you asking for you?"

He calmly met her eyes. "I'm asking for me," he said firmly.

Rebecca stared hard at him. She seemed to like what she saw in his face, because she finally nodded, and said, "Manny's a fixer. She wants to solve people's problems, and she worries at them until she *can* fix them. Her workplace, when she started, had a lot of problems—business-related, people-related—you name it. It sucked her in and sucked her dry, and she simply didn't have anything left to give at the end of day. Her friends just...drifted away. Most days, she barely found the energy for me and Daisy or our families. I'm worried she won't be able to keep herself from spiralling back into the same situation again when she goes back to work."

Zeke nodded slowly.

"So I'm torn," Rebecca continued. "On the one hand, I want her to stay on holidays for as long as she possibly can. She's rediscovering herself, and that can only be a good thing. On the other hand, she's going to continue travelling on her own, and while I know she's going to be just fine, I also know I'd sleep a lot better if I knew she was with somebody who would look out for her."

Zeke stared off into space, his dark brows low as he scowled.

"Well," Rebecca continued, deliberately nonchalant, "I guess we'll just have to find room for all the strays she brings back when she does finally wander back home."

Zeke gave her a sliver of a smile as they climbed out of the van, and Rebecca chuckled as she locked and closed the door. "Who knows? Maybe she'll finally break in that bed in there now that she's on her own. I'm sure there's at least one other Brett out there somewhere." She slanted a glance at Zeke. "Another reason not to mess up the van."

Zeke's scowl deepened.

~~~~~

Late that afternoon, Manny padded out of the bathroom in her t-shirt and boxers, warm and rosy from another too-hot bath, her hair hanging damply around her face. She jumped as her cell phone rang, then hurried across the room to grab it off the dresser. She checked the caller ID, frowned, then cautiously answered the call.

"Manny? This is Leah Huxley again."

Manny huffed a sigh. "What, exactly, do you want? I've already told your boy to go home."

"I know. And I don't blame you. Look—"

"Tell me—did you make a lot of money from Zeke's blogs about me?"

"Money? Not really—but our traffic's increased dramatically. Listen—"

"Why?" Manny asked bluntly.

"Because—because—aren't you *curious* about why I'm phoning?"

"It's not to apologize, is it."

"No, but I do want to explain a few things."

"Why bother?"

"Because—I want to."

"What about what I want?"

307

"Please, Manny. Let me have my say, and then you can hate me all you want, okay? I'll just keep calling until you do listen to me, you know."

Manny growled a sigh. "Fine," she snapped. "What do you need to tell me?"

"Thank you," Leah said gratefully. "Okay. Sending Zeke with you was my idea. Keeping the truth from you was also my idea. He wanted to come clean when he rejoined you at the park but I wouldn't let him."

Manny paused, considering, then said, "That doesn't make it all better."

"I'm not trying to make it all better. I just wanted you to know Zeke wanted to do—well, what you think would have been the right thing."

"You disagree."

"It was an awesome story! It's *still* an awesome story! And my subscribers love it—they love you! And they love Zeke's reactions to you! Which brings me to the real point of my call. How would you like to write a blog of your own for *What Women Want*? Your first one can be in response to Zeke."

~~~~~

"What did you say?" Rebecca breathed, wide-eyed. She was sitting with Manny and Daisy in a small restaurant, the remnant of their suppers in front of them.

Manny shrugged as she sipped her coffee. "I told her I'd think about it," she said, putting the cup down.

"For God's sake—why?" Daisy demanded.

"Because she offered me a lot of money for just one blog post. I mean, outrageously a lot. But..."

"But?" Daisy prompted when Manny simply stared off into space, frowning.

"But then I'd actually have to read his posts. And I'm not ready for that. Not yet, anyway."

"Have you talked to him since you told him to leave?" Rebecca asked casually. A little too casually.

Manny shot her a suspicious look. "No," she said

slowly, "and I don't expect I will, either."

"Well," Daisy said, delicately wiping her lips with her napkin, "he'd just better not be flying home with us—or if he is, he'd better not talk to us, anyway."

"Somehow, I don't think that'll be a problem," Rebecca murmured and smiled as she sipped her coffee.

~~~~~

As he packed, Zeke kept up a steady stream of curses and mutterings about stubborn, mule-headed, unforgiving women and what the hell did he care anyway—wait until they got to the blog he was going to write after *this*.

He crammed the last of his clothes into his travel bag, then stood back and scowled at it, hands on his lean hips, and thought about what Rebecca had told him about Manny continuing on alone. After a moment, he shook his head, stomped to the desk and threw himself into his chair.

He'd rent a car, book the first flight home he could find, and see how Little Miss Prissy liked travelling by herself from now on.

By the time he finished booking the car, he'd remembered Las Vegas.

By the time he found a flight, he was thinking of Brett from the park and shuddered at the thought of her coming across another ladykiller with a weakness for repressed, naïve older women with no sense of self-preservation. Sanity had prevailed in that instance for Manny, but what if next time she wasn't so smart? Or the guy wasn't as understanding?

He thought about the Misfit Toys, and the dance contest; the way her ass looked in that little blue dress and those shoes that were most likely illegal in some states. What if she broke a leg in those things?

He thought of Dixie, and the women before her, and how easy it had been for him to walk away from all of them—well. Except the first. He shook off the momentary pang. This should be even easier, he told himself

309

staunchly. Hell, she was just his Auntie Em! No, not *his*. Just Auntie Em, trying to pretend she wasn't as prudish as she truly was.

Nobody *important*.

He stopped and stared sightlessly at the computer screen feeling cold and hollow, his stomach churning.

He'd walked away from so many things. He'd walked away from his father, from his home, and from more women than he could truly–or wanted to–remember.

He didn't *want* to walk away from her–his Ma–Auntie Em. He didn't *want* to walk away from her fondness for Misfit Toys; from her rather subdued demeanour that she'd suddenly throw off when he least expected it; from her ability to talk to anyone and from her willingness to try anything–and from the way she always seemed to be having an inner dialogue about just about everything.

Damn it.

He liked her–and she was, really, completely clueless when it came to other people, especially men.

He sighed. He'd never forgive himself if something happened to her. He couldn't, in good conscience, let her travel alone.

Damn it.

Day 123

"You're what?" TJ croaked incredulously.

"I've rented a car," Zeke repeated patiently, "and I'm going to follow her."

"How are you going to keep track of her?" Leah asked, equally incredulous.

"I'll...figure that out when I get to it. I know her current itinerary, thanks to Rebecca, so I'll be able to at least follow at a distance."

"Isn't this a little...stalkerish?" Leah asked carefully.

"It's only stalkerish if I'm..." he hesitated. "Okay. Maybe a little. But I'm doing it more for her own protection than anything else. I mean, she's clueless! A babe in the woods! Even Rebecca admitted Manny would be bringing home every stray she found between now and the end of her trip. What if she finally runs into one who isn't all that nice?"

"Is that the only reason?" TJ asked skeptically.

Zeke paused. "What other reason could there be?"

TJ took a breath, choked on it, and began to cough, a harsh, dry, wracking sound. He gratefully accepted Leah's offer of water, and said, "To get her to accept your apology."

"I'm not going to apologize!"

"Uh–yeah. Okay."

"Do you have any idea how many times I've already apologized to that woman?" Zeke snapped.

"About half a dozen," Leah said brightly.

"That all?" TJ asked.

"Hey!" Zeke protested, then shook his head. "It doesn't matter–I'm not following her in order to apologize. I just don't want anything to happen to the little idiot."

Leah and TJ exchanged glances and raised eyebrows over the speakerphone.

"I think Manny's pretty used to taking care of herself, Zeke," Leah said, then grinned as TJ rolled his eyes and shook his head.

"Oh, God–if you can call what she does taking care of herself!" Zeke paused. "Okay, okay–you're right–there's another reason why I'm following her."

"I knew it!" Leah crowed.

"I don't want to fly home on the same plane as Daisy and Rebecca, or have them hunt me down if anything happens to Manny after we part company."

"I have *got* to meet these women," Leah said. "They sound like my kind of people."

"Oh, God," Zeke groaned, "don't go bonding with them! You're the reason I'm in this mess in the first place! Shit. I'm sorry, Leah. I didn't mean that the way it

311

sounded."

Leah blinked. "I think that's the first time you apologized about something you said without somebody pointing out you'd just said something that hurt someone's feelings."

Zeke frowned. "I...think I got all that...but what's your point?"

"Go. Follow Manny. Call us for bail money when she has you arrested. She's been...really good for you, you know."

Zeke hesitated, then said softly, "I know."

~~~~~

Manny stood with Rebecca and Daisy in the parking lot beside their rented car.

"Drive carefully," she told them, hugging each in turn, "and call as soon as you get home."

"We will," Daisy assured her. "You drive carefully, too. I'll expect a call every night. Maybe every afternoon, too. Possibly even every morning."

Manny laughed. "Don't worry, Daisy. I'll be fine."

"I know. But call me anyway."

"All right." She turned to Rebecca, who seemed to be watching, with a slight smile, something behind Manny. Manny frowned and turned to look behind her. She didn't see anything unusual and turned back to Rebecca, her frown deepening.

"Are you okay?" Manny asked.

Rebecca blinked and refocused on her. "I'm more than okay," she said. "Never mind," she added quickly and Manny closed her mouth with an audible snap. "Come on, Daisy. We better get going."

Daisy hugged Manny tightly. "We'll talk later tonight, okay?"

"You bet," Manny said.

Manny hugged Rebecca just as tightly, and Rebecca murmured into Manny's ear, "You should read the blogs, and then talk to Zeke."

Manny pulled away with a scowl. "What for?"

Rebecca grinned. "Trust me," she said, then hugged Manny again.

~~~~~

"What was that all about?" Daisy demanded as they pulled out of the parking lot.

Rebecca nodded towards a car, parked on a side street with Zeke behind the wheel. "I don't think he's going to let her go alone if he can help it."

Daisy snorted. "More fodder for his blog?"

Rebecca slid a glance at Daisy. "I think you need to read his stuff, too," she said, and refused to say any more on the subject.

Day 125

It was late by the time Rebecca got home, and the next morning was rushed as she slept in and had to hurry Tris out the door to catch the school bus. It wasn't until supper that night–their designated portion of the day to spend together without any other distractions–that Rebecca had a chance to really sit down and talk with her.

Tris rather disconsolately picked at her food and asked without any real interest, "So, Manny's out of jail?"

Rebecca nodded as she covertly watched her. "Yeah. A good story for the grand-nephews and -nieces someday."

"Yeah?" Tris said bitterly. "Well, I had a long talk with Jakob and Janika while you were gone."

Rebecca nodded carefully. "Okay. What about?"

Tris slammed down her fork. "You have to pay them to spend time with me! If you have to pay somebody, then pay a stranger, not people I thought were my friends!" she yelled before she burst into tears and bolted from table.

~~~~~

Rebecca lightly tapped on Tris' door and was answered with a muffled and tearful, "Go away!"

She sighed and opened the door.

"No, I don't think so," she said gently as she walked in.

Tris huddled on the bed in a ball, her back stubbornly turned to Rebecca. Rebecca sat down, but made no move to touch her granddaughter.

"We need to talk," Rebecca said firmly.

Tris snorted.

Rebecca said, "I'm not going to apologize for hiring Jakob and Janika to look after you when I'm not around. I hired them *because* they're your friends. In fact, they volunteered; I made them take the money."

Tris hunched her shoulders a little higher.

"Tris, they would have done it for nothing," Rebecca continued, "but they were sacrificing their own free time. Besides, if you guys wanted to go to the movies, or...or...or wherever it is kids go to have fun, then they needed money to pay for that."

She paused. "I'm sorry you feel your friendship is somehow...diminished because they were paid. It's not, you know. They're still your friends. They'll always be your friends." She paused again, frowning. "I told you about all this—that they would get paid for looking after you. Did you forget?"

Tris shrugged slightly.

"What happened while I was gone?"

Tris mumbled something.

Rebecca frowned. "Sorry?"

"He won't wait for me."

Rebecca leaned back, her eyes wide with surprise. She hesitated, then, "I'm sorry," she said sadly.

"Why won't he wait?" Tris asked plaintively.

Rebecca said, gently serious, "Because you're only ten years old."

"Almost eleven!"

Rebecca smiled a fleeting smile. "Yes, almost eleven. Tris—honey—you're still a child, and you have a lot of living to do before you're ready for any boy. Don't rush it. It'll happen—maybe it'll be Jakob—maybe it won't. But you don't need to be in any hurry."

Tris rolled over and stared at Rebecca with a pout and tear-reddened eyes. "It's never happened for Manny. It's never happened for you. What if no boy ever wants me, either? I mean, no one wants me now, not you, not Jakob, not Gran and Pappy, not even Mom and Dad."

"Oh, Tris," Rebecca sighed sadly, "you're far too young to be concerned about this—"

Tris abruptly sat up. "I love him! Why won't he love me?"

"Because you're still just a child—but you won't be one forever. Your future is vast and full of possibilities. And someday, when you're a little older, we'll talk about Manny and her choices, and we'll talk about me and mine. For now..."

"For now?"

"For now, you have enough to deal with—including your broken heart. I can't help you with that, except to tell you...it will get better. Really. It will."

Tris stared at her hands, tightly clutching the blanket. "I told him I loved him," she mumbled.

"And I'll bet he was flattered, right?"

Tris shrugged. "So he said..."

"Then believe him," Rebecca said simply. "And you should be proud of yourself. It takes a lot of guts to tell somebody you love them."

"Did you ever love somebody?"

"Of course," Rebecca shrugged with a small smile. "I love you."

Tris rolled her eyes. "I meant a boy."

Rebecca laughed. "Oh, yes. A couple of them even. And *those* are stories for when you're *much* older!"

She awkwardly patted Tris' leg. "Now. I can't do anything about Jakob. But I *can* do something about your parents. And it's past time I did."

~~~~~

"Now what?" Jackson asked, his voice warm and concerned on the other end of the phone.

"Now I need to put Tris first. And..."

"And?"

"It's time to stop being understanding. Jaime needs to come back to her daughter, or..."

"Or?"

"Or she gives Tris to me. Legally, I mean. Tris needs a home; she needs to feel secure. Although God knows I obviously screwed up one child; I'm not sure I should try again."

There was a long pause, then Jackson said, "You mean my kids too, don't you?"

Rebecca's mouth opened and closed as she struggled to find something to say.

"I was afraid of that," Jackson said finally. "Rebecca, you don't have to do this alone this time. I want you to meet my kids and I want to meet Tris–"

"I *never* allow my lovers to meet my family," Rebecca blurted.

"Why *not?*" he demanded harshly.

Rebecca blinked in surprise. It was, she thought, the first time Jackson had pushed her; the first time he actually seemed...angry at her desire to keep him at arms' length from her family.

"Why do you want me to meet your kids so badly?" she shot back.

"Because they're a part of my life. They're a part of me!"

"I've never tried to interfere with that!"

"But you've never wanted to be a part of it, either! Why?"

"Because kids shouldn't be hurt by their parents' mistakes!" she snapped.

"I'm a *mistake?*" he demanded hoarsely.

Rebecca sighed and wearily rubbed her forehead. "No, I don't think you're a mistake," she said quietly. "We're having fun, Jackson. I enjoy your company and I know you enjoy mine. But that's *all* we're doing–that's all we can ever do. I don't want your kids to get to know me and then..." she bit her lip, then continued quickly, "and then, when we're no longer dating, they're left wondering why I'm no longer coming around. And that's assuming they even like me in the first place!" She vigorously shook her head. "It's better to keep your sex life away from your kids."

"I told you I love you," he said softly, and Rebecca imagined how his dark eyes would be huge in his face, serious and sad. "You're more than just my sex life."

"It's not going to work, Jackson. I can't—I can't risk hurting your kids or Tris. I'm sorry," Rebecca whispered.

"Me too," Jackson managed, his voice thick with emotion as he ended the call.

Rebecca held the phone against her chest and struggled to hold back her tears.

Day 126

Daisy sighed as she disconnected from the call with Rebecca. She was more sorry than she could say that Rebecca had decided to end things with Jackson. They'd seemed to be truly happy, and Daisy thought Rebecca honestly loved him. But like many things in Rebecca's life, she wasn't about to listen to any advice about that decision—not even from Daisy or Manny.

Daisy shook her head and glanced at the clock. She frowned when she saw lunch was almost over and Max still hadn't returned to the office. He hadn't been in all day, in fact. She mentally ran through everything he was supposed to be doing the night before and that morning, and relaxed slightly when she realized there was nothing on that list that should cause him to end up in the hospital or at the police station.

Max gave her a lot of freedom to manage her day, but she'd wanted to let him know she'd be gone for most of the afternoon, first to meet with her lawyer and then to meet with her bank manager. She didn't want to do either of those things but she was discovering that dissolving a marriage was complicated, no matter how simple the settlement or how amicably the people involved were behaving.

At least the house was paid for, she thought thankfully as she sent Max an e-mail explaining her absence, then stuck a post-it note to his computer screen for good measure.

She put the sign in the window telling people to call or drop by the next day, closed the door with a sad sigh and headed to her first appointment.

~~~~~

Daisy slammed into the house, her face flushed a deep, dark red. Jakob and Janika both turned to stare, their eyes wide as they took in the look on her face.

"Mom! What happened?" Jakob said, heaving himself up from the couch and limping towards her.

Daisy closed her eyes and took a deep, calming breath. She realized her hands were clenched into tight fists and she forced them to relax. She opened her eyes and smiled at her kids.

"Nothing you need to be worried about," she assured them, "but I need to talk to your father as soon as I possibly can." She glanced at the clock. "He'll be here to pick you up any minute now. Could you please tell him I need to talk to him before you guys go?"

"It's never good when she refers to Dad as 'our father'," Janika muttered to Jakob.

"True," he agreed.

Daisy reluctantly smiled, but "I need to talk to him alone," was all she said, before she headed down the hall to her bedroom.

She tried calling Rebecca but there was no answer. She tried Manny next, but there was no answer there, either. She sighed, then dialled a third time to check in with Max.

"Three strikes and you're out," Daisy muttered crossly as her call went to his voice mail. She huffed as she tossed the phone on the bed.

There was a knock and Hub poked his head around the bedroom door.

"The kids said you wanted to see me," he said.

She bared her teeth in a caricature of her normal smile. "That's a bit too generous," she said, "but I want to talk to you, that's for damn sure. Get in here."

Hub came into the room, closing the door behind him, an annoyed frown on his face.

Daisy stood and faced him, her hands planted firmly on her hips.

"I had a very interesting meeting with our bank manager today," she said coldly.

Hub's frown deepened. "So?"

"So? *So!* So there's no fucking money in our accounts! What did you do with it?"

Hub paled. "What do you mean there's no fucking money in our accounts?" he demanded.

"I mean," she hissed, "they're empty! All of them! Zeroed out! Not a penny to be seen! What did you do? Did you move everything to a–a–an account in the Caymans or something?"

"Jesus, Daisy–" Hub muttered, sinking down on the bed, his face grey, "I didn't do anything with the money–I swear!"

She scowled furiously at him. "Then what the hell *happened?*"

He dazedly shook his head. "I don't–" Suddenly his head snapped up and he glared at her. "Wait a minute– how do I know you haven't taken the money to pay off gambling debts?"

Daisy gaped at him, then burst into bitter laughter. "I don't gamble that much! And I sure as hell wouldn't lose over six hundred thousand dollars in one shot! And no, I don't owe money to the mob, nor were they the ones who really broke Jakob's leg! God, Hub–give your head a shake!"

"Well, if you didn't take it, and I didn't take it—" Hub snapped.

They stared at each other, eyes huge.

"Then somebody stole it," Daisy said flatly. She shook her head and scrabbled her cell phone out from the blankets.

"Who are you calling?" Hub asked.

Daisy laughed a short, sharp, almost hysterical laugh. "Who do you *think*? The police first, then my lawyer, then I'm going to call Max. Again. And I'm going to keep calling him until he picks up his *fucking phone*!"

"Max?" Hub asked sharply. "What for?"

Daisy rolled her eyes and shook her head. "He's a private eye—why do you think?"

~~~~~

Rebecca stared in horrified disbelief as Daisy finished speaking.

"Sweet Jesus," she murmured, then she shook her head and said, "We need something stronger than tea."

Daisy huffed a watery chuckle. "That—would be good."

Rebecca bustled to the wet bar and came back with a bottle of tequila and a couple of shot glasses. Neither woman said another word until they'd each tossed back two shots in rapid succession.

They sat back with a sigh.

"Any leads?" Rebecca asked.

Daisy shrugged. "The police are investigating now. The only thing we know for sure is that the money was stolen over a relatively long period of time—a couple of weeks for sure; possibly even a month. Whoever did it is pretty sophisticated, too—they're still trying to find the trail."

"But—I mean, over six hundred thousand dollars, Daisy! You never noticed when it—I don't know—dipped under four hundred thousand?"

Daisy shrugged helplessly. "I only checked the accounts once a month at most even before we separated. Then savings accounts were frozen while we worked out a settlement. Well, I mean, the bank required both of our signatures before they would release any money to either of us. Honestly? I haven't even looked at the accounts since I started divorce proceedings. Hub was the same way. And here we are."

Rebecca frowned, her eyes narrowed as she rolled the shot glass against her lips.

"That's pretty dangerous," she said slowly. "Somebody stealing over a period of time, I mean, even if it's no more than a month in total. They would have had no way of knowing when the thefts would be noticed. Unless..."

"Unless it's somebody who knows us," Daisy said flatly.

"And knows you well," Rebecca agreed.

They stared silently at each other.

Finally Rebecca said, "What's the other woman's name?"

Day 127

"TJ, I'm home," Leah said hurrying into the bedroom. "You should have been up by now. The new nurse will be here any min—" She stopped short as she took in his flushed face and labored breathing.

She frowned as she perched on the bed beside him and felt his forehead.

"You're burning up," she said, concerned.

"I think I'm having a relapse," TJ croaked, his words coming in short, painful spurts. Leah's frown deepened.

"You sound awful," she said.

TJ leaned his head back. "I feel worse," he sighed, his eyes closing.

"The nurse will be here in less than half an hour," Leah soothed. "Maybe she can give you something to help."

He barely nodded, a frown on his face as he concentrated on his breathing.

Leah sat with him, watching his chest rise and fall, and the seconds crawled by as she waited for the nurse.

TJ didn't stir when the doorbell finally rang.

Leah raced to the door, and she babbled all the information she had to the new nurse as they walked up the stairs.

The woman, a comfortably cozy figure, soothed Leah as much as she could before she went into the bedroom. Leah waited anxiously as the nurse gently called TJ's name. She straightened sharply when the nurse called TJ's name again, and then again, each time louder and more urgent than the last.

Leah burst into the room just as the nurse lifted her cell phone to her ear with one hand, her other hand on TJ's wrist. The room spun as Leah heard the nurse speaking, but nothing made sense. Through a dull roar, she heard words like unresponsive and erratic and numbers like 104.5, and all she could do was stand there, feeling useless as her world trembled beneath her feet. The trembling built to a quaking as the ambulance arrived, the paramedics swarmed into the house, and TJ was finally wheeled out on a stretcher with an oxygen mask over his face.

The nurse put a gentle hand on her shoulder.

"I'll drive you to the hospital," she offered quietly.

It took a moment for the words to sink in, then Leah jerked a short nod, gathered her purse and keys with shaking hands, and followed the nurse outside without a word.

EPISODE ELEVEN
Day 128

"How bad is he?" Zeke demanded. He scrubbed the sleep from his eyes–what little he'd managed–and felt the rasp of stubble against his palms. He wondered if he looked as bad as he felt; the rental car wasn't as spacious as the van.

"He's stable," Leah sighed wearily. "He's going to get worse before he gets better, but the doctors have assured me he's in no danger of dying–at the moment, anyway."

"Leah–"

"I'm sorry, Zeke. He's very sick, but he's going to be okay. I promise."

"I'm about an hour out of Orlando. I'll head straight to the airport and catch the first plane I can get," Zeke said grimly.

Leah hesitated, then said, "No–don't."

"What?" Zeke exploded. "TJ needs me! *You* need me!"

"There's nothing for you to do here, Zeke, except hold my hand."

"He'd want me to hold your hand! He'd want me to take care of you!"

"I know," Leah said fondly, "but while I would love to have you here, taking care of me–I don't *need* you here taking care of me."

Zeke drew in sharp breath, hurt in his wide hazel eyes.

"Zeke, I'm okay. He's stable—and he's been asleep more than he's been awake. But he has been awake and talking to me. If you come home, all we can really do is sit and watch and wait for him to get better."

"I can do that."

Leah laughed shakily. "I know you can, but you have some fences to mend where you are."

"Manny? She doesn't even know I'm still here, and I have no idea where she is right now either, since I stopped following her in order to get to Orlando faster. Whether I stay or go—it doesn't make a difference. Not here."

Leah lowered her head, and pinched the bridge of her nose. She hadn't slept since they'd taken TJ out of the house, and she had a pounding headache.

"I would love to have you here, Zeke. To have you hold my hand as we watch him sleep. And TJ would be touched beyond belief."

"I'll get on the next plane."

"Zeke...Manny's the first woman you've ever chased after."

Zeke scowled as he stared out the windshield.

"She means something to you," Leah said gently. "I mean—she really *means* something to you. I think Manny's the only woman you've ever actually liked—besides me, I mean."

"I like women!"

"No—you're attracted to women—but you don't like them very much. You're not even always sure about me."

Zeke hesitated, then muttered, "She could have been a friend."

"Do you still have a crush on her?"

Zeke huffed a laugh. "No. You were right about that. But—I like her. And I don't want her to think I—I just used her."

"Then find her. TJ's stable. If that changes, I'll call." She laughed shakily. "You can be damn sure of that!"

Zeke hesitated, biting his lip, scowling as he wavered.

Leah sighed. "How about this? You talk to Manny and if you can't get her to see the light, come home."

"Are you sure you'll be okay on your own, Leah? I mean really okay?"

"I'm sure. The doctors are optimistic even though they still don't know exactly what's wrong. I'm going to go get some sleep in his room and then head to the office for a few hours. See what's happening there."

"Okay. I'm going to head into Orlando and find a place to stay. If anything changes, Leah—seriously. No matter the time—I'll get home as fast as I can."

"You're a good guy, Zeke," Leah said softly, "and a good friend. I'll call you later."

Zeke disconnected the call and blinked away sudden hot moisture from his eyes before he started the engine and continued on to Orlando.

~~~~~

Manny stared up at the motel room's ceiling and tried to will herself to sleep. She was planning on spending the day exploring Disney World and she wanted to be rested before she braved the crowds and lineups.

I'd be able to get to sleep if you would just shut up, she complained to Harvey.

Harvey propped his head on his hand as he rested on his side beside her.

You should read the blogs.

No.

You don't know what he said about you.

I know enough. I read the first few. I know what he really thought of me.

Prudish. Repressed. Timid.

Don't remind me.

To be fair—really, what did you think your image was like?

Professional. Competent. Composed.

You say potato—

Shut up.

Look, you could at least give him the benefit of the doubt–at least until you read all of the blogs.

He used me! He _used_ me!

And you thought he liked you.

Yes. Yes! I thought we were starting to be _friends_. I thought...God–I'm so pathetic. No wonder I hid from the world for the last fifteen years. I can't figure anything out.

What did you think?

Just...there was the possibility of a little excitement in my life when I got back to reality. You know? Zeke's– Zeke _was_ interesting and mysterious and different. And it would have been..._fun_ to have a friend like him when I'm once again immersed in work and...and I'm back in my world made of grey.

Maybe he'll still be a friend like that.

Look around–he's gone. And good riddance.

Are you ever going to read his blogs? **All** of them?

I don't know. Now go to sleep.

Day 129

Max shoved a cup of coffee in front of Daisy's face and she jumped.

"Jesus!" she yelped. "You're as silent as a cat!"

He smirked his crooked smirk, the deep grooves in his cheeks that weren't quite dimples on full display.

"I'll put on a bell," he promised in his quiet voice that still held an edge of danger no matter how gently he spoke. Maybe it was the bald head, she thought. "Come on," he urged, "you haven't done anything but stare at that computer screen for the last ten minutes. Come talk to me."

Daisy blinked, and glared at him. He raised one eyebrow, his green eyes intent on hers, and her shoulders slumped. She nodded as she took the coffee and followed him to the armchairs by the office doors.

They sipped their coffee in silence for a moment, then Max said, very gently, "Just how much trouble are you in?"

Daisy's eyes slid away from his, and she shifted uncomfortably. She shrugged.

"Daisy," he snapped, and she jumped guiltily. His voice was no longer gentle. Instead he was in full investigative mode, putting the suspect on the run and getting answers. It wasn't a tone he used often with her, and Daisy realized she liked it better when he used it on other people.

She rallied and glared at him. "It's not your concern," she said with as much dignity as she could muster.

They were in a standoff of wills, and Daisy wondered why she'd never noticed just how green and piercing his eyes could be.

Max finally relaxed and sighed. "I'm asking as your friend, Daisy. I want to help—I mean more than just tracking down who took your money and where it's at now. Do you need a loan? Are you okay to pay your bills?"

Daisy's anger melted. "You can't help me, Max. You can barely afford to pay me—I know! I do your books, remember? I owe more on my credit cards than you make in a year." She had a sudden, horrifying thought as she considered his dropped jaw and staring eyes. "And if you think for even one minute that I'm going to start embezzling, well, you can just kiss my lily-white ass!"

"Huh? What–? Now you're just being stupid," he scoffed.

Daisy began to puff up, eyes glinting dangerously as she opened her mouth to tell him where to go.

"For God's sake," he snarled, "just *shut up*!"

She snapped her mouth closed, and sat back with a huff, her arms crossed tightly across her chest.

He leaned forward, his eyes intent on her face.

"You're not angry with me, Daisy. I didn't put you in this situation."

She looked away, chagrined. "I know. I'm sorry. I just..." she shrugged. "Besides the sheer devastation of having our entire life's savings stolen practically overnight, I've forgotten what it's like to be worried about paying my bills. I don't like feeling this vulnerable. I don't like feeling like my children are vulnerable. At least Hub's still making his big bucks, so I know—logically—the kids are secure—even though my heart is still terrified for all of us. One thing I do know for sure: I'll be damned if I'm going to ask him for alimony!"

Max nodded. "I can understand that." He paused. "You don't know everything about me, Daisy. If you need help, you'll let me know—right?"

She nodded, then frowned. "What don't I know?" she asked.

He simply smirked and sipped his coffee.

~~~~~

Manny sighed as her cell phone rang and Zeke's name and picture appear on the screen.

Again.

You may as well answer that.

She glared at Harvey, looking handsome and smugly amused.

Why?

If nothing else, to get him to stop calling.

She scowled at the phone until the call went to voice mail.

Every hour on the hour, Harvey noted. **The boy's persistent if nothing else.**

Manny shrugged. *I don't care. Now, I'm at Disney World—let's have some fun.*

~~~~~

Manny walked tiredly into her motel room and flopped face down on the bed.

"I'm wiped," she groaned out loud.

Me too, Harvey sighed, flopping on the bed beside her.

Considering you're not real, I'm not feeling a lot of sympathy for you.

Thanks.

Anytime.

Manny's cell phone rang and she groaned again, burying her face into the pillow.

Talk to him—even if it's just to tell him to fuck off.

I've already told him to fuck off. Besides, he should be home by now. <u>Why</u> is he <u>calling</u>?

You're whining.

I know.

The phone fell silent, and Manny sighed then heaved herself off the bed and headed to the bathroom.

I need a bath. Then food.

Better hurry—he'll be calling again in an hour.

Only he didn't. He didn't phone in the next hour, either, or by the time Manny trudged back to her motel room, changed into her boxers and t-shirt and crawled into bed. She tried to read, the words swimming in front of her eyes, and even when she could make out the words, she couldn't focus on the story.

She tossed the book aside with an irritated huff, then hunched under the blanket and resolutely closed her eyes.

Well, I guess you've done it. He's given up.

Manny frowned. *I <u>want</u> him to give up.*

Do you?

...yes.

Harvey sighed and sadly shook his head. **You almost believe it, too.**

Go to sleep.

Day 130

Manny started when her phone rang at ten in the morning. She fumbled for it, and cursed the rush of relief that turned her knees to water when she saw Zeke's picture on the screen.

She glared at Harvey, who simply smirked and raised a knowing eyebrow as he nodded at the phone, urging her to answer.

She hesitated, biting her lip, then took a deep breath

and picked up the call.

"Hello, Zeke," she said.

There was a moment of silence, then, "Manny?" Zeke said, stunned.

"Were you calling someone else?" she asked drily.

"No. No! I just wasn't expecting you to pick up the call."

"Why were you calling then?"

"I...wanted to talk."

"We've already talked."

"Manny," Zeke groaned helplessly, "look. Could we get together?"

Manny frowned. "Well—I won't be home for a while yet. So if you still want to by the time I get back—why are you laughing?"

And what a laugh! Harvey sighed.

Shut. Up!

The shitty part was Harvey was right. Zeke was chuckling a low, husky sound that Manny was positive she'd never heard from him before. It was...*intimate*, that was the word, and it was doing strange things to her nerve endings.

Hormones. I keep telling you—

Oh, sweet mother of God...

"I'm not at home," Zeke told her.

Manny blinked and refocused on the conversation.

"Then...where are you?" she asked, confused.

"Orlando."

Manny's jaw dropped. "Did you *follow* me?" she said, her voice dipping into dangerous territory.

"Well, I'd intended to," Zeke admitted, "then I had to get to Orlando as fast as possible. TJ was rushed to the hospital two—three days ago now."

"Oh, my God! What happened?"

"Massive lung infection. The idiot thought it was just the flu and downplayed everything to everybody. Anyway, it was a bit nip and tuck there the first night. I talked to him very briefly yesterday. He's nicely stabilized now and once he's more with it, he'll be appropriately apologetic to both me and Leah for scaring the crap out of us."

"I'm glad," Manny murmured softly, then paused, frowning. "So—wait—you followed me?"

"Only part of the way," Zeke protested weakly.

"That's...a little creepy," Manny said.

"So I've been told," Zeke sighed. "Apparently it's not considered romantic anymore."

Romantic? Harvey blurted.

"*Romantic?*" Manny squeaked.

"In the broad sense of the term," Zeke hastened to assure her, "not in any *feelings* sense of the word."

Oh, Harvey pouted.

"Oh, of course," Manny said, relieved and disappointed all at once.

"Anyway. Can we get together?"

"Are you going to apologize?"

"About the blog?"

"Of course about the blog!"

Zeke paused, and Manny held her breath.

"I don't know, Manny."

Now it was Manny's turn to think.

Harvey shook his head and refused to say anything.

She sighed. "Okay. Okay. Where are you staying?"

Zeke told her.

"How about I meet you in the lobby at six?"

"Okay," Zeke agreed. "See you then."

Manny disconnected the call and shook her head.

Are you going to forgive him, even if he doesn't apologize? Harvey asked with interest as they continued on their way.

What do you think? Manny sighed.

Harvey was ominously silent and she glanced at him to find him frowning darkly at nothing, his dark brown eyes thoughtful.

What? she demanded.

...you're really going to miss him when he's really gone.

...I know.

~~~~~

Manny and Zeke rode the elevator in silence. They stared straight ahead and said nothing until the door to Zeke's hotel room closed behind them.

"Do you want a drink?" Zeke asked, hazel eyes intent on her face.

"Not right now."

She shook her head as she wandered restlessly around the small room.

"Why did you follow me?" she blurted, not looking at him.

"Because...I was worried about you on your own. Because I didn't want you to think I just used you. Because..."

She glanced at him from the corner of her eyes. She raised an eyebrow in question as he scowled at her, his brows lowered.

"Because I didn't want it to end like that," he muttered.

"But not to apologize," she said drily.

His lips twitched into a smile. "Not to apologize," he acknowledged. "Look. I'm not a nice guy—you know that."

"You're an arrogant guy—and pretty clueless. But overall, you'd been..."

"Nice? Really?"

"Polite, anyway." Manny shrugged at Zeke's skeptical expression. "Most of the time. After the first couple of weeks you actually looked out for me. Sorta. Okay, you weren't such a jerk all the time."

"Look," he said again, crossing his arms, "I'm not always a nice guy. My blog is meant to provoke, to cause debate—to draw traffic and readers to the site, and yet never go too far and alienate that audience. One of the ways I do that is to write truth. I may be opinionated, cynical and sarcastic—but I share the truth as I see it—and I don't—I won't—apologize for that.

"I wrote—I write—about you and your...your mid-life crisis as honestly as I can, while retaining all those elements my readers love—or hate. My readers also want me to write about my feelings, what I've been learning, what's changed for me. They want an emotional connection to my blog, and by extension, to me.

"Think of me as a...a tabloid reporter. I'm pretty sure the people who write articles about a celebrity don't ask permission first, or apologize afterwards."

"Unless it's libel."

"Unless it's libel," he agreed solemnly.

"I'm not a celebrity, Zeke."

"You actually kinda are."

She frowned.

"It's gone viral," he said.

Her frown deepened. "What does that mean, exactly?"

"It means my blogs about you are pretty much everywhere, and are being shared and discussed all over the Internet."

Manny laughed. "I get that! How many hits?"

"We've levelled off at about 250,000 a day."

She stared. "Holy shit," she breathed.

Zeke shrugged sheepishly.

"And they all think I'm prudish and repressed and—and—and why are you laughing?"

"Because the majority of commenters are firmly on your side. A couple have made some rather nasty threats against me, and a few have even offered you marriage."

"What?" Manny said. She plopped down on one of the beds and gaped at him. "*Marriage?*"

"Well, I'm not sure how serious they are," Zeke acknowledged as he tentatively sat beside her, "but some of them have included links to their pictures."

"Really?" Manny asked, intrigued in spite of herself. "What do they look like?"

"I'm too scared to find out."

Manny dissolved into helpless giggles. She clapped both hands over her mouth as she slowly flopped back on the bed.

Zeke grinned, laughing too, and laid back on the bed beside her.

She finally stopped and wiped her eyes. She sighed heavily.

"Those blogs...really *hurt*, Zeke."

"I'm truly sorry about that," Zeke said softly. "I didn't know you–"

"That doesn't make it okay."

"I'm not trying to make it okay, Manny. You can't un-ring a bell; all you can do is..."

"Yeah, where's that metaphor going, Mr. Writer Man?"

He turned his head and gave her an exasperated glare. "All you can do is live with the memory of the sound. Mr. Writer Man?"

She shrugged and turned her eyes back towards the ceiling.

"Well, you're not a multimedia developer, are you?"

"Actually, I am. The writing is something I do on the side."

"Really?" she asked skeptically.

He glanced at her. "Really. Manny, everything I told you about myself was true. All of it. The only thing I didn't tell you was the fact I was writing about our trip. Everything else–*everything*–was–and is–true."

Manny looked solemnly at him.

"It's a little tough to trust you right now," she said.

"I know." He turned his attention back to the ceiling.

The ensuing silence was sad, but surprisingly companionable.

"Do you want me to leave?" Zeke finally asked softly.

"It's your room," Manny replied.

He snorted. "You know what I mean."

"I do." She blinked up at the ceiling.

Zeke waited.

"I don't know," she finally said.

"Okay."

"That's it?"

"I'm not sure what else to say. I never meant to hurt you. And I'm sorry you found out the way you did. I wanted to tell you myself. Tell you *differently*."

"You wrote the blogs, knowing they'd hurt me."

"I–" he paused, scowling.

"If you say it was your job..."

"Well, it's why I was being paid to travel with you. But–yeah. I could have done things differently once I realized–once–well. I could have done things differently."

Manny gave him a slight smile. "Is that an apology?"

Zeke's scowl deepened.

Manny laughed as she sat up and patted him on the knee. "All right, don't worry your pretty little head about it," she soothed.

He stared. "Did you just patronize me?"

"Yep."

"That's supposed to be my attitude," he pouted.

Manny shrugged. Zeke sat up and leaned forward, his elbows resting on his knees, his hands loosely clasped in front of him.

"What now?" he asked.

"Now I could use a drink," she said firmly and stood. "Take me to the bar downstairs and ply me with alcohol and maybe I'll decide to let you stay."

"Are you saying I need to seduce you?" he teased, his voice low and husky, one eyebrow raised in question.

"God forbid," she said drily.

"Hey!"

"Stop pouting and let's go. I need a drink."

Zeke scowled as he stood, then laughed as he followed her from the room.

Day 131

"So...all is forgiven?" Daisy asked.

"Well. There's a truce. We're going to Disney World once he gets moved into this motel." Manny paused. "You sound tired," she said, concerned.

"I'm...I feel beat down, you know? There's not a whole lot the banks or the cops can do—and Max hasn't found any trace of the bitch. Yet. In the meantime, I'm not sure how I'm going to pay my credit card bills, and Hub's suggesting he move back in."

"Say *what* now?"

"He wants to reconcile."

"Because his mistress stole all your money? What the hell?"

"He said he wanted to suggest it before—when he brought the papers over for me to review. Then you called, and I went to Florida, and then all hell broke loose when I got back and he didn't know how to broach the subject. But—yeah. He wants to get back together."

"What do *you* want, Daisy?" Manny asked.

Daisy was silent for so long Manny checked to make sure the call hadn't been dropped.

"I...don't know," Daisy said softly.

"Well...I'll support you, no matter what you decide. You know that," Manny said. "Do you want me to come home?"

Daisy laughed. "No! My life isn't hanging in the balance."

"How much do you need for your credit card bills this month?"

"Manny..."

"Daisy," Manny said warningly. "I have the money to help you. Keep track and consider it a loan. I'll help you—Rebecca will, too—until you figure out what you need to do to get your head above water. In fact, I can pay them all off for you, and then you can pay me monthly payments you can afford. How much do you owe?"

"I...I don't really want to say..."

"Daisy! Come on. If I can help you—"

"Almost a hundred thousand dollars."

"Holy shit!"

"I know."

"From your gambling?" Manny asked, her voice squeaking.

"Yeah. Mostly. But it never really mattered before when I was with Hub because we shared the house expenses, and the savings I accumulated over the years were there for me to dip into when I needed to make up any shortfall. Those savings are pretty much gone now that Hub's moved out and I've had lawyer fees to pay. Anyway, I'd planned to pay all the cards off and cancel all but one after the divorce was settled and I got my share of the money. Now..."

"Wow. Okay. Wow. Look. I'll transfer whatever you need into your account; you pay off the cards and make payments to me."

"Manny–I can't do that! When you get back, you'll need enough to live until you get a job."

"What–you wouldn't give me a room in your house? You wouldn't feed me if I was starving?"

Daisy sputtered a laugh. "Fair point."

"Besides, between my pension payout and what I got for the house, I'll be okay–you know that. I can sleep on your couch, or Rebecca's, until I find a job, so I don't need to worry about buying a house right away. And you'll pay me something every month–it'll be fine."

Daisy sniffed. "You're a good sister, Manny," she said, her voice watery.

"It's what sisters are for, isn't it? To watch out for each other?"

"Yeah. Yeah. And you have the floor in the living room whenever you want it."

"Wait–not the couch?"

"That thing's expensive! I don't want your dirty feet on there!"

"Hey!"

"Anytime."

Day 132

Rebecca breathed in the aromatic steam rising from her teacup. She closed her eyes and sipped, then looked at Daisy and smiled ruefully.

"You look like shit," she said fondly.

Daisy sputtered on her own sip of tea. "Thanks," she said drily, "so do you."

Rebecca gave her a half-smile and a shrug.

It was true. Daisy looked worn, her skin sallow, dark circles beneath her blue eyes. Rebecca knew she herself was almost a mirror image, her own eyes bright with fatigue, her skin pale, her face drawn.

Daisy sighed, put her cup down and leaned back.

"I don't get it," she groaned, rubbing her eyes. "I barely lost any sleep at all when I found out about Hub's affair. I ended the marriage and slept like a baby. This? Who knew money meant so much to me?"

"Not to you," Rebecca absently corrected, "to your kids' future."

Daisy considered the point. "Maybe you're right." She stared hard at Rebecca. "What's your excuse? Are you that scared of possibly taking full responsibility for Tris?"

Rebecca snorted. "Surprisingly enough–no. Once I made that decision, I knew it was the right one, and I haven't felt a moment of doubt since. Although Jaime hasn't picked up my calls or returned any of my messages or texts or e-mails. The letter I couriered there a couple of days ago was returned unopened. If she hadn't actually called Tris yesterday, I would have called the cops to report her as missing. But even that's not it."

Daisy frowned. "Then is it your split with Jackson that's keeping you up at night?"

Rebecca shook her head, but her gaze dropped to the cup she still cradled in her hands. She smiled a brittle smile. "You know me, Daisy. I've loved 'em and left 'em before and never thought twice about it."

"Hmm," Daisy replied, her eyes shrewd, "and Jackson's just another one in a long line of discarded lovers, huh?"

Rebecca shrugged, but her eyes narrowed and her mouth tightened. "Of course," she said lightly. "What else could he be?"

Daisy let it go. "Then what's keeping you up at night? Anger at Jaime?"

"I'm beyond angry at Jaime. She can turn her back on me all she wants–I'm used to my family doing that, after all–but to turn her back on her child?" Rebecca pressed her lips tightly together. "Maybe it's genetic," she muttered bitterly, "this ability to turn your back on your children without a second glance."

Daisy stared sadly at her, knowing Rebecca was remembering the night her parents threw her out of the house with nothing but the clothes on her back and the baby in her belly. Now that baby had also rejected her, along with her granddaughter.

"Rebecca," Daisy said softly. Sadly.

Rebecca waved away her sympathy and the dark memories of the past without quite looking at her.

"I could forgive Jaime for leaving me," Rebecca said slowly, "but not for leaving Tris."

"So what are you going to do? She's not taking your calls or your letters...maybe when your lawyer starts to send her letters...?" Daisy trailed off.

"My lawyer's ready to start the formal proceedings, but I've asked her to hold off until I get back."

"Back?"

Rebecca smiled a tight, bitter smile that didn't quite reach her eyes. "It's time Jaime and I faced each other, don't you think?"

Daisy's breath caught, her eyes widening as she searched Rebecca's expression.

Rebecca nodded. "For the first time in twenty-eight years, I'm going home."

EPISODE TWELVE
Day 133

"I. Hurt. All. Over," Manny groaned at the hotel room ceiling.

"Me, too," Zeke agreed.

She turned her head and stared at him where he was sprawled face down, half-on, half-off the other bed.

"I think we've officially seen every. Inch. Of Disney World," he added, turning to look at her.

"I think you're right," she agreed, "but I'm a little surprised you're so worn out."

"So are you!"

"I'm old–you're still a puppy. What's your excuse?"

"Keeping up with the old broad has taken it out of me."

"Glad to hear I can still teach the puppies a thing or two."

"Well, only in terms of stamina," Zeke said, then grimaced as he realized what he'd said.

Manny started to laugh and Zeke joined in.

"Ow, ow, ow–that hurts," Manny groaned.

Zeke grinned at her, then said, "You know–I don't think–no, I know–I've never been just friends with a woman before."

Manny half-smiled and raised an eyebrow. "What about Leah?"

"She's my boss and my best friend's wife, and I like her. But I guess I feel like TJ's my friend. I mean—I can't imagine talking to her the way I talk to you."

"Oh," Manny said softly.

After a moment Zeke said, "That's it?"

"Well, I'm...honoured. But if you say I 'complete you', I will hurt you so bad."

"Well, if you say I had you at hello, I'll have to return the favour."

They laughed and winced.

"How are you gonna write about this in your blog?" Manny asked.

"Honestly. My readers wanted to me learn something—and I think I have." He paused, then said softly, sincerely, "Thank you."

Manny chuckled slightly. "I didn't do anything...but you're welcome anyway."

Day 136

Rebecca slowly drove the streets of her old home town and marvelled at how much had changed. She marvelled even more at how much had stayed the same. The town layout, of course, although some of the familiar landmarks were gone, with nothing to mark their places except empty lots and, in a few rare cases, new buildings. Downtown was deserted compared to the old days, and only one of the three hotels that had once stood in the heart of the town was still there. The bar where Mr. Mankowski used to hold court almost any day of the week was long gone from the looks of it. Just like him, Rebecca thought and her heart clenched from a stab of grief.

Twenty-eight years, she thought, pulling into a parking spot in front of a small cafe and grabbing her purse as she left the car. Twenty-eight years, and there was still such a void left in her heart by the Mankowskis' absence.

She pushed away her thoughts as she pushed her way into the cafe. She took off her sunglasses and glanced around. The place was half-full, with a couple of tables of families, but most of the clientele were retired men and women sitting at several tables pushed together.

"Seat yourself, hon–I'll be there in a minute!"

Rebecca jumped slightly at the cheerful voice and she watched as the waitress, harried and plump and about Rebecca's age, grinned and waved her towards an empty table as she hastened to refill the cups of the residents of Coffee Row.

Rebecca slowly smiled, somehow soothed by the thought that some things like Coffee Row never changed as she made her way to a table by the window. She grabbed the menu and waited patiently.

"Coffee?"

Rebecca glanced up, smiled and nodded.

The woman stared, her eyes widening before she said, loudly, "*Rebecca?* Rebecca Hayworth?"

The sudden silence in the cafe was deafening and Rebecca suddenly found herself the focus of everyone's attention. She flushed, remembering her behaviour immediately after Jaime was born, her notoriety, her carelessness with her own reputation and–yes, her own body. It was very possible, she thought, shame burning every inch of her, that she'd slept with at least one of the men in this cafe. She'd slept with a lot of men in town before the Mankowskis had given her the wake-up call she'd needed.

She bit her lip then pasted on a resolute smile and said clearly, "Yes. I'm sorry–you are...?" she trailed off delicately.

The waitress grinned, her plain, plump face transforming into something remarkably pretty. "I'm Heather. Heather Padloski. I don't expect you to remember–"

Rebecca gasped, jumped to her feet and hugged

Heather. "Heather! Of course, I remember! You look great!"

And she did. Heather had been even more shy than Rebecca, grossly overweight and slow-moving, picked on unmercifully by their schoolmates, often to the point of tears. She'd sometimes shared Rebecca, Daisy and Manny's table in the cafeteria, where she huddled in on herself as she ate unbelievable mountains of food silently and as rapidly as a starving puppy. Heather had kept her head and eyes down and never, ever spoke at the table unless spoken to, and even then she replied in mumbled monosyllables. Rebecca remembered she always looked like a startled rabbit when they spoke to her outside the cafeteria, or outside of school.

Now she was smiling and open as she hugged Rebecca back and giggled.

"How could I not look great—considering the shape I was in the last time you saw me!" she said cheerfully. "Listen, I'm alone here right now so I can't stop for long. Are you staying in town or are you just passing through?"

"I'm...going to be here for a couple of days, I think," Rebecca said carefully.

"Then how about supper tonight? If you don't have any other plans, that is. You can meet my family and we can get caught up. You look *fantastic*!"

Rebecca hesitated then smiled and nodded. "I'd love that."

~~~~~

That evening, Rebecca followed Heather out onto the back deck, a cup of coffee in her hand. They settled into the patio furniture, and Rebecca admired the yard that was screened from prying eyes with lush plants, mostly fruit trees and bushes.

Rebecca sighed with satisfaction. "*Amazing* meal," she said.

Heather grinned. "Thank Willis. He made it."

"There are definite advantages to having a husband

who's a professionally trained chef," Rebecca said approvingly.

"And a nutritionist," Heather agreed, "although there are days I would absolutely *kill* for an hour alone with an assortment of cakes and cookies made the old-fashioned way. You know, three pounds of butter and four pounds of sugar."

Rebecca laughed and nodded. They sipped their coffee in silence for a moment, then Heather said, "You're here for Jaime, aren't you?"

Rebecca coughed a little on her own sip of coffee and looked ruefully at Heather as she caught her breath. "I'd forgotten what a small town is like," she muttered.

Heather grinned and shrugged. "It's also just basic deduction. Jaime showed up, looking for Devon and now here you are, looking...well. Stressed."

Rebecca shrugged. "It's...complicated."

Heather raised a hand. "I know–I know. You don't really know me, not even when we went to school together, let alone after thirty years! I don't mean to pry, but you looked pretty scared when you walked in today. And, well, Jaime hasn't exactly been...ummm...*kind* when she talks about you."

Rebecca grimaced. "Why does that not surprise me?"

"I don't mean to speak badly about your daughter, but she comes across as, well...complaining about nothing, actually. Her life hasn't been that difficult, as far as I can tell."

"Depends on your definition of difficult, I suppose," Rebecca shrugged. She hesitated, then said, "Is Devon in town?"

"As far as I know." Heather gave her a comforting smile. "He's changed a lot. I think you'll be surprised."

Rebecca raised an eyebrow. "I'm not here to see Devon," she said coolly. "It's not like we have anything to say to each other."

"No? I'd think you'd have lots to say to each other."

Heather took a sip of coffee in the sudden, tense silence, then said, "But enough of that. Tell me about Daisy and Manny."

Rebecca gratefully began to tell Heather about Daisy and Manny.

Day 137

Rebecca was back in the cafe for breakfast, sitting at the same table as the day before. She sipped her coffee as the morning waitress cleared away her half-eaten breakfast and pondered what she was going to say to Jaime.

"Rebecca? Is that you?"

Rebecca glanced up at the man standing by her table and froze, her eyes wide, her mouth dry. All she could do was nod wordlessly.

The man stared back, his own eyes huge in his face. They stared silently at each other, the woman beside him looking curiously and a little resentfully at Rebecca, until he finally gestured helplessly and said, "May I join you?"

She nodded numbly and watched silently as he murmured to the woman then slipped into the chair across the table from Rebecca. The woman shot her an angry look but said nothing as she took a seat at a distant table.

Rebecca stared at the man across the table. She searched his features, seeing how the shape of his eyes was the same as Jaime's, as was the line of his jaw, the tilt of his nose. She searched for the boy she remembered, the boy she'd once so desperately loved with every ounce of her being.

Until he deserted her, that is.

He was older–of course. Who wasn't, after thirty years, she thought dimly. He was a little softer, but he'd kept himself in good shape over the years. He still had bottomless brown eyes and cheekbones models would kill for, and as he smiled at the waitress, Rebecca saw he still had the same old sexy smile, albeit a little forced at the moment.

He gave the order—a fresh coffee for him and a refill for her—and then they sat in awkward silence.

Devon was the first to speak.

"You—uh—you look...great."

"Thank you," she managed. She didn't smile.

"I didn't know you were in town," Devon continued cautiously. "I—Jaime said you'd never come here."

"My daughter doesn't know me very well," Rebecca replied, a slight emphasis on the "my".

Devon placed his palms flat on the table and met her eyes.

"I'm...glad I ran into you. I'd hoped you'd come back. I'd even thought of calling you. Asking you to meet with me."

"Why?" Rebecca asked, a puzzled frown on her face.

"I wanted to see you and...apologize."

Rebecca blinked.

"I know what I did was...well, it was unforgivable. And I deserve whatever you want to throw at me. I thought—well, since I met Jaime, I thought you deserve the chance to say everything you've ever wanted to say to me. I am sorry, Rebecca. I really am. If I could change the past, I would."

Rebecca simply stared impassively when he finished speaking. He began to fidget under her steady, unblinking gaze.

"You know," she said slowly, "even five years ago I would have taken you up on that offer. Your ears would have exploded with all the vitriol and anger I had stored up inside of me."

"And now?"

Rebecca's shoulders moved in an almost imperceptible shrug. "And now I couldn't care less. It was a long time ago, and I survived. Jaime survived. In fact, we thrived."

"I tried to find you, you know. About two, three years after the Mankowskis died."

She raised a skeptical eyebrow.

"I...didn't really try that hard," he admitted sheepishly. "I was already drinking pretty hard by then and–" he shook his head. "You and Jaime were better off without me. Trust me. You really were."

Rebecca's face creased with a slight frown. "Drinking?" she asked.

"Jaime hasn't told you yet?" Devon grimaced ruefully. "I'm an alcoholic. I've been sober now for almost four years but I had to hit a pretty awful rock bottom before I finally decided I didn't want to live like that anymore." He glanced over his shoulder at the woman sitting at the distant table. "I put my wife through hell. My kids, too." He shook his head as he turned his attention back to Rebecca. "You and Jaime really *were* better off without me."

Rebecca cocked her head to one side as she considered him. "I didn't think so at the time," she said drily.

Devon grimaced again. "I'm sorry, Rebecca. Really, truly sorry. I was so irresponsible, and such..."

"An asshole?"

He barked a sudden laugh. "Jaime said you don't pull any punches."

"I had to learn to stand up for myself," she said quietly, "especially after the Mankowskis died."

"I know. I'm glad you ended up being stronger than you seemed when you were a kid."

Now it was Rebecca's turn to give a short bark of laughter. "You and me both," she said. She considered him carefully. "Was that the only reason you wanted to see me?" she asked.

"I wanted to apologize. Face-to-face. Yes."

"Especially since Jaime's found you now, and wants you to be an active part of her life. Right?"

Devon slumped back in his chair. "I deserve your suspicion. I'm not going to bother pretending I have a hope in hell of ever making up for the last thirty years. I don't expect us to ever be friends or to be an actual part of each other's lives. But I would like us to be civil."

"Jaime's thirty years old. It's not like you have to pick her up from my house every other weekend. So yes, Devon, I think I can manage to be civil for those few odd occasions when our paths will cross."

"Well, they're going to cross more often now—this is a small town after all."

Rebecca frowned. "I'm sorry?"

He closed his eyes and swore. "I'm sorry, Rebecca—Jaime asked me not to tell you; she wanted to do it herself." He opened his eyes. "She's moving here."

~~~~~

Rebecca stood when Jaime walked into the motel lobby. Their eyes met and Rebecca was pleased to see a flash of guilt in Jaime's eyes before the usual disdain descended once more. She stopped walking and tightly crossed her arms as Rebecca walked over to her.

"What are you doing here?" Jaime snapped.

"I've come to tell you it's time to come home."

Jaime snorted. "What? Is Tris too much trouble? Is she interfering too much with your lifestyle?"

Rebecca glanced around the small lobby that was thankfully deserted except for the woman at the front desk, watching with avid interest. Rebecca gave her a small, brittle smile then turned back to Jaime and said through gritted teeth, "Do you really want to do this here?"

Jaime made a show of looking around the lobby. She nodded at the woman behind the counter.

"Why not? Grace is a friend of mine."

Rebecca turned to look again at the woman in question. Grace quickly dropped her eyes and made herself busy on the computer, turning half away from the other two women.

"All right," Rebecca said as she turned back to Jaime, "if that's the way you want it."

"I do."

"All right," Rebecca said again. "You've been here for

over four months, heading towards five, doing...whatever it is you're doing here."

"I'm getting to know my father and my family with him," Jaime said coldly.

"Without including your own daughter in that equation."

"This isn't about Tris. This is about me and my father."

"And I'm here to talk about Tris and her mother. She needs you. She wants to be with you. If you don't want to come home, then I'll bring Tris to you."

Jaime snorted and looked towards Grace as she loudly said, "Sure. You just don't want the responsibility of looking after your granddaughter. What a *wonderful* grandmother you are, mother."

Rebecca gritted her teeth and said just as clearly and loudly, "I've paid my dues, Jaime! I was a mother at seventeen, and I did my best. I worked long and hard to give you a stable, safe childhood. I love you—you're my daughter—but you're not my *life*. Not anymore. And I love Tris—but she's my *grand*daughter. *Your* daughter. She needs to be with you. And I need to be a grandmother."

Jaime snorted. "No, you don't. You just want to be with Jackson."

Rebecca's heart ached at the mention of Jackson, but all she said was, "You're not a child anymore. You're a mother yourself. It's time to act like one again."

"A good mother would do this for her daughter!" Jaime shot back.

Rebecca took an iron grip on her slipping self-control. Through tightly gritted teeth, she said, "This has nothing to do with me and whether I'm a good mother or a good grandmother. This has everything to do with a little ten-year-old girl who's asking why her mother isn't coming home!"

"She's never asked me to come home!" Jaime angrily protested.

"No, because she doesn't want to hear you say you

don't want her! So she asks me instead, and I have no answers for her! I don't understand what you're doing—or why! If you don't want to come home, then at least have Tris with you!"

"Oh, sure! Two of us staying in one room here?" Jaime expressively indicated the motel lobby and by implication the small rooms for rent.

"For God's sake, Jaime!" Rebecca burst out. "What the hell is wrong with you?"

"I'm experiencing the family you denied me!"

"Are you insane? *They* denied you! I raised you! I gave you everything you ever wanted! And *this* is the result? *How* the hell—!" Rebecca stopped abruptly and stared at the alien creature standing in front of her. It was obvious her words were falling on deaf ears.

She straightened her shoulders.

"I've come to tell you to take your daughter back—or else."

Jaime snorted a laugh. "Or else what?" she sneered.

"Or else I'll be filing for custody. That girl needs somebody who's there for *her*. Blake's still off in some monastery or something and you're here, living in some kind of fantasy world that I made your childhood a living hell because you grew up without knowing your father."

Jaime snorted skeptically. "You don't want Tris either."

Rebecca's eyes widened then narrowed at what Jaime had just admitted. She stared coldly, then turned her back to gather up her coat and purse.

"You have two weeks to return home or to ask me to bring Tris to you," she said, facing Jaime again. Her voice was deadly quiet and even more deadly cold. "If you haven't done either of those things, I'll be filing for custody. You can continue spending your time here, weaving your delusional fantasy world, or you can come home and focus on what's real, which is your daughter. The choice is yours."

Rebecca walked towards the front door on shaking

legs. She turned around at Jaime's harsh laugh.

"You're bluffing," Jaime sneered.

Rebecca smiled tightly. "I guess we'll see, won't we."

She turned towards the door then paused.

"Oh, by the way—I had coffee with your father this morning."

For the first time in years, she'd finally taken Jaime completely off-guard.

"It was very enlightening, particularly when it came to your future plans," Rebecca continued. "He was very surprised—and touched—to hear he's a grandfather. I learned you haven't exactly been a hit with your half-siblings. Or your stepmother." She levelled a steady look at her. "A fantasy world is all well and good, but it's hard to maintain when you're the only one living in it."

Day 138

"Wow," Manny breathed, stunned by everything Rebecca had told her. "How did she react?"

"About as well as can be expected," Rebecca sighed.

"You know, maybe it's time you guys got professional help. Family counselling, or something."

"I'm way ahead of you, at least when it comes to me and Tris. We're going for our first session the day after I get home, and we're both going to have private sessions as well."

"How's she dealing with all of this?"

Rebecca laughed bitterly. "About as well as can be expected," she said again. "She doesn't believe I'm going to fight for custody any more than her mother does. I've also tracked down Blake. He's still holed up in a monastery in France and...I'm not sure what's happening with him, but he says he's in no shape to take full responsibility for his daughter, and he's definitely not ready to come home. He's promised not to fight me for custody."

"What the hell?" Manny sputtered.

"He dropped some hints that he's dealing with more

than a crisis of faith. There's something very deeply wrong going on with him."

"Shit. That's awful."

"Yeah–poor guy. He said he's finding his way back–but slowly. I just asked him to keep in touch with Tris much more than he has been, and he agreed to do that. Tris talked to him for a couple of hours yesterday."

"Good. I'm glad."

"Me, too. As for Blake's parents, I finally tracked them down as well. They're in the Philippines."

"Yeah? And?"

"Well, they're sailing around the world, and weren't exactly enthusiastic about coming back to take care of Tris or in taking her with them and all that would entail. Home schooling, that sort of thing," Rebecca finished vaguely.

"Jesus. That poor kid!"

"I know. Worst of all, this means she's now stuck with me, the grandmother she doesn't like all that much."

"That hasn't gotten better?"

"A little. I guess. But I'll never be her most favorite person in the whole world."

"She's only ten. Who knows how she'll feel by the time she's twenty?"

Rebecca frowned. "Why twenty?"

"Teenagers don't like anybody."

Rebecca sputtered a laugh. "Unless you're Daisy's kids."

"True." Manny paused. "So what now?"

"Now I wait," Rebecca sighed. "My lawyer's ready to file the papers as soon as I give her the word." She sighed again. "Am I doing the right thing, Manny?"

"What do you think?" Manny replied.

"I don't know. I don't know! The last few months I've been focused on Jaime and her problems and actions, and I've been blaming myself for all of it–wondering–and terrified I'm screwing Tris up as much as I obviously screwed up her mother. But in spite of how obviously bad

I am at raising children, I keep thinking...that...I—I think I made another huge mistake, and one that, no matter what I said at the time, had absolutely nothing to do with Jaime or Tris, and everything to do with my own fear that he'd leave me first."

"Jackson?" Manny asked sympathetically.

"*Yes!* I can't—I can't even—" Tears sprang to Rebecca's eyes, her voice thick with emotion. "I think my heart is literally breaking. I've never felt like this before. I...if I think about it too much, it...Christ, it *hurts*, and it's like I need a moment to get back on my feet."

"*Wow*," Manny breathed, "I don't think I've ever heard you say that about any man before. Not even Devon."

Rebecca sniffed as she brushed her tears away. "Even losing Devon didn't feel like this! Don't get me wrong, Manny, I *can* live without Jackson—I just can't, for the life of me, remember why I'd want to."

Day 140

"Hey," TJ said as Leah walked into the hospital room.

She grinned as she dropped a light kiss on his lips. "Hey," she said, "I haven't missed the doctor, have I?"

TJ shook his head just as the door opened again and Dr. Valesquez bustled in. Leah settled beside TJ and laced her fingers through his.

Dr. Valesquez smiled and said, "I believe we've finally got the infections under control."

"Believe?" TJ asked sharply, raising an eyebrow.

"You don't know for sure?" Leah added with a frown.

"Your lungs are much clearer, but the infections are lingering longer than we expected. When we send you home, you'll have to make sure you continue taking your medication properly otherwise you could get sick again, and perhaps even worse than before."

"Great," TJ groaned.

"That's the infection," Leah said firmly. "*Infections*, actually. What about the cancer?"

"Good news on that front. Based on the tests we did yesterday, we appear to have caught the tumor early enough. At this point, it appears you won't even need chemo. We'll do another round of tests in six weeks, and if that's still clear, we'll go to every six months."

TJ groaned.

Leah patted his hand. "That's better than having the tests every month."

"No, no," TJ protested, "I think I'm beginning to like them."

Leah and Dr. Valesquez laughed.

Dr. Valesquez said, "I'd like to keep you here for another day and then send you home."

"With that cute, blonde nurse?" TJ asked hopefully.

Leah rolled her eyes and smacked him lightly on the shoulder.

"Hey—I'm a sick man, here!" TJ protested. "Besides, you'll like him."

Leah burst out laughing. "I'm so glad you're back," she said, and dropped another light kiss onto his lips.

Dr. Valesquez watched with a beneficent smile, and said, "You're very lucky, TJ. Both with the cancer and the lung infection. Another day, and you wouldn't have made it, you know."

"I know," TJ said solemnly, his fingers squeezing Leah's. "I won't take that risk again."

"Good." The doctor stood. "No offense, TJ, but I sincerely hope I don't see you very often after you leave the hospital tomorrow."

TJ grinned. "None taken, and trust me—the feeling is entirely mutual."

Dr. Valesquez grinned, shook TJ's hand then Leah's and left them alone.

Leah and TJ shifted until she was lying down on the bed beside him. He was no longer on intravenous although the needle to allow the nurses to take blood samples was still embedded in the back of his hand. Leah and TJ carefully adjusted until they were snuggled comfortably on the bed.

"I'm so glad you're getting better," Leah said softly, burying her face into his neck.

"Me, too," TJ sighed. He rubbed her back, and Leah finally allowed herself to cry.

Day 141

Daisy opened the door for Hub and gave him a slight smile. "The kids are running a little late," she said. "They were out with Tris and lost track of the time. They'll be here in about half an hour."

"That's okay, I wanted to talk to you, anyway," he said as they walked into the living room and sat down.

"Okay," Daisy said, "what about?"

"Have you made up your mind about what we talked about a couple weeks ago?"

Daisy frowned. "Anything in particular? We've talked about a lot of stuff since your ex-girlfriend took off with all our hard-earned cash," she said drily.

Hub scowled. "You know what I'm talking about. Stopping this divorce. Getting back together. Trying again. Come on, Daisy. What do you say?"

Daisy considered him thoughtfully. "I don't get it," she finally said. "Why are you pushing so hard to get back together?"

"You're my wife!"

"You should have thought of that before you got yourself a mistress! Come on, Hub. What's the *real* reason?"

Hub deflated. "You're...familiar," he muttered. "Comfortable. I know the battles, I know the foibles. I know how you think, what buttons to push, what turns you on." He looked soulfully at her. "I miss you."

Daisy tried to push aside the red tide of rage that rose up at his words.

"We've been together for twenty-four years," Hub

continued persuasively, "you *can't* just want to throw all that away."

"Why not? You did."

"Daisy—"

"Do you know you've never once apologized to me? You've never once said you were sorry you betrayed me, or sorry you hurt your kids, or sorry you threw our marriage away. I may be 'comfortable' and 'familiar' but I'm not an old pair of shoes! I'm not a favourite pair of jeans you haul out every now and then to remember the days you were skinny! Twenty-four years—" Daisy's voice broke, "twenty-four years, and starting over scares me. *Terrifies* me! But taking you back after everything that's happened? Not a chance in hell."

~~~~~

"And then what happened?" Manny asked.

"Nothing. He sat there in silence until the kids arrived, then they all left."

"Are you okay with this?"

Daisy paused, thinking. "Yeah," she said softly. Firmly. "Yeah, I'm really okay with this."

Day 143

Rebecca tightly gripped the steering wheel and stared at the house. The lights burned cheerfully in the windows, making the place look warm and inviting. Rebecca wondered if she'd find the warm welcome those lights promised. She felt the sweat break out on her palms.

For a moment she thought of driving away, pretending she'd never been here, pretending the Jackson-shaped place in her life wasn't there, and wasn't aching from his absence. She straightened her spine and took a deep breath.

She wasn't a coward, she told herself stoutly, and she could survive without him. If he told her to go, she'd go.

But she had to try.

She took another deep breath, then abruptly left the car

and walked briskly to the door. She rang the doorbell, and rubbed her palms nervously on her jacket as she waited for the door to open, which it was by a girl a couple of years older than Tris.

Rebecca blinked. "Uh, hi. You must be Dayle."

Dayle frowned slightly. "Yeah. Who are you?"

"I'm...a friend of your father's."

To Rebecca's shock, Dayle's face lit up in recognition and a huge grin spread across her face before she turned her head and yelled at the top of her lungs, "*Dad!* Rebecca's here!" She turned back to a stunned Rebecca. "Come in!" she said and stood aside to give Rebecca room to step into the foyer.

Rebecca hesitated, wondering how Dayle had known who she was. She opened her mouth to ask just as Jackson ran into the foyer, skidding to a halt at the sight of her. His dark brown eyes were huge as he simply stared while a boy about Tris' age and a lovely, dark-haired woman came rushing into the foyer behind him.

Rebecca flushed painfully as she stared at the dark-haired woman. "Oh! You have guests–I should have called first–I'm sorry–I'll just–"

The woman stepped forward and cut Rebecca off in mid-babble. "I'm Jasmine. Jackson's sister?"

Rebecca actually staggered a little with relief. "Oh! Oh. Oh...well...nice to meet you."

Jasmine grinned with delight. "Come in, Rebecca. No need to stand on the doorstep."

Rebecca hesitantly stepped into the house, once more rubbing her hands nervously against her jacket. She glanced at Jackson, then quickly away, the hunger and burning hope in his eyes causing her to shift uncomfortably.

Jasmine spoke into the tense silence, "You've met Dayle. This is Ryder."

Ryder was a miniature Jackson, with the same vulnerable brown eyes and thick, unruly black hair. He smiled almost shyly at her, and Rebecca's heart clenched because it was Jackson's smile, in miniature.

"Hi," he said.

"Hello," Rebecca said faintly.

"And now, kids, let's leave them alone for a while," Jasmine said firmly, and quelled Dayle's protest with a single look. Dayle's shoulders slumped as she nodded and followed her aunt and brother out of the foyer, although both kids watched over their shoulders until they were in the next room.

Rebecca stared around the foyer, fiddled with the edges of her coat, and looked anywhere but directly at Jackson, who was staring fixedly and silently at her.

She fidgeted uncomfortably once more, then glanced at him from the corner of her eyes and said, "Aren't you wondering why I'm here?"

"Yeah," he said softly.

"So why aren't you saying anything?"

Jackson moved towards her. "Because I'm still trying to get my breath back," he said as he wrapped his arms around her, and kissed her.

Day 144

"Awww..." Manny said as Rebecca described Jackson kissing her in the foyer.

"And then," Rebecca continued happily, "I had supper with him and the kids and Jasmine—her ex had her kids—and we watched a movie, and then I went home. I'm going to introduce him to Tris tonight."

"That's awesome, Rebecca! I'm so happy for you!"

"I've never introduced a man to my grandchild before. Hell, I never even introduced one to my child! How did this happen to me?" Rebecca groaned.

Manny laughed. "Just lucky, I guess. And I've met Jackson, remember? Did you really think you had a chance of resisting him?"

"Better than even!"

"Oh, he had no chance of resisting you, of course! Seriously, Rebecca–I'm...I'm so happy for you."

"Almost forty-eight years old, and I'm in love–who'da thunk it?"

"According to Angeline, you can fall in love at any age. And Leila says the same thing. And Simon-Simone says there's someone out there for each of us, if we're willing to take the chance and if we remain true to ourselves in the process."

"When did Simon-Simone say that?"

"She sent me an e-mail the other day. She's in love and wants everyone else to be, too."

"Ah. Anyway, Jackson and I are going to take it slow. Dayle and Ryder have known about me for a long time– but knowing about me and potentially living with me are two different things."

"Or you guys may choose to not live together until they're out of school. High school, I mean."

"That would be a long time..." Rebecca sighed.

"Okay. Stupid idea."

"Not stupid. It is something to consider. But no matter what else happens, I think we'll figure something out."

Manny laughed, "Somehow, I think so, too."

EPISODE THIRTEEN
Day 164

Manny lay flat on her back, eyes wide, staring at the ceiling while she waited for her clock to hit 7:00 a.m. It was her last day on the road. They'd be home tonight and she'd be sleeping in her new apartment that Rebecca had leased for her. Tomorrow morning, there'd be no place to go next, no tourist site to visit, no Zeke beside her. She would finally stop moving and it would be time, she thought, to make a reckoning.

The jarring noise of the alarm had barely begun when she clicked it off. She sighed, threw back the covers and got out of bed. She padded into the bathroom and looked with interest in the full-length mirror that doubled as the hotel room's shower doors. For the first time in six months she stood and took her morning inventory.

Plain face? Check.

Looking tired? Check. But they'd been driving almost non-stop for the last four days.

Thirty pounds overweight? Well, she looked like she'd lost a couple pounds—but, yes, check.

Dark circles under deer-caught-in-headlights eyes? Check and check. Then again, tomorrow she would start looking for work, and that was something she hadn't had to do for almost sixteen years.

She shuddered, then refocused on her reflection in the mirror.

Her hair was shorter, but it was still limp, still not-quite-brown-not-quite-blonde...and she was still old.

She smiled ruefully.

She had some pretty good memories, she thought as she dropped her clothes on the floor and stepped into the shower, and on the inside she felt reconnected to a larger world, but on the outside—well. Not much had changed there.

She turned on the water, positioned herself under the hot stream and closed her eyes as it cascaded over her shoulders and back.

She smiled.

After all was said and done—and there was a lot said and lot more done over the last few months—she was still *her*.

She was okay with that.

~~~~~

Zeke and Manny drove in silence. Another three hours and they'd be home, and the adventure would be at an end. The silence stretched between them, comfortable, yet rich with things left unspoken.

Almost six months, Manny thought. It was a very long time to spend together, and had been filled with more than its fair share of ups and downs, although the last few weeks had been almost serene. She suspected Zeke had been on his best behaviour ever since she'd found out about the blog.

Her feelings were mixed. She knew he was being paid to travel with her; she knew he was still writing about her. On the other hand, he'd been more than willing to do whatever she wanted to do. It had been rather fun to watch him squirm a little when she pushed his buttons, and grit his teeth before he agreed to something. Fun, but also a little irritating, and even a little sad, and she found she missed their earlier, less suspicious, more trusting relationship.

Regardless, it was all coming to an end now, and the future she'd so diligently ignored was standing on her doorstep, and would soon demand answers and decisions and a reckoning.

She thoughtfully chewed her thumb as she stared out the van's window.

"Did you find what you were looking for?" Zeke asked suddenly, startling her.

Manny carefully considered the question, then nodded. "Yes, I think so. Did you?"

Zeke laughed ruefully. "I found things I hadn't even known I was looking for."

Manny laughed too, then asked, "What are you looking forward to the most about getting home?"

Zeke frowned as he thought about it. "Sleeping in my own bed," he said. "Seeing my friends. Not moving. You?"

"Settling into the place Rebecca found for me. Seeing Daisy and Rebecca and everyone else. Looking for a job. Not moving."

"Has anything really changed for you? I mean, in real life. You still need to work. If you're not careful, you'll be back where you started."

"Maybe. Most likely. I'm still me, after all. But at least I know—at least I have the memory of a time when I did something...*more*–something different–something...a little less ordinary."

"But now it's done."

"Yes."

"Then...maybe nothing's really changed at all."

"Maybe not," Manny agreed sadly and turned her face away to look out the window again.

After several minutes, Zeke said very quietly, "We're not gonna be the same, are we?"

Manny turned her face towards him and smiled sadly at him as she shook her head. "No."

"That's *it?*" he asked indignantly.

"It's gonna be a long trip," they said together and burst out laughing, laughing much louder and longer than the situation truly warranted.

Zeke sighed and said ruefully, "I don't even know why I said that. It's not like–it's not like it's a surprise."

"No. Real life has a way of taking over–that's why it's real life."

"Do you think you'll go back to–you know–how you used to be?" Zeke asked with genuine interest.

"Prudish, repressed and timid?" she asked drily.

Zeke grinned even as he winced. "Yeah."

Manny grinned, too. "I hope not. Those are fifteen years I'll never get back."

"Were they all bad?"

"No, of course not. I learned a lot–did a lot–did things I never thought I'd do–but I allowed myself to pay a high price. That's the part I'm truly sorry about. Nobody forced me to give up everything for my job. I did that to myself. The danger is that I'll do it to myself again, because I don't really know how else to be."

"That's...pretty...scary," Zeke said slowly, frowning.

"But this time around, I can blame you," she said brightly.

Zeke grinned, giving her a sidelong look. "You do that."

Manny nodded with smug satisfaction and lapsed into silence again. Then she said, "Are you glad you came with me?"

Zeke nodded slowly. "Yeah."

"That's it?"

Zeke laughed. "Hey–I learned a lot–did a lot–been in more jails than I care to remember–"

"One! *One* jail!"

Zeke laughed harder then grinned at her, his eyes warm with affection as he nodded.

"Yeah. Yeah, I'm glad I came with you."

She slowly smiled back with equal warmth.

"Me, too."

~~~~~

After leaving Daisy's place, Zeke walked Manny to her new home on the fifteenth floor of a downtown apartment building. She opened the door and turned to face him.

"Well," she said.

"Yeah."

"I guess...this is..."

"Good-bye."

Manny nodded, blinking sudden moisture out of her eyes. "Yeah."

Zeke took a deep breath, then stuck out his hand. Manny slowly grinned, before she carefully placed her hand in his. His grip was warm and firm.

"It's been a pleasure, Manny Mankowski," Zeke said softly.

She smiled and inclined her head in acknowledgment. "Thank you. And the feeling is mutual, Zeke Powell."

They lingered for a long moment, simply holding each other's hand, looking into each other's eyes, then, with an almost soundless sigh, they relaxed their grips and let their hands slide apart.

Zeke took a step backward. "See you around."

Manny nodded, blinking against that sudden moisture again. "You bet."

With one last smile, Zeke lifted his hand in a half-hearted gesture then turned and walked briskly to the elevator. Manny stood in her doorway and lifted her hand in good-bye as the elevator door closed.

She felt suddenly very lonely as she went into her new apartment and closed the door behind her.

You know, you guys could be friends, Harvey said, leaning gracefully in the entryway to the living room. **Real ones, I mean.**

For some reason, I don't think our real lifestyles would match all that well.

What does that have to do with anything?

I don't want to talk about it.

Okay. But you're going to be lonely. Maybe you should actually consider dating.

Dating? Like...<u>really</u> dating?

Sure. If there's one thing Zeke proved to you: you can actually have a conversation with a good-looking guy.

But I obviously can't sleep with one.

Then find one who's less good-looking.

Manny laughed. *You've ruined me for normal men, Harvey.*

I'm not sure that's a good thing to think.

Probably not. But...seriously...do you really exist? Not you, obviously–but a man like you?

Harvey laughed. **Well, I highly doubt there's a man out there willing to wear frilly shirts open to the navel while he rescues you from pirates. And let's face it–some of those sex scenes you fantasized would cause a lesser man to throw out his back.**

Manny chuckled. *They'd be pretty uncomfortable for an ordinary woman, too. But you know what I mean.*

Yeah, I do. I think, if you took a few chances, you might be surprised.

Manny ruefully shook her head.

I'm not sure I'm ready to take those kinds of chances.

Harvey smiled at her, his dark eyes warm and affectionate, and a little bit sad.

Then I'll be here until you <u>are</u>.

~~~~~

Change sometimes feels like it happens without our knowledge or consent.

Zeke sat at the desk in his new apartment, typing furiously.

Sometimes the changes we make lead us places we didn't expect to go.

Rebecca and Jackson shared a smile as they sat down

on either side of the three kids on the couch and settled in to watch TV.

Sometimes we try to run from change, only to realize that change is the best thing for us.

Daisy stared at the papers sitting on the table in front of her. She squared her shoulders, and signed her name. She leaned back in her chair, tossed her pen on the table, and sighed.

Sometimes we fight to hold on to something real and true in the midst of changes we don't want to face.

TJ smiled at Leah as he walked into the bedroom. She put aside her book as he slipped under the covers and reached for her, and she melted against him as they kissed.

Sometimes the changes we try so desperately to make seem as substantial as the breeze—the more we change, the more we stay the same. Which makes me wonder: does anything truly change?

Manny stood in the middle of the living room and turned slowly, carefully assessing the space. With a final deep breath, she turned off the lights and left the room.

And so the grand adventure has come to an end. We're home again, and back where we began. It already feels like we were never gone. Does anything really change?

Manny groggily groped for the shrilly ringing cell phone that had startled her awake. She fumbled it to her ear and croaked, "H'lo?"

"What're you doing tomorrow?" Zeke asked, his voice low and husky in her ear.

"Unpacking," she muttered, her eyes drifting closed.

"Sounds exciting."

"Hmmmmmm."

"So, around eleven, then? I'll bring lunch."

"'kay," Manny mumbled, and disconnected the call, already asleep.

Zeke thoughtfully tapped the edge of his phone against his lips as he re-read the text on his screen. He put the phone down and reached for the keyboard.

Maybe it does.

AUTHOR'S NOTE

A funny thing happened on the way to participating in ScriptFrenzy 2011 (www.scriptfrenzy.org).

I had a vague idea of a plot–a 45-year-old woman decides to throw her life up in the air and departs on a road trip to rediscover herself.

Yep.

It's been done before–and better–but what the hell–it wasn't like I was writing it for money! The sad part was, though, that that was pretty much it. That was all I had– and April 1st was looming large on the horizon.

Then a LiveJournal friend published a meme, which was: "leave a comment, and I'll give you seven actors and you have to come up with a TV series starring those seven actors." I thought–what the hell–and left a comment.

She gave me:

> Megan Follows (Manny)
> Meg Ryan (Daisy)
> Gillian Anderson (Rebecca)
> Michaela Conlin (Leah)
> Kevin Bacon (TJ)
> Esai Morales (Harvey)
> Karl Urban (Zeke)

then I added:

> Bruce Willis (Max)
> Robert Downey Jr. (Jackson)

Suddenly, my vague plot had shape and form and characters I could define and see, and in no time at all, I came up with a thirteen episode miniseries.

With Jimmy Buffett's "Take the Weather With You" and the Barenaked Ladies' "Maroon" on endless repeat for the soundtrack (with a little Billy Joel, John Berry, even more Jimmy Buffett and Barenaked Ladies, along with songs from a variety of random artists), the story practically wrote itself. I whipped past 100 pages of scripts in no time, although I didn't even come close to finishing all thirteen episodes.

Several months went by and then I read the scripts over again—and you know what? I *liked* them. I thought they had potential. Shortly after that, I discovered BigBangs on LiveJournal, and stumbled upon the 100K supernova challenge. I looked at the unfinished scripts and said, "I can write another 100,000 words on this thing"—and took on the challenge.

Here's the result.

With special thanks to:

S. on LiveJournal who came up with the fantasy "cast list", beta'd the drafts, and told me she loved it even when I felt like this fic had a face only a mother could love.

The actors on my fantasy "cast list" (none of whom know anything about this book (and therefore do not endorse anything about it in any way), or me, or that I've used their pictures and their work as props to help me create the characters in these pages but to whom I nonetheless owe an enormous amount of gratitude) especially:

Megan Follows—for having that air of tough vulnerability that Manny needed to give her shape.

Esai Morales—for inspiring me to begin writing again with his far-too-short turn on the television series *Jericho* as Major Edward Beck, and for managing to steal my heart and my imagination in just seven (!) episodes.

Karl Urban—for being adorably curmudgeonly and sexy as Dr. McCoy; for giving Bruce Willis a solid run for his money in RED; and for having eyebrows that are practically characters in themselves—without you, Zeke would never have been so clear in my mind!

Bruce Willis—because, honestly? Who wouldn't want a Bruce Willis character in their story? And Max really didn't have any shape until I realized he was soft-spoken, bald and a bad ass with a smirk.

and

Robert Downey Jr.–for being the personification of the phoenix; for being funny as hell; for having chemistry with literally everyone including the dog–and for having beautifully vulnerable brown eyes and a sensitivity that gave me the outline for the perfect match for Rebecca (she can thank me later).

And finally, my enormous appreciation and love to:

The Barenaked Ladies–for being Canadian; for having a great sound and great voices and great songs and especially for "Maroon" which fit Manny's mood (and my own) so perfectly as I was writing this story.

Jimmy Buffett–for being the best damn singer of Jimmy Buffett songs there can be; for songs that have lifted me up, mellowed me out, and sound the way I sometimes feel. I don't think Manny and Zeke would have had nearly so much fun if it hadn't been for "Take the Weather With You" and various others songs from various other records.

––Victoria Bernadine, December 2012